P9-DNE-619

UNDER A GRAVEYARD SKY

BAEN BOOKS by JOHN RINGO

BLACK TIDE RISING:

Under a Graveyard Sky • *To Sail a Darkling Sea* (forthcoming)

TROY RISING:

Live Free or Die • *Citadel* • *The Hot Gate*

LEGACY OF THE ALDENATA:

A Hymn Before Battle • *Gust Front* • *When the Devil Dances* • *Hell's Faire* • *The Hero* (with Michael Z. Williamson) • *Cally's War* (with Julie Cochrane) • *Watch on the Rhine* (with Tom Kratman) • *Sister Time* (with Julie Cochrane) • *Yellow Eyes* (with Tom Kratman) • *Honor of the Clan* (with Julie Cochrane) • *Eye of the Storm*

COUNCIL WARS:

There Will Be Dragons • *Emerald Sea* • *Against the Tide* • *East of the Sun, West of the Moon*

INTO THE LOOKING GLASS:

Into the Looking Glass • *Vorpal Blade* (with Travis S. Taylor) • *Manxome Foe* (with Travis S. Taylor) • *Claws that Catch* (with Travis S. Taylor)

EMPIRE OF MAN:

March to the Sea (with David Weber) • *March to the Stars* (with David Weber) • *March Upcountry* (with David Weber) • *We Few* (with David Weber)

SPECIAL CIRCUMSTANCES:

Princess of Wands • *Queen of Wands*

PALADIN OF SHADOWS:

Ghost • *Kildar* • *Choosers of the Slain* • *Unto the Breach* • *A Deeper Blue* • *Tiger by the Tail* (with Ryan Sear)

STANDALONE TITLES:

The Last Centurion

Citizens (ed. with Brian M. Thomsen)

To purchase these and all Baen Book titles in
e-book format, please go to www.baen.com.

UNDER A GRAVEYARD SKY

JOHN RINGO

UNDER A GRAVEYARD SKY

This is a work of fiction. All the characters and events portrayed in this book are fictional, and any resemblance to real people or incidents is purely coincidental.

A Baen Books Original

Baen Publishing Enterprises
P.O. Box 1403
Riverdale, NY 10471
www.baen.com

ISBN: 978-1-4516-3919-3 hardcover
ISBN: 978-1-4516-3925-4 signed limited edition

Cover art by Kurt Miller

First Baen printing, September 2013

Distributed by Simon & Schuster
1230 Avenue of the Americas
New York, NY 10020

Library of Congress Cataloging-in-Publication Data

Ringo, John, 1963–
   Under a graveyard sky / John Ringo.
      pages cm
   "A Baen Books Original."
   ISBN 978-1-4516-3919-3 (hc)
1. Airborne infection—Fiction. 2. Marines—Fiction. 3. Survival—Fiction. I. Title.
   PS3568.I577U53 2013
   813'.54—dc23
                                                        2013017370

10 9 8 7 6 5 4 3 2 1

Pages by Joy Freeman (www.pagesbyjoy.com)
Printed in the United States of America

For my daughters Jennifer and Lindy,
for what should be obvious reasons.
Good writers create. Great writers steal.
And some people are just characters too great to not steal.
I am blessed with two daughters who meet that description.

and

As always
For Captain Tamara Long, USAF
Born: May 12, 1979
Died: March 23, 2003, Afghanistan
You fly with the angels now.

ACKNOWLEDGEMENTS

The problem with acknowledgements on this book is remembering all the people who've contributed over the last two plus years to its development. So let's start with a limited list of the people who've kept me from looking like a complete fool.

A good place to start is probably Dr. Robert Hampson, Ph.D. (Pharmacology, Physiology) for help with, well, gosh, everything, mostly the neurological effect of the H7D3 virus, some details on vaccine production and, oh, yeah, pointing out (as several did) that influenza viruses use RNA, not DNA. (Which I knew but I also once had a manual safety on a Glock. Sue me.)

Kelly Lockhart (yep, real person) for doing enough research so some of the discussions between experts was at least vaguely reasonable handwavium. Also for occasionally coming over to the house to kick my butt into finishing the book. (I'd "finished" it already but there were, shall we say, some gaps to fill in. Like most of one chapter.)

Then there's Douglas Wyatt, USCG, for pointing out about a billion things I'd gotten wrong (that fortunately you gentle readers will never see) about the most basic aspects of sailing, not to mention "There's no way in hell they'd have parked in the East River or the sound. The currents are ferocious." When I asked for some details on the USCGC *Campbell* his reply was "Yeah...most of that's classified but I'll give you what I can..." Which, alas, is what what many of my technical experts often are forced to say since I have, I think, some really cool friends.

Speaking of Michael Massa, former something something special operations, former Head of Security and Disaster Response for "a major international bank," and who has no resemblance whatsoever to either Thomas the Tank Engine or Mike Jenkins, I'd like to thank him for his assistance on aspects of, well, it should be obvious. Alas, I never did write "the battle of the BERTs." As a singer once said, most of writing is "what to leave in, what to leave out." This is another universe I've created that is made for anthologies of "the other stories." (For one of which I only have the title, "Something funny happened on the way to Peoria." Which would also work for the Posleen, Special Circumstances and Vorpal Blade universes.) If only I was an editor. Anyway, thanks again, Mike.

Deborah Fishburn and Brian Carbin for straightening out some of my Aussie slang as well as general edits and suggestions.

Michael "Subdude" Gants for some unclass details of life on a fast attack. Sorry, Mike, Dallas stays for now.

There will be a much longer list for the sequel, *To Sail a Darkling Sea*. But I gotta get this to the publishers, like, now.

—John Ringo
Chattanooga, April 2013

UNDER A GRAVEYARD SKY

BOOK ONE

LIGHT A CANDLE

At the end of the river the sundown beams

All the relics of a life long lived

Here, weary traveler rest your wand

Sleep the journey from your eyes

from "Turn Loose the Mermaids"
Nightwish
Imaginaerum

CHAPTER 1

"*AlasBabylon Q4E9*," the text read.

"Bloody hell." And it really hadn't started out as a bad day. Weather was crappy but at least it was Friday.

Steven John "Professor" Smith was six foot one, with sandy blond hair and a thin, wiry frame. Most people who hadn't seen him in combat, and very few living had, considered him almost intensely laid back. Which in general was the case. It came with the background. Once you'd been dropped in the dunny, few things not of equal difficulty were worth getting upset about. Until, possibly, now.

He regarded the text from his brother and wondered if this was how morning walkers on 9/11 felt. He knew the basic code. *Alas Babylon* was a book about a nuclear war in the 1950s and survivors in the aftermath. The novel by Pat Frank was still one of the best looks at post-apocalyptic life ever written. And he and Tom had agreed that it was the best choice for a code indicating a real, this is no shit, general emergency. Not "I've got cancer" but "grab the bug-out bag and activate your Zombie Plan." Which was why he wondered if this was the same feeling those morning New Yorkers had felt looking up at the gush of fire from the side of the Twin Towers. Disbelief, sadness, even anger. His mouth was dry, palms clammy, his sphincter was doing the bit where it was simultaneously trying to press neutronium and let go all over his seat. He felt all the cycles of grief go through him in one brief and nasty blast. Tom was not a guy to joke about the end of the world. Something had hit something or another.

Despite *knowing* it'd gone tits up, he hit reply.

"Confirm."

The return message was immediate.

"*Confirm, confirm, CONFIRM. Q4E9. CONFIRM!!*"

Shit.

The rest of the codes were the problem. Stacey and Tom were the crypto geeks. Of course, calling Tom a geek was a stretch. Nearly two meters tall and a former Australian SAS commando, the "General Manager for Security and Emergency Response" for the Bank of the Americas might have a background in crypto and enjoy the occasional alternative clubbing night. Geek was still a stretch.

Tom's penchant for code, however, was part of that geeky side. While the games growing up had been a pain in the ass, Steve recognized them as a necessity in this case. Tom had come into possession of information that was still closely held. His text was a violation of not only his employment contracts but, probably, federal law. He wasn't going to send "Asteroid INBOUND" over an open network.

Stacey would know what the code meant in a second. Despite his para nickname of "Professor," Steve was unfazed by both his wife and his brother being smarter than he. He was laid back and preferred to be surrounded by people who were smarter, more effective and more dangerous. Made his life a whole lot simpler.

He looked up at the class full of teenagers working on their Friday afternoon history test. Byzantine emperors were about the last of his problems at the moment. He still wasn't sure about the codes but he knew that he'd never see most of them again. Dead or alive, his life and theirs was about to change.

He was going to miss some of them but the protocols were clear. It was much the same as being a spy, really. If you'd been burned you didn't hesitate. When the world was ending you didn't worry about anything but the most basic issues. Notably, Stacey, Sophia and Faith. In no particular order that, he desperately hoped, whatever this was might test. Okay, even Stacey would agree Sophia and Faith first. Just in no particular order.

He therefore calmly bent over, picked up his backpack and stood up to leave.

"Mr. Smith?" Chad Walker said, looking at him quizzically.

"Just going out for a bit," Steve said. Chad was one of the good ones. Most of the kids were good for values of good. As good as American kids got, anyway. Coddled, yes, but bright by and large. Most didn't apply themselves and the parents were mostly a pain in the ass. But it had been a good job. Past tense.

He walked down the mostly silent halls in a bit of a daze. At one level it was senseless. Nobody walked out of a job they'd done for ten years without a wrench and on the basis of two text messages. But it was what you did if you'd prepared. You just walked away.

He stopped outside the school's office and tried to assume an expression suitable for a distraught husband.

"Janice," he said, stepping into the office and brushing at his eyes. "Stacey's been in an accident at the plant. They're taking her to the office. I need to pull Sophia out of class."

"Oh my God!" the heavy-set brunette said, her eyes wide. "What happened?"

"Unclear," Steve said. "I'll call you from the hospital. Just please page for her to be brought up here while I talk to Mr. Navas."

"Okay..." Janice said, fumbling at the intercom.

The woman really was someone Steve was looking *forward* to leaving behind.

He knocked on the principal's door and opened it without waiting for a reply.

"Steve?" Mr. Navas said, cocking a quizzical eyebrow. Alvaro Navas was a decent assistant principal, all things considered. Another person, among many, Steve figured he'd never see again. However it worked out.

"Stacey's being taken to the hospital," he said somewhat shakenly. "Injured at work. They... it sounded quite serious. That guarded 'we're sure it's going to be fine' from HR which means it's not. I'm pulling Sophia out to go with me to the hospital and I'd appreciate it if you'd call Angleton Middle and have them bring up Faith so I can pick her up on the way by."

"Of course, Steve," Alvaro said. "Anything we can do."

"I'll call you as soon as I know what's going on," Steve said. "I think Janice is bringing up Sophia."

"So no idea what happened?" Navas asked.

"They wouldn't say," Steve said, shrugging his shoulders help-lessly. "I...I need to go check on Sophia..."

"Of course, of course, Steve," Navas said, getting out of his chair. "Whatever you need...If you need some time."

"Well, it's the weekend, fortunately," Steve said. "I'll know more when I get to the hospital."

"Which hospital?" Navas asked.

"Not even sure of that at this point," Steve said. "Mercy, I assume. It's the closest. I've got to call back about that...Just...I've got this handled. I'll get to you about what's going on."

"Call me at home if it's after work," Mr. Navas said, patting him on the back.

"Dad?" Sophia asked, her eyes wide. The fifteen-year-old had gotten her father's looks and her mother's height. It wasn't a bad combination. With sandy blond hair, and five-five, she seemed to have stopped growing up or out. "What's up?" She had her backpack over her back. If she had anything left in the locker it was going to have to stay there.

"Your mom..." Steve said, then paused. "We'll talk about it in the car."

"What happened to Mom?" Sophia said.

"We'll talk in the car," Steve said, taking her arm. "She was injured at the plant. Mr. Navas, if you could call the middle school?"

"Of course," Mr. Navas said. "And *call* me."

"I will," Steve said. "Oh, release slip?"

"Oh...!" Janice said, fumbling with the papers piled on her desk.

"I've got it," Mr. Navas said, trying not to sigh. He pulled the form pad out from under a pile and quickly scribbled the necessities. "There."

"Thank you, sir," Steve said. "Good luck."

"Thank you," Mr. Navas said, frowning slightly. "I think I should be wishing you that."

"Yes, yes," Steve said, gesturing for Sophia to precede him through the door.

"Dad...?" Sophia said.

"In the car," Steve said as they walked out of the building. It was a thin, nasty rain, cold for late spring even in Virginia. Which just fit his mood to a T.

His car was most of the way across the teachers' parking lot so he continued:

"Don't stop moving when I say this. It's not your mother. Apocalypse code from your Uncle Tom."

"What?" Sophia said, stopping and starting to turn.

"I said keep walking," Steve said, grabbing her arm. "Which is why you're going to drive. I need both hands free."

"You pulled me out of a test for some code from Uncle Tom?" Sophia said angrily. "What about the dance tonight?"

"By eight PM we're going to be in full bug-out mode," Steve said. "This is not a drill, Soph. I still need to check the codes but it's an apocalypse code. As in 'end of the world.'"

"What *end*?" Sophia said, gesturing around. There certainly didn't seem to be any major issues. Cars continued speeding past the school. None of them seemed in any more a hurry than they ever were. "Missing the dance is going to be the end of the world!"

"Not time for drama, miss," Steve said, getting in the passenger side. "Drive."

"Ooookay," the fifteen-year-old said nervously. "You want me to drive in an apocalypse."

"The apocalypse isn't here yet," Steve said, pulling out his phone again. "Now be quiet. Head to Faith's school."

"Dad, this is crazy!" Sophia said, starting the car.

"Just drive," Steve said. "No music and no talking. Hello? This is Steve Smith, Stacey Smith's husband. Our daughter... Sophia..." He let a little check enter his voice. "She's been hit by a car in the school parking lot. I really need to talk to Stacey immediately... Yes, I understand..."

"I got hit by a *car*?" Sophia whispered.

Steve waved his hand at her angrily, then nodded.

"Stacey! Alas, alas, alas... Sophia... has been... struck by... a car... in the parking lot," he said, robotically. "I'm picking up Faith right now. Yes. I'll meet you at home, then we'll go to the hospital. You have your phone again? I'm forwarding you a text... Okay. Call me when you're on the way." He hung up the phone, then pulled up a file.

"What was the robot voice about?" Sophia asked, pulling carefully into traffic.

"False information versus true," Steve said. "I mean, you could really have been hit by a car. The 'alas' code told her it was a real world emergency but not the one that I was conveying."

"Mom is going to be that pissed, you know," Sophia said.

"Part of our bargain was that if something hit the dunny she'd go with it," Steve said, looking at a file. "Oh... Bloody hell."

"What?" Sophia asked.

"Just concentrate on getting us to the middle school intact," Steve said, consulting his smartphone. He pulled up an app and punched in certain parameters. On the third hit he'd found what he was looking for and dialed a phone number. "Hello? My name is Jason Ranseld with the Aurelius Corporation. We need to rent a boat matching the parameters of the one you have for sale. Is there any way that we can get a two-week lease? No? We'd consider buying if we could talk about the price. And I'd need to look it over... Would Saturday afternoon work for you? This is a snap-kick for a major client... Of course, three would work perfectly... Thank you, I'll meet you there..."

"Sailboat?" Sophia said. "That's full up bug-out for a biological emergency!"

"I finally got to pull up the code sheet," Steve said. "Biological, viral, latent, wide-release, previously undetected, currently no vaccine, hostile activities parameter."

"I got all of that except latent and hostile... Wait! *Zombies?*"

"Something similar," Steve said as they pulled up to the fortunately close middle school. "Cell phone."

"Dad!"

"Cell," Steve said, pulling a burn phone out of the bag. "This is your new one. *Only* the numbers on contact list."

"I have friends who..."

"No!" Steve said. "You know why. I walked away from several people I like, to maintain your uncle's cover. If it gets out..."

"Uncle Tom loses his position," Sophia said, pulling out her phone and handing it over. "And any support he can give us. But Brad Turner..."

"Is going to have to take his chances," Steve said, taking the phone, then pocketing the burn phone. "You get this when I get back."

"Thanks for all the trust, Dad," Sophia said, crossing her arms.

"I'm going to be trusting you to keep us all alive," Steve said, then handed over the phone. "I guess that starts now. Prove you deserve it by not using it."

"Okay," Sophia said.

"Emergency conditions," Steve said.

"Yes, sir," Sophia said, then shrugged. "I'll believe zombies when I see one."

"Despite the fact that I've just burned my job and your mother's, let's hope this is a false alarm," Steve said getting out of the truck.

"What happened to Mom?" Faith blurted the minute he walked into the school's office.

"Still not sure," Steve said. "Can I get a release slip?"

"What do you *mean* you don't *know*?" Faith practically shouted. The thirteen-year-old had gotten her dad's height and her mother's looks, which, honestly, was a bit of a challenge for her older sister, whom she already overtopped. Another inheritance was her mother's temper but twice as passionate. In a guy the term "aggressive" would be more commonly used. She also had something like male muscle density and pain tolerance a Delta would appreciate. She only played soccer because there wasn't a rugby team. On the rare trips to visit her Aussie grandparents she positively delighted in Australian Rules football. Although she just as passionately hated "Rule One": No Weapons.

"Kintronics HR would only say she'd been 'Injured,'" Steve said, taking the release form and signing for his daughter. "On the other hand, the person I was talking to was pretty shaken up. So it's serious."

"Well then, let's *roll*!" Faith said, snatching up her bag and darting out of the door.

"Good-bye," Steve said, waving as he went out the door.

"Apocalypse code from Uncle Tom," Sophia said as soon as Faith was in the car. "Not a drill. Dad's already arranged the boat to steal."

"So...Wait..." Faith said. "Mom's not—"

"She's on her way home," Steve said, gesturing for Sophia to get in the passenger seat and climbing in the truck. "We're in bug-out mode. And with any luck at all we won't have to steal it."

"But what about—" Faith started to ask.

"Phone," Sophia said, holding out a burn phone to her. "Yours."

"You're *serious*?"

"Zombies," Sophia said.

"No way!" Faith said. "We're not having a ZA! Where are the wrecked cars? The screaming people? Nobody's rising from the *grave*! False alarm!"

"I've got a confirm from Uncle Tom," Steve said, pulling out of the parking lot. Parents were already forming up to pick up their precious snowflakes. "Viral, not mystical. Zombielike actions. Previously undetected. Pull the batteries."

"Already done on mine," Sophia said, pulling out Faith's. "Okay, now it's done."

"Code indicates it's already spread," Steve said.

"So we could already have it?" Sophia asked. "That's...not good."

"That's all we've got right now," Steve said. "We'll get the rest as things go on."

"This had *better* be for real or I'm disowning this stupid family," Faith said, leaning back with her arms crossed and her head set.

"Put on your safety belt," Steve said. "Safety just got much more important."

"If I had your phone I could be checking for indications," Sophia pointed out.

Steve considered that for a moment. The original plans hadn't included either daughters capable of information gathering or smartphones. The first requirement was gather the clan. Second was go off-grid. Going off-grid wasn't strictly necessary but it reduced distractions. And Tom had the number for his back-up just as Steve had Tom's. Third was gather material. Then bug out. Only last, look for indicators. Among other things, indicators were a way to track information security.

"Not on the phone," Steve said. "If Tom's usage is being monitored, it could give away his tip if you search for 'zombie' or 'plague' off my phone. Just work the plan."

"Yes, my bug-out bag is packed," Faith said and grimaced. "'Where's your bug-out bag?' 'Is your bug-out bag packed?' 'What's your inventory?' 'Why did I get the *insane* parents?'"

"We're packing the trailer," Sophia pointed out. "When do we go to biocon?"

"I'm torn," Steve admitted. "We can't meet about the sailboat with masks on. On the other hand, any meeting is a danger."

"Speaking of which," Sophia said, dipping into her bag. "Hand sanitizer." She rubbed some on her hands, then passed it over.

"Which is why I have you along," Steve said, smiling. He wiped not only his hands but the steering wheel.

"This had *better* be for real," Faith said, rubbing her hands vigorously.

"You just want to fight zombies," Sophia said.

"Which is why I have *you* along," Steve added with a grin.

"Derp," Faith said. "Of *course* I want to fight zombies. Who doesn't?"

"Me," Sophia said.

"Me," Steve said.

"Yeah, well there had *better* be zombies or I'm shooting *somebody* and two guesses who. Oh, wait, they're *both* right..."

"I read the code but I'm still not one hundred percent on this. Note that I just threw away a perfectly good job."

Stacey Smith was five six with dark blue eyes and dark brown— or occasionally auburn—hair. Two children had caused her to "chunk" a bit, but she still was pretty much the attractive geek girl Tom had met in Melbourne eighteen years ago. One who agreed that the world was occasionally a hostile place and did not so much "indulge" her husband's penchant for preparation as drive it.

"I knew this day might come..." Steve said, shrugging. "Tom wouldn't jest about something like this."

"I'm going to go look for a confirm," Stacey said.

"Just..." Steve said, grimacing.

"I'll use a proxy," Stacey said, patting him on the arm. "I'm not going to go shouting 'Zombie Apocalypse' to the rooftops."

"And I'll go take care of packing the trolley."

Steve considered most "preppers" to be short-sighted, at least those portrayed in the media and even those on the various boards. Having all sorts of preparations in an urban setting was a good way to have them taken away at the first hint of trouble. If the government didn't "gather" what you had or had produced, then gangs would eventually. And those that moved to distant zones... Well, if the end didn't come, you had better enjoy the rural life, and good luck finding a decent job in the meantime.

"Prepping" or survivalism is about Maslow's hierarchies. The first three are ostensibly "food, clothing and shelter." What Maslow left out was "security." And in a real, serious, end-of-civilization-as-we-know-it, security was the single greatest concern.

So Steve and Stacey's plans were... flexible.

The house they lived in was subtly fortified. Most of it had to do with living in Virginia where the threat of an occasional hurricane or severe storm meant having plywood ready to cover the windows was just good sense. The house had been chosen for various "real world" factors: jobs, schools, the neighborhood. But it also had fieldstone walls, which meant it was somewhat bullet resistant. Also hurricane resistant, which was the point that they tended to make to casual friends and neighbors. There was a sizeable and quite dry basement. There was a generator, ROWPU water purifier and various supplies against both hurricanes and ice storms. Their neighbors were always commenting on how well prepared they were for emergencies. Which was nice until the second or third minor "emergency" when you were the only one who noticed that the lights did occasionally go out and grocery stores tended to run short when there was the slightest news of a possible disaster. Yes, we have spare toilet paper.

Incoming comet? Landward ho. They had some "true" friends, including a few Ami paras and special operations Steve had met in Afghanistan and kept in touch with. Together with Tom, the group had bought an old house in the Western Virginia countryside. More or less a "time share," they used it as a weekend or summer get-away. Its actual purpose being, well, a get-away. Staffed by six former soldiers and their generally well-prepared families, it was going to be a bit of a tough nut to crack.

But there were a few events that called for heading seaward. The first was any sort of biological. Boats were designed to take stores, and modern boats had water purifiers to draw fresh water from the sea. Once they were loaded up, you could stay away from other people for a looong time. Longer if you had a sailboat with "green" recovering power such as wind generators and recovering propeller generators. A little fishing, plenty of vitamins, and barring running into a bad storm you were good for months. And missing storms was mostly a matter of being where they didn't go. Assuming the biological was bad enough, afterwards you could probably scavenge with care. Thus the full hazmat clothing in the stores.

"Zombies" had been, generally, considered one of those stochastic low probabilities that were more for fun than serious consideration. A zombie shoot was particularly fun. But because it was the sort of thing that the kids could get into, with some humor, that had been part of the planning as well. If for no other reason than it gave them a chance to take a "prepper" cruise to the Islands on a sailboat. The kids had enjoyed the time in the Abacos and learned the basics of sailing as well as maintaining a boat.

Survivalism. Good clean fun for the whole family. At least if you didn't take it to excess.

"The cans go on the *bottom*!" Sophia shouted as Steve entered the basement garage. "Heavy stuff *down* and forward!"

"Bite me, Soph," Faith snarled. "*I* wasn't the one who already loaded the toilet paper!"

"Then move it around," Steve said. Good clean fun. "Soph, into the trolley. You load, Faith and I will toss."

"Yeah," Faith said, grinning maliciously. "'Cause you're so short you can fit inside."

"We shall soon be armed, sister dear," Sophia said, sweetly.

"That assumes you can hit me at the range of sitting next to you," Faith said, staggering over under the weight of three cases of water.

"Which you know I can do at any range you'd care to name," Sophia replied.

"She's got you there," Steve said. "She's a better shot and you know it."

"Not at *combat* shooting," Faith argued. "She's better when she takes all day to pull the trigger."

"I'm going to have all day to listen to your bitching," Sophia pointed out.

The trailer was a ten-by-six, bought used and improved and maintained by Stacey. She tended to do the mechanical and electrical bits. In this case, new plywood floor, new bearings, wiring and a new coat of paint. Hundred dollars used, a bit more in repairs, and it was practically a brand new trailer. Which was rapidly filling with gear and supplies.

"We couldn't load the gen by ourselves," Sophia pointed out. "And if we're going to, we'd better soon or it will unbalance the trailer."

"We're not taking it," Steve said regretfully. The generator wasn't new but it was in good shape, and with care, which Stacey was obsessive about, would last for years. "The boat has one."

"Spare?" Faith asked.

"Rather take more supplies," Steve said, tossing a case of bottled water into the back of the trailer. "The way to avoid loading the heavy on light is to move heavy first."

"What about ammo?" Stacey asked.

"Ammo, guns, first aid, one case water, one general case mountain house in the car," Steve said. "Bug-out bags and webbing. Hook in. We're on short time."

"Know it's bad," Faith said, grinning. "Da's going DU, then."

"Hooking in, Dad," Sophia said, then paused. "Dad... Are we really, *really* sure?"

"No," Steve admitted, tossing a case of rations onto the trailer. "Not until we have a confirm or I can talk to Tom in the open."

"I don't want all my friends to die," Faith said softly.

"I don't want either of *you* to die," Steve said. "Which is why we're hooking in."

"And there's a partial confirm," Stacey said, walking down the stairs. "There have been three reported incidents on the West Coast. People are putting it down to drugs but it's zombie-istic."

"The bath salts thing again?" Faith asked. "That's *it*?"

"No," Steve said. "That's a *confirm*. Tom's message indicated that it's already out there. Those are infected people. Presumably. We'll get a solid confirmation later. I'm hoping that guy makes the meeting tomorrow."

"Then you'd better get upstairs and call him," Stacey pointed out. "He's probably getting ready to close up shop."

"Boat broker," Steve pointed out. "He's connected to his cell. But... yeah."

CHAPTER 2

"Hem, hem . . ." Steve said, dialing the number. "Aggravated and harried . . . That's easy enough . . ."

"Mr. Resto? This is Jason Ranseld again . . . Can I call you Felix? Absolutely, call me Jason. Felix, there's a problem. Here's our deal. We're trying to close an investor and he's into sailing. The last time I did this it was some schlub that just won a big settlement and he wanted to go out on a cigarette boat. Got him into a Fountain Lightning and it just about scared the shit out of him . . . Yeah, you know the type. Thing is, the fricking meeting got moved up to Sunday and we don't have a boat available on the East Coast . . . Yeah. So I convinced the partners to just go for the whole thing . . . Yeah, purchase order is *in* place . . . We'll sell it later. Maybe to the client. Happens that way sometimes. But we've got to close this *tomorrow* so I can make sure everything's in place for Sunday . . . I know it's a snap-kick . . . We're going to have to move up the meeting to either tonight or tomorrow morning . . . Late tonight: I'm in Richmond . . . Sorry about that. You want the commission or not . . . ?"

"Yes, hello? You rent luxury cars . . . ?"

"Found the house . . ."

"Jason Ranseld's identification," Stacey said, handing over the driver's license, American Express card and Australian passport. Steve had set up the identity years before and carefully maintained it. "Jason Ranseld's photos of his kids and Mrs. Ranseld. Cute kids. Wish they were ours..."

The rain had at least passed but the sky was still gray and the wind outside the Nissan looked to be biting. It would be a great day to go sailing. Not.

"Hey," Faith said, sleepily. "I bet they're real snowflakes."

The sun was barely up and the drive had been long. The girls had been able to rack out in the back but Steve and Stacey had had to drive separate cars. Then there had been the recon of the marina...

"They are," Steve said. "My daughter Faith Ranseld just had her thirteenth birthday for sixty kids at Disneyworld in Orlando. *And* their parents. We had to pay for the whole damned thing. Sophia Ranseld's sweet sixteen is coming up and God *knows* what she's going to want, the spoiled little brat!"

"I want a cake that looks like a full-size dragon and has real flames," Sophia said. "And Disney is sooo kitsch. I want mine at...Uhm..."

"Keep working on it, Sophia Ranseld," Steve said.

"Why are we having to change our names?" Faith asked. "We're not meeting this guy, right?"

"No," Steve said. "But I need to remember my 'real' name."

"Okay, Mr. Ranseld," Stacey said. "Conspiracy to commit fraud and grand larceny. Great."

"Nothing really turning up on the radio," Steve said. "We need to get internet access."

"We need more supplies," Stacey pointed out. "We've got at most thirty days. Not food, other consumables."

"And you can't *make* toilet paper," Faith pointed out.

"Make a stop," Steve said, getting out of the Nissan. "Level One protocols. Best we can do without freaking people out. I'll meet you at the rendezvous."

"Felix," Steve said, stepping out of the rental Mercedes. "Glad you could meet me so early."

"You know the drill," Resto said, sipping his coffee. "We also serve who sell boats," he added with a grin.

"Tell me about it," Steve said, shaking his head. "Speaking of which—boat?"

"Follow me," Resto said, walking over to his BMW.

Steve kept his eyes open and carefully, if covertly, examined the marina. There was a guard shack but a drive-by the previous night had shown it to be unoccupied at night as well as day. They'd staked out the marina for two hours and had seen no sign of any roving guard, although a security car had passed at 4:23 AM. Probably the marina had once featured "guard on duty twenty-four hours" but had cut back with the current economy to an occasional drive-by. The gate had a keypad lock, which Resto opened. Which gave at least one code to the lock, given the punch-tracker that Stacey had installed. If the con didn't work they could always slip in and slip out with the boat. Assuming the owners hadn't removed something critical from the ship systems.

Better to just buy it with fake money. Money was basically fake anyway. At least the way his source did things . . .

"Tom," Richard Bateman said. "You're the man at this meeting."

Dr. Richard Bateman, Ph.D. Econ, was CEO of Bank of the Americas. Tall and nearly as broad as his security chief at six foot four, he had the de rigueur height for a Fortune 500 CEO and graying temples so perfect everyone wanted to know what hairdresser he used. "Yes, sir," Thomas "Train" Smith said, standing up and going to the end of the board table.

Tom's full nickname was "Thomas the Train Engine." This was given to him back in officer's Basic Course and had stayed as his handle ever since. The joke around the office was "Clark Kent turns out to be Australian." In his "banker suit" and Birth Control Glasses he did rather look like a sandy-blond Clark Kent. And the typing pool generally agreed that when the suit came off he looked *exactly* like a blond Superman.

When the young ladies he met in clubs asked him what he did, he generally just said "Investment Banking" because that meant he had money, and he'd get laid. Well, the dancers and actresses. The Goth and Emo chicks at the alternative clubs seemed to prefer his other answer: "I'm the bad guy that gets killed second to last in the movie. You know when the villain turns to his boss henchman and says 'Take care of it'? I'm that guy." With some who were *way* out there, this occasionally backfired. The one time he got a call to come help him move a body he'd agreed to meet her, asked where, then politely called the police. Fortunately, it turned out to be an OD, and NYPD had limited their questions.

In fact, he had yet to be told to "take care of it" in any extreme manner. When he'd taken the job he'd wondered if dirty work was in the offing, and even, tactfully, checked during the very long vetting process. The response had been, for bankers, humorous at best. Bankers didn't have to have their employees kill, defame or otherwise destroy enemies. There were lots of people that just did it for them because, well, people wanted their money. When a new dam was being negotiated in some developing country, it wasn't banks who paid "laborers" to go beat up "protestors." That was the local government who was going to make money off of the dam. To the extent that investment banks did anything along those lines, it was to quietly protest "No. Stop. No. Seriously... It *looks* bad..." and then lend them money anyway.

Tom was still unsure if he was disappointed or relieved. Most of his job came down to making sure that servers had distant off-line backups and checking to see what Shining Path was up to lately.

Saturday morning was not a normal time for all the senior executives of the Bank of the Americas to meet. And since they were only one of many such groups meeting all over the world on this particular Saturday, the cat was going to be out of the bag by noon, latest.

"This is the issue," Tom said, bringing up a photo of the pathogen in question. "The pathogen is currently called H7D3. There is no common name associated. It is definitely man-made and has been widely spread. Spread method is currently unknown. Currently there are no manifestos or declarations related to it. FBI is trying to trace the source, but they're barely getting started, and this isn't the movies. They don't find the culprits overnight, if ever. For details on the pathogen and immunological response I'm going to turn this over to Dr. David Curry. Dr. Curry is a virologist who has consulted with us on emergency response as well as business risk management in biological investments. Dr. Curry."

"I always start with 'excuse mah accent.'" Dave Curry was a bit under six feet tall with dark brown hair and bright brown eyes. "I was born in lower Alabama and ain't quite got rid of my drawl.

"The pathogen is, as Mr. Smith noted, definitely man-made, antiviral-resistant and very sophisticated. For one thing it is both an airborne pathogen and a blood pathogen. First one of those in, well, *ever*. Otherwise I won't bore you gentlemen with the technical details, they're in my lecture notes. Progress appears to be as follows: Normal flu nonsymptomatic infective period of about five to seven days. To refresh you from Swine flu: Influenza, unlike some other stuff like SARS, is infectious for a period of time, generally around seven days, *before* you get your first sniffle or fever. Which, by the way, is a bugger and a half. Individuals are, again, nonsymptomatic but infecting everyone and every-*thing* they come into contact with. And it means that the origin, assuming some sort of device, is going to be hard to pin down. Then flu-like symptoms. No major differences between this and any other sort of flu. Somewhat worse than seasonal but not as bad as, say, swine flu or SARS. Not a patch on avian flu. But it's *extremely* infective. Upper respiratory, which is the easy stuff to catch. Lots of coughing, hacking, spitting, and occasional pneumonia for those who are susceptible. Current model is about five percent mortality in the flu stage, mostly in the old and young. Not much worse, as I said, than seasonal. Usually lasts twenty-four to forty-eight hours. Then there's a dead period. Most symptoms except low-grade fever disappear. This is the first point that it becomes *non*-flulike.

"After a period they're trying to pin down, looks like two to five days, neurological symptoms start. Probably, and it's only *probably*, that is the point where subjects become blood-pathogen infectious and may, again, *may*, no longer be airborne infectious. Best to assume all subjects are both vectors until we've got a better handle on this. Initial presentation of neurological symptoms are, in no particular order, palsy, disorientation, dizziness, blurred vision and, notably, formication. Note: I said 'for-*mi*-cation.' This refers to a form of paresthesia or 'itching, tingling' which feels like ants crawling on or biting the skin. Series of presentation is somewhat random, but at a certain point the patient tends to strip to get the 'spiders' or 'ants' off."

"Strip?" Richard said.

"Yes," Tom said. "In all of the cases that have come to the attention of the police, the subject has been naked."

"That seems..." Dr. Bradford J. Depene was not as tall as his boss, by nearly a foot, but he weighed at least twice as much. He and Tom were not by any stretch of the imagination best buddies. Depene had been born with a silver spoon and had apparently used it as hard as he possibly could his whole life. Tom really wasn't as bothered by the gross obesity as by the fact that, while unquestionably brilliant, Depene had the common sense of a duckling. "That seems sort of..."

"The term you're looking for is *obscene*," Richard said. "Any idea...why? Just for the embarrassment factor? Pornographic?"

"If it's intentional, it's smart," Dr. Curry said. "But can I cover that later?"

"Continue," Bateman said.

"After the formication period things vary. There are so far twenty-four identified patients in the U.S. None of those have gone through the full series while under observation. Most have presented symptoms outside quarantine: In other words, they were picked up by the cops as crazy, naked people before they were identified as being H7 infected. There have been nine of those in the U.S. so far who were in advanced neurological stage. One has died while under care and one is critical. That's not a statistical study, but it looks as if this is also a real killer neurologically."

"Twenty percent death rate?" Bateman asked.

"Right at that is what it looks like," Curry said, shrugging. "Data is still firming up. However, in the meantime they're a handful. 'Extreme homicidal psychosis with reduced mental capacity' is the current psychobabble diagnosis. Think lobotomized and violent as hell. *Very* bitey. No coherent sentient response. No language per se. Just basically animal responses, and aggressive animals at that. L.A. General is starting to fill up their padded rooms. One customer per or they try to kill each other.

"Currently there's a statistical lean to male. Of the twenty-four, sixteen are male. All three of the terminal were male, two of the three critical are male. But that could be from any number of factors including where the infection started and how it spread. SARS looked male-leaning for a while due to how it was spreading. Again, we'll know more in a week. They're still examining suspect patients and known subjects who are identified as infected or probably infected. There's a slightly less-strong lean to male among those. Stats and other indicators as well as potential treatments will start firming up over the next few days. Again, first identification as an outbreak was only yesterday. These are early days."

"What do we do about it?" Bateman asked. "*We* being the bank as well as in general."

"If it had been a normal and natural outbreak I think we could get ahead of this thing," Curry said, shrugging. "As it is… It's spread all over, it has delayed onset of symptoms, two delays, and it's infective as hell. Airborne *and* blood pathogen with a violent vector on the latter? That's infective as hell. There are probably people going into neurological state all over the place that are being viewed as 'the usual sort of thing.'"

"The usual sort of thing?" Depene asked. "Naked people are *normal*?"

"Police have to deal with naked subjects more than most people realize," Tom said. "Any large department will deal with someone nude and incoherent at least once a week. Often extremely violent. In New York as often as once a day. It really was only when L.A. was dealing with six in one day that anyone started looking for a central source, and even then they were looking at drugs. Surprisingly it didn't make the blogs at all. At least, not noticeably. It will soon."

"We'd been tracking this new 'flu' already, mind you," Curry said. "It took about a day for UCLA Med to put two and two together. The sort of people who are naked and crazy normally have other illnesses, and this sudden, outbreak 'seasonal flu' was considered to be symptom rather than cause. Then CDC noted that this was not a seasonal flu, so the alerts starting going up, given the locus and spread was not following standard models. Then one of the police who had dealt with Patient Zero, and been bitten, started to manifest neurological symptoms. At that point they realized they were dealing with a neurological pathogen.

"To answer the original question: The only real chance we have is general public and government response. Strong influenza protocols along with some changes in Rules of Engagement by law enforcement will slow this, maybe even stop it. It's less about the bug right now than it is about general immunology protocols. Your offices already have hand sanitizers. Ensure they get *used* and if somebody won't, well, send 'em home or fire 'em. Ditto anyone showing any flulike symptoms. Don't shake hands. *Don't* shake hands. Ever. For any reason. Wash your hands thoroughly several times a day. Right now, usual drill is all we've got. Ask me again in a week if there's a change.

"As to the nastier symptoms: This is New York. Telling the difference between a crazy homeless guy and one of the infected is going to be a bit dicey at first. But if somebody is clean-cut, basically clean and running around screaming, biting and naked, they're probably in advanced neurological stage. Be warned: It definitely has a blood pathogen component. And the onset is direct to neurological and fast. The police officer who was bitten started beginning symptoms of neurological stage in six *hours.* So for our security personnel, Mr. Smith, at the first sign of incoherence on the part of an employee or visitor, especially if they start gittin' nekkid, you need to taser first, then ask questions from hazmat. Do *not* allow yourself to get bitten."

"Roger," Tom said, making a note. "Mr. Bateman?"

"Confirmed," Bateman said. "We'll promulgate that."

"If I may, sir," Tom said. "Best to promulgate that anyone acting incoherent for the purposes of humor will be fired if found to be noninfected. There are people who are going to push this."

"Also agreed," Bateman said. "This is nothing to joke about."

"And, sorry, gentlemen, that has to go for any rank," Dr. Curry said, looking at the assembled executives. "If one of you has any habit of bipolar reactions or schizophrenia, if you go off your meds, just figure you're going to get tasered. And if it's just a freak-out, say 'Thank you, Mister Security guard, for tasering me' when they determine you're not infected. On that: Right now there's no way to tell short of a blood test. They're rolling out nasal antibody tests sometime this week. But that's for the flu. We're not sure if they work for the neurological since we've never seen a dual-expression rhinovirus. Also everybody and their brother is looking for a vaccine. Any hint on that, I'll pass through Mr. Smith. Questions?"

"No antivirals that it's not resistant to?" Bateman asked. The CEO was clearly unhappy that there were essentially no useful measures to take. "There are ways to get antivirals which...aren't available in the U.S."

"None," Dr. Curry said, grinning mirthlessly. "Whoever did this armored it up. There aren't even any that are near approval in *Europe.* Which tells me there is a vaccine. You're not going to create something that you're not going to survive. The combination of 'intelligent enough to create a world-killer flu,' 'crazy enough to do it' and 'suicidal' is too small a pool. Similar personality types, mind you, but not overlapping. Whoever did this intends to survive it. Which means there's a vaccine. Not a *cure*, mind you. So you'd better hope there's a vaccine before you or your family catch it. Next."

"Cover the 'making it so they strip is smart,'" Tom said.

"I'm going to have to say a word everybody is avoiding," Curry said with a snort. "Starts with a *z*. Anybody want to say it before me? Mr. Bateman?"

"Zombie?" Bateman said. "As long as it doesn't leave the confines of this room."

"One thing that always bugged me about biological zombies," Curry said, musingly, "at least the ones that were something like realistic. Say, *I am Legend.* They've got to crap. Every species eliminates waste. If you can't figure out how to use a door handle, how are you going to take off your pants to take a crap? And modern clothing is going to plug it up. Eventually the subject dies of impaction and necrosis."

"So you really think that was built in?" Depene asked.

"The words that are on every message about this are 'lethal and sophisticated,'" Curry said. "It's why people are saying it has to be a nation-state. But I don't buy it. If it had been a nation-state there would have been an unusual round of vaccinations somewhere. Trust me, WHO looks for those as much as it looks for plagues. There haven't been. Not even, say, the Iranian Supreme Council. And what you can do with bugs these days with stuff off of eBay is insane. At least if you know what you're doing. And not even that. A reporter built Spanish Flu in his damned *kitchen*! Then there's people all over hoping to be the next biological Wozniak playing around in their houses with ... *stuff*. Usually not pathogens, but there's an entire industry of tinkerers with *biology*! Okay, I'm one of them but I know what I'm *doing*! This isn't inventing a new computer or the model T. This is the basic building blocks of *life* and you don't go playing with them like they're *Legos*. Or you eventually get something like, well ... This," he concluded with a sigh.

"Ten to one what we're going to find is this is some kid, under thirty, probably with a bachelor's degree, didn't complete his master's, and angry at the world. *I* could figure out how to do this pathogen. The people at, well, my level admit we've *all* figured out how to do a 'zombie virus' given current tech. But nobody has been *stupid* enough to actually *do* it. Until now."

"How?" Depene said. "I mean in general. That sounds like... science fiction?"

"Tell that to your smartphone," Curry grumped. "In case you hadn't noticed, we live in a science fiction world. Okay. One: Rabies doesn't just make the brain swell. That's a side effect of what it's doing to the brain. That foam doesn't come from nowhere. Rabies works by effecting production of certain neurotransmitters. Two: There are other, lesser known, pathogens which have a targeted effect on other portions of the brain. Three: There's a lot about the brain we don't understand, but we *do* know how to mess it up. We know the basic centers and neurotransmitters for about everything simple: Love, anger, hunger, memory, pattern recognition... Four, open the door: From AIDS research we know how to stick genes in eukaryotic cells and even target the type of cells. We know how to get cells to sequence certain proteins, also known as neurotransmitters. Put all that together with the pathogens we already know, like toxoplasmosis, modifying them to mess up the brain is *easy*. You can even make them only target certain individuals or groups genetically. Well, I could. But I didn't do it. I've got an alibi."

"How long have people like...yourself...?" Bateman asked, frowning.

"People who are actual researchers," Curry said with another of those mirthless grins, "Or who work as consultants to afford all the conferences and papers? And who understand them? About two years ago it was generally recognized that you could do a zombie virus. Which is one of those 'Only adults in the room and we've had too much scotch' discussions. Not for open conference. We'd estimated the general 'monkey in the basement' would be able to do it in about five. So they're three years ahead of our most optimistic schedule. Which is why those same sort of people—on closed boards and who know about this—are arguing for it being a major effort, something big, expensive and noticeable. This kind of breakthrough generally is at the beginning. Maybe an experiment at one of the universities or research centers that was in development and got swiped. One of the reasons bandied around in those drunken discussions to come up with one is that you were guaranteed to make headlines, and headlines mean funding. I'm one of the minority arguing for mad scientist. Or mad, angry, former grad student. Bright, mind you. Brilliant, even. Skipped right past three or four steps. That takes real mad-scientist genius."

"Quite mad," Bateman said. "Doctor, what are *your* plans?"

"I'm thinking island in the Caribbean," Dr. Curry said. "But Mr. Smith has made me a very generous offer of semi-permanent consultant until this is over one way or the other. I've been around enough research and on WHO teams to have stared this sort of death, in general, in the eye before. Not looking forward to losing my mind, mind you. It's my only real asset. If you're asking if I'll hang in there with one of the richest and best prepared banks in the world...We'll talk. Depends on the fringe benefits."

"Such as?" Bateman asked.

"I understand you have a retreat point," Curry said, shrugging. "I don't, really. Assuming we get to that point, I and one other are guaranteed a slot on the planes or whatever."

"*Do* we have a retreat point?" Depene asked. "And why aren't we going there *now*?"

"Because we're not anywhere near that point, Brad," Bateman said with a sigh. "It's not about a downtick in the stock market. We evacuate only when that point has been reached."

"And when is 'that point'?" Depene asked.

"I'll let Mr. Smith cover that," Bateman said. "Tom?"

"There is a specific condition under which the Federal Reserve 'temporarily' terminates operations," Tom said. "For the duration of a global emergency. But upon either suspension of trade 'for the duration of the emergency' or upon vote of the board to suspend business activities for same, we then and only then activate the Executive and Special Personnel Evacuation Exercise. Which is generally called E-S-P. Meaning 'when' is ultimately up to Mr. Bateman and/or the Board and/or the Fed, which means *I'll* be reading my crystal ball. If, in my opinion, the security situation, including biological security situation, has degraded past operability I will *request* Mr. Bateman to so inform the Board. But that is only if the Fed doesn't act first. So... You may know before *I* do, Dr. Depene. As to Dr. Curry's request, I'd suggest that that be discussed in a separate meeting as well as any hostile-environment business plans."

"Agreed," Bateman said. "Dr. Curry, your contract is at the least extended for the duration of the emergency. Usual bonuses. And we'll be with you by Monday on inclusion in the evacuation plan."

"I can wait that long," Curry said. "I need to get back into the information stream."

"We all do," Bateman said, blowing out a heavy breath. "And I need to get a statement prepared for investors..."

CHAPTER 3

"Is the boat going to be able to hold all of this?" Faith asked. "And how are we getting it there? Pushing?"

When you've basically bought a Costco out of toilet paper and feminine hygiene products, these were reasonable questions, if poorly timed.

"We can strap some to the roof of the Nissan," Stacey said, looking around the pile of toilet paper on the pallet. She certainly couldn't see over it. They'd gotten some very odd looks but no serious questions. "Stocking up for hurricane season" was the simplest answer. And it wasn't like anyone in Williamsburg knew who they were. She grimaced in annoyance when her phone rang. But it was Tom's burn-phone number.

"Tom?" Stacey said. "Hang on a second. We're walking across a parking lot."

"Roger," Tom asked. "What's your status?"

"Nominal so far," Stacey said, keying open the doors. "Inside for the chat, girls."

"Public places are to be avoided," Tom pointed out.

"Toilet paper is a right, not a privilege," Stacey said, getting in the car and putting the phone on speaker. "Okay, we're all in. Go."

"Everybody there?" Tom asked over the speakerphone.

"Steve's negotiating the boat," Stacey said. "Go."

Tom covered the highlights, such as they were, of Dr. Curry's analysis.

"*Naked* zombies?" Faith said. "Gross!"

"Makes sense to me," Stacey said. "If they kept their clothes on and are still 'alive' they'd have difficulty with waste passage."

"That means they couldn't shit, Faith," Sophia said.

"I know what it means!" Faith said. "Yuck again!"

"Short time, here," Tom said seriously. "End-of-the-world stuff."

"Sorry, Uncle Tom," Sophia said, just as seriously. "We're just having a hard time..."

"Go, Tom," Stacey said.

"Increasing incoherency to an essentially animal state. In that state, hyperaggression. May be just the cases so far identified, but aggression seems to be increased. Very bitey, from the reports from the West Coast—which also spreads because of the blood-pathogen effect. At least one cop who dealt with a case is infected. Six confirmed cases on the East Coast, *four* in Asia. Confirmed. CDC has decided to go public at noon. News media is already asking questions.

"They're looking at a vaccine. Go."

"Any pre-symptoms notable other than 'flulike'?" Sophia asked.

"Nothing particular," Tom said. "Not until second stage. May not be blood pathogen until then. General flu-prevention procedures, which is what the 'powers-that-be' are going to be calling for. Swine flu again, but this is already spread, probably worldwide, and spreading fast. Stand by... Pasteur confirms cases in England and France... Six now in Hong Kong alone...I need to cut this short. I've got another meeting."

"We're using the Aurelius Corporation plan," Stacey said. "Can you...do something about it? We'd prefer to avoid actually *stealing* the yacht."

"How much?" Tom asked.

"One forty," Stacey said with a wince.

"Done," Tom said. "I'll authorize the transfer as soon as we're off the phone. What's the cover name?"

"Jason Ranseld. R-A-N-S-E-L-D."

"I'll take care of it. Just get offshore."

"How is *your* jump plan?" Stacey asked.

"If they come up with a vaccine, nominal," Tom said. "If they don't, you don't want me infecting you. Out here."

Steve waved to bemused looking Felix as the wind carried the boat away from the dock. He could tell that the broker was wondering if he'd somehow been taken.

It certainly would hold for a couple of weeks. By which time this would either be a false alarm and the Smiths, one and all, would have to start their lives over, probably in Australia, or the world would be so clearly headed to hell in a handbasket that nobody would care.

"Jason Ranseld" had some very interesting papers indeed. Among others was a mate's license. It wasn't forged. Steve had gotten it while he was living the "Jason Ranseld" life many years agone. So he had some experience working with boats this big. In wind even. Twenty years agone.

He thus managed to maneuver out of the marina without major incident. What he hadn't thought to bring was a coat. And it was bloody chilly. The clouds were high, thin and rippled in a regular humped pattern, and the sun shone through them weak and gray. There was a name for that type of cloud formation, but Steve couldn't quite recall it.

He was worried about Stacey and the girls. Against direct threats they could take care of themselves, but a plague... There just wasn't any way to truly prevent it absent quarantine gear. And it was in the general population....

He looked up at the scudding clouds and still couldn't remember the official name for the formation. But he remembered the day he'd asked his Grandfather Smith about them. Gran had been a veteran of WWII starting from his days as a militia man in New Guinea and always knew everything.

Gran had looked up, said it was called "a graveyard sky," then walked back in the house and had gotten very drunk.

"Come on, honey," Stacey said. "Where *are* you?"

It was a nice neighborhood despite the relatively low occupancy. The housing downturn in the Virginia area had tended to impact high-end homes more than lower end. And it was a very nice neighborhood. Which was why the beat-up Nissan Pathfinder with something piled on top under a tarp was getting a lot of looks from the remaining residents. Before long she'd have to explain their presence to the police. And since there *wasn't* a good explanation...

"Jail?" Faith said.

"I don't need that right now, Faith," Stacey said. She didn't want to call Steve in case there *were* problems. He didn't need her nagging. "Besides, the check is good. Sort of."

"Have a little...faith, Sis," Sophia said.

"Oh, that's sooo *wise*," Faith spat back.

Stacey started as her phone rang. She checked and it was Steve. Which could be good or bad...

"Tell me you're not in jail," Stacey said.

"Inbound to the rendezvous," Steve said. "Glad you got that payday loan from Tom. The seller wasn't impressed by lots of important-looking paperwork. I think he's still wondering about the wire transfer."

"Which, as I understand it, we'd better be able to cover, or things have to go to hell in a handbasket quick," Stacey replied, putting the idling car in drive and creeping forward.

"Any problems on your end?"

"Just keeping the toilet paper on top of the car."

"Okay, I see what you mean," Steve said, chuckling.

The house was about ten thousand square feet and right on a navigable "creek" that would meet most areas' definition of river. And it included a very nice T dock with enough room to tie up, say, a 45-foot Hunter sailboat named *Mile Seven*. There was even a convenient drive to bring a car around to the end of the dock. Which Stacey was, cautiously, doing as the girls ran down to the dock.

The reason for the caution was apparent by the cargo. Stacey was, in Steve's opinion, an unrecognized mechanical and electrical genius. On the other hand, *he* had a tendency to hit *other* people's thumbs with a hammer. That being said, as a former para he always handled packing. Especially if it involved anything torqued onto the roof of the Pathfinder.

Stacey had apparently gotten two of the spare tarps from the trolley and done...something with a great deal of twine and *far* too much para cord. He'd seen some smaller cars more over-burdened in the Stans. However, those drivers had a bit more understanding of things like aerodynamics. And load shifting. The tarp looked a bit like a wind-battered green-and-brown potato.

"I can't remember how the knot goes..." Faith said, pulling the stern line in and then bracing as the boat started to head out to sea again. "Help?"

"I've got it," Sophia said. She'd already secured the fore line. Between them they got the stern of the boat alongside, and the older sister quickly had it secured with a double hitch. "It's simple."

"Simple is a shotgun and a zombie," Faith said.

"Quit arguing and start unloading," Steve said, shutting down the boat. "We're on short time."

"Shaking it for all we're worth, Captain, sir!" Sophia said, saluting sarcastically.

"That's more like it," Steve said.

Besides the mass of material, the main problem was first in was also first in. That is, just as the trailer had had to be packed with the heaviest items on the bottom and forward, the boat had to be packed with the heaviest items first. Which required unloading the entire trailer before they could get started on loading the boat.

They had just gotten the trailer completely unloaded when the visit Steve was dreading occurred.

"Dad," Sophia said, glancing around the trailer. "Cop."

"Roger," Steve said. "Start the load."

"Can I ask you what you're doing, sir?" Officer Jason Young, Williamsburg PD, asked.

The morning shift had started slow. A couple of kids speeding, couple of burglary reports from Friday night. The usual.

Things seemed to be picking up, though. He'd just heard two separate 10-64, indecent exposure, calls, then a 10-64, 10-28, fight or disturbance. Whatever, things were picking up and here he was dealing with...well he wasn't sure *what* he was dealing with. The call had been 10-37: suspicious person. The people just seemed to be loading a boat. But according to the neighbor who had called it in, the house connected to the dock was in foreclosure and nobody was supposed to be using the property. And the car, with badly secured materials on the roof, had been hanging around the neighborhood for nearly an hour.

"Loading my boat, Officer Young," Steve said.

"This is private property, and according to the neighbors, not *your* property," Young said. "Which means you are trespassing, sir."

"A valid position, Officer Young," Steve said. "The dock was convenient and the property is clearly not being used. It was, at best, a minor transgression and we'll be gone within the hour."

"Mind if I see some ID, sir?" Young asked. "You're not American. Irish?"

"Australian," Steve said, pulling out his driver's license and trying not to wince. Americans could never sort out Commonwealth accents. "And I'm a naturalized American citizen. Not a resident. I have a passport, American, as well."

"Says here you live in Warrentown," Young said. Which matched the plates on the Nissan.

"Yes, Officer," Steve said, politely. "The address is correct."

"Mind if I see your registration and proof of insurance?" Young asked.

"Of course," Steve said, turning around.

"Before you open the car," Young said. "Are there any weapons in the vehicle?"

"Ah," Steve said, turning back to face the officer. "I was wondering when we'd get to that part. Yes, as a matter of fact. They are all in locked cases in the rear. My wife and I also have CCLs but we are not, at this point, carrying."

"Okay," Young said, his brow furrowing. "All?"

"There are quite a few," Steve said. "Would you like to see? They're rather buried still. We were loading from the trolley first."

"Trolley?"

"Sorry," Steve said, too calmly, "trailer."

Young looked at the ladies continuing to load the boat. They didn't look as if they were preparing for a trip to the Caribbean. They looked nervous. And this cat was just too calm.

"Don't open the vehicle," Young said. "Please do not *approach* the vehicle. I need to talk to the ladies."

Steve started to open his mouth to ask why, then just nodded.

"As you prefer, Officer."

"Officer, sorry about this," Stacey said as the cop walked over. "I know we're sort of trespassing but the house is empty. It looks like it's in foreclosure. And it was *so* convenient to load! I'm really sorry but we won't be long."

She didn't do bimbo well but she was going to give it her best shot.

"There are marinas for that sort of thing, ma'am," the officer said. "Everything else okay?"

"Yes?" she asked, looking past the cop to Steve and trying to catch a clue. "What do you mean?"

"Are you under any form of duress?" the officer asked. "I mean, is this your idea? Are you okay, ma'am?"

"I'm fine," Stacey said, frowning. "We're fine. We just want to get loaded and off to sea!"

"And you are married to Mister...Sorry, what was the name again?" he asked, glancing at Steve's license.

"Oh," Stacey said, laughing. "You mean Steven John Smith, my husband of seventeen years? Would you like to meet our two children, Sophia Lynn and Faith Marie? Yes, he's my husband, these are our children and we're all real people."

"May I see some identification, ma'am?" the officer asked.

"It's in my purse in the car..."

"Which I'd like to hold off opening until I've examined the weapons inside," the officer said.

"You're in for a treat then," Faith said, stopping. "What's this about?"

"Just keep loading, Faith," Stacey said.

"What?" Faith said. "While you and Da stand around talking to the cop?"

"Just keep loading, Faith," Stacey said evenly.

"What's the rush?" the officer said.

"Trying to make the tide, Officer," Stacey said.

She knew immediately she'd said something wrong.

"The outgoing tide?" the officer asked, suspiciously. Any cop on the coast knows the tides, and the tide was currently inbound and would be for twelve hours. "Can I see the registration for the boat, please, ma'am?"

"I'll have to ask Steve where it's at," Stacey said.

"I'd appreciate it if you'd stop loading until I can get this cleared up, ma'am," the officer said.

"Of course, officer, if you insist," Stacey said, trying not to curse. "Okay, Faith, Soph, you can knock off."

"About time for a break!" Faith said.

∽ ⊖ ∾

"Problems, officer?" Steve asked as Young walked back to him.

"I'm trying to figure that out," Young said. "There's enough material here for an army, you've certainly got enough *guns* for one. You're trespassing on private property and you're in a hurry. And not, as your wife said, to make the tide. On the other hand, you don't look like a drug gang and the material doesn't look stolen. Nothing adds up. Call me suspicious."

"The dock is convenient to load on," Steve said. "Much more so than a marina."

"How long have you had the boat?" Young asked.

"Just bought it," Steve said. "This morning. Wire transfer from my brother's corporation."

"Okay, Mr. 'Smith,'" Young said angrily. "Cut the crap. What the hell is going on? Really?"

"Mind if I pull out my cell?" Steve said carefully.

"Why?"

"I'd like to check the time," Steve said. "Or you can give it to me."

"Why?" Young asked.

"I need to know what time it is," Steve said calmly.

Young stepped back and carefully, keeping half an eye on the man and group of women, checked his watch.

"Eleven forty-seven," Young said.

"Long day," Steve said ruefully. "I hadn't realized it was that early. Can I wait...thirteen minutes to answer that question?"

"What happens at noon?" Young asked, his eyes narrowing.

"An announcement," Steve said. "Probably a carefully worded one. Which will not give you enough information to protect yourself or your fellow officers. If we can continue loading until noon, and there is such an announcement, I can then give you more information. Information which may keep you alive. But I'm constrained not to until then. I will give you *one* piece of information. If you find yourself sometime in the next few days dealing with an incoherent naked person who is acting in a violent manner, my suggestion is to shoot him or her, dead if necessary, and avoid the blood splatter. That way you'll be placed on administrative leave pending the shoot investigation. And that will significantly increase your chances of survival."

Young stopped and thought about that. Guns. Supplies. Sailboat. In a hurry...

"You're joking," Young said. "That's impossible."

"Noon," Steve said. "At least I was told there would be an initial announcement at noon—"

Young's radio beeped urgently and he held it up to his ear.

"*Ten twenty-seven! Ten twenty-seven! Multiple hostile three—*" There was a series of shots, then the call cut off.

"*Ten twenty-seven, Four-one-three Elmshore Road. Ten twenty-seven, Four-one-three Elmshore Road... Break, break. Ten twenty-seven. Seven-two-seven-six Waterson Avenue... Ten Twenty-Seven...*"

"You need to go, Officer Young," Steve said. "Do *not* let them bite you under *any* circumstances. The blood pathogen is particularly potent."

"You have *got* to be kidding me!" Young said.

"Officers in trouble," Steve said, thumbing at the cop's car. "And good luck."

CHAPTER 4

Young peeled out of the driveway and checked his car's computer. He was designated to respond to the Waterson Avenue call. It was about six minutes ETA. He thumbed open his cell as he took the turn, blowing a stop sign and nearly getting T-boned by an Expedition, *then* hit his lights and sirens.

He hit speed dial three and waited impatiently.

"What? We've got multiple officers requesting back-up and youse got time for a *personal* call?"

Sergeant Joseph "Joey" Patterno would never have made sergeant in a previous Williamsburg administration. He had plenty of credentials. Fourteen years on SFPD in some of the toughest districts. He was physically fit, a short, barrel-chested Jewish-Italian from New York with time not only as a beat and operations sergeant but leading one of SFPD's premier SWAT teams. He'd moved to Williamsburg, which entailed a big pay cut, when his partner got a much better job offer than he'd had in Frisco, and the department here had, after much head scratching, taken Joey on.

The headscratching was pretty much covered by the word "partner." In fact it was—legally in California—"husband." In Virginia it was still a bit ambiguous. Joey had at least gotten over

37

his tendency to freak people, intentionally, by talking with a lisp. And he took the occasional ribbing about his "preferences" pretty well. When it got to be too extreme he'd just do a little twist or a moue and the joker would generally shut right the hell up. And if that didn't work, he had a font of other practical jokes—not to mention a right hook that was legendary.

"Not personal," Young said. "The ten thirty-seven was a family using an abandoned dock to load a mass of guns, food and toilet paper onto a brand-new boat."

"Which has *what* to do with ten sixty-fours piling on officers?" Patterno asked.

"The husband, who was one cool cucumber, suggested to me, just *before* the eleven ninety-nine, that if I had a ten sixty-four acting in a hostile nature to shoot first and just take the admin leave. And avoid the blood spatter. When I got the call, he added to absolutely under any circumstances avoid the bite. I quote, *'the blood pathogen is particularly nasty.'*"

"You're shitting me," Patterno said. "No way!"

"He mentioned ten sixty-fours *before* the call," Young said. "*Hostile* ten sixty-fours. He said there was going to be some sort of announcement at noon."

"Son of a...I'd heard about *that*," Patterno said. "The CDC was scheduling a joint press conference with the Fibbies. Okay, meet you at Waterson...Shit, change in call..."

Young glanced at his board and shook his head. There were alarm calls going up all over the place. Including...

"I've got a..." he said, then braked, hard. A naked girl, teenager, had just run in front of his car. Her face was... He keyed his radio as the girl jumped onto his hood then started smashing at the glass. Her face was distorted, insane. She looked pasty as if she'd been sick. Just...something wasn't there.

"Unit eight-seven-three to Base. Hostile ten sixty-four. Female. Four-six-zero Butterworth Drive. Attacking my car. Request female officer assistance."

"Eight-seven-three. Ten-zero. Protocol five-one five-zero. No assistance available."

"Base, eight-seven-three. Say again female, expand, teenage female, three-one-one."

"Roger. No assistance available, Eight-seven-three. Ten-zero. Five-one five-zero. Transport to Emerson on Secure."

"What the fuck?" Young swore. Use caution. Crazy person. Duh. No assistance? No female officer for a naked teenage girl? He was going to get the *crap* sued out of him.

He was avoiding using a certain word even in his head. Not that not thinking "zombie" was keeping him from thinking "zombie." Problem being, the girl was not the level of threat that *permitted* the use of a firearm. If he shot her he'd be lucky to get just administrative leave. He'd be looking at assault or manslaughter at the very least.

He caught movement in his peripheral vision and saw a man, probably the girl's father, staggering across the lawn. He had multiple bite marks on his chest and arms, both of which were bare. He'd apparently just thrown on some shorts to follow his naked daughter into the street.

The girl was going absolutely insane on his windshield, hammering it so hard her hands were bleeding, and she was biting at the recalcitrant glass. The car had been upgraded with a stronger type of auto glass, or she'd probably have shattered the window.

Young didn't hear what happened, but the girl suddenly looked to the passenger side of the cruiser. The word "feral" came to mind. The look of a wild predator that had heard the sound of prey. She leapt off the hood and charged the man on the lawn.

Then Young bailed out. He wasn't sure how he was going to handle the wild child. The department, after a series of lawsuits and protests to the city government, mostly over YouTube videos that hadn't happened anywhere *near* Williamsburg, had taken Tasers away from all officers except sergeants and above who had had the state course in same.

The girl was already on the man before Young could even get around the cruiser. She was—not howling, not screaming—*keening*, he thought, was the word. A high, long, weird sound. And she was thoroughly locked onto the man's left arm with hands and teeth biting and ripping at it.

"HELLLP!" the man screamed, looking at Young while struggling to free his arm. He was pulling the girl's hair half frantically, half gently, as if afraid to actually *hurt* her. "FOR THE LOVE OF GOD, HELP ME! JESUS CHR—! CHELSEA! *CHELSEA!*"

Young just stood there for a moment, hands on his hips, then opened up the back of his cruiser. In a box there was a bag that was for "assistance in securing hostile animals." Generally called a snake bag, it was just part of the kit. Cops didn't secure wild animals, but if they had to back up animal control they carried "snake bags." Like the M4 he was seriously contemplating, for if they had to back up SWAT. He regarded the bag for a moment, judging the size of the opening. About large enough to fit over a teenage girl's head.

There were also tactical gloves. The Diamonds were a pain to wear all the time, but if there was ever a time to put on a set of gloves it was now. He wished they were thick leather. As long as he kept her off his arms he should be good.

He took the bag in hand and duck-walked up behind the girl, gaze fixed on the back of her head.

"Would you *hurry*?" the man snarled, then screamed wildly as blood began to spray all over the freshly cut green lawn.

Young paused behind the girl for just a moment, then snapped the bag across and down. The girl's mouth was locked on her father's arm, but as the bag went over her eyes she reared back, clawing it, permitting the man to fall back onto the grass. He pushed himself backwards toward the house, trying to staunch the spurting artery his daughter had torn into.

Young, meantime, had his own troubles. The girl had started spinning before he could get the bag fully over her head, and had one hand under it. He was afraid to simply yank the closure line too hard. It could permanently choke her. But the bag had at least slid down enough to cover her mouth. She was no longer keening, just gutturally grunting.

He also wasn't sure where to put his hands. Freaking cameras were *everywhere* these days. He wasn't in direct view of the car, but people were probably breaking out their cell cameras for the spectacle. Although, come to think of it, distribution or even ownership would, probably, assuming the girl was under eighteen, and she looked more like fifteen, be a federal crime. In fact, his car camera might just be considered a federal violation. Cops weren't automatically exempt. Of course, he couldn't, legally, turn it off, absent orders or completion of the call. Which was not yet complete. So he was probably covered. Probably.

Which is *exactly* what he expected to be thinking when fighting his first zombie. Not.

First incredibly strong, wiry, excessively underage, fast, naked, *female* zombie.

Then he heard the screams behind him.

Looking over his shoulder, he saw a woman running out of a home down the street. She was clothed, but the clothing was ripped. Pursuing her was a naked man covered in blood. And she was, naturally, running towards the policeman for help. With the subject in hot pursuit.

"Screw this," Young said, holding the bag barely closed with one hand and drawing his Glock. He placed it against the girl's quadricep and pulled the trigger. The girl shrieked and fell to the ground, grabbing at her leg.

"What are you *doing*?" her father shrieked.

"Trying to save your life, her life and mine," Young said, spinning around. "Come on!" he said, waving at the woman to pass him. "Come on!"

Don't let them bite you...

"Don't," the woman said waving her hands. She was dressed in jeans and a nice blouse as if she had been headed out to the store when her world came apart. The blouse was now rent and bloody and she had a large bite mark at the juncture of her shoulder and neck. "Please don't! I don't know what's wrong with my—"

"*I* do," Young lied, targeting the oncoming man's chest. He was big enough and violent enough it *might* be ruled a good shoot. If what appeared to be happening was, well, what *was* happening, *probably* would be ruled a good shoot. Virginia wasn't quite San Francisco. In Frisco he'd assuredly be fried.

"HALT OR I WILL FIRE IN DEFENSE OF SELF AND OTHERS!" It was usually a phrase used by civilians. Cops were supposed to use anything *but* firearms to resolve the situation. You only drew a gun if there was another gun. Maybe a knife. But the guy was big and the girl was going to be up and hopping any second now and he had *no* backup. Young was out of options. "HALT! HALT! *HALT!*"

He waited until the charging man was under five meters, then, following training, double tapped: One upper chest, then, following the natural climb of the recoil, one to the head.

The man plowed the ground at Young's feet as his wife started to scream. Louder.

It was Young's first official shoot, but he'd previously seen what a bullet did to a human skull. Best not to dwell on it.

"Officer-involved shooting," Young said into his radio as he walked to his car. There was a first-aid kit in the trunk. Not that he thought it was going to do anyone much good. He'd had a bit of trouble getting his pistol back in the holster, but his voice was clear. Even if he was falling back on older training. "One Kilo India Alpha, two Whiskey India Alpha..."

He paused as he was reciting the litany of disaster, bent over and more or less casually threw up...

"No bites," Young said, spitting. "So far..."

"And this is our culprit," Dr. Titus Wong said, sliding a cursor across the screen to point to a very obvious red nodule on the spinal material. "In a different configuration."

Dr. Curry was eating popcorn as he watched the video conference. Arranged by the WHO for "interested parties only," the more or less continuous, and continuously encrypted, conference was collating the ongoing study of the Pacific Flu. Curry's new employers had ensured he was included in "interested parties." With the news out, carefully avoiding the word "zombie," the news media was going nuts. As was every epidemiology group in the world. This was the first real "wildfire" they'd ever contained, and it was turning out to be a doozy.

"This is a SEM view," Wong said. Wong was the Los Angeles Medical Examiner's Office specialist in infectious diseases. A certified ME, an MD with a pathology specialty and an additional specialty in infectious diseases, he was still considered a bit of a plodder by most of the people viewing the slides. On the other hand, he was at the epicenter, which, for once, was not in some remote, usually tropical, country. Well, remote to the developed nations. It was local to the people dying. "Natural color SEM. That is, in fact, its color..."

"Question from Dr. Sengar, Stockholm..."

The conference was currently under control of Dr. Addis Bahara, deputy underminister for Operations and Response of the WHO. Dave knew Addy and liked him. He was one sharp Ethiopian. And he was a professional, unlike the head of the WHO, who was chosen mostly for his connections.

"That has a remarkable resemblance to rabies," the senior WHO representative for Sweden said. "With the exception of the color. There have been no indications of motor impairment."

"We have seen patients with notable motor impairment," Dr.

Wong replied. "Information lag. Yet I take your meaning. The nodules are grossly similar to rabies but they seem to have a different effect. And rabies is not airborne."

Telling Sven Sengar, who'd earned any award in virology you'd care to name short of the Nobel, that "rabies wasn't airborne" was one of the reasons that Wong was a pathologist buried in the basement of the L.A. morgue.

"I said 'has a resemblance to' rabies," Svengar replied, evenly. "Have you attempted to test the Pasteur method for a vaccine?"

"We don't do vaccines," Wong said. "Just autopsies."

"CDC..."

"We'll begin examining it immediately." James Dobson, like Addis, was one of the "tech" specialists at CDC but also a decent political animal. "Decent" being defined as good at politics while still holding onto some semblance of a brain. "I'd have said a week ago that Pasteur method was cracked but this pathogen has me wondering if I know basic biochemistry."

"Dr. Kwai, Thailand..."

"Is there any additional information as to the origin?" Dr. Kwai asked.

There was a brief pause as people wondered who was supposed to answer that one.

"CDC..."

"No," Dr. Dobson said. "Computer analysis is showing that it was probably distributed in public venues, notably airports and bus stations on the West Coast of the United States, beginning some two weeks ago. Method of vectoring is still unknown and there are no known suspects. For that matter, models indicate it's *still* being spread, including in airports and bus stations. FBI has various ideas but quietly they're admitting that there are no hard leads. We and USAMRIID are...cooperating. But after the anthrax debacle, getting cooperation is...harder."

"No shit," Curry muttered. The entire anthrax investigation had put researchers on notice that the FBI cared a lot less about science or rationality than politics. That, in fact, the DOJ didn't have the slightest clue about molecular biology and could care less. The only suspects who were ever identified, and they were publicly identified well in advance of even the thinnest shred of evidence, were professional researchers from USAMRIID, the U.S. Army's version of the CDC. Both of the "accused" researchers had also been on the teams at USAMRIID *advising* the FBI. In neither case was there any real indication that either researcher had created the anthrax spread shortly after the 9/11 bombings. But the FBI was Johnny-on-the-spot with accusations.

As far as most epidemiologists were concerned, if you could explain to the FBI *how* something worked, in other words if you had the *ability* to do it, it meant to whoever you were talking, *you* were their current prime suspect. Which meant that nobody in their right mind in the industry wanted to explain *anything* to an FBI agent. Of course clamming up and being "uncooperative" *also* made you a prime suspect. Catch 22.

The attack, on the basis of no real evidence except "ability," had finally been pinned on a minor researcher who had, basically, really serious personality problems, not uncommon in any intellectual community, and who very conveniently committed suicide when he realized the FBI was going to "out" him. Which just meant he was a geek, not a mad scientist. With a good scapegoat, the best kind because he was, you know, *dead*, the FBI officially closed the case and declared victory in our time.

Despite the fact that neither researcher ever was shown to have access to the specific genetic strain and that the specific method of creating the coat of weaponized anthrax was a closely held *Soviet* secret. Nobody in the U.S. had *ever* produced it or knew exactly how. And the specific genetic strain used in the attacks was found in no U.S. inventory. From a *microbiological* perspective where it came from was as mysterious as the Roswell Landings.

Pretty much anybody with a Ph.D. or master's in molecular cellular biology or related fields now considered the DOJ and Fibbies their main *opponents* in any future bioterror attacks. Which, given that both sides were necessary to work the problem, made this situation that much harder. And the FBI and DOJ had nobody to blame but themselves.

"However, there is a database of all similar experiments being conducted in the U.S. and there are none that are even close. So it didn't, officially, come from any of our universities or research centers. And there weren't any 'unofficial' ones that come close. In fact, there are so many breakthroughs on this one... No, there are no suspects. No suspect facilities, no suspect individuals and we're *still* trying to figure out the vector...."

CHAPTER 5

Nate Dolan, BS, microbiology, twenty-five years of age, five foot four in his stocking feet and world-class biology geek with a nearly complete collection of *The Amazing Spiderman* series to prove it, was regretting more and more his choice of jobs to put himself through grad school. Intergen had been a great place to work. Even if it was part-time and he had to spend most of his time in a moon suit.

Now he had beady-eyed FBI agents poring over his every move-ment for the last three days while simultaneously expecting him to "help out" for less than half what he got paid at Intergen. In a moon suit, of course.

LAX wasn't quite shut down. But since it was suspected as one of the main sources of the Pacific Flu, it *had* been shut down and might get shut down *again*. Especially if they couldn't find the source. And, frankly, anybody had to be an idiot to just go wandering the airport in open when all the "official" people were either keeping their distance or in moon suits.

The powers-that-be were sure at this point that H7D3 was a man-made virus, a really cool one for that matter, and that there had to be a mechanical spread mechanism. The technical term for that turned out to be "attack vector." Nate had learned that when he was getting in-briefed on the search. Which should have showed these bad-suit-wearing clowns *he* hadn't done it! But until they could find traces of H7 in the environment, which was sort of tough, they were stymied to find the attack vector.

They'd had all sorts of false positives. The antibody swabs they were using were a sort of general "flu" test. They pinged as soon as they hit anything that looked anything like influenza. Which turned out to be half the organic chemicals on Earth. Up until today they'd had to send them all back to various labs to be tested.

Today they had, finally, delivered a more precisely tuned antibody test. They still used the strips for an initial test, but a field re-test was now possible. Drop the strip in a test tube, squirt in magic antibody fluid and wait for results.

"I've got another," Luiz Lopez said, holding up a strip. Sure enough it was bright red.

He'd been swabbing the inside of one of the stalls. The good news was that anything in there was kept out by the moon suit. The bad news was that about half their false positives came from in the stalls. There was *everything* in those stalls. It was tough to be a germophobe and work in biology. This job was making him a germophobe. He certainly didn't ever want to have to use a public restroom again.

"And we have a..." Nate said, shaking the test-tube. The liquid was red as blood. "Positive? Seriously?"

"Did we get a sample to cross-test?" Luiz asked.

"You think they're going to hand me H7?" Nate asked, looking in the stall. There wasn't much graffiti. The problem with the stalls was that they were, yeah, cesspits on one level, but they were also cleaned regularly. They just weren't cleaned *well*. So most of the trace evidence, including any H7, should have been removed or degraded by the environment. Even if there had been some sort of vector there a couple of weeks ago, the H7 should have been cleaned away or basically broken down from heat and humidity. And there wasn't any sort of aerosol canister. That had been the first check. "I'd be too likely to slip it to our 'handlers.'"

"Don't even joke," Luiz said. He was from Argentina working, like Nate, on his master's at UCLA. "You they'd at least give *some* rights. They even *suspect* it's me and I'm on a plane to Guantanamo."

"Where'd this come from?" Nate asked, looking around the stall.

"Walls and door," Luiz said.

If there was H7 in the stall something had put it there. Recently. It had clearly been recently scrubbed. Two more tests showed that the walls, door and even *floor* were contaminated. According to the swab *and* tube.

What there *was* was a deodorizer on the door. A round, green, deodorizer with the motto: "Save the Planet. Reduce, Reuse, Recycle. SaveThePlanet.org" stamped into the plastic.

He'd swabbed those before. They were the first thing he'd hit the first stall he'd seen. And gotten back that the material in the deodorizer was giving a false positive. Which just might have been a false *negative*. If the carrier had enough chemical similarities to the protein coat of the virus, it could be construed as a false positive depending on the test. If the evaporative coating was still coating the virus, as one example.

He reached out, carefully, and cracked open the deodorizer.

"I want you to personally run this back to Dr. Karza," Nate said, using a scupula to pull out some of the beigish substance in the deodorizer. "Tell him I suggest he run it through the portable SEM..."

"Why didn't you identify that immediately?" the FBI Supervisory Special Agent asked. "Those canisters had been tested, right? I mean, they were obvious..."

"Because microbiology isn't as easy as POINTING A *GUN* AT SOMEONE!" Dr. Azim Karza shouted, his eyes glued to the SEM screen.

"There's no need to get..." the agent said, then coughed and sniffed. "Oh... shit..."

"GET THE *HELL* OUT OF MY LABORATORY!" Dr. Karza said. As the agent left he gave himself a quick blood test, then sighed in relief. Still no trace of H7D3. He'd seen the special agent using poor transmission protocols but was forced to work with him in close quarters. Which meant that the agent's sniffles were something other than H7D3. Karza could have cleared that up for him with the same sort of test. But let the myrmidon bastard sweat it for a while.

"Cune!"

"FBI sources have found the source of the Pacific Flu virus. Anyone observing green deodorizers imprinted with the words 'Save

The Planet' in public places should avoid them and immediately report their location to their local police or the FBI tipline..."

"The evaporative material was giving a false negative reaction to the antibody tests," Dr. Dobson said wearily. "We'd checked the deodorizers and given them a pass. Yesterday. Then when we got the new antibody strips one of the techs realized that there had to be a continuous source. Looking at the material under SEM..." He gestured to the image and shrugged. "I don't know if that was part of the culprit's plan, but it was effective. They've now identified them in over sixty locations. At least one per bathroom, mostly stretching up and down the West Coast..."

"So this was an eco-terrorist attack?" Dr. Xiu Bao asked. The current representative from the Chinese Ministry of Health was clearly convinced on the subject. If for no other reason than the Chinese government was already using the assumption to crack down on their environmental activists.

"The FBI isn't really commenting, but it's possible," Dr. Dobson said. "On the other hand, if you just wanted the finger pointed at eco-terrorists it would be a simple way to do it. Honestly, Doctor, I just hope nobody points out that the canisters were made in China..."

"We assuredly did not have anything to do with this..."

"*I* know that," Dobson said. "Everyone with any *sense* knows that. It doesn't mean it's not going to get pointed out by idiots..."

"This was not *eco-terrorism," the Greenpeace spokesperson insisted. "No decent environmentalist is going to do something like this! And even if one was so insane as to infect humanity with a deadly plague they wouldn't have used a* nonrecyclable *container! And might I point out, the canisters were* made *in* China! *One of the greatest eco-terrorists on the planet!"*

"Whoa," O'Reilly said. "Whoa! Whoa! So is most stuff *these days. Pointing a finger at the Chinese government is premature to say the least..."*

"I didn't say the..."

"Out of time. Next on the O'Reilly Factor..."

"If there is a next time," Dr. Curry said, shaking the popcorn bag to get at the bits in the bottom. The laboratory he'd been handed by BotA was nicely complete but at the moment he was mostly using the microwave. Mr. "Smith" had looked at him oddly when he'd requisitioned six hundred cases of microwave popcorn. But he figured that even if they lost power BotA had generators. With water, decon showers and enough popcorn he was good till doomsday. Or till they totally lost power. "I love a front row seat to the apocalypse."

"You all know what the big issue is right now," Lieutenant Simmons said. "Fortunately, other crimes are down. However, we're starting to get heavy traffic..."

"Rats fleeing the ship," Patterno said.

"People are scared," Simmons said, shrugging. "The TV's staying away from the Z word but it's all over the internet. That and it being a real and really big bioterror attack has people worried. We just work the problem. Some of the people in traffic are going to neurological stage while driving. Night shift had a lot of accidents. Every reserve officer who's responding has been called in..."

Young tuned the brief out. He was still pending a shoot review. There had been a few words at first but by the end of his shift so many officers had had to use their weapons that they didn't even take his in for the investigation. So far he'd had to shoot three "afflicted" to wound and two more to kill. They were still being ordered to "subdue and restrain" but there were more and more ten sixty-four hotels every shift. And subduing them took two officers at a minimum. Then there was the *at least* two hours of paperwork per ten sixty-four...

"For calls on this subject, the term 'ten sixty-four hotel' has been added to the callsign list," Simmons said, getting to the main point. "The count was forty-six ten sixty-four hotels overnight."

"Forty-*six*?" Patterno said. "We've only got forty officers! One ten sixty-four with transport and paperwork takes—"

"Which is why the Chief has authorized abbreviated paperwork," Simmons said, holding up a pile of forms. "Just let me finish, Joe. These are ten sixty-four, suspected afflicted with neurological stage Hotel Seven virus forms. Try to get a solid ID, transport and fill out the form. No matter the eventual disposition, the DA, with concurrence of governor pending change in actual law, has stated that nobody is going to try to try any of these people.

And...the hospital is overloaded. *All* the hospitals are overloaded. Transport of all ten sixty-four hotels is now to One-two-seven Curb Court, Warehouse Seven—"

"Warehouse district?" Young said, looking up finally.

"They're maintaining them there pending some more appropriate facility." Young said. "Just...try to get a solid ID, secure and transport. Don't call an ambulance unless you have a seriously injured civilian that absolutely requires ambulance transport. Ambulances are overloaded with injured and there's a shortage of ambulance crews... There have now been confirmed locations of the attack vector device on the East Coast. FBI is saying they may have been in place for as much as a week. One was found right here in Williamsburg..."

"Oh, holy shit..." Young said, shaking his head. He had called his parents and brother. They were all staying inside and basically skipping work.

"The one bright spot is that CDC is now saying that ten sixty-fours may, again may, not be airborne infectious," Simmons continued. "The downside is that they are infectious through the blood pathogen, and the blood pathogen is extremely aggressive. If you are exposed to the blood pathogen, either due to bleeding from the subject or due to...blood spray, decontaminate immediately. We're issuing a decon kit per car. We have them on hand. thank God."

"*Don't* let them bite you," Patterno said. "Don't."

"Young, that came from you first. I never got the story?"

"I was responding to a ten thirty-seven yesterday," Young said. It seemed like ten years ago. "Family loading a sailboat. They were using a dock on one of those foreclosure properties over in Hunter Creek. Loading it for a long trip, and they admitted to having a large quantity of weapons in their vehicle. The male subject knew about the upcoming announcement from the CDC. This was just a bit before noon. He stated that I should avoid the blood pathogen as well. Right after that things started to, well, degrade. It was one of the reasons for my decision to act with lethal force in the encounter that day. I swear to God I wasn't going rogue...something something killer. It was just I was dealing with *two* ten sixty-fours..."

"Don't..." Simmons said, grimacing. "It's not up for discussion right now. I can't comment on the shoot. On that subject, though, our rules of engagement remain *unchanged*. Use *minimum force necessary* to subdue the ten sixty-fours. Given our new understanding of the situation... The specific wording that I was given is 'use minimum force necessary consonant with a full understanding of the threat and nature of threat to protect self and others with a high priority to ensure safe processing of the presumed H7D3 afflicted subject.' Try to remember that however these people are acting, they are *people*. People sick with a god damned disease. This isn't their fault..."

"In a lot of ways it would be easier if they *were* walking dead," Patterno said, shrugging.

"Let's try to stay away from that meme if we can," Simmons said.

"Think I wanted to double tap some poor guy who was just sick?" Young asked, shaking his head.

"You're not the only one, man," Rickles pointed out.

"We're recommending that all officers dealing with ten sixty-fours in general use rain gear for the time being until there's a better fix," Simmons said, nodding.

"That's going to be hot as shit," Young said.

"Fortunately, it looks to be a cool day," Lieutenant Simmons said.

"For *who*?" Patterno replied with a snort.

"If it wasn't for the reason, I'd be really enjoying this," Steve said, glancing over at Stacey.

The wind was kicking up whitecaps on the choppy waters of the Chesapeake Bay and the Hunter was heeled over at a thirty-degree angle as it plowed north towards the Baltimore Canal. Steve was being careful to steer well clear of the main shipping channel to the east so they had a clear view of the shoreline to the west. So far there was no real evidence of societal breakdown. Which was boding well for his decision to make for the canal.

"I could wish for better weather," Stacey said, pulling her windbreaker tighter. "Warmer at least."

"This is good weather," Steve said. The wind that had followed the cold front was cool, but it was constant and that was good. "And it's giving us a chance to get our sea legs without it being too rough."

"Always the optimist," Stacey said, tightly.

"Worried?" Steve asked without looking at her.

"Aren't you?" She gestured with her chin to the cabin. The girls could be heard engaged in their more or less continuous low-grade argument. "Is one of us infected already? What do we do about it?"

"Tie ourselves up," Steve said.

"I think we're going to have to forego that for a while, honey," Stacey said, blushing slightly.

"Think with other bits, dear," Steve said, smiling. "I don't really like thinking of it in terms of ourselves. So I think what other people should do. No plague is one hundred percent effective. The black plague did, admittedly, wipe out whole families and villages. But it had a lot of help. It's unlikely that even if we're infected, all of us will go... to fully neurological conditions. So from now on when we're not actively engaged in something, we'll secure ourselves, lightly, with rope. If one of us starts to have neurological effects, the others will work to secure them until we can find an antidote or something."

"Or something," Stacey said, frowning.

"I have various smart women around me," Steve said, shrugging. "We'll figure something out. But only if we can keep from biting each other."

"Well," Stacey said, snuggling closer. "Maybe a little nibble."

"I don't know," Steve said. "Have you been a good girl? Do you deserve a nibble?"

"I've been a very *bad* girl," Stacey whispered in his ear. "So I *definitely* deserve a nibble..."

"Oh, my God," Faith said, grimacing. She'd suddenly appeared in the hatchway to the saloon. "That is sooo gross!"

"So much for a little alone time," Steve said, shaking his head. "What's up?"

"What are we going to do about dinner?" Faith asked.

"You know where the food is," Steve said.

"So we're going to have to cook in this?" Faith said.

"We're sure as hell not ordering pizza," Stacey said. "Should we break into the Mountain House?"

"Better than trying to cook a regular meal when we can barely stand up," Steve said, grinning. "Think you can figure out how to boil water?"

"In this?" Faith said. "No way! It's storming!"

"*This* is not a *storm*," Steve said. "Given the plan, at some point you'll understand what the word 'storm' means in a forty-five-foot sailboat. This isn't even a gale."

"I can do it," Sophia said. "I think."

"No," Steve said. "Stace, take the wheel. I'm going to have to give your daughters a class on boiling water and working with boiling water in light chop conditions."

"Try not to kill yourself or catch the boat on fire," Stacey said.

"Thank you for that vote of confidence, First Mate."

"The reason that it is both airborne and blood pathogen now becomes clear..." Dr. Bao said. "Researchers at University of Hong Kong have pieced out its genetic and proteinomic code. The influenza virus produces two *separate and distinct* 'child' viruses. One is a copy of the H7D3 influenza. The second is a highly modified version of the rabies virus..."

"Two viruses in one?" Dr. Curry said, leaning forward and setting down his popcorn bag. "What the *hell*?"

"Oh...Oh...Oh...Oh, no...*No*..."

Tim Shull had been following "the synbio version of Chernobyl" in real time, monitoring multiple different sources. Tim could because he really didn't have anything better to do. After dropping out of his master's program after that stupid argument with Dr. Wirta he'd moved back home. And since Starbucks had cut back on his time he could spend most of the day scanning the various synbio boards, news and blogs. It was the virtual version of watching a train wreck in slow motion. And whether the world ended or not, it was going to wreck the amateur synbio industry.

Synbio was short for synthetic biology, the creation of new or modified organisms. The "mundane" term was genetic engineering. It was a field at which Tim was a sort of "internet only" recognized expert. He'd been on the fast track to working in the professional field when he'd had a falling out with his master's advisor and quit. Subsequent to that he'd continued his work, literally, in his mother's basement until a breakthrough last year that, if he'd done it as a master's thesis, would have made him a shoe-in for prizes, maybe even a Nobel, and a guaranteed Ph.D. track. Since he'd done it on his own time in a basement the "awards" were few and far between. So all he'd done was put up a video and blog explaining the breakthrough and become a minor celebrity in the amateur synbio community. Although there had been some applications breakthroughs in basement synbio, his was really the first theoretical breakthrough. Which meant he had the largest number of followers on Twitter of an amateur synbio "pioneer," and his words were, on amateur synbio boards, given much the same weight as professionals.

Unfortunately, his "breakthrough" was how to get a virus to express two different organisms from a single virus. And he'd put it up as a *YouTube* video...

"I am soooo screwed..."

There was a thunderous crash from upstairs and he heard his mother screaming—

"DOWN! DOWN! DOWN! FBI SERVING A VALID SEARCH WARRANT...!"

He looked around but there was nowhere to run in a basement.

"The creator of the Pacific Flu virus has been identified as twenty-four-year-old Timothy Shull, a drop-out from the Stanford microbiology master's program..."

CHAPTER 6

"I didn't create the virus!" Tim said. The room was windowless, and since he'd been transported with a bag over his head, he wasn't even sure where he was. And good luck with getting a lawyer. The ride had also made him puke all over his lap and shoes. Which wasn't adding to his day. "All I did was prove it was possible to express two different—"

"All we want is the vaccine, kid," the FBI agent said, calmly.

"I DIDN'T MAKE THE VIRUS!" Tim screamed. "If I had the VACCINE I'd have VACCINATED myself! *And* my mom!"

"You've got all the materials in your basement, son," the agent said, still calmly. It wasn't like the geek could get violent chained to a chair. "So just explain how to make the vaccine..."

"AAAAAGH!"

"There is *no* RNA *or* DNA related to the pathogen in this material," Dr. Karza said, shrugging. His team had run every stored microorganism in the suspect's lab in world-record time. There was lots of other "stuff," but exactly zero was pathogenic. "Fascinating breakthrough. Brilliant. Really brilliant. But it has nothing except background science to do with the actual pathogen."

"You didn't get it right the last time," Agent Shornauer said. "Why do we trust you this time?"

"*You* want to figure it out, tough guy? Bottom line, except for pure scientific aspects, this is a dead end."

"We'll determine that."

The FBI director looked at the report and grimaced. According to not only the CDC point people but FBI labs, there was zero evidence that this Shull kid had any background, contact or access to the Pacific Flu. There was lots on his computers, not to mention his blog, the YouTube videos, which he'd actually found really useful explaining how this bug worked, about "dual expressionism." What there wasn't was a scrap of the actual bug or any references to it. All the kid had worked with was "non human-pathogenic" materials. Mostly something called "coliphage lambda," whatever the hell that was. There was less evidence of H7D3 in the Shull home than in, say, the front lobby of the J. Edgar Hoover building. Which another report had just noted was *lousy* with the stuff.

He decided to let the attorney general and the Bureau's lawyers worry about it . . .

"There are still conditions under which he could be a questionable actor," he typed into the memo. "Change his status to material witness and give him to the CDC. Keep somebody on him and don't let him slip away."

"*My client is only guilty of an extremely important scientific breakthrough . . .*"

Dr. Curry thought you really had to love the caption: "Pacific Flu Killer's attorney." They didn't even have the poor attorney's name displayed.

"*The FBI has shown no proof that my client had any part in creating the flu . . .*"

Which, from everything Curry was scanning—which was probably more than the attorney was being given access to—was true. Or at least the only part the kid had played was breakthrough synbio. Which meant he was going to have a fun time convincing the DOJ he wasn't guilty. Assuming the world didn't come apart entirely, the upside was that he'd be able to sue the crap out of the federal government and get more scholarships than you could shake a stick at.

Right now that didn't look likely.

"And I'll remind the media of the FBI's record in high-profile cases. Richard Jewel, a hero who was arrested and immediately publicly condemned. Dr. Steven Hatfill, a researcher assisting the FBI who was publicly charged in the anthrax case..."

"Great way to make friends there..."

"Shull isn't your culprit," Dr. Dobson said wearily.

"We're still trying to determine his part in this," the FBI deputy director for terrorism replied.

"His part was to create one of the necessary technological conditions," Dobson said, as patiently as he could. "That's it. He made a breakthrough. The same thing could be said for dozens of professional researchers. You might as well indict Alfred Nobel for every IED in Iraq. And I'd really prefer you didn't lock them *all* up. We need them. As we need Shull. He's the expert on dual expression. Nobody had even *looked* at it before he did. So, sure, keep him in custody, but if you don't put him on a plane to Atlanta by the end of the day, I'll let you explain it to the news media and the President. And I want *my* people talking to him within the hour. He didn't make the virus, but he understands it in a way we don't..."

"The Department of Education has mandated a total shutdown of all public and private schools starting Monday..."

"School's out for summer..." Dr. Curry crooned, looking at the latest spread graphs. Only Sunday and they'd gone from dots on the West Coast to spreading red in every reporting zone across the globe. And the "Save the Planet" deodorizers had been found in dozens of public locations stretching up and down the eastern and western seaboards. *Somebody* had been a busy little beaver. *"School's out forever..."*

"Okay, first of all..." Dr. Karza said, shaking his head at the scene in the interrogation room. "Get him out of the cuffs."

"Doctor..."

"Just get him out of the *cuffs*, you dick-brained *myrmidon!*" Karza snarled. "He's not going to be able to think if he thinks he's on his way to Gitmo and WE NEED HIS *BRAIN!*"

He waited until the agent had released Shull and left.

"Idiots," Karza said, shaking his head again. "I mean, not actual idiots. They're smart. They just aren't bio smart. And that scares them. And I didn't literally mean we need your brain, just in case you were wondering . . ."

"I didn't make the virus," Tim said, rubbing his wrists. "Please, I really didn't! *I'm* worried about catching it!"

"I know," Karza said, nodding. "My lab processed the hell out of yours. There were zero pathogens in your lab and I'm pretty sure from the looks you hardly ever went out. And eventually they'll figure the same thing out."

"I really don't," Tim said, hunching up. "Not since I left school."

"Sorry about the master's thing," Karza said, shrugging. "I know Dr. Wirta. He's a dick and not nearly as important as he thinks he is in the field. I'm Dr. Azim Karza from the CDC, by the way. And while I'll admit you have more problems than I do, try being the lead investigator on a bio-terror attack while being Islamic, born in Iran and with a name like Azim Karza."

"I can imagine," Tim said, chuckling and sniffling at the same time.

"Your mom is fine, sort of," Karza said. "She's been released and she's gotten you a lawyer. Who, for all sorts of Patriot Act reasons, isn't going to be able to help you any time soon. On the other hand, CDC is on your side. We get how the DOJ reacts in these sorts of things. They think about the perp walk and calming the public because, just because you have the culprit the plague is going to stop *all by itself!* We react differently. Which is why I'm here. We're going to be moving you to Atlanta pretty soon. Not the Pen, to CDC. FBI and DOJ are still going to be going apeshit and asking all sorts of questions you can't answer. That's because they don't know which questions to ask.

"We know you don't know how to make a vaccine, or a 'cure,' as the FBI keeps insisting. They've been watching too many movies. 'What's the cure?' They don't like 'There isn't one, even theoretically.' But what we need is your knowledge of dual expression. So what we'd like you to do is go with the flow for the time being. You're under arrest, but as of this point you're *also* one of our research associates. Until DOJ can get over 'he had to have made the virus' they'll probably insist on treating you like a criminal. Let them. Cooperate with them. Be polite. Keep your head down. If we, that meaning the CDC, can possibly get one of our people along the whole time, we will. And he or she will be there to both pick your brain and keep the Fibbies from getting berserk. Let your lawyer work on getting you out and work with *us* on finding a vaccine. Deal? At the very least it's going to make their argument that you *must* have done it because you *can* a little weaker. The term is 'cooperation.' Goes loads with judges."

"Absolutely," Tim said, nodding vigorously. "I mean, a chance to work with the CDC on this is like a dream come true. I really, *really* want to help!"

"Good," Karza said. "Good. Now: how in the hell did you get a *DNA* virus to express an *RNA* virus? That right there was effing brilliant."

"These are all the points to two hours ago where the canisters have been reported," the agent said, pointing to a dot-filled map. "The red dots are where they are presently and have been verified by removal teams or local police. The yellow dots are reports from owners or managers where they were reported to have been seen and removed prior to determining the spread method."

"That's..." the President said, looking at the map. "There's a line..."

"The unsub appears to have worked down the West Coast to Los Angeles," the attorney general said, working from notes. "Then Interstate 10 to its joining with I-20. From there the unsub continued to I-95. Indications are that the unsub then went north through the Washington–New York–Boston corridor, then down again into Florida. The indications are that it was one unsub or unsub team. If there were more they would have been expected to spread out. This is definitely a single movement. Because the pathogen was initially..." He consulted his notes for a moment. "Because it was asymptomatic at first, there was no indications for some time this was a bioweapons attack. Current estimates are that the unsub could have completed most of this spread within the period prior to the neurological symptoms outbreak."

"Any idea who he or she or they are?" the President asked.

"We have a number of working suspects, Mr. President..."

"So do we," the director of National Intelligence said. "Al Qaeda being at the top of the list..."

"That's an absolutely unfounded attack, Director," the secretary of state said.

"Oh? Really? Shall I *count* the ways...?"

∽─◯─∾

"Welcome to the Centers for Disease Control, Mr. Shull," Dr. Dobson said.

Shull started to hold out his hand, then pulled it back.

"Nothing against you," Dr. Dobson said hastily.

"No, sir, Doctor," Shull said, just as quickly. "I . . . I guess I'm having a bad protocol day."

"We're having a more or less ongoing teleconference this way," Dobson said, gesturing for the former master's candidate to precede him. "I'd like to say . . . Not sure where to start. First of all, your dualistic expression is an amazing breakthrough, especially with limited resources . . ."

"My dad had a lot of insurance," Tim said, shrugging uncomfortably. "After . . . Stanford I just sort of . . . I guess I got obsessed. And I was right. You can get a dualistic expression!" He paused as he remembered what his breakthrough had been used for. "Is this how Oppenheimer felt after Hiroshima?"

"Probably," Dr. Dobson said, nodding sympathetically. "Through here . . ."

"Mr. Shull has yet to be fully exonerated by the DOJ," Dr. Dobson said. "But the CDC is satisfied that, while he may have discovered a method of dualistic expression, he did not develop the H7D3 virus. He is, however, the only one who knows anything about dualistic expression. Dr. Addis?"

"Pasteur . . ."

"Mr. Shull, from what we have gleaned from your videos, the expression is two fully separate viruses. To be clear, the secondary virus is also able to replicate?"

"Yes, D-Doctor . . ." Tim said nervously. "It of course depends on what you want to replicate as the secondary expression. But a secondary expression can be a replicable organism. My initial experiments were with a nonreplicating secondary expression but . . . Yes, Doctor."

"Pass . . ."

"Hong Kong . . ."

"Mr. Shull, as with these others, I'd like to add my congratulations on your breakthrough," Dr. Bao said. "However it has been used. The question is whether in your opinion a vaccine against the secondary expression alone would work?"

"I believe so, Doctor," Tim said, his brow furrowing in thought.

"There is no reason that it should not. I...I was following the progress of the information about the pathogen before the dualism was identified. And I'd like to congratulate you, as well, Doctor. I read the draft paper before...before... Very brilliant. Just really...uh... The thing is that even before that I was... wonder...More like *worrying* that it was a dualistic pathogen. The...change in effect was what I would have expected to see with a dualistic pathogen. And...and...the period of fever after the primary pathogen has effectively run its course... That's signs of a dualistic. And the secondary pathogen has to then spread in the...the host.... So a vaccine targeted against the secondary expression... Yes, yes, it should work..."

"We've already started experiments with the Pasteur method here at CDC," Dr. Dobson said. "The problem is the question of if it's affecting the primary pathogen."

"...Standard influenza vaccine would not affect the blood pathogen..."

"...a secondary will not affect the primary..."

"Doctors," Dr. Addis cut in. "Stockholm..."

"The primary threat is the secondary expression," Dr. Svengar pointed out. "The influenza is a bad influenza, yes. At least at the level of swine flu. But it is not an apocalypse. The blood pathogen package should be the primary target especially given the fact that at least twenty-five percent of all infections are blood pathogen related."

"CDC..."

"Concur with Dr. Svengar," Dobson said. "If the neurological secondary packet can be stopped, even after airborne infection, we only really need a viable neuro vaccine and efforts to produce such should concentrate there."

"Pasteur..."

"While we appreciate the use of our namesake's name in this vaccine development," Dr. Phillipe Jardin said drily, "there is one problem remaining. Several, in fact. The spread on this is...enormous. At least the airborne packet. It is all over the world at this point and well established. We have produced a vaccine using the namesake method and have vaccinated specimens. And they do have antibody response against the secondary packet. However, we have also determined that it requires a dual stage injection, primer and booster."

"Confirm," Dr. Dobson said. "We're that far as well. A single

strong injection caused several specimens to develop the neurological condition almost immediately."

"As did ours," Jardin said, nodding.

"Here as well," Hong Kong confirmed.

"Which means that we now have to wait," Phillipe said. "While
the infection spreads and the blood pathogen overtakes airborne
as the most common method of transfer. Until the specimens
cook, we really don't know if the vaccine will work at all. And
even assuming it's of use, vaccines take time to produce."

"The Pasteur method is the simplest production method in the
world," Dr. Svengar pointed out.

"Ah, and that is the second problem," Jardin said. "We have
tried infecting various organisms with the blood pathogen. The
only organisms that will host it are higher order primates."

"We had noted that as well..." Dobson said, grimacing.

"This is very bad," Dr. Bao said quietly. "That is...a great
misfortune."

"*Potassium...*!" Tim blurted.

"Excuse me?" Dr. Dobson said, looking at the younger man
and hitting the button for priority.

"Potassium transfer!" Shull said, excitedly. "I...I didn't have a
lot of lab materials to work with and I was using a medium high
in potassium at first. Even though I knew I was on the right track
I couldn't get a dual expression. I ran out of the high potassium
medium and had to change to a...a cheaper one. That one, I
could get dual expression! I realized later that dual expression
is *inhibited* by potassium! I never thought to mention it in...I
think you can...We might be able to reduce the likelihood of
dualistic expression...Maybe. I mean..."

"It's something to try," Dr. Dobson said, nodding. "Thank you,
young man."

"Anything," Tim said, his face working. "I mean...This really...
I'm sorry, Doctors, but I have to say it, this pisses me OFF. I feel
like I've been *raped*. You know?"

"We'll begin immediate experiments on potassium inhibition,"
Dr. Svengar said. "As well as continuing work on vaccines. And,
yes, to have your life's great work used in this way...You have
my sympathies, young man."

"I think we all feel a bit raped by this," Dr. Addis said.

∽ ⊖ ⌒

"Progression of secondary expression *is* reduced by potassium," Dr. Karza said, looking at the printout.

"So it helps?" Shull asked, looking at the paper over the doctor's shoulder.

"Unfortunately, only in a test tube," Karza said with a sigh. "The levels of potassium that *stop* expression in a human would be terminal. However, it slows expression at lower levels. That is useable."

"This organism is much more complex than just a dual expressor," Shull said, looking at the reports from groups studying the "zombie virus" all over the world. Different groups had taken different parts of the virus to study and the total take was being analyzed by CDC, Pasteur and a series of other teams in various countries. "It only has thirty percent rabies RNA in the secondary expressor virus. Has anyone looked at, well, other people who are sort of off the radar map working on this sort of stuff?"

"What do you mean?" Dr. Karza asked.

"Whoever did this stole my process," Shull said, frowning. "Has anyone done any digging in the amateur field to see if any of this stuff is from their work?"

"You jumped out as a dual expressor pioneer," Karza said thoughtfully. "Do you have an example?"

"This," Shull said, pulling out a report and pointing to a series of gene sequences. "This looks a lot like Jaime Fondor's work. She's working on plant resistance and works with clavaviridae. I'm pretty sure I've seen her use similar sequences. It would help if I could shoot this over to her. She may know something useful."

"How do you recognize it?"

For a change the FBI agent assigned had been just quietly staying out the way and not looming menacingly. Karza understood their passion for the case but their attitude really did not help the way that most bio geeks worked.

"I . . ." Shull said, looking up nervously.

"There are . . . signatures," Karza said. "There are usually several ways to work out a genetic puzzle. In this case, I think what he's saying is that this looks like this Ms. Fondor's signature."

"Hey, hey, hey," Tim said, holding up his hands. "She's not a suspect! Jaime would *never* do something like this!"

"But you're saying that is her signature?" the agent said.

"No," Karza said. "Or most likely not. It's *similar*. Someone has been looking not only at professional synbio but also closely studying *amateur* synbio."

"And that's important," the agent said, frowning. "Here's the thing. You guys get bio. I don't. Or barely, which is why I'm in this lab. What we get is investigation. What you're saying is that the unsub has been monitoring information in the amateur synbio stream. That means they're probably members of synbio boards. You have those, right?"

"Yes," Tim said nervously.

"And you're saying that there are signatures to this thing," the agent said, getting animated. "We *love* signatures. If we can get an algorithm for the overall virus, then we can build a database to compare posted genes or whatever and look for similar signatures...If somebody has *ever* posted on one of those boards, we'll find them."

"The point being that he's copying *other* people's methods and signatures," Dr. Karza pointed out. "Which means you're going to be terrifying a lot of innocent people. Innocent people who don't work well terrified."

"We'll contact this Ms. Fondor," the agent said. "Bring her in as a material witness. *Nicely*, okay?"

"Can you control that?" Karza said.

"Just let us handle it. We *can* be polite. In the meantime, yes. Shull, you're familiar with these people's work. Keep looking for signatures. The more 'suppliers' we have, the better we can build a profile. What boards the unsub frequents. Whose methods he's been copying. It would be good if we could build an algorithm for that. Is there anything like that already?"

"So you want me to burn the only friends I have in the world?" Tim said angrily. "You're all ready to go bust down Jaime's door and you want me to do that to *how* many people?"

"I'll send up that these people are probably innocent of any wrongdoing," the agent said. "But, Tim, keep in mind. While you're worrying about hurting your friends' feelings, the world is going to hell in a handbasket."

"Point," Dr. Karza said. "Tim, do you have any personal contact information for Jaime Fondor...?"

"Dr. Curry," Bateman said drily. "Thank you so much for joining us..."

The "meeting" was taking place by video conference. At least in Curry's case. The boardroom the rest were meeting in was five floors up and a few suites over from Curry's lab. But since he'd been given it he hadn't left. And he didn't intend to any time soon.

"As you might have heard on the news, the kid who figured out dual expression has been 'cooperating' with the CDC," Curry said. "I'll take an agnostic position on whether he has anything to do, directly, with the virus. He's being helpful, he was just in a videoconference with the WHO and others and not only pointed out some helpful stuff but a possible... Call it an ameliorative. Not a cure but something that might help. Again, might. Thing is, he's a little too pat or I'm a little too cynical. Doesn't matter. The first news, well ahead of the news as it were, is potassium may inhibit the secondary neurological packet's expression. Sort of. Bottom line is we all might want to start taking potassium supplements. Which people can OD on, by the way. Too much potassium will kill you as dead as too little. But as long as the dosage isn't too high, I'd recommend them."

"That's good news," Bateman said, looking at Tom.

"I'll get that promulgated through our medical personnel," Tom said, composing a note on his iPhone.

"Then we get to vaccine," Dr. Curry said. "Turns out this is one hell of a virus. I'm not going to totally bio geek out, but not only does it express two viruses with one packet, it expresses two viruses so different they're night and day. Just to give you the short version: Influenza is an orthomyxovirus. It has a full RNA packet and is a fairly complicated virus. The neurotopic, blood-pathogen, packet is a rhabdoviridae virus. Rhabdoviridae are so different from orthomyxovirii, there are some pretty good theories that they come from two entirely different evolutionary processes. They might as well be alien lifeforms to each other. And, somehow, the mad bastard who created this thing got both to express from a single pathogen. It's like a human mother conceiving and giving birth to a hippo. Impossible. Brilliant. And very problematic for the vaccine.

"The CDC, Hong Kong and Pasteur have all produced detailed directions for their experimental vaccines. You don't want them yet. They are *really* experimental. Like 'trial and error' experimental. With lots of error. They've already mapped out a vaccine for the airborne packet. But producing influenza vaccine is ...

complicated. And it takes time. And I can't do it in this lab even if we had the design. What I can do, if it works out, is the blood pathogen vaccine. Once they work out the bugs."

"What are the differences?" Bateman asked. "And what are the risks?"

"Well, the risks right now are high," Curry said, chuckling. "They had some of their lab rats catch the bug. Which is the 'error' part. But they'll work it out. Then the real problems come. However... I'm going to have to explain how this vaccine is going to be made, in general. 'Cause I'm going to need some more equipment."

"Which is?" Bateman asked. "I thought you had everything you needed?"

"I have everything you'd have in a regular laboratory," Curry said, nodding. "For its size, even a well-equipped one. What I don't have is what you'd use to produce a vaccine. For that I'm going to have to lecture. Ahem... Vaccination One-Oh-One:

"Various ways of inoculating people against smallpox date back to ancient China and India. But the way they did it was pretty damned dangerous and was just as likely to give you the disease. There's lots of bits in the middle but Edward Jenner figured out a way to use cowpox to vaccinate and that was what really started modern vaccine methods.

"It was Louis Pasteur that figured out that there were ways to 'weaken' pathogens, what's called 'attenuation' and then use those weakened pathogens as a vaccine. The first one was a mistake with chicken cholera but it led to all his other successful vaccines. The way he did it, exactly, isn't important because it's been superseded by other methods. Modern vaccines are produced in a number of ways. Very few of them use attenuation anymore. But it's still the fastest way to make vaccine. And they're pretty sure that this pathogen can be prevented with an attenuation vaccine."

"Why did they stop using it?" Bateman asked.

"Problems," Dr. Curry said, waggling his hand from side to side. "Issues. Lawsuits. Immunology One-Oh-One. Your immune system's a lot more complex than it's explained in high school but the basics work for this. Antibodies identify pathogens and bind to them. That signals other immunobodies to attack and destroy them. However, the antibodies are originally produced because immune cells have detected that there *are* pathogens in the body. So you've got to be infected, first. And if you've got a good immune system and all's well, you shake it off after a bit. If you don't have a good immune system or the pathogen's really nasty, well, you die.

"So...an attenuated vaccine is damaged bits of a pathogen. Just enough to tell the body, 'Hey, you've got an infection! And it looks like this!' without actually infecting you. The...issues are two-fold. More. The first is that if the vaccine *isn't* strong enough your body doesn't get a good enough look at the pathogen and when you do get hit with it you're not really prepared. And then you die. Or, the vaccine is *too* strong, has too much of the pathogen left, and you get the disease and you die. Or you're allergic to the materials in vaccine and you die. Or get really sick. Or there's a scare story on TV. Or people blame their child's autism on vaccines. Or...whatever. And in all those cases lawyers get involved and there's a big lawsuit..."

"Which of those do we have to worry about?" Bateman asked.

"I dunno," Curry said, shrugging. "Is Dr. Depene getting the vaccine? There's a guy with so many risk factors, medical and psychological, the answer is all of them."

"Thanks so much," Depene said.

"If the recipe is right and I'm making the vaccine... There's still a small risk that someone may get the disease instead of be protected from it. Half a percent? And to do it I need a radiation generator. That's the big difference between Pasteur vaccines and modern attenuated. You can be much more precise in your attenuation, not to mention take less time, with irradiation..."

"Well, no wonder nobody trusts it!" Depene said. "You're not going to inject radioactive vaccine in me!"

"As I said," Dr. Curry continued, shaking his head. "Psychological risk factor which, in and of itself, can cause hypochondriatic reactions. The *vaccine* isn't radioactive, you dope. You shoot it with radiation, which goes right through. It kills the RNA of the virus. There's no residual radiation. What I'll be using, to give you an example, is a dentist's X-ray machine. Ever had your teeth X-rayed? One of the newer cesium source models is more or less vital. Which you'd better get your hands on fast or they'll be all snatched up by the time you go shopping."

"And this will work as a vaccine?" Bateman asked.

"Against the neurological packet," Curry said, nodding. "It

should. The other problem is that it's going to take nearly two weeks to be close to 'sure.' Not 'this is FDA approved and has been through all testing.' Sure as in 'This probably won't kill you and probably will stop the disease.' That's the real problem. To get either one *distributed* will require all sorts of approvals. And then there's... other problems. But once it's through the most basic checks, I'll start producing. And I'll be the first one to take it, for what that's worth to Dr. Depene. Oh, and it's going to take a primer shot and a booster and you won't really be covered until you've had the booster. And you can't have the booster until a week after you've had the *primer*. So... we're fighting the clock, the spread of the disease and the development and production of the vaccine. It's going to be close. For us. For the world? I don't give us a shot in hell."

"Is there anything else critical?" Bateman asked.

"Not that you can't get on the TV," Curry said. "But you need to get that X-ray machine. And it will require some installation. Radiation shielding among other things. But that's details I can go over with Mr. Smith. Until the vaccine is somewhat cleared, we're in a holding pattern."

"Very well," Bateman said, nodding. "Thank you, again, for your assistance in this, Dr. Curry."

"Just make sure the check clears," Curry said, chuckling.

"Break this down," Bateman said.

CHAPTER 7

"The Center for Disease Control and the World Health Organization are assembling an unprecedented group of both professional and amateur synthetic biologists in a desperate search for a cure to the ongoing pandemic..."

"The FBI is searching for a white or Hispanic male in his early twenties believed to have last been seen in the Miami area in regards to the deliberate spread of the Pacific Flu Virus..."

"With the Pacific Flu widespread throughout the Pacific Rim, science reporter Timothy Karl has this report on Chinese authorities' battle against this deadly disease..."

"Finally some good news as the World Health Organization last night reported a breakthrough in curing the Pacific Flu pandemic..."

"Any idea what he wants?" Bateman asked. All that he knew was that Curry had asked for a meeting. Given that the WHO had announced a "breakthrough" in vaccine *yesterday*, he'd been expecting the call earlier.

"No, sir," Tom said. He'd called Curry last night as soon as he got the word. Curry had been tight-lipped and just asked for a meeting the following afternoon.

"Dr. Curry," Bateman said into the screen. "Still holed up I see."

"Yes, sir," Curry said, licking his lips.

"We're all agog on how you're going to save us," Bateman said. "I'd expected the call earlier."

"Are we secure, Mr. Smith?" Curry said, temporizing.

"We are," Tom said, curiously. "It's only the three of us."

"I'll have to trust that," Curry said. "When I covered all the stuff about attenuation in the previous meeting there was a reason: The WHO was kind of ahead of itself on announcing a vaccine."

"So you *can't* make a vaccine?" Bateman said, sitting back, his face hard. "That's not good news."

"Just..." Curry said. "Let me get there. There *is* a vaccine. It's just a matter of a sort of big logistics issue. The primary vaccine method has been known the whole time. We can do a flu vaccine, given time, in our sleep. But the flu, itself, is beside the point at this point. We need a vaccine for the secondary expressor. We could build a protein sequence mimicking the binding sites for that. They're working on it. And it will take another two months, minimum. Then there's certifications—"

"Doctor, we don't have two months," Tom said. "I'm not sure we have two weeks at the rate this is spreading."

"I'm getting there..." Curry said.

"I need an *answer*, Doctor," Bateman said.

"You want me to take this slow," Curry said. "The secondary expressor turns out to be a lot like rabies. It's definitely based upon it. About thirty percent of the same RNA, similar protein coat... It infects nerve cells. Primarily central nervous system. The spinal cord and brain. That's...where you find the...face it, the zombie virus."

"Understood," Bateman said. "And the attenuation vaccine. I think you mentioned lab rats. We got you quite a few. I suppose we can find some of the virus..." he said, looking at Smith.

"I'm sure—" Tom started to say.

"I asked for them assuming that I could work with them," Curry said, grimacing. "They're...basically just eating up rat food. Although you should probably get some rabbits or monkeys to use as cover.... The thing is...Pasteur and CDC have both confirmed that this pathogen *only* affects higher order primates. That's the *only* source of the virus bodies to attenuate."

"Oh," Tom said, leaning back and his face closing down. "Oh... bloody hell."

"Higher... order... primates..." Bateman said, slowly and carefully. "That includes...?"

"Various... monkeys if you will," Dr. Curry said, gulping. "Rhesus monkeys would do. Green monkeys possibly. Rhesus definitely. Possibly chimps. Probably chimps... The problem being, the supply of those is already being eaten up by the government for critical personnel. Has been eaten up. Critical personnel and research. There's just none... None available. That was what I was checking. Thus the logistics problem."

"Of course, homo sapiens is a higher order primate," Tom said, his face hard and cold.

"And... yes," Curry said. "Homo sapiens would... Yes, we are."

"Thank you for that information, Dr. Curry," Bateman said. "Besides attenuable virii, what do you need to make vaccine?"

"It's been a week, sir," Curry said. "Everything is installed and ready to go. As soon as I can get some virus bodies I can start cranking out the vaccine."

"Understood," Bateman said. "And, again, thank you for your assistance in this time of difficulty."

"Thank you," Curry said, closing the connection.

"Now I understand his insistence that this conversation was secure," Bateman said. "And it never occurred."

"Yes, sir," Tom said.

"Dr. Curry needs some materials to produce the vaccine, Mr. Smith," Bateman said, standing up. "I'll detail a significant budget for this. Are there any questions?"

"No, sir," Tom said, standing up. "I'll take care of it, sir."

"You understand that this never happened," Tom said, suiting up.

Although he'd been told he'd never have to "take care" of something, he'd also been hired for his proven ability to plan ahead. And part of planning ahead was making sure that he had back-up in case his bosses were wrong.

Jim "Kapman" Kaplan and Dave "Gravy" Durante were part of that planning.

The term was "functional sociopath." Both were former special operations. Both had combat experience. Both enjoyed combat. People, other than those close to them, weren't really "real."

Tom understood the mindset. He had the same type of brain. Having one was almost required to be in elite military units. It didn't mean any of them were serial killers. He'd had them go through advanced poly tests to ensure that they weren't going to be an "issue" as employees of the bank. They'd never done so much as assault that wasn't under controlling legal authority. They kept their killer side under control by tight discipline. They just had the potential. In fact, they just really needed a good reason. Like, say, fighting terrorism. Or saving their bosses and family from a disease.

"Your bonus is one out of fifty doses," Tom said, putting on the gloves of the Hazmat suit. The warehouse was a nondescript property in Alphabet Soup that the bank had repossessed. It was ostensibly untenanted. Setting up the "lab" for this mission had been easy enough. "We get vaccinated right after Dr. Curry. Curry, us, Bateman and then down. You can use the doses for anyone you want and you get two seats on the evacuation plan."

"Understood, sir," Kaplan said, pulling on his own gloves and holstering the taser. "Although I can actually see some value to this. Better than NYPD's answer."

The "Afflicted Temporary Holding Facilities" had already made the news. And the term "hell hole" was generally used.

"I'd rather be turned into vaccine than be put in that place," Durante said, holstering a back-up sidearm in case the taser didn't do the trick. "And since we're bonding, that's my official answer. If I go full zombie, make me into vaccine."

"Will do," Tom said, getting an odd sensation. It took him a moment to recognize it. It was the feeling of coming home. This, really, was where he was designed by nature to be. In a team on the sharp end. "Same here."

"All for one and all that," Kaplan said, grinning through his mask. "I'm in. Strip my spine and put my head on a shelf."

"I'll do that for you, Kap," Durante said, mock sobbing. "I'll put your head on my mantelpiece and toast you once a year on the anniversary of you becoming a zombie. I swear, man!"

"Let's load up," Tom said, opening the door of the heavy emergency response vehicle. "Before you Yanks start kissing and stuff."

They rolled out of the warehouse and down Avenue B, maneuvering carefully through the traffic. The one positive to the disaster was that traffic was getting lighter and lighter as people found anywhere but New York to exist. Everybody knew that no matter what the government was saying, things were getting bad and getting bad fast.

They didn't even get to Houston Street before they had their first customer.

Corinda was cursing her choice of delis for lunch and blessing her decision to wear walking shoes. If she'd been in heels the zombie would already have caught her. Unfortunately, it seemed to be in better shape than she was and was obsessive in chasing one Corinda Carfora, wildcat marketer. She'd been running nearly two blocks and it wasn't even swerving for other pedestrians. She'd turned the *corner,* for God's sake!

And, being New York, nobody was so much as giving a second glance to a naked man chasing a woman down the street. Much less helping.

"You're passing fatter people, you idiot!" she screamed, giving a glance over her shoulder. Still there. This was *ridiculous.* The other mercy was that lunchtime walking traffic was light in Alphabet City so she didn't have to dodge much. But she was wearing out. "Look! That guy! *He's* fat! Eat *him!*"

Never a cop...

That hoary adage was belied when she was halfway down the first block of Avenue B. A big black truck marked "Biological Emergency Response Team" swerved into traffic with blue lights on and stopped, blocking half of north-bound to a blare of horns.

Puffing, she swerved towards it as a pair of men in moon suits and masks exited. One of them waved for her to pass between them as they both pulled out guns. She recognized that one was holding a taser. The other was a gun-gun. Bang, you're dead gun.

"Thank you," she panted as she passed between them. "Thank you. Thank you..."

Tom waved the woman between them and took up a position covering Durante. Kaplan was driving and prepared to move out as soon as the zombie was tagged and bagged.

"Deep breath, mate..." Tom said, sotto voce.

"Don't make me laugh," Durante replied, then took the shot.

The zombie seemed to throw off the effect of the taser at first, nearly reaching Durante, then dropped to the ground, shuddering.

"Keep up the juice," Tom said, stepping forward. He holstered his Glock and pulled out an ampule. The auto-injector drove 15 ccs of Dilaudid into the zombie's thigh. Then he stepped back.

"Let up on the juice," he said.

The zombie, a man in his early forties and previously in good condition from the looks of him, stumbled to its feet and started to lunge for the team leader, then stumbled to its knees. In a moment it was back on its face as the narcotic took hold.

"Tag and bag," Tom said, pulling out a pair of flex-cuffs. "Ma'am, do you know this gentleman? Can you identify him?"

"Never seen him before in my life," Corinda said, still gasping for air. "He just came around the corner as I was going into the deli. I've been running ever since. I mean he *turned the corner* off Houston to chase me! Why?"

"No idea, ma'am," Tom said. He and Durante had already flex-cuffed the zombie and bagged his head in case he came to. As Durante started the blood test, Tom pulled out a receipt and filled it out with bogus information. "If you know of anyone looking for him, please refer them to NYPD. They'll be able to determine his disposition." He pulled the receipt off the pad and handed it to her.

"Okay," Corinda said, looking at the paper. "Is he... Is he going to the Warehouse?"

"I'm afraid so, ma'am," Tom said. He looked at Durante, who nodded. "He's positive for neurological packet of H7D3."

"I... guess I survived my first zombie attack," Corinda said, trying to smile. "That's something."

"Yes, ma'am," Tom said, taking one of the zombie's arms. "Have a nice day."

It had only taken an hour to collect five zombies. Three male, two female. And they'd seen more "incidents" on the way back to the warehouse.

"I can't get that people are still just going to work," Durante said, hooking one of the female's flex-cuffed ankles into a hoist hook. "I mean, they're walking right past other folks being attacked and it's like 'Whatever. Got to get to lunch.'"

"It's New York," Kaplan said, bringing over the butcher knife. "What do you expect? I mean, how do you tell the difference between a zombie apocalypse and every day?"

He drove the knife into the woman's throat, then cut out and away. There was a spray of carotid blood that fell on the pre-spread painting tarp in a broad splatter of red.

"Hey, look," Durante said. "We're making modern art. We could probably sell this in a gallery for big bucks."

"Can it," Tom said. He understood. At a certain level they all really hated what they were doing. They hated that it was necessary. And they hated even more that they were enjoying it. They hated themselves. And so they joked. But if he let it go too far they might forget that they were, in fact, humans and under discipline. "Cut all the way up and back to the highest cervical vertebra."

"Roger," Kaplan said, slicing further into the neck as Durante stabilized the woman's body. The ceramic knife slid up through the muscles, tendons and arteries of the neck like butter. The cut around the spine was somewhat ragged but serviceable.

"Okay," Tom said, coming over. "This is the tricky bit. Gravy, hold the body firmly. Kap, get the clippers and bag ready..."

Tom applied a sharp twist and snapped the connections at the disk, then slowly and smoothly slid the spinal cord out of the spine.

"Don't let it hit the floor," Tom said, juggling the head in one hand and catching the falling spine with the other. "We want to reduce contamination."

"Roger," Kaplan said, holding the lower portion of the white cord. "This I've never done. I mean, slaughtering pigs, yes. I've done that. And goats. But I've never stripped a spinal cord."

"I don't think many people have," Tom said, holding up the head by the woman's hair. He tried to ignore that it was a fine, light brown. The woman was probably in her forties, but she'd taken care of herself. Until she became a zombie, of course. "Got it?"

"Got it," Kaplan said, working the cord into a ziplock bag. He gathered the ropelike material into the bag, then snipped it at the base of the woman's spine with a pair of bandage scissors. The last of the spinal cord dropped into the bag. "That it?"

"That's it," Tom said, setting the head down on the floor and taking the bag. "See that red?"

"Blood?" Durante said, leaning forward to look.

"Spinal cords should be pure white or a slight yellow," Tom said. "That red you see is virus bodies. Big bundles of millions of individual viruses. Which makes this one a winner." He carried the bag over to a cooler, opened it up and dropped the bag on the ice.

"Four more to go..."

"I assure you I decontaminated the outside before I brought it over," Tom said, setting the cooler down on the doctor's desk.

"Which is why you're wearing nitrile gloves?" Curry said. So was he. And goggles and a light respirator. He opened up the cooler and pulled out one of the bags. "Should I ask?"

"There are people in the city who have pet monkeys," Tom said, tonelessly. "They get zombieitis, too."

"It's not zombieitis," Dr. Curry said, examining the spinal cord. "'Itis' refers to inflammation. Positive for H7D3, though. Zombigenic? Nobody has a really good term yet. This 'monkey' would be about five foot seven at a guess..."

"And in good enough shape to chase a woman two blocks," Tom said. "Fast monkey. Your point?"

"None, really," Dr. Curry said. "I'll be doing the work in the hot zone. And I suppose that twitting the person who brought it to me is one of the stupidest possible things I could do, all things considered."

"Doc, as long as you're producing vaccine, you've got nothing to worry about," Tom said.

"That had a faintly sinister tone to it, Mr. Smith," Dr. Curry said, starting to suit up.

"And if you think I'm *not* feeling rather sinister at the moment, Doc, you're an idiot," Tom said, yawning slightly.

"I'll keep that firmly in mind," Curry said.

"Voila," Curry said, holding up a vial from the door of Tom's office. "Primer."

"Come in all the way, please," Tom said. "That wasn't quick."

"It is, to say the least, a tedious procedure," Curry said, closing the door. "The longest part as a process is separation through a medium. But I even checked the attenuation level. It's good."

"I need a detailed SOP on how to produce it," Tom said,

walking over and taking the vial. He held it up to the light, then paused. "Sorry about the sinister thing earlier. We need you for more than vaccine. This is an ongoing issue and I've convinced Dr. Bateman that you're definitely needed on the evac. So you're secure."

"Trust you?" Curry said with a snort. He pulled out a couple of syringes. "Ready to shoot up?"

"Very," Tom said. "And I'm, of course, trusting that this works and isn't going to give me the virus. Or be some odd poison."

"See how sinister things can get?" Curry said, pulling out a dose from the vial and rolling up his arm. "Me first. How's that?"

"I can think of at least ten ways this could be a trick," Tom said, injecting the biologist. "Starting with you've already given yourself the vaccine and this is just water."

"O ye of little faith," Curry said, shaking his head. "I take it you're on the executive evac list? Like I want a zombie your size to go nuts onboard? How are we getting out, by the way?"

"Depends on the situation at the time," Tom said. "Probably helo to the airport, then jets to the remote site. Which means I need vaccine for the pilots and crew as well. How much did you get?"

"Forty doses," Curry said. "Of the primer."

"From five ... primates?" Tom said, grimacing. "That's all?"

"That's all," Curry said. "Despite the nodules being visible, there's not really a lot of virus there. Less than rabies, for example. Roll up your sleeve."

"Okay," Tom said, taking off his shirt. There was no way he was getting the sleeves all the way up his shoulders. Then he rolled up his T-shirt sleeve. He held up his hand at the doctor. "Just ... gimme a second."

"What's wrong?" Curry said, then laughed. "Oh, my God. Seriously?"

"I'm okay with getting shot, knifed, blown up and shot again," Tom said, grimacing. "Tattoos, even. I just don't like needles, okay? Just ..." He closed his eyes and turned his head to the side. "Just do it quick ..."

"Said the virgin," Curry said, stabbing in the needle and injecting the vaccine. "There, done, you big baby."

"Uh, uh ..." Tom said, shuddering. "I hate that. I really, really do. Although I hate even more that you only got forty doses."

"And that's just primer," Curry said, handing him a small black package. "More for your bully boys. That's just the first dose for forty people. And figure on a minimum of ten percent wastage. And ten percent is low. We're going to need a lot of... primates."

"We're looking at a minimum of two hundred doses for critical personnel alone," Tom said. "Damnit."

"Two hundred?" Curry said, his eyes wide. "You've got that many planes?"

"You forget the support staff at the remote site," Tom said, putting his shirt back on. "The helo pilots aren't part of the evac but they need to be vaccinated. Nor are certain critical personnel on this end. They all know that. But they're holding out for the vaccine if nothing else. After the primaries the next goes to pilots to take vaccine to the remote site. There's a schedule. But a minimum of two hundred doses. Two twenty if you're talking ten percent wastage."

"I'm going to need an assistant," Curry said, shaking his head. "That's more work than you realize."

"I'll put out an ad, shall I?" Tom said. "'Minion wanted. Must have a complete lack of squeamishness and a sociopathic personality...' Actually, if I thought they'd keep their mouth shut, I know a couple of people in the club industry like that.... No, wouldn't work... You?"

"Not anyone I'd trust," Curry said, shrugging. "I mean... I'm trying to avoid thinking about what we're doing."

"Saving lives?" Tom said. "Come to think of it... What do you need in the way of an assistant?"

"Just someone with a strong stomach and good intelligence," Curry said.

"How old?" Tom asked. "I mean, would an intelligent and..." He paused in thought. "Would an intelligent and *diligent* teenager work? I know where I can get one of those that I'd trust."

"A teenager?" Curry said, frowning. "I'm not..."

"I'm thinking of my niece," Tom said. "She and her family are down lurking in the Hudson on a sailboat at the moment."

"Thinking of jumping ship?" Curry asked, then frowned. "Or jumping *on* a ship?"

"There's nothing wrong with a back-up plan," Tom said, chuckling. "I presume *you* have one. If *I* didn't they shouldn't have hired me. She's a straight-A student and she's interested in science. And she's closed-mouthed."

"This is a pretty big secret," Curry pointed out.

"Which is going to get out, at least as rumor, before long," Tom said. "I'll get them in here and let you interview her. I'll cover the specific details. That's on me."

"Are you going to clear it with Bateman?" Curry asked.

"He does not need to know the details of the vaccine acquisition," Tom said. "That way if it blows up in our face, he can sacrifice us both to the so-called justice system with a clear mind."

"I can just feel the love," Curry said. "You realize you're putting your niece squarely in the crosshairs?"

"She can lie and say that she was just doing lab work and had no clue what she was doing," Tom said, shrugging. "We cannot. But I'll need to get her parents' approval. Which means a trip to the River." He picked up the vial and tossed it up and down. "I'm going to need the rest of this. Any specific requirements?"

"Keep it on ice," Curry said. "Refrigerated, anyway."

"Get the rest to Dr. Simmons," Tom said, walking to the door. "He has the schedule..."

CHAPTER 8

"Dad, we've got inbound," Sophia said, ducking into the saloon.

"Harbor cops?" Steve said, setting his iPad down. He had to admit he was as bored as the girls just sitting in the harbor. But he also wasn't leaving until Tom called it.

"Small, fast boat," Sophia said. "Open. Center console fishing boat I think. I only see one bloke."

"Rig up," Steve said, stepping up to the cockpit. He picked up a pair of binoculars and regarded the approaching boat. It was probably just someone passing through the area, but people were using sailboats to evacuate. It was just as possible that someone wanted this boat. He considered the driver as it approached. Big guy... "Stand down! It's Tom..."

"You could have *called*, Uncle Tom," Faith said. She was still in her hastily donned body armor. "We nearly blew you away." She took the tossed coil of line and secured it to the stanchion.

"Why am I not surprised?" Tom said, grinning. "Sort of an opsec situation. First of all, I come bearing gifts."

"I hope that they don't include the flu," Steve said, frowning. "We've been very careful about protocols and I'd hate to catch it from my brother."

"I'm clean," Tom said, picking up a large black pelican case and hoisting it over onto the deck of the sailboat. "And so is this. It's all been decontaminated. And part of the gifts is vaccine."

"Hallelujah," Stacey said, grinning. "The news said that it wasn't going to be ready for months!"

"And we need to talk about that," Tom said, dropping another case over the side.

"What is all this stuff?" Faith asked.

"More weapons," Tom said. "Ammunition. Legal releases for holding it. First-aid materials. More masks and filters. And . . ." he said, lifting a small cooler over the side. "The first delivery of vaccine. And now," he said, climbing over the rail, "Steve, Stacey, we need to talk. Alone."

"Girls, front cabin," Steve said.

"Aww, Dad!" Faith said.

"Seriously," Tom said, pointing. "It won't be long. Sophia, no eavesdropping."

"I won't," Sophia said, grabbing Faith's arm. "Come on. We'll find out eventually."

"I'd accept a drink if it was offered," Tom said.

"What, you want to raid my bar?" Steve said, waving him into the saloon.

"We'd better talk out here, though," Tom said, following him in. "Stacey, I haven't really said hello."

"Vaccine, medicine and ammo is the best hello you could have sent," Stacey said, hugging him. "How are you doing?"

"I've been better," Tom said, taking the offered whiskey. "I probably should have brought you some of this as well."

"We're okay on it," Steve said, waving out of the saloon. "If we start using it to pass the time we're done for."

"How's it been?" Tom asked as they sat down in the cockpit. Steve tactfully closed the door.

"Boring, really," Stacey said. She'd poured herself a glass of wine. "We've had harbor cops tell us we had to move twice."

"Not much pull there," Tom said. "But the most they can do is fine you. And I'm pretty sure they're too busy to do that . . ." He paused and took another sip. "This is good. Smooth."

"Bushmills Honey," Steve said. "Why are you stalling?"

"Because I don't know where to start," Tom said. "What do you know about vaccines?"

"Depends on the vaccine?" Steve answered. "There are a bunch of different ones and various ways they're produced. Why?" he asked, suspiciously.

"You know the thing about who you'd call to help you move bodies?" Tom asked.

"Yes," Stacey said, cautiously. "Do you need us to help you move one? Who did you have to kill to get the vaccine?"

"Several people," Tom said, taking another sip. He'd been avoiding drinking since the vaccine mission. "And I'll have to kill several more."

"You're serious?" Steve said. "Tom..."

"It's more complicated than you think," Tom said. "And not. The easiest and fastest way to make a vaccine is through using killed virus. The only source of the virus, the only place it grows, is on spinal tissue. And the only species it infects is primates. And the only readily available primates are...?"

"Humans," Stacey said, turning slightly green. "Oh God, Tom. Oh good God."

"The excuse is that, unlike rabies, there seems to be no way to reverse the damage," Tom said, taking another sip. "Once a zombie, always a zombie. And vaccine will save people like, oh, you and me and the girls. But they are, also, unquestionably human. So it is just as unquestionably murder. I have people to... help me with the heavy lifting. And sedated zombies are *very* heavy. But the biologist who is producing the vaccine does not have help. So I thought to where I could find someone that was trustworthy enough to not talk about what they were doing..."

"How much do you need?" Stacey asked. "I mean..."

"I only got about forty doses from our first run," Tom said. "And after I said I needed two hundred doses, four hundred actually since there's a primer and a booster, I got the estimate upped by higher. So the answer is: a lot. The general idea is to keep producing until we hit the eject bar. Or, rather, shortly before."

"I can..." Steve said, then looked around.

"Would you like me to think ahead for you?" Tom said. "The boat needs to be secured. Although the girls and Stace are trained by you, they're not you or me. I could detail someone to secure the boat, but given the circumstance I'm not sure who I'd trust to hold a boat in the harbor. So you need to stay. And Stacey is your engineer, not to mention just about the kindest person in the entire family. I don't see her as an assistant to our resident mad doctor."

"Is he mad?" Stacey asked.

"No more than Steve or I," Tom said, shrugging. "Bit of an arse, but then so are Steve and I," he added with a grin.

"You're saying one of the girls," Steve said. "To assist you in murder."

"Assuming that this ever comes out," Tom said, "and assuming that people don't just ignore it and assuming that Sophia's role in it ever comes out, the most she could be charged with is accessory after the fact. The only persons who are going to know she knows what she is doing are more culpable by far. And you can be assured I'll be moving heaven and Earth to make sure she's not locked up when the fall comes. To the point of having the plans ready for the prison break."

"Which will be difficult for you to effect if you're in prison as well," Steve pointed out.

"Which is why *you're* going to have them," Tom said, grinning. "The other reason for you to be out *here*, brother of mine. Seriously. I need Sophia. You have my assurance as her uncle that she'll be secure while she's on the island. Oh, and she'll get paid. In gold."

"Why would people ignore it?" Stacey asked, temporizing.

"Because I know I'm not the only one with this bright idea," Tom said. "I don't have any hard data on that but I guarantee that NYPD is doing the same thing. The cops aren't going to go without vaccine. Nor is NYFD. And all the same rationales hold. One: it gets dangerous zombies off the streets without having to put them in permanent isolation. Which is consuming so many resources it's getting ineffective. Two: it saves people. Yes, it requires that some die that others live but they're already effectively no longer human. At least that's what I tell myself in the middle of the night. Oh, and for another reason to release Sophia: it gets her off the boat. That's less resource use and I know that she and Faith have been driving you nuts."

"I'd rather you took Faith," Steve said, shaking his head. "If I hear the word 'bored' out of her mouth one more time I'm going to throw her over the side."

"Which of them would you rather have producing your vaccine?" Tom asked.

"Sophia," Stacey and Steve said simultaneously. Then chuckled.

"Send them both," Tom said. "I can find something to occupy that little hellion that doesn't involve being on a BERT."

"BERT?" Stacey asked.

"Biological Emergency Response Team," Tom said. "And I'll ensure they both get the same protection as any of our execs. They'll be safe. They can quarter with me. I've got the room."

"You'll regret that," Steve said, looking at Stacey.

"We'll have to talk to them about it," Stacey said. "It's..."

"A horrible thing to ask," Tom said. "But it's necessary."

"Let me go get them," Steve said.

"We get to get off the boat?" Faith said.

"Let me get this straight," Sophia said carefully. "My uncle is chopping up people to make vaccine?"

"Possibly," Tom said, calmly. "And yes."

"And you want *me* to help?" Sophia said.

"You wouldn't be directly involved in termination," Tom said. "Or harvesting. Or certain other aspects. Just working in the lab with Dr. Curry to produce the vaccine. The worst part is the first bit. Dr. Curry will handle that. After that it's just centrifuging and irradiating materials."

"*I'll* help," Faith said. "If it gets me off this boat!"

"I'll find something else for you to do," Tom said. "Although I'm not sure what. I can't exactly put a thirteen-year-old on guard duty—"

"You don't trust me?" Faith said. "Thanks a lot!"

"At my back, sure," Tom said. Okay, a little white lie. He'd rather have her in front so he wouldn't get shot by an AD. "In a lab? Let's face it, Faith, you're not detail oriented."

"True," Faith said, grinning. "You'd trust me at your back? Really?"

"Really," Tom said. "And I'll figure out something useful for you to do. But not anything involving securing, terminating or harvesting. Oh, and if this *does* come out and the authorities become involved, nobody knows nothing. Understood?"

"Oh, yeah," Faith said, making a zipping motion on her lips. "Sealed tight."

"I'll do it," Sophia said, shrugging. "It needs to be done and I can see why you chose me. I...appreciate the trust if not... Really don't want to chop up people stuff. But...Okay."

"I'm sorry I'm asking," Tom said. But he'd already been back and forth enough on the subject. "But...yeah. Thank you. And there's another bit," he said, pulling out some paperwork.

"You need to hire me?" Sophia asked.

"You're going to be an intern," Tom said. "We'll handle that paperwork at the bank. This is paperwork making your parents 'associated security contractors' with the Bank and paperwork to permit the vast store of weapons I'm sure Steve brought to be legally held in New York harbor..."

"You can't even have weapons in New York *harbor*?" Steve said. "What the hell is wrong with this place?"

"The law on it is iffy," Tom said. "But what they'll do is have the Coast Guard board you with some NYPD harbor patrol people along. If there are weapons, they may not, legally, be able to seize them, but they'll do a bend-and-spread on you looking for an excuse. Right now, the City and various corporations, hem, hem, are hiring security contractors left and right. This is all the paperwork. You fill it out, I'll file it and get the certification back to you. Technically, you're not fully legal until the certs have been authorized by the appropriate bureaucrats. But with the certs pending review, you're covered enough. And the office that does the certifications is overrun right now so nobody should geek."

"When do we leave?" Faith asked, standing up. "I need to get dressed."

"As soon as your parents finish filling out the blanks on the paperwork and you get packed," Tom said. "Why do you think I brought the big boat? And dressed how?"

"Dressed for Zombie New York!" Faith said. "You don't think I'm going walking through the streets of a New York overrun by zombies in *street clothes,* do you?"

"Yes," Tom said carefully. "Yes, I do. Because you're a thirteen-year-old girl. If you go walking through the streets of New York dressed up like a zombie contract hunter in Fallujah, you're going to get escorted to juvie. Where, like as not, some kid will go zombie and bite you. So, yes, you're going to go dressed in street clothes. I've got security waiting to pick us up at the dock."

"Are there zombie contract hunters in Fallujah?" Steve asked.

"Yes," Tom said. "And like I said, the idea is catching on in the States. Better to have contractors securing them than police. Put a bounty on them. There are legal issues. There always are. So go get packed for a few days at Uncle Tom's cabin. Or condo, in this case."

"Can I *bring* my gear?" Faith asked. "Just in case?"

"No firearms," Tom said, rolling his eyes. "Other than that, if you can carry it, you can bring it."

"Oooo! Got that!" Faith said, darting below.

"And no bows, crossbows or blowguns!" Tom called after her. "I hate you, Uncle Tom...!"

"Well," Kaplan said, catching the tossed rope. "I can see the family resemblance..."

Sophia had packed one "good" outfit: a cream business suit and matching shoes. Which was what she was wearing. She was carrying a briefcase and had a backpack over her shoulder. And, because she wasn't stupid, she was wearing a nose/mouth respirator.

Faith, on the other hand...

She had on body armor. And a full-face mask respirator. And a tactical helmet. And a full coverage uniform. And tactical boots. And tactical gloves. And a radio. And a machete. And a kukri. And two or three more knives. And three, count 'em, three tasers, 'cause Uncle Tom hadn't mentioned tasers.

"Can you move in all that, kid?" Durante asked.

"Yep," Faith said, her voice slightly muffled. She bent down and picked up one of Sophia's duffles, then tossed it through the air to hit the former SF NCO in the chest. "Shoot, move and communicate. That get through to you?"

"Loud and clear, kid," Durante said, laughing. "Let me guess: You're the lab rat."

"Like she knows a pipette from a test tube," Sophia said, stepping delicately onto the dock. "I see you have the bags, Faith dear."

"Like hell I do," Faith shouted. It was muffled by the respirator, which sort of ruined it. "Get back here and do some *work* for a change!"

"We've got it," Kaplan said, climbing in the boat. "Just head up to the car."

"Where's the zombies?" Faith asked, jumping onto the dock.

"Faith," Tom said, trying not to laugh. "Just get in the Expedition," he added, pointing.

"Where's the screaming crowds?" Faith asked, throwing her hands up in the air. "Where's the random gunfire?"

"Queens," Kaplan said. "But that's sort of normal."

"This sucks!" Faith said. "I'm bored."

"Oh, just do not start," Sophia said.

"Me start?"

"This is going to be sooo much fun," Tom said. "I should have looked in the phone book under 'deranged minion.'"

"Craigslist," Durante corrected. "There's a whole section..."

"Mr. Smith..." the security guard said carefully. The retired NYPD cop was, after all, talking to his boss. "You realize that most of this stuff is illegal to carry in New York City, right?"

"Just humor her," Tom said. "It's not worth the argument."

They'd taken a side entrance to the building, but it still had a manned security checkpoint where Faith, over protest, was being forced to disarm herself.

"God, this is embarrassing," Sophia said, hanging her head.

"*You're* embarrassed?" Faith said, pulling out yet another knife. Then the brass knuckles... "I'm being *disarmed*! In *New York*! In a *zombie apocalypse!*"

"I'm in charge of building security," Tom said, shaking his head. "Me. I'll make sure you don't have to fight any zombies while in my building."

"Like *that's* being a friend," Faith said, dropping a sandbag cosh onto the pile. "There. Done. I need a receipt."

"Just give her one that says 'Bucket o' weapons,'" Durante suggested. "I wish you were legal, girl. I'd propose."

"Like I date old guys," Faith said, then thumped him on the shoulder. "Just kidding. You're pretty cute for an old fart."

"So you're the boss's niece," Dr. Curry said dyspeptically.

Sophia's previous experience in a lab was high school chemistry. She'd made her usual A.

She had no *clue* what most of the stuff in Dr. Curry's lab was for. There were big boxes with lights flashing on them. There were piles of complex glassware. There were computer cables snaking everywhere.

"Yes, sir," Sophia said, trying not to appear as terrified as she actually was.

"You can take off the respirator," Curry said. "This is the clean zone. The hot zone is back there," he added, pointing to a door liberally covered with warning stickers. "Wait. Have you been blood tested?"

"No, sir," Sophia said, starting to take off the respirator.

"Then keep it on for a second," Curry said, pulling out a lancet. "I don't want to get exposed if you are. Hold out your hand."

He lanced the tip of her finger, then squeezed a drop of blood onto a small white card. The blood spread through a series of channels, and as it did, it turned blue.

"You're clear," Curry said. "*Now* take off the mask."

"Yes, sir," Sophia said, finally pulling it off and shaking her head. "Whew. That feels better."

"Don't get used to it," Curry said with a mirthless chuckle. "You'll be in full gear in the hot zone. Okay, don't get freaked by all this stuff. It's useful but you won't be working with most of it. Any of it probably. What you are going to be doing is working with vaccine production." He paused and looked at her carefully.

"I understand that we're extracting the vaccine, or the virus bodies anyway, from the spinal cords of infected primates," Sophia said carefully.

"Correct," Dr. Curry said, nodding. "Just concentrate on that word. Primates. What you'll be doing is, frankly, all the scut work. There are several procedures. Some of them are tedious, and you'll be doing the tedious ones. I did them when I was in college and grad school. I'm getting too old to pipette all day. And then there's the washing up. I'll be in there most of the time, all of the time at first, working with you. I'll be doing the more complicated procedures. You just do as I tell you and you'll be fine. The only real danger, since the material is a blood pathogen, is getting it into a cut. Do you have any cuts at all?"

"None on my arms or anything," Sophia said, holding them out.

"Okay," Dr. Curry said. "I do hope you brought some other clothes."

"They're outside," Sophia said. "May I ask why?"

"Because there's no way you're working in a moon suit in a business suit and heels..."

CHAPTER 9

"Mr. Schmidt, this is my niece, Faith," Tom said.

Dave Schmidt didn't work for Tom. He was one of the building engineers, which was an entirely different company. But they were sort of friends, and if Tom didn't find someone to entertain Faith soon, all hell was going to break loose. And he was *busy*, damnit.

"It's a pleasure to meet you, miss," Schmidt said, his brow furrowing.

"It's nice to meet you, Mr. Schmidt," Faith said, waving instead of shaking his hand.

Faith was being as close as she could come to being on "best behavior." Given that not only had Uncle Tom divested her of all her weapons, most of her gear had been dropped in the security team's locker room. She didn't even have so much as body armor. In a zombie apocalypse!

"There are some real-world reasons that I'd like Faith to have a thorough grounding in large-scale building design," Tom said. "I know you have duties, but would it be too much of an imposition for Faith to assist you in them?"

"There are regulations, Mr. Smith..." Schmidt said uncomfortably.

"And we live in interesting times," Tom said, smiling broadly. "Seriously, help a guy out here."

"I..." Schmidt said, then shrugged. "Sure. No problem."

"Thank you," Tom said. "I owe you."

"Can we speak privately, sir?" Schmidt asked.

"Sure," Tom said, waving for Faith to step out. They were meeting in the engineer's very nearly subterranean office.

"I..." Schmidt said, then cleared his throat. "I understand that BotA has access to vaccine, sir..."

"That rumor was quick," Tom said, frowning. "I'll neither confirm nor deny, but for the purpose of discussion...?"

"I'd really like to get some, sir," Schmidt said, his face working. "My...my sister has already... She's in the confinement facility."

"I'm sorry," Tom said, sighing. "You understand that it's a vaccine. It's not a cure. There's nothing, currently, that can be done for your sister."

"Yes, sir," Schmidt said. "But...I really don't want to be that way and...I have children. And grandchildren."

"I can't get a lot of doses freed up," Smith said, trying not to sigh again. "I'll see what I can do. As long as you keep that Amazon out of my hair for a while."

"I heard about the security checkpoint," Schmidt said, chuckling. "A sword? Seriously?"

"Are you talking about the machete or the kukri?" Tom asked. "Yes, seriously. And okay, yes, I'll see what I can do. Just..."

"Get her out of your hair for a while," Schmidt said, standing up and sticking out his hand. He pulled it back after a moment. "Sorry. Can do. Lots to learn. And I'm a pretty good teacher."

"Thank you."

"So this is it?" Faith pounced as Tom left the office. "You're going to turn me over to some fat old engineer to go dig around in sewers?"

"Faith," Tom said, trying not to grit his teeth. "There is, in fact, a real-world reason for this."

"What?" Faith said. "What can I possibly—?"

"Building design!" Tom snapped. "Where are we?"

"I really have no clue," Faith said. "I got lost a half an hour ago."

"Which is the point," Tom said. "Let's say that things really fall apart. That you have to do stuff that no reasonable thirteen-year-old should have to do to survive. You think that knowing how big buildings like this really work won't be useful?"

"Well..." Faith said, frowning.

"Also, I am incredibly busy," Tom said. "I'm the head of security of a major international bank that millions of people depend upon in the middle of an international crisis! Are you really so selfish you think I should spend all my time pampering to your tantrums? Or that you should even be throwing them?"

"I'm sorry, Uncle Tom," Faith said. "I— It's just..."

"This will keep you occupied and hopefully interested," Tom said. "While I try to save as many people as I can. So, yes, you're going to get an introductory course in building engineering, which is at least half about how to find your way around in one. Which may just some day save your life."

"I understand and comply, Uncle Tom," Faith said. "But... what you're asking me to do is creep around the, frankly, creepy bowels of a building with, you know, people turning into zombies without any warning. This is not exactly 'keeping me safe.' Sir."

"You have a point there," Tom said. "I'd planned on keeping you up on the executive level. Where we have posted security."

"Just a *couple* of weapons?" Faith asked.

"The problem is what," Tom said. "Almost anything useful is illegal for carry by a minor in New York."

"I hate this place," Faith snarled, then got hold of herself. "Sorry. But..."

"I'll get you an issue baton," Tom said. "But that's it."

"Better than nothing," Faith said, saluting. "Reporting for duty, sir!"

"Just...Don't get yourself turned into a zombie," Tom said. "Your mother would kill me."

"I had no idea these buildings were so complicated," Faith said as they were walking down another seemingly interminable service corridor.

"Every one of these buildings is basically a self-contained city," Dave said proudly. He'd found he enjoyed the girl's company. She might be a little firebrand but she was a smart one. And willing to pitch in no matter what the weight. Strong as hell, too. She'd carried a sixty-pound circuit breaker up two flights of stairs without a single bitch. "More like a spaceship. Air has to be pulled in and pumped to everywhere in the building. Then there's water and sewage. Movement of materials. It's a dance really. A great one."

"What are those?" Faith asked, pointing to some huge...thingies.

"Air handlers again," Dave said. "Currently they're not running since the portion of the building they supply isn't in use. No need for them. Nobody's using the air."

"And that is..." Faith stopped and tilted her head to the side. "What's that sound?"

"Fluid flow?" Dave said, cocking his head. "Air flow? There's an electrical hum..."

"I was thinking of the..." She stopped at the shriek.

The zombie had been behind one of the idle air handlers. It was covered in blood, not its own. Faith really didn't want to see what it had been feeding on behind the box.

"Charlie?" Dave said, stepping forward. "Charlie, it's me, Dave..."

"Don't," Faith said, putting out her hand. "It's not going to..."

The zombie charged the twosome, keening.

It was the first time Faith had heard the zombie wail and it sent shivers down her spine. That was the sound early man had heard in the forests. It was the thing in the corner at night. The monster under the bed. In the closet. It was fear curled up into a ball and distilled. For just a moment she froze.

"No!" Dave shouted, backing up. "Charlie! No, no, no, NO!"

The zombie was fixated on the engineer. Which gave Faith her chance.

She whipped the baton into the zombie's shin as it passed. She could hear the bones snap from the blow. But it turned on her nonetheless. She captured one grasping hand in a come-along, lifted the arm and spun under, tucking it up and back.

The strength of the zombie surprised her as did its complete disregard for pain. Any normal human would have been down on the ground with a broken leg and a nearly dislocated arm. The zombie just continued until it was fully dislocated, its teeth snapping to reach its tormentor.

Faith drove the butt of the baton into the zombie's kidneys and was mildly unsurprised to get no result. It just didn't notice pain at all. With that understanding, she flipped the club out and up, then across, hard, on the upper part of the zombie's neck. There was a sickening crunch and the thing dropped to the ground.

"Oops," she said, trying not to throw up. "I think we're going to have to report this to Uncle Tom..."

∽ ⊖ ⃕

"I didn't mean to kill him," Faith said miserably. "I'd just tried everything I could to subdue him and nothing was working. I know you're not supposed to use a baton on bone or the neck but...I couldn't think of anything else to do..." She started sobbing.

"I'm surprised you could," the NYPD officer said, shaking her head. "You gonna be okay, miss?"

BotA security and the coroner's overworked office had already cleared the bodies away. As Faith had feared, the zombie had been feeding on a previous victim. Both of them had been support engineers working in the area.

Faith was meeting with NYPD under the gaze of BotA's general manager for Security and Emergency Response as well as the chief legal advisor. The experienced attorney was more used to contract law, but he could dance the tune of criminal law. Juvie was, admittedly, not his expertise.

"Are you planning on charging my client?" the attorney asked. "She has cooperated fully."

"Given the situation and everything else going on?" the cop said. "It's up to the DA's office, but I don't think so. I'd find it unlikely. Thirteen-year-old girl defends herself and another person from an H7 EDP and the EDP is killed in the process? With a *stick*? I'd say the *Post* would want to interview her but not the DA."

"I think we'll try to avoid that," Tom said. "If there's nothing else?"

"We'd appreciate it if you'd keep her somewhere safer than the steam tunnels," the cop said, standing up. "And she's going to need counseling."

"We'll get her the best available," Tom said. "Chad, could you walk the officer out while I talk to my niece?"

"Of course," Chad said. "Officer?"

"Are you going to be okay?" Tom said as the others left. "And feel free to say 'I told you so.'"

Faith grunted a laugh, then shrugged.

"I'd like to say the crying for the cop was all an act," she said tonelessly. "And some of it was. But, no, not really what you'd call okay. On the 'told you so,' 'cause among other things I had to use a MELEE WEAPON. I'd planned on killing my first zombie at at *least* twenty-five yards! Not where I could hear the *bones crack* and get blood all over myself! So, no, not okay. Okay?" She sniffed again and grimaced. "God, I hate that I cry. It's so ... *girly!*"

"Think soldiers don't cry?" Tom said. "Think your father never cried? You cry. You cry, usually, when nobody is watching. You cry in the shower. Or only when friends are there. People who know. Who understand. And you didn't cry in the crunch."

"Go me," Faith said.

"I don't think there are really words for this," Tom said, shrugging. "I can get you all the counseling in the City. But it boils down to you did what you had to when you had to. If you hadn't, then two more lives would have been lost—"

"One," Faith said. "If worse came to worse I was going to break Dave's leg and run for it."

"That's the spirit," Tom said, his hand over his mouth trying not to laugh.

"I mean, even a twenty-two!" Faith said, throwing her hands up. "That way I could have shot his leg out at a distance!"

"Dave's or the zombies?" Tom asked.

"Yes! Either! Both!"

"Well, you won't have to worry about it again," Tom said, shaking his head. "I should have been smart and kept you up here in the first place. I'll ... find some paperwork for you to do or something."

"Great," Faith said, crossing her arms.

"For now it's back to the apartment," Tom said. "I've already called Dr. Curry and told him that Sophia's done for the day. And you definitely are. I'll have someone run you over."

"I ..." Faith said, then frowned. "That's the only thing that makes sense. But ... I am *not* going to the apartment without my gear."

"Faith ..."

"Uncle Tom," she said, reasonably. "The next time I might not be able to say 'I told you so.' I know you're running us over with executive protection. Are they staying on the door till you get there?"

"Um ..." Tom said. He had had a hard enough time finding the personnel to run them home. There were a million tasks.

"There are still criminals," Faith pointed out. "And unknown threats. You're not going to leave us alone in the apartment without so much as a taser. Not this time."

"Agreed," Tom said, sighing. "I'll have the security detail transport it. But no going zombie hunting!"

"Been there, done that," Faith said. "All I really want right now is a bath."

"And tomorrow we'll...find something else for you to do."

"Filing. It's going to be filing, isn't it?"

"Miss, I'm really sorry about having to disarm you when you came in..."

It was the same security guard and he really *did* look sorry. The story was already all over the building.

"You were just doing your job," Faith said, thumbing at Durante. "He's supposed to tote all my stuff for me. Is there anything in there I *can* carry in New York?"

She'd had to turn over the baton to NYPD "for examination." But Tom had helpfully issued her a new one.

The guard leaned over and slid a taser across the table under the cover of his body.

"Drop this in one of your cargo pockets," he whispered. "And if you do get in trouble, give me a call on the cell and I'll call a few buddies..."

"Thanks," she whispered back.

"Sorry, miss, but as I said, all this stuff is illegal for carry in New York without a permit," he said loudly. He handed the tote with her weapons to Durante. "Mr. Durante will hold onto it for you."

"I understand," she said loudly. "Let's go, Gravy."

"Oh, my God," Sophia said. She was in jeans and a T-shirt after working in the lab. She was starting to wonder if body armor wouldn't have been the best call.

As they walked out of the building to the waiting car, a photographer ran up and started taking pictures. Of Sophia.

"Ow!" Sophia said, turning away. He was using a heavy-duty flash, and between her eyes not yet being adjusted and the descending sun, it was like looking into a nuke.

"Hey," Durante said, stepping between them. "Back off!"

"Miss, can we get your name?" a guy with a hand-recorder asked. "Are you the thirteen-year-old who fought off a zombie with a pair of nunchuks?"

"*What?*" Faith said.

"Out of the way," Durante said, pushing the guy back. But there were a dozen or more coming around the corner from the main entrance. He keyed his microphone. "Unit fourteen. I've got a security issue at Entrance Six. Request support. Just keep moving, girls. To the car!"

"Move, you idiot!" Faith said, bodychecking one of the mike-wielding reporters out of the way. "Follow me, Soph!"

"Watch out, rentacop!" the reporter said, pushing back. "I can get you charged with assault!"

"You want *assault*!" Faith said, pulling out her baton. "Move or I'll *show* you assault!"

"Just keep moving, Faith," Durante said, giving her a shove.

"Can you tell us what you were doing in the building...?"

"No," Sophia said, holding her hand up to shield her face from the flashes.

"What is your relationship to BotA...?"

"Say 'no comment,'" Durante said.

"No comment..."

"Can we get your name...?

"No."

"Was the afflicted hostile...?"

"You've got the wrong person..."

"Damned straight," Faith muttered.

More security poured out of the building, and with their assistance Durante managed to get the girls to the car without actually injuring anyone in the crowd. Which had grown to include the usual gawkers. New Yorkers would ignore anything except paparazzi, which generally meant celebrities.

"*Is that Lindsay Lohan...? Did she get arrested again?*"

"No!" Sophia screamed as the door closed.

"Oh, crap," Durante said. "Move it. To the condo. If we've got trailers, see if you can lose them, but don't do a Princess Di."

"Rentacop?" Faith said, buckling her seatbelt. "*Rentacop*?"

"They thought you were part of her security detail," Durante said, chuckling.

"Son of a bitch!" Faith snarled. "I make the tabloids but I *don't*?"

"You might want to remember what we're actually doing here," Sophia said, her face tight.

Durante waved his hand to indicate it was not a subject for discussion.

"New York," Faith said, looking around at the unusually light afternoon traffic. "I don't get the attraction. It stinks. It's crowded. The people are rude. And there's barely a scrap of green in the whole place."

"You wanted to come," Sophia said.

"Because it was better than being stuck on a sailboat," Faith said. "But not much."

"The food's good," Durante said. He really didn't like New York much, either, but he felt he had to come up with some virtues. "And the girls are— There's a lot of . . . art and culture . . ."

"The girls are hot?" Faith finished. "Or easy?"

"I'm not going to have this conversation with my boss's teenage nieces," Durante said. "It's got its attractions. Of course . . . a lot of them are closed right now."

"Hang on," the driver said, swerving. A naked woman was running through traffic, hitting the cars as she ran as if trying to push the traffic onto the sidewalk.

"Zombie?" Sophia asked.

"Could be," Durante said. "Probably. But this is New York. She could just be high. You don't know until you run a blood test."

"So, about the food thing," Faith said, her stomach rumbling.

"We'll get you delivery," Durante said. "One other benefit to New York. You can get any kind of food in the *world* delivered."

"I'm not really hungry," Sophia said.

"I am," Faith replied. "I need food. And after an almost continuous diet of Mountain House, I need *good* food. Is there Italian?"

"Best Italian in the world," Durante said. "Better than Italy. Although mostly it's mom-and-pop places. But we can get some delivered."

"I just want a shower," Sophia said, looking out at the city. "'Nother zombie."

"That's a zombie," Durante agreed. Two NYPD officers had the zombie restrained, but it was clear that he'd bitten a passerby. The passerby was a punk with a gigantic pink mohawk who was crying and holding his arm and appeared to be begging the officers about something. The officers didn't seem to be listening.

"And another one on the way," Faith said.

"Indications are that if you clean the affected bite quickly the chances are reduced," Durante said. "And they're saying now that if you get the flu, the secondary virus is reduced if you take potassium supplements."

"Yeah, the separation at the b phase telomerase site is inhibited by potassium," Sophia said. "But it's not an either-or thing. If you take enough potassium to totally inhibit expression, it's a lethal dose. But if you have a strong immune system, then having any inhibition of the expression gives your immune system a chance to beat the beta expressor. If you have a strong immune system. And bites are tough. The beta expressor is aggressive and resistant. It's a matter of how much viral load you get through any source—"

"I take it you were listening at work," Durante said.

"Dr. Curry has every channel that's working on this running continuously in both the hot and the cold zones," Sophia said, shrugging. "So, yeah, I picked up a little. More than I can talk about in the car. He's got the updated spread graph, for one thing. The one that's way ahead of the news."

"Can I ask..." the driver said, then paused.

"It's getting worse," Sophia said after a glance at Durante. "Lots worse. The thing is... This virus is, molecularly, 'spit and baling wire' is the way that Dr. Curry described it. After a while it's just going to burn itself out."

"Soon?" Durante asked. This was more than he'd been getting.

"Not soon enough," Sophia said with a sigh. "Look, it's... The virus, the influenza one, is really complicated. It's a dualistic expression. That right there is waaay out there. And two centers, UCLA and College of Rome, have both come back with pretty good models showing that dualistic is impossible to support over the long term. Probably why it never evolved in microorganisms. There's some fundamental problems with it chemically. And flus mutate. But the way that they mutate... they just mutate. They can get more lethal, more infective, or less lethal, less infective, stop being infective or lethal at all or any combination. This one, the real killer is the beta expressor, the zombie virus *embedded* in the flu. CDC and Pasteur both ran models of it over multiple replications and it just... breaks pretty quick. It doesn't mutate to be more lethal or more infective; it stops working at all except as a mild flu bug. It stops being able to express the zombie part."

"So the plague's just going to... stop?" the driver asked.

"Yes," Sophia said. "But it's not going to be soon enough. Look, you buy a new computer. And you don't know it, but there's something wrong with it. Every time you turn it on, one little random bit of software goes wrong. Now a computer can go a long time like that. Or it can break the first time you turn it on. It's random. That's what's happening with all the flu viruses. As they replicate, sometimes they break. Or get closer to breaking. As more and more break, the flu will burn out. The question is if it will burn out before it kills the world."

"And the zombie part?" Durante asked. "We're getting a lot of transmission from bites now."

"Yeah," Sophia said, grimly. "They've broken out the transmission graphs by bite or flu and bite, or at least blood transmission, is starting to pull ahead of flu. There was one case in South Carolina where a husband apparently gave it to his wife through, well, fooling around. Then he zombied but didn't bite her. She hid in the bathroom. And she had no flu antibodies. So they think it was sexually transmitted. And then *she* zombied."

"Ouch," Faith said, shuddering.

"The beta expressor isn't really robust, either," Sophia said. "There are four different models that people are arguing over but it looks as if it's going to slowly degrade back to basically rabies or just fall apart. Like I said, spit and baling wire."

"And with that, we're at the condo..." Durante said as the driver pulled up to the entrance. "Don't wait for me. I'll find my own way back."

"Yes, sir," the driver said.

"Dibs on the shower," Faith said.

"Age before incompetence," Sophia replied.

"This is going to be sooo much fun," Durante said.

CHAPTER 10

"So I see you made the news," Dr. Curry said, moving his cursor to highlight particular points of the virus. His voice was muffled by the moon suit.

"I didn't really have a way to avoid them," Sophia said, carefully squirting prepared attenuated virus into vaccine bottles. "Well, if I'd known they were going to be out there, we could have taken a back way, I suppose."

"This isn't something we want to end up on the nightly news," Dr. Curry pointed out.

"Tell me about it."

"Although it already has." Curry gestured to one of the plasma screens. The YouTube video was of a reporter outside a warehouse. The caption said "vaccine chop shop found by NYPD."

"I hope like hell that's not us," Sophia said. The sound was turned down.

"Drug dealers," Curry said with a snort.

"So we're in competition with drug dealers?" Sophia said. "How'd drug dealers get involved, anyway?"

"People want the vaccine," Curry said, looking around at the laboratory he'd been provided. "Drug dealers fulfill economic needs that others can't or won't."

"I don't know that I'd want to get vaccine from drug dealers," Sophia said. "Not knowing what I know about how it's produced. And that's *here*."

"In which you are wise," Curry said with a snort. "Over two hundred people have become infected due to bad vaccine. If it's not properly attenuated: Instant zombie."

"You're sure this is attenuated?" Sophia said, holding up one of the vials.

"That's what I'm checking," Curry said, gesturing at the screen he was using. "The binding sites are still there but the RNA is well and thoroughly trashed. I'd say that this RNA has less coherence than rabies but the binding sites are about as robust. That's good for vaccine. Not sure what it says about the organism long-term. What is worse, most of the 'vaccine' that's being bandied around in the City is nothing but colored water."

"Why colored?" Sophia asked. She held up one of her completed vaccine bottles to the light. "This is clear."

"Because they're drug dealers?" Curry said, shrugging. "People want to *see* something for their money. Who's going to believe a drug dealer who gives them a shot of clear liquid."

"Who's going to believe a drug dealer, period?"

"I take it you've never gotten into illegal drugs," Dr. Curry said.

"I'm not an idiot," Sophia said. "Drugs can seriously screw up your life. Of course, so can the zombie apocalypse but I didn't have any control over that. So, no, I don't do drugs. I drink a little but my parents are okay with it in moderation. Faith doesn't even do that. She only drinks water and fruit juice."

"I suppose I should be impressed," Curry said. "I've dabbled in drugs from time to time. Heck, I dealt when I was in grad school. If you have a biochemistry lab at your disposal, cranking out a little LSD is no problem and it's one way to pay for grad school."

"Seriously?"

"You might notice what we're making here, miss," Curry said mirthlessly.

"Point."

"One shot of zombie vaccine is going for fifty dollars on the street," Curry said. "Which is a good price. The question being whether you're getting vaccine or not. Or 'good' vaccine. Some of them even have mild drugs in them to give a feeling that something is happening. Which, even if the dealers get the right attenuation, can cause the vaccine to be nonfunctional."

"Seriously," Sophia said. "People who get their vaccine from a source like a drug dealer are getting what they deserve. Speaking of which, I'm done."

"Let me do a cross-check and then we'll get it over to Dr. Simmons," Curry said. "Quality control is the best control..."

It had been filing.

By afternoon of the next day, Faith had had enough. She'd had enough of the questions about her experiences in the tunnels. She'd had enough of the gossip. She'd found out, quickly, that her uncle's big "secret" was anything but. The rumors were all over the place that The Bank, capital letters, was producing vaccine. And just as many rumors about how, most of them more or less dead on. She'd gotten tired of the sidelong glances and the vaguely worded questions about where her uncle was gone to all day. People even referred to the "BERT" van in the sort of hushed tones reserved for nuclear secrets. And then there were the subtle questions about "how do *I* get the vaccine?"

And she'd had it with filing. It was boring and pointless since most of this was going to be relics of a bygone age in no time.

She'd paid attention when she'd had to turn in her stuff the first day. All of *her* stuff was back in the apartment. That didn't mean there wasn't "stuff." The locker room had *everything* she'd need to go zombie hunting.

Faith stepped out of cover, aimed carefully and zapped the zombie in the back with the taser.

"Nice," she said as the zombie dropped to the floor. She darted forward and slammed the narcotic injector into the back of its thigh, holding it as she thought the instructions indicated.

She was rewarded by the two-and-a-half-inch needle driving through her thumb and a gush of tranquilizer squirting onto her facemask.

"Shit!" she screamed, hopping around and shaking her hand. The needle steadfastly refused to exit her thumb. "Cock-suck... Fuck! Rat turds! Ow!"

She grabbed the injector and pulled it from her thumb, tossing it across the corridor.

"Well," she said, shaking her hand. "At least it's num... b. Mum... Oh cap... No... No... bad..."

The zombie was getting to its feet, which was the bad part. Besides being slightly stoned by the small dose of tranquilizer that had gotten into her system. And her right hand flopping uselessly.

"Very bad," she said, drawing another taser left-handed. She couldn't get her usual dead-on targeting since she was getting a bit of double vision. "I think he's about..."

Which was where he was. The zombie let out a screech and dropped to the floor, spasming. Again.

"Perfect," she said, then wondered why there was blood dripping on the zombie's back. She looked at her hand and thought it through. There was blood. Dripping. From her thumb.

"Blood pathogen," she said, drunkenly. "Not good."

She pulled off the tactical glove, and the rubber glove under it, and looked at her thumb. It was swollen, bleeding and discolored.

"Is that normal if you AD yourself with an injector?" she asked the empty corridor.

The answer was another zombie howl from the south.

And the zombie was getting up. Again.

She pulled out her last taser and fired, hitting it in the groin.

"I said *stay* down!" she said to the hissing and whimpering zombie.

"This is soooo not good," she said, finally injecting the zombie and then fumbling in a taser reload with one hand flopping useless. She could *hear* zombies heading her way by the flop-flop of their bare feet on the concrete. "I really, *really* need to start allowing adult supervision.... And reading the directions more carefully. And eating all my vegetables.... They need these in semiautomatic... With a magazine..."

She turned and fired the reloaded taser just in time to stop the zombie coming from the north. There were two more in the other direction....

"Durante," Kaplan said, holding up the office phone. "Your girlfriend's calling."

"I don't have a girlfriend," Durante said, working on paperwork. Turned out that even in serial killing there was paperwork. Time sheets, materials... It just glossed over a lot of stuff.

"That would be the boss's niece," Kaplan said, grinning. "She wants to talk to you."

"What now?" Durante said, picking up the phone.

"Line two."

"Hey, Faith, how's the filing going...? Uh-huh. How'd you get an injector stuck in your thumb...?"

Kaplan spun around in his chair and quirked a "Spock" eyebrow.

"And how'd you run into a zombie...? And you got the taser where...? And you ran into this zombie...? Uh-huh. Uh-huh. Okay...Okay...Sure. You just stay right there, okay? We'll be down in a jiffy. Yeah. That would probably be best.... Uh-huh. Bubye now."

He hung up the phone and looked at the wall thoughtfully.

"Problems?"

"Roll the full tac team to level B-9, section forty-two," Durante said, standing up carefully. "Loaded for bear. And I mean right GOD DAMNED NOW!"

Then he hit the door running...

When Tom got there it was all over but the flex-cuffing. Faith was still up on the air-handler, wrapping a bandage around her thumb, and there were nine, count 'em, nine zombies, male and female, on the floor. At least two, considering the cranial damage, involved the blood-splattered crowbar resting next to her.

The security team wasn't bothering to flex-cuff those.

"Hey, Uncle Tom," Faith said in a mixture of nervous and cheerful voice. "Did you know your basement was absolutely *overrun* with zombies? *I* didn't."

"Wasn't really aware," Tom said carefully. "Need to talk with Brad from building security about that. Faith...aren't you supposed to be up in the *filing* room?"

"Yeah," Faith said. "About that. Filing's not really my thing. And with the bad thumb and all..." she said, holding up the appendage.

"Hi," Faith said, hanging her head. "I'm Faith. I'm supposed to help with the mail..."

"Uh-oh," Steve said, watching the approaching boat.

The anchorage they were in was designated open. They weren't in a channel or anything. It was an out-of-the-way spot on the Hudson on the Manhattan side. But Harbor Patrol seemed to want to stop by.

"Stacey, police visit," Tom yelled through the hatch. He'd had watch.

"Roger," Stacey said. She quickly picked up the ready weapons, two Saiga shotguns, two pistols and an M4 semi-automatic carbine, and began emptying them. That was simply a matter of dropping the magazines and storing them. Then she proceeded to lock all the weapons in their containers.

By the time the boat pulled alongside, everything was locked down. And she and Steve were both in respirators with nitrile gloves on.

"Harbor Patrol," the loudspeaker boomed from the small trawler. "Permission to come aboard for health and safety inspection..."

"Granted," Tom said shouted. It was muffled so he waved for them to board. Not the best way to talk to police, wearing respirators, but they'd managed to avoid the flu so far, and the vaccine wouldn't yet have taken hold. "Stacey, paperwork?"

"On it," Stacey said, shoving the last pistol case into a locker and locking *that*.

"Good afternoon, sir," the lead officer of the two-man team said. His name tag read: Torres. They were clearly bothered by the respirators, but *they* were wearing nitrile gloves. "First question, are there any weapons on board?"

"Yes, officer," Steve said. The two officers' body language went immediately to "defensive." "We're an associate security contractor for one of the onshore banks. We have quite a few weapons on board for that reason."

"Contractors," Officer Torres growled. "Great. Just flipping great."

"May we use a certain amount of discretion in the conversation?" Steve asked.

"Anything you say we're required to restate if so asked," the officer said.

"Discretion in that is all I'm asking," Steve said, grinning. "We're a back-up jump plan for some executives. In the event that things get bad enough that protection from law enforcement breaks down, the weapons are for protection of the executives."

"How many?" Torres asked.

"With the weapons and *ammunition*, I'm sure you'd use the term 'arsenal,'" Steve said, smiling again. Stacey handed him the paperwork for the weapons as well as the stamped form that they had registered as security contractors in and for the State and City of New York. The form included a list of all registered weapons ammunition and "paramilitary equipment."

"Jesus Christ," Torres said. "Arsenal is right. You can't have all this stuff sitting in the harbor!"

"Included in the paperwork is my BATF FFL license," Steve said calmly. "As well as my certification as a Class III firearms instructor, tactical firearms instructor and law of weapons instructor. My wife is a tactical firearms instructor as well and is a reserve Virginia police officer. This is not meant to be offensive, Officer Torres, but I *teach* police officers. Part-time anyway."

"In Virginia," his partner said.

"I once taught a class for some of your NYPD SWAT people," Steve said. "A Lieutenant...Hansen comes to mind?"

"You mean *Captain* Hansen?" Torres asked, suspiciously. "Out of the One-Thirty-Second?"

"Five-ten, two hundred?" Steve said. "This was five years ago or so. Weight may have changed. Blue eyes, shaved head. I detected balding... Wife's name...Cynthia or something like that? Five years and we only chatted briefly outside of class."

"Stay where you are?" Torres said, pulling out his cellphone. He walked up to the front of the boat for the conversation.

"How's it going for you guys?" Steve asked.

"All good, sir," the officer replied.

"My two daughters are onshore," Steve said. "They paint a rather lurid picture."

"Lurid?" the officer said.

"Vivid in color," Steve said. "Presented in shocking or sensational terms. Sorry, I only instruct in firearms during the summer. The rest of the time I'm a high school history teacher."

"Got it," the officer said. "My dad's a teacher. He used to spend summers and holidays working odd jobs."

"How's your family doing?" Steve asked.

"So far, so good," the officer said, shrugging. "People are scared. I mean, what can you do about a plague?"

Steve tilted his head and tapped the respirator.

"They won't let us use those," the officer said, balefully. "I guess..." He looked up as Torres came back from the front of the boat.

"Aussie, huh?" Torres said, looking at him oddly. "I thought it was Irish."

"Australian accent mixed with Southern tends to sound that way," Steve said, trying not to sigh.

"That's a buttload of ammo," Torres said, looking at the paperwork again. "You get a fire onboard and you're a floating bomb."

"Which is why we anchored well away from other boats, Officer," Steve said. "As well as to avoid contamination."

"Can see you've got that down," Torres said, handing him back the papers. "Those weapons do not go on-shore until all your certifications have been processed, understand? We've had too many of you god damned contractors get gun-happy in the City."

"If it makes you feel any better," Steve said, "I agree with your opinion of most contractors. They tend to be unprofessional nuts with delusions of grandeur because they can walk around with the big guns. Part-time firearms instructor. Dealt with *too* many contractor wannabes."

"The captain said you were a straight shooter," Torres said. "No pun intended."

"I'm glad he's hanging in there," Steve replied. "I didn't really keep in touch," he added with a shrug.

"Not a round of ammo, not a single gun, goes on shore," Torres repeated. "I take it all your safety gear is complete?"

"Inventory, location and log book," Steve said, handing over that paperwork.

"Yeah, we'll—" He started at a honk from the boat.

"If it's clear, come back," the captain said over the loudspeaker. "Priority call!"

"Just..." Torres said, looking both ways.

"We're not going to go zombie hunting in your city, Officer," Steve said. "We're perfectly content just sitting here."

Torres shook his head and scrambled back over the side.

"You guys take care," Steve said, casting off their lines. "And hopefully that takes care of *that*. I suppose hoping that there won't be any more crises today would be too much?"

CHAPTER 11

"Where's the usual mailman?" The executive assistant for the manager of Cost Accountancy was a lady in her forties with what Faith mentally dubbed "teacher face."

Faith sort of preferred being the mail girl to filing. It got her some exercise and she got to meet and talk with people. Of course, half of them asked her why her sister was fighting a zombie. She'd given up trying to explain, which was a bit of a pain. And her thumb still hurt like heck, which was another pain.

"Didn't show for work," Faith said, handing over the next set of packages. A lot of it was actually "mail." FedEx was having trouble with deliveries. "No answer on his cell. H7? Left town? Who knows..." She was used to answering that question, too.

"Oh, my God..." the executive assistant said, looking at her computer.

"What?" Faith asked, craning over.

"Airplane crash," the EA said, gesturing at her screen. "Go ahead." She turned the sound up slightly.

"...these images were taken by a cell phone shortly after the crash..." the voiceover was saying. The plane had landed in a suburb, and the caption read "Bellefonte, PA." All that could really be seen was billowing smoke and flame. It didn't even look like a plane. *"FAA reports that based upon the truncated call from the cockpit, one of the pilots may have succumbed to the secondary H7 virus... There are no reported survivors on the flight..."*

"No wonder FedEx isn't delivering," Faith said.

"They need to get vaccine distributed," the assistant said, shaking her head. "This shouldn't be happening. Where's the vaccine?"

"Depends on the type," Faith said, shrugging. "The Pasteur method requires infected material. And it can only come from higher order primates. Since there are only so many Rhesus monkeys in the U.S., there's not much of a source from that. To do the other type requires growing the proteins. Two months, minimum, to do that. And then..."

"That's not true," the EA snapped.

"Which part?" Faith said, confused. "I mean, I've talked to—"

"It doesn't take that long to produce vaccine! They're just stalling because the vaccine companies want to run up the price!"

"They are?" Faith said, still confused. "According to Dr. Curry, you have to build the protein crystal—"

"Young lady," the EA said, calming down. "I know you think you know what you're talking about. But this is the fault of the Bush Administration allowing the drug companies to get runaway profits off of pharmaceuticals. They know that if they wait they can ask anything for their vaccine. And it will probably be dangerous to use even then. Vaccines are the cause of autism and allergies in children, another thing that the Bush administration allowed to run rampant. I think this virus was created by the drug companies just to make money. They're making money hand over fist just with the tranquilizers for those poor infected people."

"According to the FBI and the CDC, it appears to have been one person," Faith said, mulishly. "They've tracked the spread."

"Young people," the lady said, shaking her head. "You believe anything you're told, don't you? Just because it's on the TV doesn't make it true."

"Okay?" Faith said. "I guess you *could* be right."

"Trust me, I'm right," the lady said. "I don't know who's been filling your head with all that other nonsense, but this is definitely the fault of the drug companies."

"Okay," Faith said, frowning. "Well, I better get back to work. Mail to deliver."

"Yes, you should," the EA said, turning her attention away.

Faith continued on her rounds, dutifully dropping packages at offices. She got the usual round of questions. Where's the regular guy? Didn't report for work. No answer on his cell or home. Where did your sister run into the zombie? She didn't. It was a misunderstanding.

There were more rumors. Everybody had a rumor. The H7 was God's judgment on the world. It wasn't really the H7 virus causing people to go zombie. It was all a plot by, choose one or more: the DOD, the Republicans, the pharmaceutical companies, the Democrats, Greenpeace, the news media to boost ratings. Until she started delivering the mail, she'd never heard of the Trilateral Commission or Skull and Bones. She'd had to have them explained. And woe betide if she questioned the explainer's arguments. She was wrong. Anything that she'd heard from Sophia or Tom wasn't true. It was all a plot by somebody.

"Hey, Gizelle," she said, dropping off packages for Tom's office. "Is my uncle around?"

"He is," Gizelle said. "He just got back from a meeting out-of-office."

"Does he have a minute for his second-favorite niece?"

She typed a message into her computer and then nodded.

"Go ahead."

"Hey, Uncle Tom," Faith said.

"Not to be unfriendly, but can you make it quick?" Tom asked. He was reading his computer in jeans and a T-shirt. Not normal executive wear. "I'm sort of swamped."

"So, who really started the zombie virus?" Faith asked.

"Still unknown actor," Tom replied.

"So . . . not the Trilateral Commission?" she asked.

Tom looked up and grinned at her.

"Never, ever, trust a furfy," Tom said, still grinning. "Is it possible it was an organized terrorist plot? Yes. What's the rest? Big bankers?"

"That one never came up," Faith said, blinking. "Drug companies. The Bush Administration. Something called 'Skull and Bones.'"

"If you were working anywhere else, it probably would have," Tom said, leaning back in his chair. "Banks and bankers generally get blamed first and often. The blogs are full of conspiracy theories about the H7. And every group that has previously been cast as the villains in some other context is being blamed by some other group. That's the way that people handle this sort of thing. During the Middle Ages, the Black Death was due to the Devil, and they killed cats to get rid of it. Since it was carried by rats, that was the worst thing they could do. But, no, it wasn't any of the above."

"I tried to tell people that..." Faith said, desperately.

"Don't bother," Tom said, shaking his head. "They won't believe you. They only believe trusted sources like some guy who says he's a researcher for the CDC on some forum they read every day who doesn't know an enzyme from a lyse and is a janitor at a minor research lab in Peoria, Kansas. But they'll trust them over all the experts because they speak truth to power! So just listen and mostly ignore it."

"Does it really take two months to just produce a vaccine?" Faith said. "Nobody believes that."

"I suppose I should get Curry to do a simple explanation and distribute it," Tom said, making a note. "But, yes, from what I understand. The protein crystals take that long to grow on the matrix. Then you have to start making the vaccine from those. And then there's a minimum four-month approval window. And even with that, the vaccine isn't going to be the best. They rarely get it exactly right the first time. It's going to have more harmful side effects than one that's been through the full approval process. But if they can get that done before, well, everything comes apart, they'll distribute it anyway. Because, you know, the world's coming to an end." He gestured at his computer.

"Don't bother arguing, if there's something that really seems relevant, bring it to me," Tom said. "Anything else?"

"Pretty much everybody knows the Bank has some vaccine," Faith said nervously. "Some people say it's from monkeys. Others that it's from people."

"The nice thing about all the outrageous rumors going around is that that's just one more," Tom said, smiling tightly. "Which is good. Anything else?"

"No," Faith said unhappily.

"If I can get in before oh-dark-thirty tonight, we'll talk," Tom said. "But no zombie hunting!"

"Been there, done that," Faith said, holding up her thumb. "I'm sworn off until I can use a shotgun. Tasers suck."

"Thanks for this little meeting," Tom said, pointing at the door with both hands. "Now I have a boatload of work to do. And you should have a cartload."

"Actually, I'm nearly done," Faith said. "With this load, anyway."

Faith dropped off her last few packages, then headed for the elevator. Just getting to the mailroom was a pain. BotA didn't occupy the entire building, but they had the top fifteen floors. The mailroom, on the other hand, was in the basement. Faith really didn't like heights, and every time she got on the elevator she was reminded of that.

There were three other people waiting for the elevator when she got there. They waited for the group onboard to get out, then Faith apologetically pushed her cart into the corner.

"Where's the regular guy?" one of the men asked. He was wearing a BotA golf shirt and slacks, which Faith had learned was uniform for middle manager. She'd guess he was in IT from the look.

"Didn't show for work," Faith said. "No answer on his phone."

"There's a rash of that going around," the guy said, shrugging.

"You act like it's some sort of joke!" the lady snapped. She was probably an EA or typist, judging by her clothes and age. Mid-twenties and dressed to show off her talents. She grabbed the manager by his shirt collar. "Bad things are happening!"

"Hey!" the guy said. "Calm down."

"YOU calm down!" the woman screamed. Then she screamed again and started scratching at her arms. "WHAT'S ON ME? WHAT'S ON ME?" She started stripping with practiced speed.

"Oh, no, no, no, no, NO," Faith said. "Calm down! Just don't do this NOW!"

The woman shrieked and continued tearing at her clothes as the two men backed away from her.

"ZOMBIE!" Faith yelled. She didn't even have her baton, so she snap-kicked the woman in the stomach, causing her to double over. Faith picked up the cart and slammed it onto the woman's head, smashing her to the ground. Unfortunately, the cart was rather light, didn't knock the secretary out and came flying back up in a welter of undeliverable packages and internal memos.

The woman screamed again and leapt at Faith, who had exactly no room to maneuver. Faith blocked the woman's chomping mouth up and away with a forearm under her chin, then secured her wrist in a come-along. From there she was able to twist under and get a chokehold on the woman's throat. The zombie was still wearing high heels, if not a shirt or bra, and as the door to the elevator opened they both tumbled into the corridor. The group that was waiting for the elevator initially scattered, then several of them stepped around the two wrestling women and into the elevator while others apparently decided there were other places they'd rather be. The IT type darted out of the elevator and sprinted in a more or less random direction.

Faith suddenly found herself wrestling a zombie completely alone in the corridor.

"Thanks for all the help and support!" she screamed. The zombie was incredibly strong for her size and Faith could already feel herself wearing out trying to maintain the holds. "COULD SOMEBODY KINDLY CALL SECURITY?"

"I thought you *were* security?" The woman was peeking up from over her cubicle and Faith now realized she had gone from alone to attracting a crowd.

"I'MTHENEWMAILGIRL!" Faith snapped out in one continuous scream as the thrashing zombie started rolling her down the hallway. "CALL*SECURITY!*"

"Got a report of somebody wrestling a zombie on the thirty-second floor," Durante said, looking at the alert code. Doing both the BERT thing and his regular job was starting to wear on him. And this was the ninth "zombie" alert today. On the other hand, six of those had been false alarms.

"Which means two zombies," Kaplan said, standing up. "I'll take my team."

"Faaaith," Kaplan said, standing in the hallway with his hands on his hips. "I'm *sure* your uncle told you: no more *zombie hunting*?"

"She went zomb on the god damned elevator!" Faith swore. She'd finally gotten the woman into a hold where she couldn't roll down between the cubicles, with her legs scissored and one arm up behind her back. Not to mention the apparently entirely useless chokehold. She still wouldn't quit squirming, and Faith was just sooo impressed with all the help she'd been getting, meaning none. "JUST TRANQ 'ER!"

Kaplan obligingly bent over and jammed a tranquilizer injector into the woman's thigh.

"See, that's how these things work," Kaplan said. "The red end is the end the needle comes out." He took a spandex bag from one of the other guards, who were looking equally amused, and slipped it over the woman's head. "And now she's not bitey."

As the woman went flaccid, Faith pushed her away and rolled up and to her feet.

"*Please* don't let me have any cuts," she said. "Other than, you know, the *hole* in my thumb. I bashed her over the head with my mail cart, but it didn't stop her. And then she was bleeding all over me from the cut on her head."

"We'll get you down to decontamination, then," Kaplan said seriously. "I hadn't realized it was that bad." Faith's front was covered in blood.

"I just thought about a problem," Faith said.

The decontamination shower was, to her surprise, just a shower. Tile lined the whole bit. With funny-tasting and -smelling water. She'd been instructed to wash thoroughly with soap and that was about it. Kaplan had squirted betadine onto her thumb, again, for all the good it would do.

"And that is...?" the female security guard who'd been left with her asked.

"I don't have any clothes with me except what I was wearing," Faith pointed out.

"For future reference in your later years, I've always found it's best to know what clothes I'm putting on before I take clothes off. Just a tip." The guard's voice was amused.

"Very funny," Faith said. "My clothes were covered in zombie blood. I couldn't get them off fast enough."

"I noticed," the guard said. "I'll go see if we've got a set of tacticals in your size."

"Guys' medium usually works," Faith said with a sigh. It wasn't her fault she was cursed with gigantism. "Hey! And clean, please!"

"I'll see what I can do..."

"Assuming I don't have zombieitis and *have* later years," Faith said quietly.

Steve picked up his phone at Tom's ringtone. It was about time for a daily check-in. So far there had been no major incidents reported.

"Hey, Tom, how's it going...? Uh-huh..." he said, neutrally. "Right...Okay...How's she doing?"

Stacey's head came up from reading her iPad at "how's she doing?"

"Okay...and this happened how?" There was a long pause. "Hang on, Stacey's looking bug-eyed." He looked up and shrugged unhappily. "Faith ran into a zombie. Turns out it wasn't the first time. Which everybody had carefully *not* mentioned. She's...possibly infected."

"Oh, my God," Stacey said, standing up. "I need to go onshore!"

"Tom, you're my brother. And God knows there have been things I've done in my time that..." Pause. "Agreed. And my only real response is what you said. How the hell did that fall under 'I'll make sure she's safe...?'" He paused and listened and then nodded. "Okay. Agreed. Yes, it is Faith, after all. Yeah, I know. Yep... That's Faith in a nutshell. Stacey wants to go onshore. Is there a way...? Okay. Got it. Yeah. Bye."

"He's sending a boat over," Steve said. "With security for you. They're at the apartment. I guess you can stay there tonight. There's still no curfew, but you don't want to move around at night."

"What happened?" Stacey asked.

"I...think I'll let Faith explain," Steve said. "Apparently Tom's been trying to keep her from zombie hunting and failing. When she did finally give it up, some secretary went zombie in an elevator. Faith wasn't bitten, but she got blood all over herself and she already had some wounds from the previous bouts. So they're afraid she's infected. Good news is that she's had the vaccine so they're hoping between the small amount of infection and the vaccine she'll pull through. Hoping."

"I'm already packed," Stacey said, then paused. "That means you'll have to man the boat by yourself..."

"I've got it," Steve said. "I can handle a few sleepless nights. Thank God for coffee as long as it holds out."

"There's good news and bad news," Dr. Curry said.

A set of tacticals had been found in her size. Ditto tactical boots. Faith was planning on dressing that way from now on. Screw "street clothes."

"Don't keep us in suspense," Tom said.

"Her blood test is positive for antibodies, but..." he said, holding up his hand to forestall the responses, "that would be the case anyway. She had the primer vaccine. That *probably* means that those were present from her immunization shot. However, she may have gotten a solid shot of D4T6 . . ."

"What?" Faith asked.

"That's the new designation for the beta expressor virus," Sophia said. "Zombie virus, in other words."

"Oh."

"So we'll take the full Pasteur route," Dr. Curry said, holding up a syringe. "This is the primer. Again. In two days you would have had the booster. We'll give you a shot a day of primer or booster for two weeks. That should adequately prime your system even if you *did* get some viral load from your scuffle. And by pumping your body full of the attenuated virus, it will force your immune system to respond. Hopefully faster than the virus can take you over. We'll also increase your potassium supplements, pump you full of antivirals even though their effect is limited, and give you a B-12 shot to bump your immune resistance."

"And you're going to have to go into quarantine here," Tom said. "The room's fairly comfortable but it's, face it, a cell. If you haven't turned by tomorrow . . ."

"Okay," Faith said miserably. She looked around. It was only the four of them in Tom's office. "Is it cool to talk about 'you know'?"

"Yes," Tom said.

"Then if I do turn, I want to get turned into vaccine," Faith said, looking at the floor. "That way maybe somebody else won't."

"That's not going to happen . . ." Tom said.

"Uncle Tom—" Faith responded.

"I don't mean what you think," Tom said, holding up his hand. "You are not going to turn. You're not. We're not going to let that happen."

"But if it does," Faith said, tearing up.

Sophia leaned over and pulled her into her arms, hugging her.

"I'll make it myself," Sophia said, choking up. "And we'll save it for special people."

Faith sobbed. "Thank you."

"Okay," Dr. Curry said. "If we've gotten that out of our system, we need to start the procedures."

Faith stood up and rolled up her sleeve.

"Go ahead and shoot me up, Doc . . ."

∽ ⊖ ⟋

"How you doing?"

Despite all their "additional duties," Durante and Kaplan had volunteered to maintain watch on Faith.

"Sort of like a rat in a trap," Faith said.

The cell wasn't particularly small or uncomfortable as such things go. But it was still a cell.

"And when I have to go, you'd better not be watching the pick-up," she added. "Do I really have to be on camera all the time?"

"It's for science," Durante said. "Seriously. If you turn, they can watch the progress of the disease."

"Who can?" Faith said. "In case you forgot, it would be kiddy porn. 'Cause zombies, like, strip."

"You haven't been keeping up with YouTube," Durante said. "The FBI has about given up trying to police 'naked zombie girl' videos. They're everywhere. And this would really be for science."

"Which is pointless," Faith said. "I can tell you about the progress of the disease. They get real angry and snappish, freak out and start pulling off their clothes. That's when you know they're a zombie."

"Or one of my ex-girlfriends," Durante said. "Sorry. Tasteless."

"No big surprise," Faith said. "I need something to read. A book. An iPad. Something."

"I've got some technical manuals," Durante said. "You might want to read the one on injector operation, just as an example."

"Very freaking funny, Durante..."

"Oooh," Faith said, tossing off her covers. She had put on a pair of shorts and a T-shirt while Tom made sure nobody was watching. Now they were soaked in sweat. "Durante? Who's out there?"

"Kaplan."

"I'm sick," Faith said. "Burning up. Can I get some aspirin or something? And some more bottled water?"

"I'm calling the medics," Kaplan said. "Any formication?"

"I'm a little young, Kaplan."

"For-*mi*-cation," Kaplan said. "Itchy skin? Feeling like bugs are crawling on you?"

"Yeah," Faith said. "I knew what you were talking about. Little bit. Mostly I just feel sick as hell."

"Nurse is on the way..."

∽ ⊖ ℮

"Please don't bite me," the nurse said. He was in a full moon suit just in case.

He checked her BP and pulse as well as her temperature and shook his head.

"I'll do my best," Faith said. "But the difference between normal zombie irrational and how I get when I'm sick isn't much. Don't do anything I don't like and I'll try not to rip off chunks of flesh and chew them."

"I'm calling Dr. Curry and Dr. Simmons," the nurse said. "Your temperature is a hundred and five. Which isn't good. Any feeling of itchiness or feeling like bugs crawling on your skin?"

"Formication," Faith said. "Itchiness, but I've got dry skin. I get itchy pretty often. Maybe worse than normal. I dunno. I feel sucky."

"If I was still working the EDC ward we'd have you in a lukewarm shower," the nurse said. "I'll see what the doctors say..."

"I thought you said this shower would be *lukewarm!*" Faith yelled. She'd gone from fever to chills and the cold shower wasn't helping. "I'm f-f-free-zing..."

Faith barely remembered getting back to the cell. The bastards wouldn't even give her extra blankets because "they didn't want her temperature skyrocketing."

"I don't want to be a zombie..." she muttered. "But I *would* like to die...Now, please...Now would be good..."

"Faith, honey...?"

"Mom?" Faith said. She'd been dreaming a really vivid dream. More like being there. She was a knight on a horse fighting in a big battle. She wasn't sure what was reality and what was hallucination anymore.

"Oh, wait," she said, shifting up. Her mom was in a moon suit. "You're real."

"Why wouldn't I be?" Stacey said, sitting down on the bed.

"I think I was hallucinating," Faith said. "You shouldn't be here. What if I zomb?"

"It's pretty hard to bite through a moon suit," Stacey said. "And you're going to be okay. Focus on that."

"Yeah, well you don't want to get this," Faith said. "Zombie or not. I've *never* felt this bad."

"It'll be okay, sweetie," Stacey said, cradling her in her arms. "It'll be okay."

"Mom," Faith said, "when you cry like that it ruins the whole 'it'll be okay' thing." She paused and looked around wildly. "I think I'm going to throw up..."

CHAPTER 12

"Looks like you're going to make it," Dr. Curry said, examining Faith's chart.

"Don't sound so enthusiastic," Faith said. She was sipping ice water and balefully considering what Dr. Simmons had prescribed for her first meal in two days: jello and chicken broth. "As far as I've been able to figure out, the only good thing about New York is, supposedly, the food. This is not what I've been promised."

"You need to let your body get used to food again," Simmons told her.

"The emesis was a suprising response," Dr. Curry said. "And as the resident mad scientist, while I *personally* didn't want you to go fully into abnormal neural condition, the opportunity to study it would have been useful."

"I love you too, Doc."

"What is it about 'mad scientist' you don't understand?"

Faith picked up the bowl of broth, took a sip and set it down.

"God, I'm weak," she said, her hands shaking. "That's just weakness, right?"

"Should just be low blood sugar," Dr. Simmons said. "You've still got a high antibody count but your fever seems to have broken and your white blood cell count is dropping. As Dr. Curry said, it looks like you're going to make it."

"And we've now got really good data on the progress of the disease," Curry burbled happily.

"Bully for you," Faith said. "I know I'm tired. I'm channeling Da."

"Anything we can do for you?" Dr. Simmons asked.

"As soon as I'm better enough somebody owes me one good meal in this stupid stinking town," Faith said, sipping the broth again. "That's all I hear is how great the food in New York is. And so far all I've had is take-out Chinese and...soup."

"One good meal," Dr. Curry said. "I'll make sure that goes on the agenda."

"Well, this has been too much fun," Tom said. "Stacey..."

"She made it, Tom." Stacey looked nearly as washed out as Faith. "And I guess the good news is that the vaccine works."

"And she's about as resistant as anyone could be," Tom said. "I've always known she was tough.... She's saying she wants one decent meal in New York. How do you feel about that?"

"Going out to dinner in zombie-infested New York?" Stacey said, grimacing. "Have a hard time saying no. But it's not something I'm real thrilled about. She'll need a day or so to rest up."

"Agreed," Tom said. "Steve should join us. I'll scrounge up some security I can trust to put on your boat. I'll send Kaplan and a backup. He's scheduled for the primary extract, anyway. And I'll find a restaurant that's still open. Most of the really good ones are closed. I'll find one. Oh, I traded some favors. Your certification as licensed contractors has been cleared. So you can carry, heavy, in New York City."

"Does that include Sophia and Faith?" Stacey asked.

"I've got an ID printer," Tom said drily. "And some very flexible software. At this point I doubt anyone will check."

"Do you have anyone who can take you to the hospital, ma'am?" Patterno asked as Young draped a sheet over the woman's husband's body.

The man had been in his seventies and yet had thrown off two taser hits. Some of them did that. Some of them dropped and some of them just kept coming. The new ROE was clear: If a 10-64 Hotel didn't stop with the tasers, deadly force was authorized.

The department, with concurrence of the state and local authorities, had had to do it. Not only was it already the de facto rule of engagement, based upon how many shooting, had been officer-involved over the last few weeks, they'd lost too many officers to the Plague. And more than half of those had gone zombie themselves. The "squad" room meeting was starting to look like the "team" room meeting. If many more of them went down, it would be no meeting at all.

The wife had a bite on her arm and another on her shoulder. They'd hit both with antiseptic, for all the good it would do. They were probably looking at another zombie in a few hours.

"A friend is on the way over..." the woman said shakily.

"We'll stay here until they get here," Patterno said. "The coroner's office team will need to have access to your home. Can I get a verbal confirmation on that? Is it okay if the coroner's team handles the management of your husband's remains?"

"Yes," the woman said, shaking her head. "Yes, I suppose they have to... Why did you have to shoot him?" she said angrily. "He was just *sick*! He—"

The woman suddenly lunged at Patterno, howling. Joe instinctively threw up his hand to fend her off. Unfortunately, he'd taken off his tactical gloves after dealing with her husband.

The woman's teeth sank into the web of muscle and skin between his thumb and forefinger, ripping out a chunk. She lunged at him again, chewing.

At the first howl, Young had ripped out his taser, and as Patterno rolled backwards off the sofa the taser round hit the woman in the side. She fell onto the floral-print, blood splattered sofa, spasming.

"Shit, shit, shit, shit..." Patterno said as Young slapped a tranquilizer into the woman's thigh muscles. The zombie started to stand up and he tapped her, hard, on the back of the head with his baton. She might be dead or not. He wasn't really caring at the moment.

"How bad?" Young asked.

"Bad." Patterno had his hand clamped on the wound but it was still streaming blood.

"Let it bleed," Young said. "Maybe it will get some of it out."

"Shit, she turned fast," Patterno said.

"Really fast," Young replied. He opened the med kit back up and, as Patterno held out his hand, started pouring Betadine over the wound and then roughly bandaging it. He pulled out an antibody kit from the medical bag and did a quick blood test on the tranquilized subject.

"What's it read?" Patterno asked, cradling his arm. They both knew she'd zombied, but it was still possible she'd just had a really bad freak-out.

"Positive," Young said unhappily.

"Call for pickup," Patterno said. "Then back to the station. Sentara Hospital is overloaded. And there's not much they can do for me that one of the paramedics can't. Hell, there's not much they can do, period."

"Unit four-six-four," Young said into his microphone. "One sixty-four Hotel Kilo India Alpha. One sixty-four Hotel Tango. One officer possibly infected, bite. Ten-nineteen for medical..."

"Good news," Joe said, holding up his hand. "You get to do the paperwork."

"I don't want to go to the Warehouse," Joe said as they were driving back to the station. He had his hand elevated and was staring at it.

"The warehouse makes Dachau look like Disneyland," Young said.

"Billy's ... not going to be able to handle that," Joe said. "You know that, right?"

"Yeah," Young said. There was a zombie running down the street. Ten-year-old or so boy. A clothed woman was running after him. She was already bitten. Just another zombie in the making.

"We should have started at shoot-to-kill," Joe said, watching the scene unfold. The woman was waving at the cop car as it passed, trying to get help. She'd be pissed off. Maybe she'd complain. Maybe somebody would hear it. Then she'd turn and the complaint would be sort of moot.

"You've got a spare, right?" Young asked. The department required that you turn in your issue firearm as you were going off-duty. Since it was legal to carry for officers off-duty, most had at least one spare.

"Yeah," Joe said. "I'd say stop so I could shoot both of them. But then they'd lock me up. And then I'd go to the Warehouse. And either starve to death or get eaten when it all goes down. Or, worse, get free and be one of them. I don't want to be one of them."

"I'll come by after I get off-shift," Young said. "Can Billy ... secure you?"

"Heh," Patterno said, starting to laugh. It turned into a full-bore belly-laugh. He finally stopped, wiping his eyes. "Yeah, he can."

"What's so funny?" Young asked.

"You've never had a problem with my lifestyle," Patterno said, looking at him. "Any reason for that?"

"I don't give a shit what a cop does with his or her genitals as long as they're a good cop." Young answered. "And you're a good cop."

"Oh, I've had my times being a bad cop," Joe said, musingly. "But I've always appreciated that you weren't a flake about it. So I've never really tried to screw with you. Don't screw with me, I won't screw back. So just ... When you come by, just don't get freaked out that Billy is able to secure me really, *really* well."

"Oh," Young said, grimacing. "Okay. Yeah. I'd say TMI but it's useful, if, yeah, disturbing information."

"Hey," Patterno said. "Guy's got to have a hobby ..."

"Hi, Bill," Young said. He didn't want to be at Joe's house. He didn't want to go through with this. But duty was like that. "How's he doing?" he asked as he stepped through the door.

"Not ... well," Bill Jacobus said. The electrical engineer was tall and slender in contrast to his partner. Young had never seen him wear anything but a golf shirt and fine slacks, and that, at least, had not changed. The odd part was that his pant legs were covered in dirt. Then Young realized why. Bill started to stick out his hand, then remembered and ended up wringing them together. "His fever is very high. I've given him Motrin and water. He's ..." He shrugged. "Thank you for coming. You're a ... good friend."

"You know why I'm here?" Young said. "If you do ... maybe you want to go out for a walk or something?"

"At night with zombies roaming?" Bill said with a breathless chuckle. He gestured up the stairs. "My first husband died of AIDS. I was always careful, even with Thomas, so I never contracted it. The one mercy of this plague is that it's decently quick. I ... since we are in this situation, I will tell you that I ... gave the same grace to Thomas. But here ... I don't have the contacts, the materials."

"It only takes one thing," Young said, walking to the stairs.

"I could...turn up a morphine drip," Bill admitted. "Add... some chemicals. I could not have pulled a trigger. That is why you are a good friend. Would you mind if I...? No, I should stay to say good-bye."

Joe was in the master bedroom spread-eagled on the bed. There was a band across the top of the bed that restrained both his wrists and his head via a collar and his legs were spread and chained. He was dressed in black tacticals and wearing an SFPD badge.

"You guys are serious about your restraints, aren't you?" Young said.

"I said a guy needs a hobby," Patterno said. He was visibly sweating and racked with chills.

"How are you doing, honey?" Bill asked, sitting on the side of the bed and wiping his forehead. He leaned over and kissed him where he'd wiped.

"Guys, I'm real supportive of your relationship," Young said, neutrally. "But I'm still the kid who was raised Southern Baptist at some level. So I'm just going to go outside. You two...chat. When you're ready, Bill, I'll be right in the hallway. Sorry."

"Nah, it's okay," Joe growled. "I get it. I mean, I don't get it but I get it."

After about fifteen minutes, Bill came out wiping his eyes.

"Just...don't..." Bill said, his face working.

"I won't until I'm sure," Young said. This was getting to be more and more of a pain.

"I'll be in the back yard," Bill said.

Young walked back into the room and pulled up a chair.

"Before I get comfy," he said. "Piece?"

"Side drawer," Joe said, gesturing with his chin.

Young quickly found the Glock .40. He pulled the slide back far enough to see there was a round in the chamber, then slipped it into his waistband.

"Could I get a drink?" Joe asked.

"Sure, partner," Young said. There was a bottle of water with a straw in it by the bed. He reached into his cargo pocket and pulled out a pair of thick leather gloves. "Sorry. That old biddy turned so fast it has me nervous."

"She did turn fast," Joe said, taking a sip.

"How the hell do you do that?" Young said. "I can't drink from the prone for nothing."

"Years of training," Joe said. "You really don't want to know. Thanks."

"You need some Motrin?" Young asked.

"I've had enough to kill an elephant," Joe said. "It's not touching this fever. Or chills. Or aches. I mostly just want to lie here. No offense."

"None taken," Young said.

"But there is..." Joe said, then stopped. "I've got a favor to ask."

"I thought that was why I was here," Young said.

"Okay, another favor," Joe said, frowning. "It's about... Bill. He's not going to deal with this real well..."

"Joe..." Young said. "I'm willing to accept that there are some people who are just... you know, totally gay and there's no going back. You realize that there are some people who are just totally straight? And you know I'm one of them, right?"

"That's not what I meant," Joe said wearily. "He's got no skills for surviving this... shit..."

"Are you saying you want me to help your wife survive the zombie apocalypse?" Young said. "Because it would help a lot of it was, you know, an actual *wife*. Like, female."

"I know what I'm asking," Joe said.

Young thought about it for a second and shrugged.

"I'll do what I can," Young said. "But that's all I'm promising."

"Okay," Joe said. "Way things are going, not sure what you could do anyway. You going in tomorrow?"

"Not hardly," Young said. "I'm done. There's no way to survive this as a cop. We're not getting vaccine, we're not getting support and we're not doing a damned thing to stop it."

"We should have quit a week ago," Joe said, shrugging as well as he could. "I was sort of waiting for you to ring the bell."

"Ring the bell?" Young asked.

"SEAL thing," Patterno said. "When you quit BUD/S you ring a bell."

"Ah," Young said. "I didn't know you were a SEAL."

"Wasn't," Patterno said. "Guy on the team in Frisco was. Just picked up the term."

"I was waiting for *you* to ring the bell," Young said. "Bad call on both our parts."

"Yeah."

"Yeah."

Young sat in silence after that, occasionally giving Joe water, for about an hour. Then Joe started to struggle against the straps.

"Spiders!" Joe snarled. "Get the spiders off! No, no, no, nooooo, aaaaaRRRRR..."

Young waited until he was sure, then put on a pair of nitrile gloves, pulled the Glock from his waistband and put it under the chin of his struggling partner. He pulled back carefully; you could blow a shot even at this distance, and felt the hammer give. The top of Patterno's skull was taken off, blasting over the seafoam-green sheets.

Young unstrapped Joe's right hand, then wrapped it around the butt of the Glock. Last, he laid both on the upper chest. It wouldn't survive a detailed forensic examination, but there wasn't going to be one. The last forensics tech in the department had gone zombie three days ago.

He walked out and shut the door, walked downstairs and exited the house.

From here on out, it was every man for himself.

CHAPTER 13

"This place is good, trust me," Tom said. The traffic wasn't that heavy, but the car was still having trouble making its way. More and more double parked cars were turning up abandoned on the streets. And the street department couldn't get them cleared fast enough. Apparently, people tended to not only strip but bail out of the cars when they went zombie. At least most did. Some just flipped too fast and ended up crashing. "And it's still open."

"Trust me like 'Trust me, you won't get bitten by a zombie'?" Faith asked.

"Not fair, Faith," Sophia said.

"Sorry, Uncle Tom," Faith said. "That *wasn't* fair. Especially after all the crap I got into on my own." She stroked the Saiga she was toting and grinned. "But this time I'm *fully* prepared."

"I'm a big guy," Tom said, grinning back. "And if you use that you'd better make damned sure you *only* hit your primary target *and* that you have a *valid* target."

"In other words," Steve said, "*don't* use it. Your ID won't hold up under scrutiny."

"Spoilsports," Faith said. "Truth is, I don't want to take a shot. I'm still too woozy. But it's a nice security blanket."

131

"I hope you told them that they're hosting 'contractors,'" Stacey said.

"I did," Tom said. "There were some issues to work out but it's all good."

"They didn't want people with guns?" Sophia asked. She was in body armor and full covering but had settled for just a pistol and taser. Pistol on the right thigh, taser on the left.

"The restaurant is popular with a certain crowd," Tom said. "The owner was twitchy because he didn't want *them* getting… riled."

"We're here, sir," Durante said as the limo pulled up to an unpretentious brownstone building on the upper east side.

"Doesn't look like much," Faith said, opening the door and stepping out.

"You're supposed to let Durante do that," Sophia said. "You're *never* going to figure out how to make an entrance, are you?"

"Let me clear the way, first, Faith," Durante said, holding out his hand. He strode towards the door, checking side to side for threats as the driver stepped out and covered the street side.

"The good ones rarely do," Tom said. He was wearing just a business suit. Of course, he was also carrying *under* the suit. "Truth is this place is sort of used to this sort of arrival. Just not as openly armed."

"Oh," Steve said. "*That* sort of crowd."

"*What* sort of crowd?" Faith asked, looking around.

"Mr. Smith!" The speaker was a short, rotund fellow with a thick Sicilian accent. "It is good to see you again!"

"Mr. Fattore," Tom said, nodding. "I hope this isn't a bother."

"Not at all," Mr. Fattore said. "We shall feel very secure, yes? Come in, come in."

He ushered Tom, Sophia, Steve and Stacey into the restaurant like royalty. The restaurant was long but fairly narrow, with booths down the right side and tables filling the middle. It was also surprisingly crowded. The conversation muted for a moment when Faith and Durante entered, then it picked back up.

"For you and you friends," Mr. Fattore said, gesturing to a booth at the rear.

Faith found herself blocked in getting to the booth.

"Hem, hem," Faith said.

"You is sitting at the table," Fattore said in a whisper. There was an empty table by the booth which would only take four anyway. He clearly wondered why he had to explain.

"I'll take the table," Tom said, grinning. "This night out was Faith's idea."

"We can squeeze up," Stacey said. "You and Faith on that side."

"Works," Tom said, then looked at Faith. "I don't do inside."

"*I'm* the one with all the guns," Faith pointed out. "I'm not sure I *can* slide in."

"Gimme the Saiga, Faith," Durante said.

"But what if somebody zombies?" Faith said, clutching it to her chest. "I'm really serious. I am not going through that again unarmed."

"And I'm really serious that it's *my* job to take care of it," Durante said, holding out his hand. "Saiga. Then you can fit in the booth."

"Okay," Faith said, unclipping the semi-automatic, magazine-fed shotgun and handing it over. "But I'm totally hanging onto the pistols." She had three. One in a fast rig and two on chest rigs. She was also, at Tom's insistence, carrying a dual-fire taser X26 and spare cartridges. Since all those, in her opinion, might need refueling, she was also carrying more ammo than Durante.

"You can hang onto the pistols," Tom said. "Now slide in."

"Smells good," Stacey said, looking at the menu. It had been printed on paper and clearly was "this is what we could get today." "What do you recommend?"

"Anything," Tom said. "It's all good. I usually get the Frutti di Mare."

"I'm not sure I'd trust seafood in these conditions," Steve said. "Supply chain is getting totally screwed up."

"I think you can trust it," Tom said. "He's got pretty good suppliers."

"I want appetizers," Faith said. "And . . . stuff. I don't even know what to order. All I ever get is spaghetti and meatballs."

"Don't get greedy," Steve said.

"Let her," Tom said. "It's on expense account. And the money's just going to turn to electronic trash. The meatballs are to die for."

"How long?" Stacey asked.

"Depends on the model you look at," Tom said. "If we're going to enjoy a night on the town, better make it tonight is all I can really say. Don't ask me about tomorrow night. Pretty much it's things will continue limping along and then they'll stop. When the tipping point hits, it will cascade fast."

"Can we talk about something other than the end of civilization tonight?" Sophia said.

"How 'bout something interesting and peripheral?" Tom said. "They're quietly evacuating all the major art museums to an 'undisclosed' remote site. Basically, even if things fall apart completely, they'll have saved all the big artworks. Ditto classic manuscripts."

"That's nice to hear," Stacey said. "I'd hate to see Titians burn."

"What about stuff in private collections?" Steve asked.

"Not sure," Tom said. "I guess if they find out and turn them in for protection, I don't see the Museum of Art turning down a Van Gogh. Most of those 'private collections' tend to be associated with big corporations. And most of them have remote jump sites. We've already been doing that for the Board and the Corporation. I'm not sure if they'll hold. Heck, I don't know if the museum remote site will hold." He shrugged.

"How's your plan?" Faith asked.

"Solid," Tom said. "Thanks in good part to Sophia. This is on expense report because of what you've been doing, not Faith by the way."

"Well, thanks a lot," Faith said. "All I did was stop zombies from taking over your building and nearly die doing it!"

"That, too," Tom said. "Just twitting you. Richard Bateman said he appreciated both your efforts."

"Are you ready to order?" the waitress asked.

"I don't know what most of these are," Faith said, looking at the load of appetizers. Tom had basically ordered one of everything on the appetizer menu.

"This is great," Sophia said. "What is it?"

"Squid in ink," Tom said.

"Oh, gross," Faith said, setting the piece down.

"Try it," Steve said. "Just a bite."

"I'm not six," Faith said, taking a bite. "Okay, it is good. I hate the texture though."

"Works for me," Sophia said, trying another appetizer. "You're right, it's all good." She looked around and leaned over to Stacey. "It would be better with some of the wine...?"

Stacey slid her wine glass over and refilled her mostly empty water glass from the bottle.

"So that's the trick," Faith said. "Eat it with wine and everything tastes good?"

"Pretty much," Tom said. "You don't want to know some of the stuff I've choked down with alcohol."

"Monkey," Sophia said taking a sip. "Ooo. It *is* better with the wine."

"Try sloth," Steve said. "Which is, by the way, truly putrid stuff. Tried some on a bet one time. Helped that I was off my face at the time. Then I chundered. But I won the bet."

"Ate a slug once," Tom mused. "No beer involved. We'd been in the back of beyond for a bit. Looked tasty. When you're that hungry, they are."

"Uggh," Faith said. "Okay, no end of the world talk and no weird foods."

"It wasn't one of the slimy *ground* ones," Tom said. "Tree slug. Colorful. Looked a bit like a red and blue mobile banana. Turned out they're slightly poisonous. Was quite ill the rest of the op."

"No eating red and blue tree slugs," Sophia said, nodding. "Got it. Just in case it comes up."

"Speaking of which, how are you doing for supplies?" Tom asked.

"We resupplied right after we got here," Steve said. "Which means the boat is packed. But we should be good for a month or so. Depends on how long we spend in harbor."

"Not much longer," Tom said. "We'll be moving the girls back to the boat after tonight. We're shutting down the project Sophia has been working on. It's . . . as complete as it needs to be."

"Understood," Stacey said. "And I'll be glad to have them back. No offense."

"It's been an adventure, that's for sure," Tom said. "I'd say sorry again, but . . ."

"What's it you say about adventure, Da?" Faith asked.

"Adventure is something that happened to someone else, preferably a long way away and a long time ago," Steve said. "*When* it happens it's horror, terror or tragedy."

"*Someday* this will be an adventure," Faith said.

"Okay, they're right," Faith said, burping as she picked at her tiramisu. "The food in New York is incredible. I should have gotten that fruit of the sea thing. I usually don't like seafood but that was *great*."

"And this is really just a neighborhood restaurant," Tom said. "But one of the best in the city."

"Do we have to go right back to the boat?" Sophia asked.

"It's getting dark," Steve said. "And there's a curfew."

"Which is hardly enforced," Tom said. "Even with the National Guard they're too busy rounding up infected."

"And it's *getting dark*," Steve noted.

"Up to the parents," Tom said, shrugging. "There are some clubs still open, and I hear there's a more or less continuous concert going on in Washington Square Park. More of a rave, really."

"Concert?" Sophia said, her eyes lighting.

"In the *dark*," Steve said. "In zombie-infested New York city."

"I've never been to a concert," Faith said sadly. "I mean, that's one of those things you do when you're a teenager. The way things are going, I'll never get a chance. Or go to prom..." She sniffed.

"We are not going to a *concert* at *night* in a *park* in *zombie-infested New York*!" Steve said. "And that's *final*!"

"This band *sucks*," Faith shouted.

"Warm-up band," Tom shouted back. "They usually do. The good ones don't come on until later!"

Nobody seemed to care that the band sucked. With enough alcohol and drugs anything sounded good. And from the litter, it looked like the party had been going on for quite a while. The stage was set up right in front of the Arch and was apparently powered by a collection of generators that added their own cacophony to the din.

"No security?" Sophia asked, looking around. There was no sign of police presence and nobody was apparently in charge.

"I guess it's us!" Tom said, grinning. "No, this is a totally illegal gathering under New York City law. But it has sprung up so many times and there are so many other problems that they're not bothering to enforce it. You're here at your own risk. Which I would not suggest if Durante and I weren't here."

"Got it," Sophia said. The women in the crowd were either in large groups or accompanied by males. "Don't drink from an open container. Don't accept anything, and for anything else I've got this," she said, tapping her pistol.

"This will probably stop any problems in their tracks," Tom said, tapping the large BERT sign velcroed to the front of her kevlar. He'd also provided "contractor" badges for the group. The badges, on neck lanyards, read "Biological Emergency Contract Agent."

"What?" Sophia said, her eyes wide. "You mean the rumor that BERT vans are taking people to be made into vaccine? Nobody *believes* that!"

"Just keep repeating that," Tom said.

Despite the implicit warning, Sophia gently drifted to the side of the group, getting a look at the crowd. Most of them were young. Her apparent age. Or maybe even her real age. The point was that you could never tell. And the whole crowd had a funny edge. They didn't seem to be enjoying themselves as much as trying really really hard to enjoy themselves. The only ones that didn't have that edge were the ones that, before it was even dark, were already so stoned or drunk they could forget why an illegal concert *could* go on in the Park without being broken up.

"Hey," a guy said from behind her. It was as close to a whisper as you could use with nuclear level speakers blaring. "Top quality vaccine!"

She turned to look and the guy was holding a vial cupped in his hand.

"I can get syringes, too." The guy was dressed in a vivid pink rayon shirt, a Yankees jacket and jeans. He looked like some sort of walking advertisement for bad drug dealers. "Clean."

"Got some," Sophia said. "Thanks."

Sophia turned fully so he could see the sign on her body armor and neck badge and just gave him a cold, blank stare.

"Oh . . . *shit*," the guy said, his eyes going wide. He turned around and hurried away, occasionally glancing over his shoulder.

"Wow, that really *does* work," Sophia said.

"Hey," a girl said, looking around to make sure nobody could hear. "Can you score *me* some?"

"We don't *really* make vaccine," Sophia said, sighing. "And I don't even work the streets. I'm support staff."

"What do you do?" the girl's male companion asked slowly. He was pretty clearly stoned but trying to track.

"Antibody tests," Sophia said, shrugging. "Lab work. Making sure that our clients aren't infected. We're contracted to a particular corporation. The rest is sort of NDA."

"That's cool," the guy said. "Hey, want some ebomb?" he asked, holding out a handful of pills.

"You really don't want a person carrying a pistol and a taser fucked up," Sophia said, grinning. "No offense."

"You here as security?" the girl asked.

"Nope," Sophia said. "Just enjoying the show. Sort of. They really suck."

"Yeah," the girl said. "The good ones don't start showing up until after dark..."

The girl was Christine, her boyfriend "he's just a hook-up, really, 'cause he's got a source" was Todd. They were both New York natives, as were their friends. The group was huddled for protection against the increasingly rowdy crowd. There was a group right down by the stage that had created a mosh pit, which explained the fence set up to protect the bands.

After the sun went down the band changed. It was another NYC local band, but it was better. Not by much, but better.

That band changed out for somebody she actually thought she recognized, a tall saturnine guy carrying an acoustic guitar.

"Is that Voltaire?" Sophia asked.

"Yeah," Christine said. She'd been hitting a bottle of Chivas Regal from the neck and was thoroughly plastered. "He shows up every night."

"Brains, Brains, Brains...!" the crowd chanted.

Of course, he started with "Brains," then all the oldies and goodies. "Vampire Club," "Demonslayer," "USS Make-Shit-Up"... Sophia knew them all and she'd always wanted to see him in concert.

An underground concert in a park in NYC in the middle of an apocalypse was just...perfect.

He was in the middle of "Day of the Dead" when she heard the first shotgun blast...

"The 1911 is a great gun," Faith shouted. "But it's really obsolete technology. And it's only got seven rounds! I prefer the H and K."

"Try getting service out of them," Durante shouted back. They were standing side by side, with Faith watching the bands and Durante watching the outer darkness. They'd both put in earplugs even after Voltaire showed up. You could still hear him, and she wasn't a huge Voltaire fan. "And a 1911 doesn't have 'I crack if you look at me wrong' polymer frame."

"You can shoot an H and K underwater," Faith said.

"You can shoot a 1911 under water," Durante replied. "Although I don't know why you'd have to. That's called a straw-man argument."

"Once, maybe," Faith argued. "But an H and K has an octagonal barrel. It can handle a much higher load."

"We're just going to have to agree to disagree," Durante said, grinning.

"I wish they had, like, Atreyu or Avenged Sevenfold," Faith said. "Sophia must be having a blast, though." They'd all been keeping her under light surveillance.

"She seems to be," Durante said. "She seems more..." He paused and shook his head. "BOSS! COMPANY!"

"Cops?" Faith asked, looking over her shoulder.

"No."

Coming out of the shadows of the trees she could see two naked people, male and female, trotting towards the concertgoers.

"Shit," she said, drawing her taser.

"Again, let me take it," Durante said, drawing one of his. "Fewer questions."

The zombies weren't heading directly their way, so Durante trotted to the side to interpose himself between them and the crowd.

"I'm surprised it's taken this long," Tom said. A Glock had appeared from somewhere.

"Uh-oh," Faith said, gesturing to the side. More zombies were coming out of the trees. Lots of zombies. And they were moving fast. "Uncle Tom?"

"I don't think tasers are going to do it," Tom said. "DURANTE! MULTIPLES. *HOT* ROUNDS!"

Durante had already tasered the two zombies and injected one. He dropped his injector as he was preparing to inject the second, and switched to the Saiga.

"See?" Steve said. "I told you this was a bad idea." He had his 1911 in a two-handed grip, and Stacey had his back holding a SIG Sauer.

"Cell service is out," Tom said. "Shit. Engage at will."

"On it," Faith said, drifting right. Durante had gone left to engage the first two. Moving right, she was closer to covering Sophia. She and the group with her were apparently completely oblivious to the approaching threat.

Faith put her eye to the point-and-shoot scope on the Saiga and targeted the first approaching zombie.

"*This* is how you handle a zombie apocalypse," she said, just as Durante fired.

CHAPTER 14

Sophia spun around and saw Faith fire at one of the fast approach-ing infecteds. The fiftyish woman was thrown back with her chest opened up by the twelve-gauge round. But she wasn't the only one inbound for the concertgoers.

Sophia didn't even hesitate. Her father had run her through too many tactical ranges, and her actions were muscle memory. She'd been standing towards the back of the group and now stepped forward, covering their rear, and ripped her 1911 from its holster. Taking a two-handed grip, she targeted the closest zombie, put-ting two .45 rounds into his chest. She was using polymer-tipped expanding hollowpoints, which on impact spread out to make not a .45 inch hole, but a nearly inch-wide one. The "lab tech" had recently been getting an eclectic masters-level course in biology including mammalian anatomy and physiology. She could practi-cally recite the blood vessels her rounds took out without doing the autopsy. The infected took two more steps and dropped.

She'd been carrying a round in the chamber and a full maga-zine for the 1911. If she'd been in the earlier argument with her sister, she would have pointed out, didactically, that that way a 1911 can carry *eight* rounds. Which did for four infecteds.

But there were more.

141

"This job fucking sucks."

Specialist Cameron "Gunner" Randall, New York Army National Guard, was tired, aggravated and frustrated. He was a fricking 13 Foxtrot: a fire support specialist. He was supposed to be calling for artillery fire. Not roaming the streets of New York "enforcing the curfew." Among other things, they *weren't* "enforcing the curfew." There was a fucking concert going on right *there* in Washington Square Park. And he and his guys had to just "maintain presence." What the fuck did "maintain presence" mean?

What they really were were roaming zombie collectors. They carried their issue M4s but so far all they'd used were Tasers. Taser the zombie, inject, call for pickup. Tell people there was a curfew. *Tell* people. Not order them back to their flipping homes. "Remind them." And the ROE for shooting a zombie with your M4 went to ten pages. "And don't bother the concert."

It really, really sucked. He never thought that a deployment in the states would suck more than the Stan. But this *sucked*.

"Well, at least it's a slow night."

SGT James R. "Worf" Copley thought their current job was idiotic on so many levels it wasn't funny. Among other things, since "zombieitis," whatever they were calling it this week, was incurable, the "care facilities" were not only getting overrun with infected, they'd started as nightmares and just gotten worse. Killing them, sad as it was, would have been a mercy. And if they were going to have a curfew it should be enforced. But this was New York City. The city that never slept. And even with occasional power outages, food shortages and zombies it was going to go right on being "The City that Never Sleeps" until things blew over or it all went to shit.

"Maybe all the zombies are at the concert," Private Patricia Astroga said wistfully. "I don't suppose we could stop by just for a bit to...ensure security?"

"I'm not really into alternative..." Sergeant Copley said. "Besides—" He paused as he heard the distinctive boom of a shotgun from the direction of the concert, followed by a series of shotgun and pistol blasts. What amazed him was that whoever was caterwauling kept right on singing over what was working up to a full-fledged firefight.

"On the other hand," Randall said.

"Let's roll," Copley replied. "*Fours*, not Tasers..."

∽ ⊖ ⌒

Sophia was reloading, visually tracking another inbound target, when her arm was grabbed from behind.

"What are you doing?" Christine asked. "You can't shoot those zombies!"

"'Can't,' 'may not' and 'shouldn't' are three different things," Sophia said, seating the magazine and letting the slide go forward. "And what I'm doing is *protecting* you. Why the hell are you still here?" She looked over her shoulder and was amazed that the concert was still going on. Thinking about it, Voltaire hadn't even missed a beat.

"They come every night," Todd said. "It's their concert."

"What?" Sophia asked, her eyes wide. "Don't they...? Don't you get attacked?"

"They bite some people," Christine said. "Sometimes they eat. I've been waiting to get bitten. But they haven't taken me yet."

"WHAT?" Sophia screamed. The infected was inside fifteen meters, so she put two rounds in her chest and turned back, keeping her weapon pointed downrange and looking over her shoulder. "*WHAT*? Are you flipping *nuts*? You *WANT* to be a zombie?"

"There's nothing to be afraid of if you're a zombie," Christine said, starting to cry. "You just are. You just exist. It's like..."

"It's like zen, you know?" Todd said, swaying back and forth. "You just exist in the moment, man. There's no stress. No school, no work, just eat or be eaten. It's like Rousseau's noble savage, the beast inside every man."

"You are absolutely batshit fucking nuts," Sophia said, looking back to the target zone. Another inbound. "I am *not* going to be turned into a zombie. My sister got infected but she pulled through, and *we* are not going to be zombies. We are not."

"You just don't get it," Todd said. "Myrmidon."

"Idiot," Sophia said, double tapping the next inbound. She looked around and had time, so she quickly reloaded her magazines.

"And now you've brought the fucking soldiers here," Christine said disgustedly. "They're going to just blow us *all* away! Babykillers!"

"You want to be a zombie?" Sophia asked. She grabbed Todd by the arm and walked him over to the nearest fresh corpse. Then she pulled out a clasp knife. "Cut your arm. Wipe some of the blood on it. Instant zombie."

"I..." Todd said. "Let go of me..."

"You're not going to because you're afraid," Sophia said, holding the knife up to his eye-level. "You're afraid because you're not willing to *fight back*. You're the poet. What's the thing about the raging and darkness?"

"You mean Dylan Thomas?" Todd said disdainfully. "'Rage, rage against the dying of the light'?"

"Do not go gentle into this good night," Sophia snarled, waving at the darkness all around. "Old age should burn and *rave* at close of day; Rage, rage against the dying of the light.

"Though wise men at their end know dark is right,
    Because their words had forked no lightning they
    Do not go gentle into that good night.

"Good men, the last wave by, crying how bright
    Their frail deeds might have danced in a green bay,
    Rage, rage against the dying of the light.

"That is what you *should* be doing!" she finished. "Raging against the dying of the light. You're not even in *old age!*"

"You knew the poem," Todd said wonderingly.

"I got an A plus in a really *tough* AP English class," Sophia said. "*And* AP physics. *And* calculus. *And* I know how to kill zombies. What the fuck have *you* been doing with your life?"

"You want to tell us what's been going on here, miss?" the sergeant of the three-man team asked. They weren't up and pointed, but you could tell they were here for a fire-fight.

"We're having a poetry and philosophy discussion," Sophia said, holstering her pistol. "I'm glad you could join us..."

"Contractors," Copley said, disgustedly. "Never thought I'd have to deal with you guys in New York City. I had enough of you in the Stan."

"Hey," Durante said, shrugging his shoulders. "Be glad we were here. Otherwise half this crowd would be going zombie."

"From what I got from Sophia, that's happened before," Steve Smith, "President of Blue Water Security, LLC," said. He hadn't even known he was a "president" until Tom handed him the certifications. "When's NYPD getting here?"

"They're not," Copley said, shaking his head. "We're not even getting coroner's office. I'm told to take down the information, then await graves registration."

"It's gotten that bad, huh?" Tom said. "And your ROE probably still says 'do not fire until fired upon.'"

"It's better than that," Copley said. "But not much."

"So...You guys get to shoot 'em ?" Randall asked.

"Not usually," Faith said. "Usually we have to taser 'em. There were too many this time. You guys gotta wear that rig all the time?"

The National Guardsmen were in masks, hoods and ponchos.

"Keeps the blood off," Randall said.

"Makes sense," Faith said. "I got in a scuffle with one the other day and it bled all over me. Ended up very nearly going zombie myself. You do *not* want to get it even if you don't zomb. Sickest I've ever been in my *life*."

"Damn," Randall said. "So...you're not going to zombie, right?"

"Certified immune," Faith said. "My immune system got it. Low dosage of the virus I guess. Don't even have any antibodies anymore, which is medicalese for 'you're not going to be a zombie.' Shook it off completely. Not that it was much fun. Horrible sick."

"I'll keep my poncho on, then," Randall said. "Let me tell you, this shit is hot, though."

"Better or worse than the Sandbox?" Faith asked.

"Oh, better," Randall said. "But not much."

"Nice rig," Astroga said. "What is that rifle?"

"Shotgun," Faith said. "Saiga. It's an AK variant that fires twelve-gauge." She dropped the magazine and cleared and handed it over to the private. "Ten-round magazine. Which beats a pump all to hell."

"Is it reliable?" Randall asked. "May I?"

"Sure," Faith said. "As long as I get it back. Especially if we get any more visitors."

"Nice," Randall said.

"Love the kukri," Faith said, gesturing at the combat knife on his belt.

"Carried it in Iraq and the Stan," Randall said. He hesitated for a second, then handed it over. "Thought it might come in handy."

"Sweet," Faith said, examining it. It had the word "Boosh" carved on the handle. "I've got one on the boat. They said it was overkill for tonight. Famous last words."

"There is no overkill," Randall intoned. "There is only open fire and reload."

"Schlock fan, huh?" Faith said. "I knew the world was coming to an end when Schlock didn't update."

"It's heavy," Astroga said. "The Saiga."

"I'll take the firepower any day," Faith said, gesturing with her chin at the M4. "The U.S. started to go downhill when it changed from a round designed to kill our enemies to one designed to piss them off."

"Nice quote," Randall said. "That one I don't recognize."

"Read it on some blog," she said, then looked up. The entire skyline had gone black as had all the lights in the park. "Oh, that is not good. Getting home is going to be a bitch and a half."

"I wonder if the subways are out, too," Astroga said nervously. "I'd hate to be in a subway in the dark in this."

"We've got..." Faith paused. She reached for her Saiga. "Wasn't what I was going to say but what we've *got* is *movement*."

A woman was running through the park pursued by a zombie. Before she could get to the relative safety of the group of concertgoers, another came at her from the side and knocked her down. She started screaming.

"Move it!" Copley said, waving.

The threesome ran to the woman, stopping just short to fire tasers into the zombies attacking her. One of them seemed to be trying to sexually assault her.

"Okay," Faith said. "That's just gross."

She looked away and then turned back at another scream. Astroga had been attacked from behind by another infected. She was struggling to throw it off. Randall tasered it but there were more. Suddenly, the threesome was surrounded by zombies and there were now screams from the concertgoers.

Looking around, Faith realized that there were more and more of the zombies closing on the concert.

"The lights!" Tom shouted. "They're zeroing in on the lights!"

Suddenly, an M4 went to full auto and Faith heard rounds zipping by her head. Copley pushed his way through the crowd of zombies, dragging Astroga by the harness. She could see Randall, clearly out of rounds and with no time to reload, wielding his kukri and chopping zombies left and right.

"Rock and roll!" Copley screamed. "Just *shoot*! We're in *armor*!"

"Authorized," Tom said, taking a two-handed stance. "Try not to hit the good guys."

"Uncle Tom!" Faith said, backing towards her group and firing to the side. "We've got more coming!"

"This way, too," Stacey called. "They're in the concert."

Faith glanced over her shoulder and saw something she never expected to see. Ever. With the defenses around the actual stage, where the lights were, the zombies couldn't climb up. Zombies coming down Fifth Avenue had bent around the stage until they hit the dancers in the mosh pit. A naked, writhing zombie was being crowd-surfed over the group. So far, the moshers seemed to consider the zombies to be a feature, not a bug. Just more people to hit.

When it dropped into the regular concertgoers, the screams started. and there were more being crowd-surfed back.

"Remind me to pick up some mosh gear," Faith shouted.

"On you," Sophia called.

"Cover me while I reload," Faith said. There was a tidal wave of zombies coming for them, and she made, if not the fastest reload in her life, then close. She had to make sure to keep the magazine since she foresaw a time in the not-too-distant future when getting more would be a bit of a pain.

"And we're back," Faith said, taking three quick blasts to clear their side. "Where the fuck are they all coming from?"

"Thanks," Copley said as the three soldiers reached the perimeter of the contractor group. "Thanks, thanks..."

"Reload and start laying down," Tom said. "We're not out of this yet. And call for back-up."

"Roger, sir," Copley said.

"You, Specialist," Tom said, pointing to Randall. "East side. Durante, South. Faith, West. You, Private," he said, pointing at Astroga. "North towards the concert. We're going to start moving south. Steve and I will back Durante."

"That's right into most of them, boss," Durante pointed out. He was keeping up a slow-aimed fire with his Saiga. "Reloading."

"Covering," Steve said.

"Questions later," Tom said, taking down two zombies with two shots. "Sergeant, stay on the horn."

"Roger, sir," Copley said. "The NYPD liaison net is down. Ditto cell. I'm down to military radio."

"Keep at it," Tom said. "Durante, start moving forward as soon as we're reloaded."

The concert crowd had started to scatter as more and more of the infected swarmed the only light in a mile. Faith could hear screams over the music as they were picked off one by one in the surrounding darkness. She keyed on her tactical light as they moved down the road into the woods.

"No lights," Tom said.

"Boss," Durante said, firing.

"They're attracted to the lights," Tom snapped. "The reason we're going south. No lights."

"Lasers?" Faith asked.

"Authorized," Tom said, firing carefully.

"Oh, my God," Astroga said.

Faith glanced to the side and blanched. It was just possible to tell who was a zombie and who was a mosher but it didn't look as if many of the moshers were left. And the zombies were fighting their way over the fences and razor wire to get to the band. Most of Voltaire's back-up had quit, one was pounding a zombie with an electric guitar, but he was still strumming along.

"Jasper glittered all over the wall, so they /Hung him from the ceiling for a Disco Ball. /There was so much angst after the fight, /Edward and Bella broke up that night. /While some wolves chowed down on a puddle of food /That used to be some rasta vampire dude..."

There was a crackle of sparks as a zombie hit the power leads for the concert and the lights shut out with a sudden finality. Faith couldn't see what happened in the darkness. But she could hear the screaming.

"You wanna, you know, fight zombies here?" Sophia asked. "I'm borrowing a pistol."

"Go," Faith said, returning to fighting. She tried to ignore the screams from the crowd.

"Don't shoot!" a woman screamed, running towards the group. "Please! Help!" There was an infected in hot pursuit.

"Down!" Astroga shouted. "Get down!" The woman was directly in her line of fire. And she wasn't listening.

"Cover!" Faith snapped. She could barely see, her eyes were

still adjusting, but she drew her sidearm and tracked the zombie one-handed. There was a boom.

"Got it!" she shouted.

"Nice shot," Copley said.

"Thanks," Faith replied, firing into the darkness. There was a scream and something started thrashing.

"Thank you, thank you..." the woman sobbed.

"Hey, Christine," Sophia said airily. "I thought you *wanted* to be a zombie."

"I changed my mind, okay?" Christine said.

"Quiet," Tom said. Christine started to say something and he hit her on the back of the head. "I said, *quiet.* Listen."

"I *don't* like being under these trees," Faith whispered. It was darker even than in the main square and very hard to see the zombies. She flashed her laser around and was rewarded by another thrashing sound. She moved it again and there was another thrashing.

"Are you playing laser tag with a zombie?" Sophia asked.

"I think it's trying to chase it," Faith whispered. The sound of the city had nearly died and all there was was the sound of their breathing, the crashing of zombies in the trees and the occasional scream in the distance. A horn started blaring and there were howls in the distance.

"Just keep moving," Tom said. "Don't fire unless you have to."

A zombie came loping at the group and Durante turned to fire.

"I've got this," Randall said, stepping forward. He let his weapon drop on the sling and held out his left hand. "Come on, zombie, nice fresh hand to bite..." He carefully drew his kukri.

The zombie grabbed his arm and bit down on the offered hand. As he did, Randall brought the kukri down and to the side, chopping into the back of the zombie's neck. It dropped to the ground, twitching.

"Stay away from the blood spray," Tom said.

"Oh, yeah," Durante said. "Those masks and ponchos make more sense now. You get bitten?"

"Two sets of gloves," Randall said, holding up his hand. "Rubber MOPP gloves and tacticals. Didn't even penetrate the rubber."

"You've been planning that, haven't you?" Copley said.

"Since we got deployed."

"Sergeant," Tom said quietly. "Support?"

"Multiple teams in contact," Copley said. "The reaction team is in contact. The bases that aren't deep in buildings are all under attack."

"If you can, pass that they're attracted to sound and light," Tom said. "Go to NVGs."

"Wish we had them," Randall said.

They finally cleared the park. There was more light on Washington Square South but not much.

"We need wheels," Tom said. "Where's the nearest headquarters that's not under attack?" Tom asked.

"Fourteenth Street precinct reports no movement," Copley said.

"Bank's closer," Tom said, pointing with his pistol to the west. "We'll go there. We've got a heavy rescue vehicle. We can get you back to your people."

"Not going to complain," Copley said. "Wait..." He put his ear to the radio. "Roger... Is that confirmed? Roger... We've got *ten* personnel, say again, *ten*. Team eight-three, one civilian, six contractors... Okay... Roger... Do not, say again, do not use lights... Roger..."

"What?" Tom asked.

"There's an MRAP moving down university place to NYU to pick up another team that's hot. They can do pick-up for us as well."

"*All* of us?" Tom asked. "Or just your team?"

"All of us," Copley said. "It will be tight but they'll pick us up."

"East it is," Tom said. "Rotate with Durante on the park side. Faith, you're plowing the road."

"Oh, goody," Faith said. "*Which* way?"

"There," Tom said, grabbing her shoulders to point her in the correct direction. "Specialist, take the back door. Private, you cover the street side. Sergeant, back up Faith in clearing the road."

"Roger, sir," Randall said.

"On it," Copley said. "We'd better hurry, though. I'm not sure how long they're going to wait. Or if they can make pick-up if we don't make the ETA."

There was a sudden flash of light and a Yellow Cab took the turn onto the street from the direction of the university. Which meant it was going against the traffic if there had been any. It was weaving from side to side, dodging most of the zombies. As Faith watched, it hit one, tossing it halfway across the street. As it zoomed by the group it tooted its horn and a faint big band swing medley dopplered into the distance.

Unfortunately, its antics had attracted the zombies in the park. And they were now closing in on the group. Some were getting caught on the low metal fence of the park but most were successfully clambering over.

"Contact," Durante said, pulling the trigger. "Tango down. Multiple contacts my side." He fired again. "Tango down. Not clear..."

"New plan," Tom said. "Middle of the street. Plow the road and shag bloody arse."

"We are in heavy contact and moving to your position," Copley shouted over the radio. "Request support soonest." He was firing his M4 one-handed as he ran.

"Here, zombies, zombies, zombies," Faith said. She was panning the Saiga back and forth at shoulder level. As soon as the red laser would appear, meaning something was in its way, she fired.

"Oh, there's a bunch behind us!" Randall shouted. "Cover me while I reload!"

"I really wish I'd brought more Saigas," Steve said. "But what could go wrong with a concert at night in a zombie apocalypse?"

"You're never going to let go of that, are you?" Faith asked. "I'm out!" she yelled. Zombies were too close to reload, so she pulled a pistol and started firing.

"We're getting surrounded," Tom said. "We need to keep moving!"

"Take cover!" Copley said. There was a sound of a heavy vehicle moving, and a burst of machine-gun fire suddenly hit a group of zombies by the park.

"South side," Tom shouted. "By the buildings!"

"Shit!" Faith snarled. She'd dropped behind a concrete planter just as a burst of bullets ripped over her head.

"Friendlies!" Copley shouted. He was face down on the ground. He popped a chemlight and threw it in the air towards the MRAP.

The unlit MRAP continued to lay down fire over their heads as it moved forward, slowly. When it was opposite the group it stopped and the back doors opened.

"You waiting for an engraved invitation?" somebody shouted, then fired to the rear.

"Waiting to make sure you weren't going to shoot us," Astroga shouted. She was in the heavy vehicle like a shot.

"Thanks," Faith said. "I think. You nearly tagged me back there."

"A miss is as good as a mile," the vehicle crewman said. "Who's got the count?"

"Me," Tom said. "And we're good," he added as Durante boarded.

"Ow!" Sophia said, banging her head. "We should have worn helmets."

"Military vehicles are designed for them," Steve said, leaning forward. "Hunch and you probably won't hit your head as much."

"When did we go hot?" Copley yelled. The inside of the MRAP was like being in a rock crusher. It also was occasionally tossing around as if it was hitting potholes.

"When the lights went out and every zombie in New York City headed for anything with lights on," the crewman shouted. "Every team's been hit and just about every headquarters. We are 'redeploying for active clearance.'"

"About fucking time," Randall snarled.

"It's going to get *really* tight in here," the crewman said. "We've got two more teams to pick up and they've got some civilians, too. I guess the zombies are enforcing the curfew for us!"

It was nearly dawn by the time Tom was able to arrange pick-up for the group and get back to the Bank.

"So are you pulling the handle?" Steve asked.

"I'll have to see what the Fed and the Board say when they get around to meeting," Tom said. He was looking out the window of his office at the darkened skyline of New Jersey. There were a few lights. And although he couldn't see them, he was sure that each was surrounded by a wall of "infected persons." "I can't pull the handle until the tipping point has clearly been reached, the Fed orders temporary suspension of all operations or the Board orders suspension."

"I'd say last night was a tipping point," Steve said.

"For us, maybe," Tom said. "But I've got to stay until they pull the handle. You can go. The evac plan is solid. Everybody involved in critical actions or in the evac group has been vaccinated and boosted." His phone rang and he picked it up.

"Smith... Roger, sir... Understood... I'll send a team to pick them up... Roger, it's under control..."

"Pulling the handle?" Steve asked.

"Sounds like it," Tom said. "The chairman and his family are holed up in their apartment on Park Avenue and apparently they can't get out. Zombies, don't you know? Do me one last favor?"

"Short on teams?" Steve said.

"Very," Tom said. "Take the BERT truck and go get them. There's a few other board members as well. Then take it over to the dock and trade places with Kaplan. I'll send Durante with you, but he may need some fire support."

"I'll contact you on Channel 47," Steve said, standing up wearily. "I'm getting too old for this shit."

"We both are," Tom said. "Brother..."

"We'll see you when we see you, Tom," Steve said. "You going to say good-bye to the girls?"

"Faith would blow me away like a zombie if I didn't."

"As a last job for Uncle Tom, that *sucked*," Faith said, collapsing onto a couch in the saloon. "I'm done. I'm sooo done."

It was nearly sundown. They had been up all night, and the way things were going they were going to have to be up another night.

The thirteen-year-old was barely out of the hospital. She was toast.

The "simple" job of moving the chairman of the board of the Bank of the Americas—along with his "immediate family," which included not only children and grandchildren but some cousins he thought would be helpful, other board members, their "immediate family" and some hangers-on that Steve thought probably fell into the category of "mistresses," or in one case "boyfriend"—had been a *nightmare*.

The only people who seemed to understand words and phrases like "urgency," "emergency evacuation" or "get in the fucking truck, lady" were the chairman and his wife, Nancy. The chairman had had to leave in the first lift to get to the meetings at the Bank. There were essentially no electronic communications working. That left his wife trying to persuade a group of wealthy, entitled cats that they needed to move. Didn't happen quickly and it wasn't helped by the fact that they had to ride in the BERT van.

In one of the last lifts, Faith had finally lost it when she heard:

"I am not riding in the back of a simply horrible vehicle like that!"

The woman was the wife of a president of something or another at the Bank. A president, as she repeatedly had pointed out. Hubby had long since left to attend "meetings."

Faith, who was working the loading point, pulled her .45 and put it to the woman's head.

"You can get into the van or I can turn you into vaccine," she said, coldly. "Your call."

"You wouldn't!" the lady snapped.

"Look in my eyes, lady," Faith said. "Get in the fucking van and get in the van now!"

The lady got in the van.

"Well, I don't think we're going to be asked for our services again, all things considered," Steve said now. "I understand there were complaints."

"I hope so," Faith said. "I thing a was a..." Her eyes closed and she started to snore.

"It reminds me of when she was four and she used to fall asleep in her plate," Stacey whispered.

"The difference being she's not four, she's not small and she's still got all her gear on," Sophia said tiredly. "Faith!" She shouted, kicking her sister's boot.

"Wasat?" Faith said, sitting up and reaching for her pistol.

"Whoa," Steve said, clamping her hand. "You need to get undressed and into bed."

"Ogazada..." Faith said and her eyes closed again.

"Mile Seven, *this is Thunderblast,*" the radio crackled.

"That's Tom," Steve said, stepping into the cockpit and keying the radio. "Thunder, *Mile Seven.*"

"Code is Goose, say again, Goose."

"Confirm, Goose," Steve said. As he replied there was the sound of a distant explosion behind him. Looking north he saw the center of the George Washington Bridge collapsing into the river. "Bloody *hell*...Roger, Goose. Good luck."

"Same, same," Tom replied. *"Out here."*

"And we are away to better climes," Tom shouted. He hit the anchor winch switch and looked towards the darkened skyline. There were fires burning out of control in Harlem and more from the direction of Brooklyn. The same seemed to be the case on the New Jersey side with widespread fires in every direction.

He raised the mainsail and jib, catching the strong northeast breeze, then straightened away to the south.

When he was underway he pulled out his iPod and scrolled through it for the playlist he'd created. There was a recessed input for it right on the console so he plugged it in and started the playlist.

"*Speed bonnie boat like a bird on the wind...*" he crooned. "*Onward the sailors cry. Carry the lad that's born to be king, over the Sea to Skye...*"

BOOK TWO

I WILL NOT BOW

Watch the end through dying eyes

Now the dark is taking over

Show me where forever dies

Take the fall and run to heaven

All is lost again, but I'm not giving in

I will not bow, I will not break

I will shut the world away

I will not fall, I will not fade

I will take your breath away

"I Will Not Bow"
Breaking Benjamin
Dear Agony

PROLOGUE

"It is requested that passengers move to their designated lifeboats..."
the enunciator purred over the screams.

"Gwinn! Come *on!*" Chris Phillips yelled from the lifeboat.

Chris had spent ten years in the Royal Navy as a chef. That was not a cook, as he liked to point out. He was a Royal Navy *chef*. There was a difference. And Steven Seagal *didn't* know the difference.

But after a while, the "allure" of Navy life palled. He still enjoyed the sea. The problem was he never got to *see* it except from land. He was a very good chef. Good chefs served admirals, and admirals generally were also land-bound.

So he'd quit and put out some resumes. Which was how he ended up as a chef for Royal Caribbean Cruise lines and met the love of his life, Third Officer, Staff, Gwinneth Stevens. After years of bachelorhood that had most people joking about his actual tastes, he'd proposed only two months ago.

Then the H7 virus had broken out.

They'd pieced together that the bastard who spread it had left one of his calling cards at the cruise terminal in New York. Which meant that there were at least fifteen "patient zeroes" on the boat. And by the time they found that out, there were more.

The boat had been put in "at sea" quarantine. Then the "afflicted" had started to turn. And without antigen testers, they couldn't screen for who was infected and who wasn't. And then it spiraled.

The captain and other "ship" officers were already gone, taking all the powered lifeboats. But Staff Side had stayed on. The ship officers, Greeks, as was common, considered themselves only responsible for the ship. When it was clear the infected had control and there was nothing to do about it, they had given an almost Gallic shrug and fled, the bastards.

Staff Side was responsible for the passengers. And they were chosen from people, like Gwinn, who took that job seriously. The senior officer, Staff, had already turned when the first officer gave the order to abandon ship. Thomas, though, was still standing his post. He intended to go to full lockdown as soon as the boats were away. Since passengers had been issued water and food in their quarters, assuming that help arrived soon, a major assumption, perhaps a few would survive.

Gwinn kept looking for one more passenger who could make it.

"There might be more—" she said.

The infected came from out of nowhere and hit her like a rugby player, taking her down and biting at the back of her neck.

"Gwinn!" Chris yelled, scrambling up the short steps. He grabbed the infected and punched him in the back of the neck, hard. It knocked the thing out for a moment.

"Gwinn, come on, honey," Chris said, pulling her up. "Please..."

"Go," Gwinn said, holding the back of her neck to staunch the blood flow. "Just go..."

"I can't, honey," Chris said. "Please! Darling—"

"Go!" Gwinn screamed. "I'm *infected!* I *can't* board! GO!"

She stood up and pushed him to the boarding steps. Normally the slight woman couldn't have moved his nearly two-meter, fifteen-stone mass. But he backed up.

"It's duty, darling," Gwinn said, sobbing. "Just duty."

"One last kiss?" Chris said.

"One..."

He gave her a hug and kissed her, then allowed her to push him into the raft.

"Love," Gwinn said, tears streaming down her face. "And survive..."

Gwinn closed the hatch and Chris took his seat under the big red lever that said "Do Not Pull."

"Ladies and gentlemen, please assume what are called in the airline industry 'crash positions' bent over at the waist, arms wrapped around your legs," he said tonelessly to the mostly shocked or crying passengers. "There will be a brief sensation of falling, then a light impact. I'm told it's a bit like a carnival ride." He reached up to the bar and pulled down, hard. "Last ride of the day..."

CHAPTER 15

Blood-splattered blue curtains rippled to the rocking of the boat as Steve stepped over the corpse of the former owner. From the loose skin, the man had probably been heavy-set before turning zombie. By the time they boarded the boat, he was clearly on the edge of starvation.

"Who chooses blue curtains with a maroon interior?" Faith asked, her voice muffled by her respirator.

"At a guess?" Steve said, gesturing at a gnawed corpse in the corner. "Her."

The body had been chewed down to the bones. There was still a mass of goo from decomposition staining the maroon carpets.

They'd lured the zombie to the rear sliding doors, then when Faith jerked them open Steve had "terminated the hostile infected." At least that was how he was going to write it up in the ship's log.

"This one useable?" Faith asked.

"Too early to tell," Steve said. "But we're definitely going to have to fumigate."

The Hunter was about done. Three weeks after leaving New York harbor they'd hit a heavy tropical storm that had ripped away the wind-generator as well as half the deck rigs and railings.

Steve had seriously reconsidered his choice of zombie plans as the craft pitched uncontrollably through fifty-foot swells.

But, based upon what they were getting, or had stopped getting, from land, a tropical storm was better than a zombie storm. One by one, shortwave radio stations had stopped broadcasting. First the major commercial news stations, then governments. The last "official" station to broadcast was the Beeb from "a location in Scotland." And then one day it was silent.

That left only amateur ham radio operators, who reported large crowds of zombies roaming even through rural districts. One station, Zombie Team Alpha, from Kansas, had boasted it was prepared for any zombie attack. Then an attack. Then silence. There were still a few broadcasting out there, mostly from deep in the arctic, but they were doing it quiet.

What puzzled Steve was that GPS was still up. As he understood it, GPS depended upon an atomic clock somewhere in Colorado. Since it was unlikely that that facility had held out, he wasn't sure why it was still working. But he was glad it was. Sophia and Stacey had waded through a book on celestial navigation and learned how to do it, but he wasn't looking forward to the day they had to use that method.

Whatever the case, they needed a new ride. And the Fairline 65 twin diesel, christened _Tina's Toy_, looked to be a pretty good choice.

The boat was the first they'd tried to board. They had had a few of what might have been attacks in the couple of weeks after leaving New York. The waters, then, in the area were fairly crowded, and the sailboat filled with mostly women must have looked like an inviting target. But whenever a boat tracked towards them, they'd just started breaking out the equipment, and as more and more body-armored and heavily armed people came on deck...boats would just sort of turn away.

To avoid the crowded NYC-Bermuda-Norfolk corridor, Steve had turned northeast into the deep Atlantic. The family had basically sailed in the direction of Iceland, then back down into the U.S. region. By the time they came back, there were far fewer boats. At least, boats under power and control. They had seen several boats, and even freighters, under power but clearly not in control. One encounter at night had nearly resulted in what would surely have been a fatal collision. Only quick action on

Sophia's part had gotten the tiny sailboat out of the way of the massive freighter.

Just adjusting to being shipboard had been hard. None of them had any serious at-sea experience. It was the one flaw in Steve's zombie plan, and a couple of times it had nearly cost them. Forget that the girls had to learn to find their own "space" on the relatively tiny craft. And learn that there were tasks that had to be completed. And that they had to find their own entertainment. Some of the tasks, like fire drills, had proven out when they had their first galley fire. Then there had been the possible "attacks," the tropical storm and just learning to adjust to being on a boat, which was a big enough problem.

In the last two weeks they hadn't had any similar problems. They hadn't seen many small boats, but floating freighters and tankers seemed to be everywhere.

However, in the two months they'd been cautiously avoiding contact, they'd also used up the bulk of their stores. They were flat out of fuel for cooking, nearly out of fuel for the generator and when that ran out they wouldn't be able to produce drinkable water.

Definitely time to find another home.

"Ooo, I want," Faith said, getting a good look at the saloon.

"Even with the maroon interior?" Steve asked.

"The maroon I can handle," Faith said. "It's the blue curtains that suck."

"Oooo," Steve said, stepping forward. "I want."

"Nice helm," Faith said, looking at the enclosed helm forward of the saloon. "Who came up with this idea?"

"I dunno," Steve said, examining the controls. "We'll need to get it powered to check its fuel and water stores."

"You gonna be able to figure all this out?" Faith asked.

"If I can't, your mom and sister can," Steve said. "Now to find the way down."

They quickly found a companionway, which was blocked by a hatch.

"Hello!" he shouted, banging on the hatchway. "Any zombies down there?"

"I think I hear something," Faith said, taking out an earplug. "Yeah, I hear something."

"Is that a zombie?" Steve asked, cocking his head.

"I don't think so," Faith said, then cocked her own. "Wait . . .
I dunno."

"It's not on the other side of the hatch," Steve said. He readied
his shotgun anyway and then pulled at the hatch. Which was
stuck. "I don't think this has a *lock . . .*" he said.

"You've sort of got a master-key," Faith pointed out.

"Yeah," Steve said. He pulled out his magazine, ejected the
round in the chamber, then pulled another round out of his vest,
loaded it in the chamber and reinserted the magazine. "'Ware
bouncer."

"Roger," Faith said, turning and ducking her head so any
bounce-back from the door would be taken on her body armor
and helmet.

Steve tapped the edge of the hatch until he found where something had been installed to make it lockable. He placed the barrel
against the blockage and fired.

The frangible round blew out the light latch, and the hatch
opened on darkness.

"Zombies in the darkness," Faith said. "That brings back
memories."

"And whose idea was that?" Steve asked.

"Uncle Tom's?" Faith answered. "I don't know why you keep
blaming *me!*"

"'But I've never been to a concert, Da!'" Steve mimicked.

"You've gotta let that go, Da," she said. "We going or not?"

"Let the—" Steve said.

"—zombies come to you," Faith finished. "You've covered that.
They're not coming to us. Hello! Zombies! Hello!"

"What's that?" Steve asked as a zombie came around the corner
of the companionway.

It was emaciated and could barely stumble along. Steve wasn't
even sure it was a zombie. Except for being naked it could have
been a nearly dead human.

It stumbled on the stairs and started clawing upwards, snarl-
ing in a weird, dry tone.

"Jesus," Faith said, stepping forward. She'd drawn her .45 and
fired one round into the zombie's back, then another into its
head. "That was a mercy killing."

"There's still some sound," Steve said and pulled out his earplugs. "Hello! Zombies! Hello!"

"...lo..."

"I don't think that's a zombie," Faith said, stepping forward.

"Wait," Steve said. "Just take our time. If that's a survivor, they'll keep ten minutes while we make sure we're safe."

"Roger," Faith said.

"I've got point," Steve said, stepping past her. He had to step on the zombie's body to get down the narrow companionway.

The lower passageway was just as narrow and had a host of hatches. It also was covered in feces. Steve had wondered if he'd gotten his seals seated on the respirator. He knew, now, that he had. Otherwise he'd be smelling all this filth. One of the hatches, leading to a stateroom to port, was open. That floor was covered in feces as well. The sounds were emanating from a hatch forward. Which was covered in scratches and badly battered.

Steve tapped on it with the butt of the Saiga.

"Hello?"

"Hello?" a weak female voice answered.

"Jesus," Faith said. "Survivor."

"There goes this salvage," Steve said. "Miss, we need you to just hang on..."

"...water?"

Faith pulled off her assault pack and pulled out a bottle of water.

"I've got it," she said. "Hey, passing through some water. You gotta open the door, though."

"...zombies...?"

"We're inoculated," Faith said. "And we've cleared all the ones in this area. You can open the door. You're safe. I mean, I'm a girl. You don't have to worry about me or anything. And the guy with me's my Da..."

There was a sound of a bolt being pulled and material being moved. Slowly, as if the person moving it could barely manage. Finally, it cracked open.

"Here," Faith said. She clearly was trying not to react.

The girl was probably a little younger than Faith but was emaciated and haggard.

Faith opened up the water and started to hand it to her, then held it up for her to drink.

"Don't drink it too fast," Faith said. "You'll just puke it back up."

"Thank you," the girl said, taking careful sips and treasuring them. "Thank you."

"Sorry it took so long," Steve said. Emotionally he'd known that there were going to be survivors on the boats. The law of the sea sort of mandated that they rescue people. Which they'd been ignoring because, well, there wasn't anywhere to take them and there wasn't much "law of the sea" anymore.

Seeing the survivor drove it home, though.

"Where's Charlie?" the girl asked after a few sips.

"The infected?" Steve said. "We...took care of him."

"Oh..." the girl said. "I sort of thought so. I heard the guns."

"Family?" Faith asked.

"No," the girl said, slowly. She seemed to be trying to remember how to speak. "He was the captain. He put the bolts on and told me to lock myself in here after...after Dad..." She started to sob.

"Miss, we sort of need you to stay here until we're done clearing," Steve said. "We'll get you over to our boat as soon as we can. But...you want us to clear up some before you go through. Okay?"

"Okay," the girl said. "Is there...anybody else?"

"How many on the boat?" Faith asked.

"Four," the girl said. "Me and...Mom and Dad and Captain Charlie."

"Then...no," Faith said. "You're it."

"Okay," the girl said, tearing up again.

"Just hang in there," Faith said, handing her the bottle. "Sip this. Slowly. We *will* be back."

"Okay."

"*Seven*, Away Team," Steve said over the radio.

"*Away*, Seven. *Everything okay?*"

"Nominal," Steve said. "One survivor. Female, early teen. Non-infected. Will clear before transporting."

"*Okay*," Stacey replied. "*We'll get ready for her. Is it useable?*"

"Unknown at this time," Steve said. "No power. Prep for engineering survey."

"*So you want me to get ready to come over and see if I can get it running again?*" Stacey replied.

Steve hung his head. Stacey was never *ever* going to get military radio discipline.

"Yes, dear," Steve said.

"*Then why didn't you just say so? Get the survivor back here and we'll talk.*"

Steve and Faith checked the rest of the hatches. A series of homemade locks had been put on them, reinforcing the ones already there. They had to resort to a crowbar to get the master cabin door open.

"Nice," Faith said, waving her taclight around the cabin. "I don't suppose I get this one?"

"I'd say that the survivor will get the forward cabin again," Steve said. "If she wants it. She might be tired of it. Your mom and I in this one."

"So Soph and I get the *little* beds again," Faith said, disgustedly.

"There are probably more cabins in a boat like this," Steve said. "So at least you should have your own."

There were a total of five cabins. The master and forward were both queen beds. The two smaller forward cabins had a double in the starboard cabin and bunks to port. The rear cabin had two bunk beds and a daybed couch. And there were no more zombies.

"I'll take this one," Faith said when they found the last cabin. "No zombie poop."

"We'll see," Steve said. "Right now we need to get the remains gathered up and the survivor back to *Mile Seven*."

"Captain Charlie" was fairly easy to move, despite the tight quarters. He hadn't been a big guy *before* starvation had gotten him. They took him up to the aft-deck, tied some metal they'd found in the engine room to his ankle and heaved him over the side.

Despite his own starvation, the father was a bit more of an issue.

"Take the legs," Steve said, getting his hands well locked into the corpse's armpits.

"Why are dead bodies so heavy?" Faith asked, heaving the legs up to clear the railing.

"I'm not sure," Steve said. "But it's what they mean by 'dead weight.'"

The father, like Charlie, disappeared into the depths with barely a splash.

"Okay, this one..." Faith said, looking at the mother's gnawed and decomposed corpse. She turned her head away and retched slightly.

"Don't throw up in your respirator," Steve said. "I'll get it."

He got a plastic trash bag and gathered the mother's remains up. There wasn't much he could do for the pile of goo that had been most of her intestines. And when he tried to gather it up he found himself retching.

They loaded the bag with more metal and made sure it sank.

"Dear God, we commend these people to the depths in the sure certainty that in the end of times the sea will give up its dead, amen," Steve said quickly.

"Amen," Faith said. "I didn't know you were even a Christian, Da. I knew Gran was Catholic but..."

"The girl's going to want to know that we did more than just pitch her parents over the rail of their boat," Steve said. "Besides...keeping up the niceties to the extent you can isn't hard and enough people think it's worth it that...it's worth it. Taking thirty seconds to say a prayer sort of shows that we're still civilized or something."

"How's it going?" Stacey called. The *Mile Seven* was tied up to the bigger boat with every fender and bolster they had alongside to prevent them from banging together in the light swells.

Steve started to shout through the mask, then keyed his radio.

"That's the last of the bodies," Steve said. "We're bringing the survivor over now."

"Okay," Stacey yelled, waving.

Steve changed his gloves before opening the hatch to the cabin.

"Miss," he said, turning around and squatting down. "Let's try piggy back. Will that work?"

With Faith's help he got the girl back onto the *Mile Seven* and cast her off.

"What are you doing?" Stacey asked.

"I want to take off my respirator," Steve said. "And I don't want to do it alongside that boat. Not until it's cleaned out."

"Thank you for this," the girl said.

"I still haven't asked your name, miss," Steve said.

"Tina Black," the girl said. She was a tiny thing with black hair and blue eyes.

"Let's get you inside..." Stacey said, wrapping her arm around the emaciated girl.

"Despite her condition, we need to decontaminate, first," Steve said.

"Steve," Stacey said dangerously.

"We've got some water in the tank," Steve said, relenting. "Use the fresh-water shower."

"A shower?" Tina said. "Is that what you meant? I thought it was... I don't know what I thought."

"We need to get you cleaned up is what it means," Sophia said. "I'm Sophia Smith, the second mate. That's my mom, Stacey. The guy who can't seem to use normal words is my Da, Steve. And the hulking moron with a shoot-first attitude is Faith."

"Bite me, Soph," Faith said through her respirator.

"Don't mind her," Sophia said, wrapping her arm around Tina's shoulders. "She's adopted..."

"When Dad went I was down in my cabin," Tina said, sipping tomato soup. She'd had a shower and her hair was combed. All three of the Smith women were larger than her, so the sweats she'd borrowed from Sophia made her look even tinier. "I heard Mom... screaming. Captain Charlie blocked the door and put some food and water in my cabin. Then he made all the locks and told me to lock myself in the cabin. He'd... he'd told Dad that was what we should do in the first place. All of us in different cabins with a way to make it hard to get in or out. Then he... he went."

"How long ago?" Stacey asked.

She'd geared up and gone over to check out the Fairline after Sophia had taken charge of the survivor. After a bit, and some toting of materials from the Hunter, she'd managed to get the engines running. The boat still had nearly two-thirds of its fuel and the water tanks were full up. The reason that Tina had run out of water was the batteries supplying the pumps had finally gone dead.

"I don't know," Tina said. "There was a big storm..."

"We got hit by that, too," Sophia said. "That was about a month ago."

"Then... about a month and a half," Tina said. "I ran out of food after the storm sometime. And... as long as the water lasted I'd drink a bottle of water, then fill it. Then the water shut off and I couldn't flush or anything and..." She curled up into a ball.

"I can't promise that nothing bad is ever going to happen again," Steve said. "And I can't bring your parents back. But I promise I'll do my best. Okay?"

"Okay," Tina said. She leaned into Sophia and tucked in her head.

"Hey," Faith said, standing up. "Somebody should probably be on deck making sure we keep the boat in sight. I volunteer for watch."

"Go for it," Steve said. "I'll be up in a bit."

"Don't mind her," Sophia said. "She's good at fighting zombies. Not so big on the whole helping others thing."

"I guess you need people who are good at fighting zombies," Tina said. "Can I ask... What did you do with my mom and dad?"

"We gave them a decent burial at sea, Tina," Tom said. "The best we could under the circumstances."

"Thank you," Tina said.

"There's something we need to talk about," Steve said.

"Now?" Stacey asked.

"If not now, when?" Steve said. "It's about your parents' boat. This one is about done. The law of the sea, such as it is right now, is that if a boat is unoccupied it's salvage. But you were on your boat. So it's yours by right. Not to mention it's got your name on it..."

"But you need to use it?" Tina said. "If you can take me back to Virginia..."

"Virginia's not there, Tina," Sophia said. "I mean, the land's there but it's all zombies."

"All?" Tina said. "I mean... All?"

"We've been inshore a few times," Steve said. "Everywhere we've been there are zombies on land. No lights at night. No sign of civilization."

"Everything?" Tina said, looking at Sophia for confirmation. "New York?"

"We sailed out of New York harbor when they blew the bridges," Sophia said. "We actually attended the last concert in New York."

"And there hangs a tale," Steve said. "But the point is, we need your boat."

"You can *have* it," Tina said. "I never want to see it again!"

"And that won't work, either, honey," Stacey said. "After we get it cleaned up, we're all going to have to go back onboard."

"Oh," Tina said. "I'm not sure... I really don't want to go back."

"Cross that bridge when we come to it," Steve said. "But we have your permission to use it?"

"Yes," Tina said. "I mean, I'll give it to you. Just for getting me out of there."

"Probably ought to get that in writing," Steve said. "But I'm not really worried about it."

"Is Washington still...?" Tina asked.

"Let me see if I can put this in perspective," Sophia said, getting up. She turned on the shortwave receiver and consulted a chart. "Hear that static? That's the primary U.S. Federal Emergency Channel, the one that FEMA used to broadcast on. This..." she said, changing the channel. "That's the BBC... This is ABC... CNN...Fox Radio..."

"Oh, my God," Tina said, her eyes wide. She started crying again.

"You survived, Tina," Steve said, taking her chin and making her look at him. "You survived. And as a parent I can tell you that it was more important to your parents that you survive than that they survive. You were important to them. So your job, from here on out, is to not only survive but do the best you can at it. Understand?"

"Yes, sir," Tina said.

"As I said," Steve said, standing up. "It's not going to be easy. But we are not only going to survive. We are going to *win*."

"That's the first time I've heard you use the word 'win,'" Stacey said. She'd brought him a cup of coffee. That was one thing they'd taken off the yacht first off. They'd been out for two weeks. "Penny for your thoughts."

"I'm not sure I have any," Steve said, looking at the other boat. "But so far all we've been doing is running and hiding. That was the right thing to do. Now...I'm not so sure. My basic plan was to find an abandoned island somewhere and set up shop. Maybe there's a house somewhere with a harbor or something. Seeing Tina... Honey," he said, taking the coffee and setting it down. He turned to her and shrugged.

"There are people out there, just like Tina. Hiding in compartments. Starving. Dying of dehydration. On life rafts. We've been avoiding them for fear of someone going zombie. But by now, most of them will have gone through the cycles. If they haven't, we've still got some of Tom's vaccine. We can *save* people."

"Are you sure that's a good idea?" Stacey said. "I mean, Steven, there's only four of us. We're not exactly the Coast Guard. Just tying up to Tina's boat was tough."

"Compared to, say, going to a concert in New York in a zombie apocalypse at night?" Steve asked.

"You're never going to let that go, are you?" Stacey said with a breathless laugh.

"Zombies don't think," Steve said. "But whoever *created* that virus does. And I bet they had a plan to survive. I bet they're out there. And that person thinks humanity is beaten. There's no indication that anyone is doing anything. Everything is *gone*. There's no government, no Army, no Navy, no Coast Guard, no Homeland Security. No Homeland for that matter. It's all gone. The bastard *won*. Well, I'm *not* going to be beaten. I'm *not* going to have my children and grandchildren grow up hiding from the zombies. I'm *not* going to let that happen. I will not *bow* to the zombies!"

"Do you have a plan?" Stacey said.

"I have an inkling," Steve said. "I have a goal. I have the goal of a zombie-free world. I don't know if I'll see it in my lifetime. But I'll start with the U.S. and that's going to have to be good enough."

"Big plan," Stacey said, shaking her head. "Steve, I love you for your paladin side. But 'saving the world' is usually a metaphor."

"If not us, *who*?" Steve asked. "Tom, if he's out there still, is locked into a fortress and can't get out. Ditto any remaining government groups. There probably are government secure points that held out. But they're trapped by the zombies. *We* have mobility. And there are other boats, ships, survivors out there. We'll rescue them and organize."

"You think they'll go for it?" Stacey asked. "Tina's a lovely child but she's not going to be much help. They're all going to be traumatized, terrified..."

"Some will," Steve said. "Those that don't..." He shrugged. "Cross that bridge when we come to it. We'll cross *every* bridge when we come to it. We're going to *win* and I'm not going to let the bloody damned zombies stop us. I will not bow."

CHAPTER 16

Cleaning the *Toy* was an unimaginable pain.

The two zombies had crapped and pissed everywhere. Not just on the floor but on the seats and walls. Stacey had taken over checking the electronics and engineering while Sophia did an inventory of stores. Which left Faith and Steve to clean up, ripping up the carpet and ripping out the seats. The Fairline wasn't going to be nearly as comfortable when they were done but it was going to be livable.

The bunks in the port cabin were ruined. But they were the same size as the ones on the *Mile Seven* so they could be switched out. It was mostly a matter of ripping out the fabric and then application of elbow grease.

Tom took a break after two hours and went up to the helm. The seats there were just as messed up as the rest of the saloon but Stacey had ripped them out, stuffed in some pillows and started to work on the electronics.

"Figuring it out?" Steve asked. The console was so much more complicated than the Hunter's he found it intimidating.

"Fortunately, Tina's father was detail oriented," Stacey said. "There are manuals for everything. He wrecked a couple of the screens, but they were for peripheral systems. The whole thing is networked and it was mostly the secondaries that were damaged.

So, yes, figuring it out. Here's one thing that you'll find interesting, given our conversation last night."

She flipped through a touch-screen menu on one of the screens, then brought up one that was a map of the Atlantic. A false-color image of weather.

"What's that?" Steve asked.

"Tina's dad was a techie," Stacey said. "It's a weather satellite image."

"A file copy?" Steve asked.

"No," Stacey said. "Current. The GOES for the Atlantic. And here . . ." she said, changing screens. "That's North America."

"We've, sort of, got weather reports," Steve said, sighing in relief.

"Sort of," Stacey said. "All it gives us is the satellite."

"I can't believe it's still transmitting," Steve said. "They're still transmitting. I thought they had to have ground stations."

"I guess it's like the GPS," Stacey said, shrugging. "That should have gone down with Boulder. Didn't. Secrets of the universe I guess. But then there's this," she added, bringing up a screen filled with red dots.

"Okay, lots of red," Steve said. "That's bad."

"Little context," Stacey said, zooming out. As she did, the outline of the North American continent came into view. The dots were in the Atlantic. And they were everywhere.

"Distress beacons?" Steve asked.

"Two different types," Stacey said. "Three, really. One is EPIRBs," referring to Emergency Position Indicator Radio Beacons, "the other is AIS."

"AIS?" Steve asked.

"Automated Indicator System," Stacey said, hitting a control. Most of the indicators disappeared. "AIS is a system on large vessels. Those are big ships or boats that are in distress."

"Jesus," Steve said, shaking his head. "I didn't realize there were so many ships at sea at any time." He leaned in and looked at something. "What are those clusters?"

"I wondered the same thing," Stacey said, zooming in on Bermuda. There were a cluster of distress beacons along its southern shores. "Those are run aground. Seen enough of those."

Every time they had run in sight of shore there had been ships and boats run aground. One time they even saw what looked like a submarine. It was partially submerged and it might have been the bottom of a boat turned turtle. But it looked like a sub. And not an American one.

"EPIRBs are going to be lifeboats," Steve said. "We might find survivors on those."

"And then there's the third system," Stacey said, zooming in on their position and hitting the menu again. "You know that emergency GPS thingy on the Hunter?"

"Right," Steve said. "Push the button on the radio for five seconds and it sends out your location? Is that AIS?"

"No," Stacey said. "That's Digital Selective Calling. And that is ... these."

"How far?" Steve said, looking at the screen. There were at least twenty indicators on the screen.

"That's fifty miles," Stacey said. She pointed to an indicator at the bottom. "Twenty-four DSC in one hundred miles. And..." She touched another control and more dots popped up. "Sixteen EPIRBs, four AIS. So ... there. Boats and potential survivors."

"It's going to take all day to get this boat even vaguely livable," Steve said. "Then cross-loading. After that, we'll get to the real work. Thank you, milady. That would have taken me days and I'd have been tearing my hair out."

"That's why you have me around, my charming knight," Stacey said, patting him on the arm. "I'd kiss you but then I'd have to take off my respirator."

"And from the little bit that's been getting through, you don't want to smell this," Steve said. "Or me."

"And that is what saltwater showers are for..."

Steve took off his respirator and took a whiff.

"Ugh," he said, shaking his head. "*Still* stinks. What did we miss?"

"I think it's just baked in," Sophia said, grimacing.

"I think we're just going to have to get used to it," Stacey said. "Once we get moving we'll get some of the forward hatches open and air it out. Maybe that will help."

"Hopefully," Steve said. "Well, it's as good as it's going to get for now, and people are waiting. Time to cross-load..."

"What are those?" Tina said, wrinkling her brow at the small and obviously heavy cases.

"Ammo," Faith said. "Bullets."

"You've sure got a lot," Tina said. She'd asked if she could help but had been told to just keep building her strength. She still could barely totter around.

"Not as much as we used to have," Faith said, hefting two cases of 7.62x39. "And I think we're going to need lots more if Da's going to seriously clear every boat in the Atlantic."

"Can you do that?" Tina asked, following along behind as Faith carried the cases up on deck.

"One boat at a time," Faith said. "But I'm going to rebel if I *also* have to clean them all up."

Sophia sounded the bullhorn as they pulled up to the inflatable life raft. There was no response but they hadn't really expected any. They could see a zombie onboard.

"So how do we handle this?" Faith asked. She was rigged up and had her respirator on.

"Carefully," Steve said, drawing his .45. He fired twice, missing both times. The combination of the roll of the boat and the lifeboat, called "catenary," was something he was still getting used to. It wasn't something he'd trained for in the paras or since. He hit the zombie on the third try. It clawed at the wound in its stomach and dropped back into the lifeboat.

"Mark this one for later," Steve said. "He'll bleed out or die of sepsis. We'll clear it later."

"She," Faith said.

"Easier for me to just call them all he or it," Steve said, waving to Sophia. "Next beacon!"

"I don't think anybody's home," Faith said.

The lifeboat was much more substantial. There was a deck aft and a solid covered area with portholes. It was marked "Carnival Cruise Lines 4416," which meant that some cruise ship had, not surprisingly, ordered abandon ship. The one problem, indicated as Sophia had circled the boat, was that there was a hatch and it was shut. Which meant *anything* could be inside.

"Get the grapnel," Steve said. "We'll see."

Moving from the *Toy* to the lifeboat in armor was unhappy-making. The waves had increased, probably because of a distant storm, and Steve had to be careful jumping from one boat to the other. If he went in the drink, the combination of armor and equipment would carry him down fast.

"We need to figure out life vests for this or something," Steve said as he landed on the deck of the lifeboat.

He tapped the hatch with the butt of his Saiga and waited. He was fully expecting a zombie to hit the hatch running.

He opened the hatch and looked inside, then stepped back, turned to the side, took off his respirator and puked over the side of the raft.

After a bit he spit to clear his mouth, put his respirator back on and entered the cabin.

There were shots from the interior. Steve hurried back out, unhooked the grapnel and crossed back to the *Toy*.

"What were you shooting?" Faith asked.

"The deck," Steve said. "I think that's one of those no-sink hulls but it was the best I could do. I pulled the EPIRB before I shot. Hopefully, nobody else will have to see what I just saw."

1436 26JUL EPIRB 1164598, loc: 33.797409,-70.927734. Four dead, no survivors.

1623 26JUL EPIRB 2487450, loc: 33.797326,-70.926289 2KIA. Nosurv.

0814 27JUL DSC: Cost Estimate, 45ft sportfisher. Loc: 33.797298,-70.926327. 1 H7. 2KIA. Nsv. Cleared. Disabled. salvaged materials, fuel, water (see inventory). Scuttled.

"EPIRB," Sophia said from the helm. "Looks like one of those good lifeboats."

"I hate those," Faith said. "I'm getting to hating this whole idea."

"There *are* survivors," Steve said. He was starting to realize what luck finding Tina on their first boarding had been. "And it's not about how many dead we find but how many alive."

"If we find *anyone* alive," Faith said.

"Faith," Stacey said from the galley.

"Well, I keep getting rigged up!" Faith said. "And for what? There's *nobody*!"

"I survived," Tina said. She was carefully cutting up a blackfin they'd caught earlier in the day. They always had a line running behind the boat.

"I'm sorry, Tina," Faith said. "I'm just frustrated."

"What you're doing is important," Tina said. "You don't know what it's like, thinking somebody is going to come and they never do..." She paused and wiped her eyes. "And then you *did*. Faith, you're a *miracle* to somebody. You were a miracle to *me*. You just have to keep looking."

"Horn," Sophia said a minute later. She'd started to slow to come alongside.

The horn blasted, then blasted again.

"Bloody hell!" Sophia said. "Survivors!"

"Chris Phillips," Chris said, holding out his hand. "Thank you."

"Steve Smith," Steve said, taking his hand and pulling him aboard. "Are you the last off?" Steve asked.

"Last off," Chris said. "Pulled the EPIRB as you requested."

"We're going to be tight as hell," Steve said, looking at the group on the aft deck. There had been *seven* survivors from the lifeboat. "And we're going to have to be careful with rations. You're the senior officer?"

"As such," Chris said. "I was a chef onboard the *Voyage Under Stars*."

"Damn," Steve said. "No offense, but I was hoping for engineering or ship's officer."

"They scarpered long before," Chris said. "Aussie?"

"Got it in one," Steve said. "Brit?"

"Former RN," Chris said.

"Para," Steve said. "Okay, as we announced, we need to do a saltwater washdown. We got some slops from the boats we've cleared and we'll try to find clothes for everyone. Males are forward..."

"We're a bit past that," Chris said. "We'll just wash down here."

"Uh..." Steve said.

"Sir," one of the ladies said. "Captain. First, again, thank you. Second, we've been on that tiny little boat for two *months*. There is absolutely *nothing* we don't know about each other including what we look like without clothes."

"Well, then," Steve said, shrugging. "We're already rigged for washdown..."

"You'll probably get tired of us saying thank you," Paula Handley said, sipping tomato soup. Not only had they included it as a major store item, they'd found more on the *Toy* and the one other boat they'd cleared. Paula was the lady who had pointed out that group washing was not going to be an issue. In her late twenties with fine, reddish-blond hair, she looked as if she might once have been plump. Two months under starvation conditions had changed that. "But thank you, thank you, thank you..."

"Where the hell is the Coast Guard?" one of the men asked truculently.

"Gone," Faith said. She was looking nervous with all the people on the boat and had kept her sidearm. She was clearly trying not to tap it. "No shortwave from any governmental agency. The few ham radio operators on land say that they can't move outside of their compounds and spend a lot of time hiding even then. There are some towns that survived in the high arctic but they're back to basically living like Indians."

"Show a light, have a gen and you're hit by the zombies," Steve said. "I'm wondering about my brother. He had a professional fall-back point. But I just hope it was strong enough."

"Everything can't be *gone!*" the man said. "That's not true!"

"Mister... sorry, name?" Steve said, calmly.

"Isham," the man said. "Jack Isham."

"Mr. Isham, I can't prove to you that it's gone," Steve said. "But there is a shortwave receiver. I can pull up the frequencies of the few hams that are out there. If they're broadcasting. If they're not gone as well. And you can then check the Beeb, FEMA, what have you. They are *gone*. Check for yourself."

"Well, where are we going to go, then?" Paula asked, looking around. "There's not enough room on here for us to stay forever. I appreciate the hospitality, but..."

"Other boats," Steve said. "There are more. Some of them larger. For the time, we'll need to be a floating community, as it were."

"I want to get my feet on dry land," one of the women said. She was probably a well-preserved sixty and had the remains of a strong dye job. Her natural hair color was now clearly gray.

"I'd say I'd be happy to drop you off on some nearby landfall," Steve said, shrugging, "where you can compete for resources with the zombies. But we're still in clearance mode. We are, clearly, going to have to find more boats. But that is the point. There are other people out there who need to be rescued as much as you did. Once we find another boat, it will go to people who want to continue the rescue. If we find an excess, I'll be glad to turn some over to people who don't support rescuing others. They can then go do whatever they'd like. But in the meantime, there are people to be saved. We're currently on our way to another distress call..."

"'Wherever a Tardakian baby cries out...'" a young man said, grinning.

"Oh, please, Pat," Paula said, despairingly. "Not *that* again."

"Well, it's what he's saying," Patrick Lobdell said.

"I'm sorry?" Steve said.

"As Paula said, we've been in each other's pockets for two months," Chris said drily. "Pat is an SF movie nerd par excellence."

"I can quote over thirty movies," Pat said. "Verbatim."

"As he has repeatedly demonstrated," Chris said. "If I recall correctly, that was a quote from *Galaxy Quest*. One of his favorites."

"'Whenever a Tardakian baby cries out,'" Patrick said, thrusting his fist in the air. "'Wherever a distress signal sounds among the stars, we'll be there... This fine ship...'"

"'This fine crew,'" Paula said, shaking her head.

"'Never give up,'" the entire group chorused, tonelessly. "'Never surrender.'"

"Oookay," Steve said, putting his hand over his mouth to contain the chuckle. "I can see that it's a bit of a sore point..."

"And, Jack," Paula said, dangerously, "*don't* get started on football scores..."

"If you will stop talking about *sewing*," Jack snapped.

"And we're going to go back to the original discussion," Chris said firmly. "In which Mr. Smith was outlining his plan to clear... How much?"

"You want to see the EPIRB map for the North Atlantic?" Steve said. "There are over two *thousand* distress beacons. About ten percent are hard aground and, well, they're screwed."

"One boat of people cannot clear two thousand lifeboats," Isham said.

"When we find a functional boat," Steve said, "as previously noted, it goes to someone with something resembling experience and agreement to keep searching. And so on and so forth. I'd guess Mr. Phillips."

"I'm a cook, not a ship's officer," Chris protested.

"Ever conned a boat?" Steve asked. "Something this size?"

"Well, bigger, actually," Chris said. "But..."

"Sophia, what had you driven before you started conning the *Mile*?" Steve asked.

"My bike?" Sophia said from the helm. "You might remember I'm still fifteen, Da."

"Fifteen?" Paula said.

"Faith's thirteen," Steve said, gesturing to the girl lurking in the corner. "And she plowed the road out of Washington Square."

"Excuse me?" Isham said. "Washington Square Park?"

"We are four of the ten survivors from the last concert in New York City," Faith said. "Which we got out of by blowing away so many zombies you could follow our path by the bodies. So don't get me started on how hard it's going to be to clear a bunch of boats. Boats are *easy*. Hey, Patrick, is it? Bet you've played all sorts of video games. Want to fight some *real* zombies?"

"Uh..." Patrick said nervously.

"Faith," Steve said.

"No, Da," Faith said angrily. "What Tina said. They wanted to be rescued. I bet you were praying to God every *day* that somebody could come to rescue you. And now you want to... what? Curl up and *cry*? While there are people out there that *need* you? Screw *you*."

She turned and stalked out of the saloon, slamming the door behind her.

"Bloody hell," Chris said.

"Faith is a little passionate," Steve said in apology. "We don't expect any of you to go charging aboard zombie-infested freighters any time soon. You need to get your strength back. But you need to start thinking about how you can help and if you want to. If you don't... well, we'll find something to do with you eventually. For now, just rest up."

"Da, this is another sportfisher," Sophia called. "About five minutes."

"If you'll pardon me," Steve said, standing up. "It probably is a derelict but there may be some supplies."

As Sophia blasted her horn, a zombie stumbled out onto the aft deck of the yacht. Female, she was in surprisingly good health.

"I guess we'd better rig up," Faith said, drawing her sidearm. She fired one-handed and hit the zombie in the upper chest. The woman had been at the rail, clawing in the direction of the *Toy*, and flipped forward into the water. "That made things easy."

"Don't fall in," Steve said, pointing at the water. A fin cut through the water and the shark rolled over and tore into the still thrashing zombie.

"Guess not," Faith said, holstering her pistol. "I think I just figured out why you'd want a gun that shoots underwater..."

The 50-foot sportfisher, christened *Reel Fast*, had two more zombies, one dead of apparent starvation, four other dead bodies, including two children, all well gnawed, and no survivors. The dead zombie had been in the engine room and before succumbing to starvation had well and truly trashed it. The engines would probably still work but every other system was damaged. Beyond repair from their point of view.

What it did have was stores. The group had stocked up heavily and apparently been hit by the plague shortly after setting to sea. The reason the female zombie was in such good shape was that a large amount of the stores had been freeze-dried rations, ubiquitously called "Mountain House" although most of these were a different brand. Many of the boxes were in the saloon and open. The zombie had figured out how to rip them open, with her teeth from the look, and had had plenty of supplies for the voyage.

"Where'd she get water?" Faith asked after they'd pieced it together.

"Rain?" Steve said. "The self baler was stuck. There's a puddle."

"You'd think she'd get sick," Faith said, pointing to the water. It was mixed liberally with fecal matter.

"Surprising what people can survive," Steve said. "They're still homo sapiens after all. And we're a resilient species."

CHAPTER 17

"Can I help?" Chris said to Stacey.

"I don't know," Stacey said, smiling. "Can you help?"

"I may be somewhat unconfident about your husband's plan to clear the seas of zombies," Chris said, grinning, "but I am a past master of galleys the world over."

"I was just putting some sushi together," Stacey said. "We caught a big blackfin. I wasn't sure what people—"

"Please," Chris said. "It would help me to spend some time in normal conditions. I'm a chef."

"Oh," Stacey said, stepping back and raising her hands. "Go right ahead. I'm not even that good a cook."

"Do you have a primary role?" Chris said, starting to expertly slice the tuna. "I mean, your daughter . . . Sophie, is it?"

"Sophia," Stacey said. "Or Soph."

"She's the helmsman," Chris said. "The other one is the bruiser . . ."

"Call it 'clearance expert,'" Stacey said, grimacing. "I really hate it, but it's what she enjoys and she's good at it. And I guess you'd call me the ship's engineer. I'm . . . mechanically inclined. Mechanical, electrical. I'm just good at it. Geek stuff, sort of."

"I note you're all armed," Chris said.

"Is that an issue?" Stacey asked.

"No, I'd say it's wise," Chris said. "For myself . . . I spent ten years under discipline in the RN. Not great discipline, I was a cook, then a chef. But I am familiar with the need for discipline and authority at sea. Especially in small boats. I'm fine with taking orders from your husband, and you, at least for the time being. I even agree with his plan, grandiose as it seems at first glance. But others . . ." He shrugged. "Keep your weapons."

"Any particular others?" Stacey asked, quietly.

"Jack Isham owned a small manufacturing company in the States," Chris said. "Nori?"

"We packed loads," Stacey said, gesturing to a cupboard. "We figured we'd be eating a lot of sushi. When we ran out of gas for the stove . . . When we were *running* out, I boiled up a bunch of rice. And it was sushi for the next week until we got this boat."

"As I was saying," Chris said, laying out the nori. "Jack is not a bad person. But he insists on being in control. I guess it's from being his own boss for so long. So he's not going to just take orders and will, frankly, be a right pain to have around. Tom Christianson was a drug dealer taking a cruise with his stripper girlfriend. They both made it to the boat. She turned. He really didn't seem to care. Not someone who looks out for others and I suspect not someone to let into your weapons stash."

"I'll keep that in mind," Stacey said, tapping her pistol. She shook her head. "I guess it was sort of a bad idea for there to be only two of us on the boat, huh?"

"They're tired," Chris said quietly. "They're getting used to being safe. Somewhat safe, anyway. But, yes, there may be problems in the near future. Sushi." He presented the expertly arranged plate. "I'll continue on this. You probably should be near the companionway below and the helm."

"Got it," Stacey said, taking the plate. "Why? I mean, not why I should be there . . ."

"I agree with your husband's plan," Chris said. "I'd even say I'm trustworthy enough to arm, but I wouldn't suggest you believe it until I've proven it. And having survived everything I've survived, I don't want to be caught in a firefight."

"Sushi," Isham said. "That's it?" He took two, though, and stuffed them in his mouth.

"Your stomach has to get used to food again," Stacey said,

sitting down between the group and the helm. And by the companionway below. "Sushi's surprisingly easy to digest."

"We've been eating a lot of raw fish," Paula said, taking one and biting it delicately. Her face assumed a beatific expression for a moment. "With rice and nori it's *exquisite*."

"Anybody who has any energy and a strong stomach?" Steve asked. "Boat's trashed. Zombie in the engine room. But there are a lot of supplies and we can cross-load fuel and water."

"I'll help," Patrick said, standing up. "I'm not exactly feeling great but the soup helped."

"Jack?" Steve asked.

"Do *I* get a gas mask?" Jack asked, taking another sushi roll.

"Sorry," Steve said. "All out."

"Then I'll pass," Isham said.

"Anybody else?" Steve asked.

"Steve," Stacey said. "Let's hold off on cross-load. We have enough stores for now and we know which EPIRB it is. We can always come back. And there are more lifeboats to check. Just leave the EPIRB going and we'll come back. Let's get you and Faith back aboard."

Steve started to speak, then noted where she was sitting.

"Okay," Steve said. "Sophia, next EPIRB?"

"About ten miles," Sophia called. "Lifeboat."

Faith jumped aboard the inflatable life raft and cut the wire to the EPIRB with her kukri. She jumped lightly from the side onto the back deck of the yacht, then bent down and poked the fabric of the raft, holing it.

"I hate the ones that are just *empty*," Faith said as the lifeboat started to deflate.

"How many have you cleared?" Paula asked.

"I don't know," Faith said, shrugging her shoulders. "You'd have to check the log. Bunch. Clear, Da!"

"Roger," Steve said. "Next one, Soph."

"I sort of like the boats," Faith said, shrugging. She hadn't bothered to rig up for this one. "Creeping around in the dark looking for zombies may not sound like fun to most people, but it is to me."

"To each their own," Paula said, laughing. "I'll leave it to you."

"But the lifeboats and life rafts?" Faith said, frowning. "Usually everybody's dead. And usually 'cause the zombies got them. What happened with you guys? No zombies?"

"No," Paula said, her face closing up. "There were infected."

"So how'd you make it?" Faith asked. "You didn't have any guns."

"Right after we hit the water, Chris had us put on light restraints," Paula said carefully. "Just light knots. When somebody started to... turn, we could... restrain them."

"There weren't any when we got there," Faith said, then stopped. "I just realized this is something you really don't want to talk about. Sorry. Me and my big mouth."

"No," Paula said. "And, yes. I guess... I'm afraid it would be hard to understand. It's not something that we even talked about on the boat. Chris and, while he was still with us, a guy named Donnie would... take them out on the aft deck and deal with them."

"Do I want to ask?" Faith said.

"We never did," Paula admitted. "The first time Donnie and Chris took a woman, it was Tom's girlfriend. They went out back and then Donnie came back in and then a bit later Chris. And he just said he'd handled it. That happened nine times. Then Donnie got bitten and *he* turned. He stayed out on the back deck, tied up, knowing he would turn. He said he'd been special forces and he... he really went out like a hero, you know? And you could hear when he turned and Chris just went out and... Came back. And then it was just Chris. Nobody would help him with them. I... I wanted to but I... I'm not like you."

"I didn't get bitten but I screwed up and got a cut," Faith said, showing Paula her thumb, which still bore the mark of the injector needle. "Then I got into a fight with one on an elevator and the bitch bled all over me. And I got it. But I'd had the vaccine, at least the primer, and I only got a little. So I just got sick. *Really* sick. It's the worst sick you can imagine."

"I sort of saw," Paula said. "Donnie didn't go down easy. You know what was really crazy about Donnie?"

"What?" Faith asked.

"He was missing both his legs above the knee," Paula said, shaking her head. "He said he'd lost both of them in 2001. In Afghanistan. Then went through all the process to go back on active duty and went back to Afghanistan."

"That's double tough," Faith said, shaking her head. "I can only wish I was that tough."

"So . . . What was the thing about the last concert in New York?"

"We need to have a crew meeting," Steve said, poking his head out the back door. He wasn't sure what Faith had been telling the survivor, but the woman's face was dripping with tears. "You okay?"

"Oh, my God!" Paula said, howling with laughter. "I can just *see* Voltaire doing that!"

"It was sooo not my fault," Steve said. "It was *her* idea!"

"It was Uncle *Tom's* idea!" Faith said. "And at least *I* remembered my *shotgun!*"

"Anyway," Steve said. "Crew meeting. Chris is taking the helm."

"Okay," Faith said, getting up. "Work, work, work . . ."

"At least I didn't have you clean up that last boat," Steve said.

"That boat needs to be sunk, not cleaned," Faith said.

"We have a potentially serious security issue," Steve said.

"Who?" Faith asked.

The meeting was taking place in the master cabin, which was the only place outside the saloon or the back deck that would take them all.

"All of them," Stacey said.

"I like Paula," Faith said. "You're talking about them taking over the boat? I don't think she'd take over the boat."

"I like Paula, too," Steve said. "Paula, Chris, Patrick, I like all three. I'm not sure about the lady with the white hair."

"Jack's a dick," Faith said.

"But I don't fully trust any of them," Steve said. "And, yes, Jack's a dick. That was one of the big glaring holes in my plan that I can see but not really fill. There's no . . . the term is 'controlling legal authority.' There's no government to enforce anything. If one of them tries to take over, the best we're going to get is a firefight."

"There's guns," Sophia said. "And we've got all the guns."

"Which is the point," Steve said. "And we're going to have to keep it that way for a while. But that means keeping someone on the guns at all times."

"I don't want to just sit in a cabin, guarding guns," Faith argued.

"Isn't how we'll do it," Steve said. "We're going to have to hot-bunk, anyway. So . . . all four of us will hot bunk in here. With the door locked and bolted, whoever is in here will have plenty of time to respond if anyone tries to break in. Carry at all times. We were when they boarded. We're just 'one of those families.' Gun nuts. And if anyone goes for a gun, we'll deal with it."

"That's a way of putting it you might want to avoid," Faith said. "'Deal with it' has a really special meaning for these guys . . ."

"You guys have been asking about the land," Steve said as they left the next EPIRB. The life raft had held only two corpses. "We're going to kill two birds with one stone. Bermuda is about two hundred miles from our current position. We'll clear in that direction. When we get there we'll spend some time in the harbor. You can get a look around."

"I could do with a Bermuda vacation," Tom Christianson said.

Until the conversation with Stacey, Tom hadn't really been on his radar. Now he was keeping him under more or less constant covert surveillance.

"Like I said," Steve said, shrugging. "Anybody who wants to get eaten can go ashore. Up to you. This is an all volunteer operation."

"If it's all volunteer, where can I get off?" Isham scoffed.

"You want off?" Steve asked, calmly. "There's a great big ocean. Go jump in it."

"Fuck you," Isham snapped.

Steve drew his pistol, walked over and put it to the man's head.

"When I kill a zombie, I kill a human being," Steve said. "I am fully cognizant of that. Zombies are not, by a long stretch, the first people I've killed, Mr. Isham."

"Mr. Smith," Paula said, shakily. "He was just—"

"He was just being Jack," Steve said, pulling back the hammer. "Mr. Isham, there is no controlling legal authority, period. Now I've said, as soon as I can find a place to put you, I'll move you off this boat. You can go ashore. But if I put a bullet in your head right now, who can gainsay me nay?"

"Wh . . . what?" Isham stuttered. "Can you just put the pistol down?"

"No," Steve said. "That's the problem, you see. I *can't* put it down. Because I can't trust you, Jack Isham. Because you are a revolving pain in the ass, want to be the boss and contribute *nothing.* Why, exactly, *shouldn't* I put you over the side? You're just consuming stores that others need and everything about you tells me you're a threat to this boat, myself and especially my family." He pulled the pistol back, decocked it and holstered it.

"I swear to God I won't try to take over your boat," Isham said. "I mean, if you're mad about me not helping..."

"'If it's all volunteer, where can I get off?'" Steve quoted. "You've said repeatedly that you're not interested in helping others, period. You dominate and wrest for control—"

"You've been talking to Chris too much," Isham growled.

"I didn't have to have Petty Officer Phillips's confirmation," Steve said. "I don't care who or what you were before this plague. What you are, now, is a passenger on my boat. I am the captain, the chief, the boss, the head guy. And given the situation, I cannot afford or abide any threat to that authority. So, Mr. Isham, you will need to swallow your pride, swallow your sarcasm and understand that you are under discipline on this boat or I will, I assure you, put a bullet in your head and put you over the side. Do you understand?"

"You wouldn't *dare*," Isham said.

"How 'bout me?" Faith said coldly. "'Cause I really, really think you're a prick."

Isham felt the barrel of her pistol against the back of his neck and blanched.

"Ah," Steve said. "*That* you can believe, I see. Now, I'm going to give you some words to say. And if you cannot say them, then Faith *will* pull the trigger."

"Please let me pull the trigger," Faith said. "I bet you dollars to donuts this guy's hurt plenty of people in his time."

"I—" Isham said.

"Repeat after me," Steve said. "I, Jack Isham..."

"I...Jack Isham..."

"Hereby swear..."

"Hereby swear..."

"To do my level best..."

"To do my level best..."

"To quit being a prick..."

"To quit being a prick..."

"To follow the orders of the crew..."

"To follow the orders of the crew...?"

"Without the question mark, Mr. Isham and, yes, that includes the young lady with the gun to your head...to follow the orders of the crew..."

"To follow the orders of the crew..."

"Of the rescue boat *Tina's Toy*..."

"Without backtalk..."

"Or sarcasm..."

"To the best of my ability..."

"Until I can get the hell away from these nutjobs..."

"So help me God."

"You can holster, Faith," Steve said.

"Damn," Faith said, decocking and holstering.

"For everyone else," Steve said. "I was a para in the Australian Army. I am a combat veteran long before this current brouhaha. I am a naturalized American citizen. Immediately prior to the plague, I was a history teacher. I actually understand these times because they have been common in history. Oh, not zombie plagues, but similar situations. Once we have more than one bloody boat for people to be on, we can determine who gets the boat and who goes on it. And we'll do that by vote. Not that you get a vote about taking *this* boat anywhere. But when one comes open, anyone who fears for their safety with us mad people, or who is unwilling to aid in this Great Endeavor, can move to that boat. Or, as I've said repeatedly, when we approach shore you can take your chances. But until I'm assured that you are not going to mutiny, do not become a security threat. Do I make myself *very* clear? A chorus of 'yes, Captain' would be appropriate."

"Yes, Captain," the group said.

"Aye, aye, captain," Chris said from the galley. He was spinning a rather large knife. "I've got asahi coming up, if that meets with the captain's approval?"

"Thank you, Chris, that would be superb," Steve said. "The next boat that we come to, if there are no security threats, you'll be clearing the EPIRB, Mr. Isham. Clear?"

"Yeah, sure," Isham said nervously.

"Clear, Captain or Aye, aye, Captain," Steve said, trying not to sigh. "There really *is* a reason for it. So...Try it again..."

CHAPTER 18

"Toy, *this is* Cooper."

"*Cooper, Tina's Toy*, over," Sophia said.

Sophia sometimes thought about complaining that she was on the helm about fourteen hours a day. She, like, *never* got a break. The problem being, she knew she *loved* being at the helm.

They'd picked up two other boats and six more survivors. Isham, Christianson and four others who volunteered to leave had been put on one of the yachts and told they could go anywhere they wanted, don't let the door hit you in the ass and don't get in our way.

Chris was now running the *Daniel Cooper*, a 75-foot "flush deck trawler." It wasn't as cool-looking at the *Toy*, but Sophia had to admit it had more room. And it had taken less of a beating from zombies.

"*Uh, Captain Chris wants you to come over here . . .*"

"Where is here and why, over?" Sophia asked.

"*There's a big boat here. He says it's a Shewolf job.*"

"Give me your location, over," Sophia said, trying not to snort. She was actually at fault for the nicknames. She'd been talking to Paula, at the helm as usual, and telling some stories from Da's old days. His old para nickname of Wolfsbane had come up. That got changed to "Captain Wolf." Then people started calling her, Sophia, "Seawolf." So now it was "Papa Wolf" or "Captain Wolf," "Mama Wolf," "Seawolf" and "Shewolf."

She took down the coordinates, then another voice crackled over the speaker.

"Seawolf, Cooper, *over*," Chris said.

"Roger, *Cooper*," Sophia replied.

"Need to talk to your Da, over."

"Da," Sophia said, keying the intercom. "Cookie's on the horn. Says there's a boat that's a 'Shewolf job.'"

"I hate you!" Faith yelled from the saloon. She was engaged in cleaning some of the guns.

"It's not my fault you're adopted," Sophia sang out.

"I'm *not* adopted," Faith said.

"She's not adopted," Steve said, walking onto the bridge. "*Cooper, Toy* actual, over."

"Got a big job here, Toy. Forty, fifty-meter tug. Zombies, plural, on deck. Lots of corridors. Not our cuppa."

Steve had supplied Chris with some weapons to clear open boats, but not something like that. Besides, he'd expressed an unwillingness to do serious clearance. "I was a chef, not SBS."

"Roger," Steve said, thinking about it. "We're about to clear a purb. We'll vector after that."

"Roger. We're on to other clearance then?"

"Roger. Continue clearance. We'll handle the big job."

"Better you than I. Cooper, out."

"Shewolf job?" Faith said. "Big job?"

"You are about to get your wish, I think," Steve said. "Big ocean-going tug. Hundred and fifty feet or so. Zombies on deck."

"Which means zombie city," Faith said, excitedly. "Boo-yah!"

"You're too weird *not* to be adopted..."

The EPIRB had been another bust. The tug was another matter.

"Assuming it didn't run its engines out and it's diesel, that's a boomer of fuel for the taking," Steve said.

The tug was enormous. Next to it the *Toy* looked like, well, a toy. And, as reported, there were zombies on the deck.

"I can get an AK and try to shoot them off," Faith said.

"You mean *I* can try to shoot them off," Steve said. They were certainly lining up for it. "I'm a better hand with a rifle."

"Bet I get more than you," Faith said. "Bet you dishes."

"The problem is bouncers," Steve said, considering the angles. "We're going to hit low some of the time. We don't want them bouncing back. That would be unwelcome."

"I was thinking from the flying bridge," Faith said. "But if we fire from down here, they're going to bounce up, right?"

"There's a bit of a lip," Steve said, pointing to the metal bulwark. "Either way, we're going to have some come back and down. Seven six two tends to keep going, you know. Like going through your mother, going through the hull—"

"Frangibles?" Faith said.

"We're a bit short on those," Steve said. "Full-up body armor, ballistic glasses, shotgun, and hope like hell we don't kill anyone but zombies or sink the boat."

"Shotgun spreads, Da," Faith pointed out.

"It also is relatively low-velocity," Steve replied. "When, not if, it bounces, it hopefully will not go all the way through the hull. The family will rig up, everyone else below decks."

"Think you put enough holes in the boat, honey?" Stacey asked nicely. There was a large one right in one of the saloon windows.

"I'm just glad nothing worse happened," Steve said. He was finishing rigging for the entry. This time an assault pack made sense. But they'd put life vests on outside everything. They were going to have to climb a boarding ladder to get up to the tug's deck. That was going to be a new experience. "We're going to have to figure out a better way to clear zombies off the deck."

"Like water cannon maybe?" Sophia called. She'd taken off her helmet but was still in armor. And she hadn't liked it when a bouncer had come through the cabin.

"As I said," Steve said, "we'll have to find something better."

"I'll go get the fiberglass patches..." Stacey said.

"I still got more than you did," Faith said. "You're on dishes tonight."

"We need to use the dinghy for this," Steve said, grimacing. "I don't want to put the boat alongside until we can get some of those big balloon things from the tug."

"Going up there from the dinghy is going to be tough," Faith said.

"Which is why we're going to do it very carefully," Steve said. "And wear life vests."

"Pirates make this look so easy," Faith said, throwing the grapnel again. "Damnit!"

"Don't hole the dinghy," Steve said as she pulled the rope back in.

"Son of a b-blug-blug..." Faith spit out a mouthful of water and flailed at the surface. "This vest isn't... Blug!"

Given the weight of her gear, the vest was barely keeping her at the surface.

"Grab the *rope*, Faith!" Steve yelled. He was up on the deck already and dangling a recovery line to her. Fortunately, the vessel wasn't moving much in the light swells.

"Ow!" Faith said, as the hull hit her helmet and pushed her under. She managed to get a hand on the recovery line, though, and Steve pulled her back out from under the tug.

"Tell me there aren't any sharks," Faith said, flailing with one free hand for the boarding ladder.

Steve looked around and considered his answer carefully. The recently terminated infected had, after all, bled out. The scuppers were, in the old term, running with blood. And, yes, there were a few shadows. And fins...

"You might want to hurry..."

"We need a better way to get onto boats," Faith said. She was sprawled out on the deck of the tug.

"You realize you're lying in infected zombie blood, right?" Steve said.

"I sooo don't care," Faith said. "We're going to wash down when we reboard, anyway. Christ, that sucked. I was getting ready to dump my gear. If we didn't need it and if I could figure out a way to do it without taking off the vest, I would have. But all I could think was if I took off the vest I was doing the deep dive with sixty pounds of gear to take off on the way down."

"We're going to have to figure out better protocols," Steve said. "That's for sure. But we're still going to have to use the ladder."

"I hate those," Faith said. "I really do."

∾ ⊖ ∾

"Zombies, zombies, zombies!" Faith yelled, pounding on the exterior hatch with a crowbar. "Come to Papa Wolf! Zombies, zombies...And we've got customers, Da."

"Roger," Steve said, taking a free-hand stance back from the hatch. "Make sure to cover yourself with the hatch."

"Try not to nail me with bouncers," Faith said, undogging the hatch. She pulled it all the way open and hid behind it.

Four zombies stumbled out into the light, blinking.

"HERE!" Steve called, taking the first one out. "Here, here, here!"

The zombies, half blinded by the light, stumbled towards the shouts and were dropped in a line.

"All clear?" Faith asked, sticking her head around the hatch.

"Step away and we'll see," Steve said.

She moved back to his position and considered the darkened interior.

"We're really going to have problems with adjustment," she pointed out.

"I read an article where the reason that pirates wore eye patches was to keep one eye available for moving into darkness," Steve said. "Go into a hold and switch it to the other eye."

"I guess maybe we should have flip-up sunglasses or something?" Faith said.

"Maybe," Steve said. "Zombies! Hello...ZOMBIES! Anybody home?"

"Zombies, zombies, zombies!" Faith yelled, banging on the deck with her crowbar.

"Ah, that's got one," Steve said as another zombie stumbled out into the light.

"Wait," Faith said, dropping the crowbar and drawing her pistol. "We've still got more forty-five than twelve-gauge."

"Point," Steve said as she fired. "I was afraid you were going to use the crowbar."

"Been there," Faith said. "Prefer shooting them."

"Let's dog it again and check the bridge," Steve said. "Then we'll clear down from that."

"Okay," Faith said, shrugging. "Any particular reason?"

"More light up there?"

There was a zombie on the bridge. A well-fed one. Which was explained by the two corpses also on the bridge.

"So..." Faith said, tilting her head. "One was wearing clothes. The other looks like he wasn't..."

"Zombies eat each other," Steve said. "Interesting factoid."

"Whoops," Faith said as a zombie came up the companionway. She fired and it tumbled back down. But there were sounds of more stumbling in the darkness below. "Think we've got a nest here, Da."

"If we have to, retreat through the door," Steve said, stepping next to her. Another headed up the companionway and he terminated it. The following zombie stumbled over that one and then started crawling up the stairs.

Faith let her Saiga fall on its sling and drew her .45. One shot to the head terminated that one.

"I think I've got this," Faith said.

"I don't think they were all crew," Steve said, letting her take the shots. He had the Saiga up and pointed if any got past her. "This is too many for crew."

"And there are women," Faith said as she took one down.

"There are women in merchant marine," Steve said. "But... yeah. I think they took on refugees."

"Or family," Faith said, pausing. "Da?"

"Got it," Steve said, dropping his Saiga to its sling and killing the child zombie with one round of .45.

"I hate shooting the kids," Faith said. She didn't have any trouble with the grown male following.

"Here's a puzzle," Steve said thoughtfully. "Zombie up here is dead and eaten. I'd see them killing the weakest first. Why did the *child* survive?"

"You're asking *me*?" Faith said. "That sounds like a Sophia question. I think it's clear."

"We certainly made enough noise," Steve said. They'd given up on earplugs, and his ears were ringing. "We're going to go deaf with all this fire."

"I'll take deafness in old age over being eaten by zombies," Faith said, shrugging. "Why are my ears ringing in rhythm?"

"Because that's metal pinging on metal," Steve said. "I think we got us a survivor."

"*Another* salvage operation ruined!" Faith said.

"Ah, Jesus," the man said, turning away from the taclights and holding up his arm.

"Sorry," Steve said, turning the light away. The locker the survivor been hiding in had no portholes and the lights must have been like a nuke going off.

The survivor was skinny as a rail with long, shaggy hair and a beard that must have started out long and gotten longer. He was also wearing only a pair of shorts. If he hadn't responded verbally to their bangs, Steve would have thought he was a zombie.

"I'm not going to be able to see for a day," the man said. "Sorry, let me start again. Thank you."

"You're welcome," Steve said. He pulled a chemlight out of a pouch and dropped it on the floor in the compartment. "Here's some water," he said, taking the bottle from Faith and getting it into the man's hands. "We're going to keep clearing and come back when we're sure we can extract you safely. Just hang in there."

"Not a problem," the man said, taking a swig of the water with his eyes still closed. "God, that's good. God almighty, that is sooo good."

"Just hang in there," Steve repeated. "We'll be back."

"This place is a maze," Faith said, swinging her taclight around. "Do you know where we left that guy?"

"I think we're going to have to find the bridge again and follow the trail of bodies," Steve said, opening a hatch. He held his hand up to the descending sun and grimaced. "Okay, based on the bodies, this is where we first were..."

"Then the bridge ladder should be up and to the...left? Port, right?"

"Starboard," Steve said. "See why that's important on a boat?"

"Let's just see if we can find that guy again..."

"Some of the guys brought their families," the survivor said, pulling the blanket up as he sipped tomato soup. He still was wearing the sunglasses Faith had found for him. "We figured if we stayed at sea we could avoid it. Somebody, maybe a couple, were infected..."

The survivor's name was Michael "Purplefly" Braito, deckhand and assistant engineer on the oceangoing tug *Victoria's Boss*.

"Anybody else?" he asked, pushing up the sunglasses and grimacing.

"I didn't hear any more banging," Steve said. "But that doesn't mean it's *clear*. It was sort of a maze."

"Not if you know it," Braito said. "I could...Christ, I don't want to go back on, but I could help you find your way around?"

"Tomorrow," Steve said. "And we're going to need to figure out some better protocols for boarding and clearing..."

"Okay, why didn't we do this the first time?" Faith asked. She had a line clipped to her gear, which was being belayed by Steve from the deck. She'd held a line from the dinghy as he'd climbed the ladder.

"Because I didn't think about it," Steve admitted as she cleared the railing. "Makes a lot of sense in retrospect."

"So does marking everything," Faith said, pulling out a can of spray paint. "We're going to need more of this. Okay," she continued, unclipping and throwing the line over the side. "Your turn, Fly."

"Zombies, zombies, zombies?" Faith said, banging on the hatch with the butt of a knife. "Sounds clear, Da."

"Open," Steve said, taking a two-handed stance with his .45, covering the opening hatch. He'd picked up a head-lamp and had two more lights duct-taped to his gear pointing forward.

"Stuck," Faith said. The dog had released but the hatch wouldn't open.

"Crowbar," Steve said. "Carefully."

"There is no careful with a crowbar, Da," Faith said, pulling it out.

"Wait," Braito said. "There's something better..."

"I need, like, a sheath for this," Faith said, hefting the Halligan tool. "This is, like, totally made for zombie fighting."

She jammed the adze portion into the seal of the door and pushed on the bar. The hatch gapped slightly.

"There's a rope holding it closed," Steve said, shining a taclight into the interior. "No zombies. Not alive, anyway."

"Can you get the rope?" Faith grunted. "Hang on, let me—" The tool slipped, fortunately missing Steve. "I need this in farther."

"Hammer," Mike said. "And you might want me to do it next time."

"No way," Faith said, hefting the Halligan. "I *love* this thing! I wanna have its babies."

"No survivors," Steve said. Getting the hatch open had involved hammering in the Halligan, gapping the hatch and cutting the rope with a machete.

The room had held five people: male, female, three children. Now there were five corpses.

"One guy with a gun," Faith said, picking up the pistol. "Wife and kids went zombie and he killed himself?"

"Looks like," Steve said. "One of the kids is still dressed. Trapped in the room, no food, zombies outside... Murder-suicide is my guess."

"Bill Carter," Mike said, shaking his head. "He's the engineer. Sort of my boss."

"Sorry," Faith said.

"He wasn't the greatest boss in the world," Mike said. "But I sort of liked his kids. Can we..."

"We'll clear all the bodies," Steve said. "They're people. We don't do the full flag-and-sheet thing, but we give them a burial at sea. We try not to just toss them to the sharks."

"Thanks," Mike said. "That's... good."

"Onward," Faith said, spraying a C on the hatch then putting an arrow on the bulkhead next to it pointed to the nearest entry point. She shook the spray can. "I don't suppose you guys have some more of this onboard?"

"Lots of supplies," Steve said, whistling thoughtfully. The small hold was packed with cases of Number Ten cans as well as general "groceries." It looked like the back room of a grocery store except for everything being tied down under cargo nets.

"We were figuring on being at sea for a while," Braito said. "We were going to need it."

"So why the hell is she dead?" Faith asked, looking at the bloated corpse. "I think *she*. She's been dead a while."

The corpse was clothed and lying up against the bulkhead. She, probably, didn't have any evidence of wounds and was in a hold packed with food.

"Remember how sick *you* got?" Steve asked. "The *virus* kills people twenty percent of the time."

"Moving all these stores is going to be a pain in the patootie," Faith said.

"We've got cranes," Mike said, pointing up. "Open up the top hatch, winch it out."

"That... works," Steve said. "If it's flat calm."

"You can tow a tug boat," Mike said. "The main transfer is

shot but that doesn't mean you can't tow it. How far to the nearest harbor?"

"Bermuda's about a hundred miles away," Steve said. "Last time I checked the position. Put it in Bermuda harbor and call in the boats to load up? Hell, it's got enough *diesel* to keep us running for months."

"What about Isham?" Faith asked.

"I think we can spare some," Steve said.

"I hate to point this out," Braito said nervously. "But this isn't, technically, salvage."

"You don't have to finger your pistol, Mike," Faith said. They had loaned him one for his own security on the boat as well as body armor. "And it makes me nervous when you do. You don't want me nervous."

"Down, Faith," Steve said. "Mike, you can claim it as last survivor, I guess. There's no owners anymore that we know of. But what, exactly, are you going to do with it? You don't have a boat to tow it to Bermuda. It's drifting."

"I'll, you know, cut you in on it...?" Mike said.

"That's what we were looking at anyway," Steve said, shrugging.

"So...what do I get?" Mike asked.

"You mean *besides* being rescued?" Faith replied.

"What do you want me to offer?" Steve asked. "Mike, what you get in this world is what you make for yourself. I suppose at some point there will be enough people mobile that you can add 'what you take from others.' But right now all there is is either running and hiding or doing what we're doing, trying to save people like, you know, *you*. If you want some help to try to find a boat...I'm getting stingy with those, really. But I'll do that. Trade you this for a functioning yacht and as much stores as you can carry. Hell, refuel as often as you'd like until the tanks are dry. But what are you going to *do*, Mike? Keep running and looking for that one 'safe' place? Good luck finding it. I haven't heard where it might be."

"I know boats," Mike said, his brow furrowing. "I mean, I'm not a captain, but, hell, none of you are. But...I know repairs. And we've got repair materials. I don't want to go around scavenging. Being in here...It's scaring the shit out of me. I want the lights on and the whole thing cleared out. But I can repair boats..."

"Okay, we anchor the hell out of this in a protected part of

Bermuda harbor," Steve said. "And you can act as a base station? If we get a tanker or something, we'll bring it in for fuel?"

"I'm getting the feeling we need to talk about how to organize this whole thing," Faith said. "But can we finish clearing the boat first? Or do we let Fly do the rest?" she asked with a feral grin.

"Please, no," Braito said.

"There," Steve said, cocking his head. "The reason you're willing to share the boat, then."

"Point," Braito said.

"So, let's get finished clearing," Steve said, heading down the corridor. "Then we'll figure out how this is going to work in more detail. Zombies! Zombies! Any zombies...?"

"*Toy*, away team," Steve said, taking off his respirator. They were running out of filters, which was going to suck pretty soon. It wasn't bad on the deck but the air was still thick with rot.

"Away team, Toy."

"Where's the *Cooper*, over?"

"About fifty miles northeast."

"Ask them to vector here," Steve said. "There's supplies and we need to have a meeting."

"Roger."

CHAPTER 19

"Chris, I swear to God I should have just kept you as a cook," Steve said, wiping up the spaghetti sauce with garlic bread.

"It's nearly as good as that place in New York," Faith said, then grimaced. "Sorry, Chris, but—"

"Nah," Chris said, taking a bite of green beans. "I know what you mean about those places in New York. Some of those old guys are wizards. And there's only so much you can do with canned meat. Besides, much of it was Tina."

"It's great, Tina," Sophia said. Stacey had stayed on the boat after talking with Steve and giving him her proxy.

"I didn't do much," Tina said shyly. She'd transferred to the *Cooper* to get away from the *Toy*, which still had too many bad associations.

"I think I might transfer," Patrick said. He'd been acting as assistant helmsman and deck hand on the *Toy*.

"Which kind of brings up the subject of this meeting," Steve said. The saloon in the *Cooper* had enough room for most of the crowd and most people were done with dinner.

"I'd wondered what the agenda was," Chris said, arching an eyebrow.

"This is Mike Braito," Steve said, gesturing to Mike. "He's the only survivor we found on the *Victoria*. Being a professional seaman, he's been a real help with figuring out how to board without killing ourselves—"

"Hear, hear!" Faith said.

"And in finding our way around the tug. Which is full of diesel and packed with stores, by the way..."

"That's good to hear," Chris said. "We could use a refuel."

"And being a professional seaman, he also pointed out that since he was alive it's not, technically, salvage."

"I'm not saying I won't *share*," Mike said as heads swiveled towards him. He held up his hands in surrender. "I just wonder what *I'm* going to get out of it. Okay? Is that so wrong?"

"People didn't ask what they were going to get out of it when they rescued you," Paula said snappishly.

"Yes, actually, we did," Steve said.

"What?" Paula asked.

"Well, I knew there was a good chance that it would have fuel," Steve said. "And that it might have supplies. There was an— There was an economic reason to clear it. Call it logistic if you want. But there was a thought beyond 'might there be survivors.' Which brings up the point. I am going to go right on clearing as long as it takes. And I've got some ideas about how to clear the land..."

"How?" Patrick asked. "I mean... That's a lot of bullets. We don't have that many, do we?"

"No," Faith said. "We're even getting a little short on shotgun ammo."

"I said ideas," Steve said. "I'm not really willing to talk about what they are right now because they change based on what we find. But the point is... I think we need to talk about the... the theory of this whole thing. *I'm* going to go right on clearing and saving people. But how do we make some of the decisions that need to be made? What right, really, does Mike have to that boat? I'm not saying that he *doesn't* have rights. I'm saying that, face it, this is not before the plague. There are laws of the sea. But those have changed over the years. Forget the *laws*. For one thing, there's nobody to enforce them. How do we organize ourselves? Example: I said that if he wanted I'd try to find him a decent yacht and he could take as many supplies as he wanted in exchange for the tug—"

"Can we use the tug?" Chris asked. "That's a lot for a derelict. Does it run?"

"No," Steve said. "We need to tow it to Bermuda. But we'll need Mike's help to do that. But the real point is, do I have the authority to make that promise? That was the thought that crossed my mind after I said it. Chris, when we found the *Cooper*, you were the obvious choice to take it over..."

"You giving him my boat?" Chris asked.

"No, but the point is I said 'Chris, this is your boat.' I said it. And I gave Isham that forty-five footer. Is that my decision to make?"

"We're sort of following your lead, Steve," Paula said. "I don't have a problem with that."

"Uhm..." Patrick said, raising his hand. "I've sort of been thinking about that."

"Go," Steve said.

"You said you were a history professor," Patrick said. "One of the groups I was thinking about is the Italian *companeres*."

"Okay, not a reference I'd expected," Steve said with a laugh.

"*Companeres*?" Chris said, blinking. "What?"

"Simply put, they were mercenary bands during the long wars in the late Middle Ages and the Renaissance in Italy," Steve said. "They're where we get the word 'bravo,' which was what they were called individually. It just means 'the courageous ones.' They basically fought for shares and elected their leaders rather than having them appointed or fighting for lords directly."

"Ronin," Paula said.

"Ronin were radically different," Patrick said.

"They're better known and there are some similarities," Steve said. "The big difference being that *companeres* came from multiple backgrounds whereas ronin were samurai that lost their lords and had no one to be loyal to afterwards. So you're saying we should vote?"

"I think..." Patrick's face worked. "I don't explain stuff very well sometimes. But *companeres* were one of the bases of the *Star Trek* universe system."

"We're all over the map, here," Paula said, sighing exasperatedly.

"The *companeres* were sort of share and share alike," Patrick said. "Which is how the Federation was based..."

"You mean the stupid liberal 'we don't have money' bullshit?" Faith said.

"It wasn't stupid," Patrick said, shaking his head. "They had so many resources that trade in terms of money was left behind. Cory Doctorow explained it better in—"

"Stop," Steve said. "You have already done two digressions. I used to think the *Star Trek* thing was an example of Roddenberry's liberal side as well. But once I got my head around the economics it made sense."

"It does?" Faith said.

"I won't say it wasn't procommunism political speech disguised," Steve said. "But in the Federation, anything was available at the touch of a button. There weren't any basic resource restrictions. If you didn't want to work, you didn't have to. On the other hand, there was no economic drive to be, say, a starship captain. You did it because you *could* and you *wanted* to. The question I've always had is why there was a restriction on how many *starships* a group like that had. Why couldn't *anybody* have a starship if there were exactly *no* resource restrictions? But that's besides the point. And I think Patrick's point is that as we get better at clearance, resource restrictions aren't going to be an issue after a while. Patrick?"

"Right," Patrick said, pointing. "That. What you said. In Starfleet you didn't want to get promoted for the stuff. You wanted to get promoted to run stuff. To be a Star Fleet captain. Not for the money. About all you got in terms of stuff was a bigger cabin."

"How did they do promotions?" Sophia asked.

"Ummm..." Patrick said.

"Through Starfleet based on presumed merit," Steve said. "Which doesn't help us. And it's more than promotions, although that's part of it. But on that point, when we find the next boat that's useable, assuming we don't have the question of legitimate salvage, who gets it? And who decides?"

"You do," Chris said.

"Really?" Steve said. "Because the next person I'd give a boat to is Sophia."

"What?" Sophia said, her eyes wide.

"Uh..." Chris said, frowning.

"*Sophia?*" Faith said angrily.

"She has more boat handling experience than anyone else we have," Steve said, ticking off his points on his fingers. "She's engaged in the program. She's not only a good helmsman, she understands the logistics side. She's diligent and people like her.

She gets things done. Oh, I'd choose the crew carefully, but those are my points."

"Okay," Chris said, his brow furrowing. "She's kind of young—"

"Yeah!" Faith said. "And...and..."

"Faith, you don't even like driving when it's your watch," Steve said.

"Yeah, but..." she said, frowning.

"You want to do the paperwork?" Steve asked. "Figure out the fuel use? Try to figure out which EPIRB to do next?"

"Well, no, but..." Faith said. "Damnit!"

"How 'bout me?" Paula asked, cocking her head.

"There are other potential choices," Steve said. "But the best choice, in my opinion, is Sophia. Actually, if he wanted it and agreed to fully join the program, I'd now say Mike."

"Uh, I don't want to clear boats," Mike said, holding up his hands.

"Sophia hasn't cleared an actual powered boat since we started," Steve said. "My point is, Chris, you said I get to decide. Should I? I'm not saying I shouldn't. I think, for now, that's the way to go. But what's my authority? What's it based on? Saving people?"

"That's a pretty good basis," Paula said. "Why don't we put it to a vote?"

"Because if we'd put it to a vote at a certain point when Isham was onboard I might have lost?" Steve said.

"So you want to stack the deck?" Chris said.

"Not stack the deck," Steve said. "But who we get off of boats is a crap shoot. Do we automatically give them voting rights? How often do we have elections?"

"You want a charter?" Patrick said. "Like I said, *companeres*. And I was serious."

"There's no Starfleet, Patrick," Paula said.

"There wasn't with the companeres," Patrick said. "I think... Okay, pirates, then."

"Oh, great choice," Faith said, rolling her eyes. "We're not *pirates*!"

"When pirates captured a ship, they had to decide who got it," Patrick said. "And they were freebooters. They worked for shares. The shares were based on... Actually, I'm not sure what the shares were based on but they voted on the basis of their shares."

"Okay, now you're talking *my* language," Mike said. He'd been looking puzzled through the whole exchange.

"Go," Steve said.

"Lots of boats, tugs, fishing boats, are share boats," Braito said. "When you make money off something like salvage, part of it goes to the cost. Like, the food, fuel, some for maintenance. Then the profit's split between the owner and the crew. Sometimes it's not a direct split but it's pretty close. Then it's broken up. The captain gets part of the share, then the other bosses, then the crew. Usually it's the captain gets twenty, thirty percent, the other senior guys, deck boss and engineer usually, share another twenty and the hands share out the rest. Newbies don't get a share, just straight rate. To get to be share hands, they have to be voted on by the crew."

"You're talking about *Deadliest Catch*?" Faith asked.

"That's how they do their shares," Braito said, nodding. "And when you have something that's a question that the crew gets rights on having a say, they vote their shares."

"Freebooters," Chris said, rubbing his beard. "Heh. I always sort of wanted to be a pirate."

"What about larger decisions?" Steve said. "No, back to the point. Is that the way that we should organize ourselves? Does it make sense?"

"For this level," Paula said. "But your point about larger is valid. We're planning on being bigger, right?"

"And what about salvage?" Chris said. "Mike, I get the point that the *Victoria* isn't 'legal salvage.' But we need those supplies."

"I'll share, man," Mike said. "I'll even help. But I really don't want to go around clearing boats. Not my thing. Especially after sitting in that fucking hole listening to the zombies howl for months."

"Fifty percent," Steve said. "When we clear a boat, any survivors get fifty percent of the materials the boat is carrying for trade. Crew or passengers. If you were on the boat, you get fifty percent of the *material*. The *flotilla* gets the other fifty percent and the boat unless it's turned over to one of the survivors for reasons determined by . . . well, we'll get to that. Of that, some amount goes to the boat that cleared it, some to the boat that found it if it's not the clearance boat. The rest goes to support the overall flotilla."

"I can go fifty percent," Mike said, grimacing. "Do I keep the boat?"

"Mike, we're probably going to be using it for storage," Steve said. "Until we get something better. You're not going to go hungry again. You okay with that? Being the base station? And your share is fifty percent of the materials to trade if you want."

"I can do that," Mike said, nodding. "Not sure what I'll trade."

"Okay, first, do we have a second that boats organize on the basis of shares?"

"Second," Paula said. "Wait—are we voting on a shares basis?"

"Not yet," Steve said. "We have a second. Objections?"

"It's out of order," Chris said. "But before we vote, what *are* the shares?"

"Figure that out after we determine if we're going to do it on a shares basis..."

"Okay," Steve said, looking at Sophia's notes. "I think we've got the beginnings of a working governmental organization here. Each boat votes and shares materials on the basis of shares. Captains have the right to choose their crews. Crews can call for a vote of no-confidence and oust the captain, but since, if it fails, the crew can then be fired by the captain...better be careful with that. New captains are sent to the captains' board from the commodore and must be approved by a majority of the captains' board. Currently, that's me, Chris and Mike. Captains have pre-modern rules of the sea, but do *not* have the right of corporal or capital punishment. All lower order crimes, petty theft, assault, fighting among the crew, are handled at the discretion of the captain of the boat. All higher order felonies, notably rape, mutiny or murder, must have a trial by jury or, if that's infeasible, agreement of three captains who have been shown good evidence. Captains follow the orders of the...Agh, 'commodore,' currently one Steven John Smith, captain of the *Tina's Toy,* in all normal day-to-day operations of the flotilla.

"Newly rescued persons do not have the right to vote until agreeing to become members of the flotilla *and* being accepted as full crew members. All large decisions are by vote of the captains' board or all flotilla members, depending. More complete charter to be written up at a later time. Charter to be voted on by *straight* vote of all members of the flotilla. And I foresee a couple more meetings, at least at long range. Persons who choose not to be with the flotilla will be organized in groups and then at some point put off on functioning boats to do whatever the hell they want."

"Shunning," Paula said.

"Should such persons attack or steal from the flotilla... Pretty much all we've got right now is shunning or capital punishment. Cross that bridge—"

"Motion," Chris said. "I motion that this organization hereafter take the name Wolf's Floating Circus. Can I get a second?"

"Damn," Patrick said. "I was hoping for Sea Quest."

"Second," Paula said. "Get me a screen printer and I can make an awesome T-shirt for that!"

"I think you need to call for a vote," Chris said, grinning.

"I'm trying to remember Robert's Rules of Order to see if I can quash it," Steve said, frowning. "Okay, okay, all in favor?"

"Well, that was a pain in the ass," Steve said as the *Victoria* dropped its final anchor in Jew's Bay.

Tug operations turned out to be anything but straightforward. Trying to do it with an untrained crew had turned out to be a right pain in the ass.

But they'd finally gotten the tug into place. Jew's Bay was about the most protected spot in the complex of islands that made up "Bermuda." At least the most protected that they could tow the *Victoria* into safely. There were some tighter and better protected creeks, but there was no way they were getting the *Victoria* into them.

The edges of the bay were littered with small craft, proof that "sheltered" was a relative term. The tropical storm that had made their life hell had driven them all onto the islands. And while there were "open" areas, areas free from obvious zombies, on the surrounding islands, just scanning they could see zombies moving around. Not much and not aggressively. But zombies were there.

As soon as all of the anchors on the *Victoria* were down, the *Cooper* moved up cautiously alongside. The new crew of the *Victoria*, four volunteers who had been "supernumerary" on the *Toy* and *Cooper*, started inexpertly throwing balloon "fenders" over the side. As one that was badly secured fell in the water, "Captain Mike" started bellowing from the wheelhouse.

"One of these days we will find real professionals to figure this out," Steve said.

"That'll be the day," Sophia said.

"But to do that, we need to clear more boats," Steve said. "As soon as we're replenished . . . Back to sea."

"Da," Sophia said quietly. "You're serious about me taking a boat?"

"I'll need to find the right crew," Steve said. "I don't want you kidnapped in a mutiny. But, yeah. We need captains. And you've got more experience than anyone but Chris and Mike. And Mike's content to sit on the *Victoria*. So . . . yeah."

"Thanks, Da," Sophia said.

"Thank me after you've had the responsibility for a while," Steve said, rubbing his forehead.

"You okay, Da?" Sophia asked.

"There are people dying out there, right now," Steve said. "There were people dying that we could have saved a long time ago. I'm regretting just hiding for so long."

"We'll get there, Da," Sophia said.

"Toy, Victoria," Mike growled over the radio.

"*Toy*," Sophia responded.

"*Now that we've got this ratfuck cleared up, come alongside port. We'll start filling you up.*"

"Roger, *Vic*," Sophia said. "Da, you want to get ready to handle the lines?"

"Yes, ma'am," Steve said, grinning.

"While we're here," Steve said, looking at the coast of the nearby island.

"What are you thinking?" Stacey asked.

"Nothing worse than going to a concert . . ."

Steve slipped over the side of the dinghy into the water carefully. All he was carrying was a pistol in the event there were some zombies around. Mostly, he planned on out-swimming them if it came to it.

"One last time," Faith said. She was rigged up in case swimming didn't work. "You sure about this?"

"I can see the utility," Steve said. "I think it's a good idea. If I can't find any or I get eaten, it was a bad idea."

He quietly swam ashore, keeping an eye out in every direction he could. The zombies seemed to barely notice human activity in the harbor except at night when there was light. Then they'd lined the harbor, trying to find a way to the boats.

There was plenty of junk along the shore but what he was looking for wouldn't be found there. He let his nose do the work for him, moving carefully through the sea-grapes of Gamma Island, following the smell of rot.

It was, unsurprisingly, a human corpse. Probably a zombie that had lost the zombie-eat-zombie battle of survival. And very putrid. It was covered in flies, which weren't of interest to him. But it was also covered in small black beetles.

Those he collected, quickly, and popped into a ziplock bag.

He stopped as he heard movement in the trees and looked up. There was a zombie crouched under the bushes. A young black woman. She was regarding him ferally, apparently trying to work out if he was worth attacking.

Steve stood up, slowly, and then leaned forward, raising his shoulders and grunting at her.

She ducked back into the bushes and disappeared.

Steve snuck back through the bushes, trying not to think about the interplay in which he'd just engaged. He had to pay attention to keeping alive. But it was interesting, nonetheless...

"Seriously?" Faith said, looking at the beetles crawling over the tuna guts. "That's it?"

"You'll see," Steve said. "They'll be useful."

CHAPTER 20

"We've got survivors on this one," Sophia called over the intercom. "Life raft. Looks like two people. People, people."

"Roger," Steve said, looking up from his paperwork. He'd known there was going to be paperwork, but there had to be a better way.

They'd been clearing for two weeks since towing in the *Victoria* and picked up two more useable boats. Both had survivors, and a) they had agreed to help out and b) they were experienced and c) it was their boat. So Sophia was still running the con. They also had found more than twenty survivors in life rafts and lifeboats, including more from the *Voyage Under Stars*.

Steve didn't even sway as Sophia swung the boat around to back up to the life raft. He did check his pistol and taser, though. A couple of the survivors had been problems. They'd settled by pulling two wrecked sailboats off the shore of Jew Bay and putting them on those, solidly anchored in the harbor. One for men, one for women. That had come about due to the accusation on the part of one of the female survivors that she'd been raped by one of the males. And it just made sense. Mike didn't think that he'd want to be on those boats, but there wasn't much else they could do at the moment.

Steve stepped out onto the back deck as Sophia backed up towards the life raft.

"Throw your line to the man on the deck," Sophia said over the loud-hailer. "Exit junior person first, senior last. Last person out, pull the wire on the EPIRB before boarding. After boarding you'll have to wash down on the back deck to decontaminate. After that we'll get you some food. By the way, welcome to Wolf's Floating Circus and Rescue Flotilla. You're welcome."

The man threw the line, then pulled the wire from the EPIRB. Steve pulled the raft alongside and helped the woman onto the deck, then the man.

"Thank you," the guy said. He wasn't exactly ugly looked at in the right light. But he wasn't a beauty, either. Big as hell, his skin was flat black as an ace of spades. "Who's Wolf?"

"My actual nickname in the paras was Wolfsbane," Steve said. "Got around due to one of my daughters and got changed to Wolf or Papa Wolf. Steve Smith, captain of the *Tina's Toy* and, somewhat against my will, and I quote, 'commodore' of this lashup. And the name wasn't my idea."

"I really don't care if you're called the Devil's Own," the woman said, grinning. "I'm just *so* glad to be off that boat! I'm Sadie Curry, Captain Smith."

"Thomas Fontana," the man said. "Paras... Not Brit or Irish. Aussie with lots of time in the States. *Southern* States. Paras or SAS?"

"Paras," Steve said, surprised. "Brother was a goldie."

"Sorry," Thomas said, shrugging. "Any idea on him?"

"Last I heard he was on a flight to a secure point," Steve said. "Long story. Let's get you washed down and some food in you..."

"There is probably something worse than being stuck on a cruise ship, unarmed, in a zombie uprising," Fontana said, popping two sushi rolls in at a time. "Food..." he muttered past the mouthful.

"Thomas was special forces?" Sadie said. "I think I got that right. I didn't know anything about the Army until we ended up on the... raft." She grimaced and shrugged. "That was right, Thomas? Green Berets?"

Fontana nodded, trying to clear his mouth of rice and tuna. He took a sip of tea and just sighed through his nose.

"God, this is good," he muttered.

"Most of the boats from the cruise ships are, well, boats," Stacey said.

"I couldn't make it to one," Fontana said. "There was an open door and I went out. Outside. There were rafts in the water—"

"I was running from a zombie and he saved me," Sadie said, grabbing his arm. "My hero."

"I threw him over the side," Fontana said, shrugging. "Then I had to deal with him when we went over. But we got into a raft. There was another guy, Terry—"

"Can we skip that?" Sadie asked, looking pleafully at Steve. "He had to do what...He had to do it. He...turned."

"Strangulation?" Steve asked, taking a sip of tea.

"Yeah," Fontana said, looking at him oddly.

"The only people who have survived in the lifeboats are people who have killed zombies," Stacey said, shrugging. "And generally the only way to do that is strangulation. On a life raft you can't even avoid it."

"It was horrible," Sadie said, tearing up.

"Most of this world is," Steve said. "But it has some compensations."

"What?" Fontana asked.

"We're doing good work?" Steve said. "The sea is beautiful when it's not trying to kill us."

"Need help?" Fontana asked. "I sort of need to get some food in me, but if I can help I'd like to."

"We always need help," Steve said. "What did you do in the—Rangers, was it?"

"Bite your tongue," Fontana said. "Fifth special forces group. I was an Eighteen Bravo. Cross train in Eighteen Echo and Delta. Six times in the Stans, some training time in Africa. You?"

"Rifles sergeant," Steve said. "Also in the Stans. Then later a history teacher. Question: did you happen to know someone named 'Donnie' who was a special forces officer?"

"Know him, no," Fontana said. "He was out before I joined. But I've heard of him. Missing both legs?"

"He was, unfortunately, a casualty," Steve said, nodding. "Okay, I'd say you're in."

"No, I'm not a poser," Fontana said, grinning. "And I notice your wife's wearing a pistol and you're wearing a pistol and taser. Still. Problems?"

"Some," Steve said. "But we deal with them as they come along. How do you feel about clearance?"

"With a crowbar?" Fontana asked. "Not so happy. With a firearm? Please!"

"Are you sure, honey?" Sadie asked unhappily.

"We're not going to send him in unprepared," Steve said. "Among other things, we still have some vaccine. That goes first to clearance personnel. And we're careful to avoid bites and blood spray. But we do need more people willing to do active clearance. We have two vessels waiting for clearance teams. We were on our way to one of them. And right now it's only myself and my daughter doing it."

"You're afraid if you give me a gun I'll try to take over," Fontana said, nodding. "Makes sense. All I can say is that until something better comes along, I'm your man. I'd like to get a piece back from these zombies. And I'm seriously missing my gun collection. The one thing I'd like to know, though, is there anything in it? I mean, I'll help out but what is it, share and share alike?"

"More or less," Steve said. "Clearance teams get a spif on every boat they clear. Besides first choice of loot, which is pretty obvious. The real question is, how open-minded are you about your partner...?"

"So, how do you usually handle this?" Fontana said, trying not to be amused by the thirteen-year-old girl in full assault rig.

"Usually like this," Faith said, drawing her H&K. She measured the catenary carefully and shot the zombie clawing at them from the back deck of a 60-foot fishing boat.

The round hit the zombie high on the right chest. It clawed at the wound for a moment, then slipped on its own blood and fell over the side.

"Then the sharks take care of it for us," she said.

"Works for me," Fontana said. "You got a handle?"

"Shewolf," Faith said, reloading the expended round in her magazine, then seating it again. "Got a problem with that?"

"No, *ma'am*," Fontana said.

"Seriously?" Fontana said, as he levered open the stuck hatch. "I'd heard of Voltaire but I never really got into that kind of tunes."

"Seriously, it was a hoot," Faith said as a zombie arm clawed out of the compartment. "Hang on a sec." She lifted her Saiga and put it to the doorway. "'Ware bouncers."

"Roger," Fontana said, holding the hatch gapped.

"You want some?" Faith said, firing the Saiga. The arm started spasming. "Who else? Huh?"

"Watched a lot of *Aliens*, have we?" Fontana said.

"Love that movie. *You*? *You want some...*?"

"Wait," Faith said, holding out her hand as Fontana started to step over the coaming.

"Looks clear," Fontana said, flashing his tactical light around the compartment.

"Zombies do not like impolite people," Faith said. "Always announce your presence. ZOMBIES, ZOMBIES, ZOMBIES! OLLY OLLY OXENFREE!"

"That is so...wrong," Fontana said.

"You're used to trying to sneak up on people," Faith said as there was a scuffling sound. "There..." The zombie was emaciated and clearly on its last legs. She put a round through the infected's chest as it stumbled towards the lights.

"Where the hell did it come from?" Fontana said, waving the light around again.

"Da thinks they spend a lot of time sleeping really deep to conserve energy."

"So...make enough noise to wake the dead?" Fontana said, chuckling.

"Something like that. ZOMBIES, ZOMBIES, ZOMBIES... COME TO SUPPER!"

"I wonder what most of this stuff does?" Fontana said, looking around the engineering compartment. "I mean, obviously, there's the engines—"

"Yeah," Faith said. "Never futz with the engineering compartment. If there's a zombie in it, let it out and take it out in the corridor. You get one bad round in engineering and you don't know what's going to go wrong."

"I think we need a manual," Fontana said.

"I think we need to find a SEAL or something who *knows* how to do this..."

"Pistol," Faith said, shaking her head as the zombie came up the companionway.

"Ooo-kay," Fontana said, changing weapons. He put a round into the zombie's chest, then went for a double-tap and missed the headshot.

"Damnit," Faith said, ducking back as the round caromed off the deck and, fortunately, into the darkness below. "That's why I said *pistol. One* round. Targeted! One zombie, one round, no bouncers!"

"Roger," Fontana said. "Sorry."

"I shouldn't have snapped," Faith said. "I sunk a boat that way, though..."

"How many times have you *done* this?" Fontana asked.

"I dunno," Faith said, drawing her H&K and tagging the next zombie coming up the companionway. "I'd have to check a log. Boats this size only...three. Small yachts? Twenty or so?"

"Jesus. And there I was floating around in a raft."

"So, now, we use Da's superty-duperty new gimmick," Faith said, looking at the beetles askance. They were clambering around the interior of the bag—that made her more ill than bloated zombie bodies.

"Think it will work?" Fontana asked dubiously.

"He said give it a few days and leave the interior hatches open," Faith said, dropping the beetles into the interior and shutting the exterior hatch. "We'll see..."

"Holy cow," Steve said as they approached the target boat.

"Oooh," Sophia said. "Can I have *that* one?"

It wasn't so much that the boat was large; the *Victoria* was larger. It was that it was just enormous and *beautiful*. Sleek as hell. It looked fast *and* it was *darn* big.

"It's probably trashed," Steve said. "And it'd be a bitch to maintain."

"I'll do it," Sophia said.

"You sound like you're asking for a puppy," Steve said. "Besides, *I* want it. The problem will be finding anybody who knows how to run the engine room. And it will be up to the captains' board. Assuming it's not trashed."

"No zombies on deck," Sophia said, circling the drifting yacht. "Did they even *board*?"

"*His Sea Fit*," Steve said. "I'll go get rigged up."

"I'm going to turn over to Paula," Sophia said, picking up the intercom mike. "You're going to need somebody who knows how to run the dinghy."

"Dinghies and lifeboats are all gone," Steve said, boarding the yacht on its flush transom deck. It was just about the easiest boarding he'd done in some time.

"Did they abandon ship?" Sophia asked.

"You tell me," Steve said.

"Want me to back you up?" Sophia asked.

"Up to you," Steve said. "You're not in armor, and if there are bouncers that's an issue."

"I'll take my chances," Sophia said, tossing him the mooring line. "This I want to see."

"Oh, Da, I want," Sophia said, sighing at the helm.

The 92-foot Hatteras Elite dubbed *Livin' Large* was only about thirty feet longer than the *Toy*, but that made a huge difference. And the interior was that much nicer. Not to mention being in *much* better shape. In fact, except for signs of rapid exit from the boat, there appeared to be no damage at all.

"Log," Sophia said, pulling out a standard logbook and flipping to the last page with writing, then flipping back. "Chief engineer and a mate went zombie. According to the log they're locked in the crew compartment. Ran out of fuel. No power. The rest of the people abandoned ship off an island in the Bahamas and went ashore." She flipped through a couple more pages then shrugged. "I think this is valid salvage. And really *nice* salvage. I can't believe they abandoned ship."

"Which island?" Steve asked.

"Great Sale Cay?" Sophia said.

"Occupied," Steve said. "Well, if we ever run into them, and if they survived, I'll have to thank them. Now to check for zombies..."

"I don't hear anything," Steve said, banging on the hatch again. Chairs had been barricaded against it but they had been easy to clear. The rest of the ship, absent the crew compartment, was clear. And again, except for the debris of rapid exit, remarkably clean.

"You're the expert, Da," Sophia said nervously. She had a

headlamp and a flashlight but she was still keeping an eye behind them. "You and Faith *enjoy* this?"

"Faith does," Steve said. "'Enjoy' would be too much of a stretch for me." He levered the hatch open and flashed a light inside.

"Anybody home?" Sophia asked.

"Not alive," Steve said, stepping into the compartment. One of the bodies had been partially eaten. The other was cut and bloated but didn't appear to have died from violence.

"Probably the one killed the other, then died of dehydration," Steve said checking the toilet. It was empty of water. "Which makes this perfectly legal salvage. Not to mention easy to clean."

"That's going to be nasty," Sophia said, looking in the room. "Oh, gross!"

"Yeah, that's not the worst I've seen by a stretch," Steve said, taking out a baggie. "We'll just seal the room up fairly tight. Vent it to the rear. And let these do their work." He dribbled the beetles on the corpses. "Say hello to my leetle friends..."

"Steve, these are *way* beyond me," Stacey said, looking at the engines.

"We've got fuel in the tanks," Steve said. "Some. And a jumper battery. Can you get them running?"

"I don't know?" Stacey said. "I mean, that's the *point*. These are huge professional engines! I'm not sure where to *start*!"

"I think that's the start button," Sophia said, pointing.

"I can see *that*, Sophia," her mother said tartly. "Just let me look over the manuals..."

Steve looked up at a rumble from below. A moment later the lights in the saloon came on.

"I knew I married that girl for a reason..."

"Think you can get that alongside without wrecking it?" Mike called over the radio.

"Trying," Steve said to himself. He wasn't going to pick up the radio when he was trying to con the *Large* up to the *Victoria*. The *Large* really was. And it had a lot more sail area than the *Toy*. He picked up the radio. "Just have the bloody balloons down."

"There is no such thing as too slow..." he muttered.

∽ ⊖ ⌒

"That wasn't the worst coming-alongside I've ever seen," Mike said, looking around the interior. "Say, you know how you told me I could have a boat...?"

"We'll have to call a captains' conference," Steve said. "This is, among other things, going to take some serious crew..."

CHAPTER 21

"I think the *Large* needs to be a harbor queen for now," Steve said over the radio. "It drinks fuel, we don't have that many people that we need a boat this size, and it's a bitch to actually use. If we did use it I'd see it as an at-sea base. If we can find enough fuel for it."

"*Cooper* here," Chris said over the radio. "I can see that, but what about theft?"

"Just about out of fuel," Mike said. "We'll drain it down and it's not going anywhere. Leave it alongside the Victoria. We might have a use for it later. It runs, anyway."

"*This is* Endeavor. *We're getting beat up in this minnow. Could use a bigger boat.*"

Stephen Blair, the sole survivor of the 35-foot Viking *Worthy Endeavor*, had had issues from the beginning. But he'd also cleared more than forty rafts and lifeboats since taking over the battered ship.

"*Endeavor*, Seawolf," Sophia said. "You do *not* want to con this thing alongside a raft. Concur, Da, this is a support ship. Better in harbor for now."

"*Endeavor*," he thought for a second about the growing fleet. "*Sea Fit*. You are both next up for a bigger vessel. Will determine that when available. But this is a *monster*. Any likely candidates?"

225

"Endeavor. *We just relayed another. About sixty-five. Wouldn't mind if it's useable.*"

"Do we have a location on that?" Steve asked.

"Yeah," Mike said. "Back at the *Vicky.*"

"I've got it on the *Toy,*" Sophia said.

"My recommendation," Steve said. "Use this for harbor base. Staff with reliable personnel. Bring in new personnel for rest and recovery prior to assignment. Comments and response for vote? *Sea Fit.*"

"*I'm fine on my boat for now,*" Captain Sherill replied. George Sherill, sole survivor on the 35-foot Bertram, was less than enthusiastic about ever seeing another zombie in his life. Possibly because the entire "charter" he'd had had zombied on him. "*And, yeah, that sounds like a plan.*"

"Endeavor?"

"*We need a bigger boat,*" Blair replied. "*But agree.*"

"Knot?"

"*I'd go for a bigger boat,*" Gary Loper of the *Knot So Little* replied. "*I guess I'm next after Blair?*"

"Other discussion," Steve said. "Not saying no, just later discussion. Agree leave *Large* harbor for rest and refit?"

"*Yeah, I can go with that. But about a larger boat?*"

The truth was that Steve didn't think that Loper and his crew *deserved* a larger boat. They just seemed to be cruising around and coming in from time to time to draw on supplies.

"Captains' vote for next upgrade," Steve said. "Cannot nominate self." He thought about it for a second and tried not to grimace. He knew he was playing politics. By the real rules, Blair should be the first to nominate. But if he nominated Loper, which was the only real choice, others might follow. But Sherill not only liked his boat, small as it was, but liked Blair.

"*Sea Fit.*"

"*Blair from the* Endeavor," Sherill replied, instantly.

"*Endeavor.*"

"Seawolf," Blair replied.

"Seriously?" Sophia asked.

"*Knot So Large.*"

"Uh...Seawolf."

"Damn," Sophia muttered.

"*Daniel Cooper.*"

"*Blair.*"

"That bastard," Sophia said.

"*Victoria.*"

"Blair," Mike said into the radio.

"Thanks for the vote of confidence!" Sophia said.

"You don't get it, do you?" Mike said, grinning. "You're going to get the *Endeavor.*"

"Oooh," Sophia said, then grimaced. "It really *is* small."

"It's a good learning boat," Steve said. "*Tina's Toy* abstains. Any votes against Captain Blair for the next upgrade...? The ayes have it. Next good boat goes to Captain Blair and his chosen crew. Any old business we really need to cover, 'cause I'm going to have to head out to that sixty-five?"

"*Commodore,* Cooper," Chris said. "*We're in position and have Clearance team bravo. Will vector to clear.*"

"Roger, *Cooper,*" Steve said, trying not to let the surprise enter his voice. He'd started to forget he didn't have to do it all.

"*You don't have to do it all, Comm,*" Chris said.

"Any other business?" Steve asked.

"*We'd like a bigger boat as soon as possible,*" Loper said.

"We'll discuss that when the question comes up," Steve said. "Anything else?" He looked over as Mike raised his hand. "*Victoria.*"

"We're burning an awful lot of diesel," Mike said over the radio. "I mean, try to refuel from derelicts if you can, or tow them in here and we'll get it out. But we're going through diesel like crazy."

"Keep an eye out for small tankers," Steve said. "Anything else critical?"

"*Can we get some of that vaccine?*" Loper called. "*Some of my crew are asking.*"

The radio tech leaned forward, clamping his earphones to his ears.

"What?" Petty Officer Second Class Stan Bundy asked, picking up his own set.

The Los Angeles Class attack boat SSN 900, USS *Dallas,* had been tracking the formation of this "at-sea militia," as it had been classified, for the last three weeks, ever since radio communication between multiple boats between Bermuda and the U.S. had been detected.

"*Vaccine,*" Electronics Mate Harry Fredette whispered.

$\backsim\!\ominus\!\backsim$

"Son of a bitch!" Steve swore, then keyed the radio. "Okay, *Knot*, first of all, *thanks* for bringing any pirates that may still exist down on us. Like we covered, that is *not* for discussion over the radio. But since we're discussing *something*, no, the supply is *limited* and it is *only* for clearance personnel. You want some, do some clearing. Or, even, maybe, pick up some *survivors!*"

"Upload this for priority exam," Bundy said, hitting a key and backing up the recording..."

"Hey, we're busting our ass out here in this dinky little boat and we don't need your shit, 'Commodore'! We've been clearing these damned lifeboats. There's nobody home."

"Loper, you're full of shit," Blair called. *"We've cleared twenty lifeboats in the last couple of days. And, yeah, there's not much. But we've picked up* six *people. On our even dinkier boat..."*

"Clear the channels," Steve said as the channel got cluttered with people screaming at each other. "Clear the... Ah, shit."

"Christ, I want to cut in."

Commander Rex Bradburn was frustrated, angry and scared. Which described his entire crew. They'd started to sea before the plague was spread and had remained at sea since. Because to make contact meant dying. Like their families on shore.

But a sub could only stay at sea for so long. Sure, the pile would last twenty years, more if you only used low power. But all the other systems? Not to mention food. They had gone on short rations as soon as they found out they were on "extended deployment." That only lasted so long. And that went for all the surviving boats. Some of them had already dropped off the screen, just lost. Possibly mutinied but more likely something vital broke at the wrong time or the wrong depth. Others had snuck into deserted harbors and put their crews ashore to survive as best they could.

But if they had *vaccine*...

"Monitor only, sir," Lieutenant Commander Joseph Scholz reminded him.

"Knot So Little," Steve said as the shouting died down. "We still don't have a protocol for this. But I think that a captains'

vote would be sufficient. If you don't start showing that you're working the problem, I see no reason for you to get diesel or fuel. You can put some welly in it or turn over your boat and join the lost and useless. Or try to make it without clearance teams."

"*Just 'cause you got all the guns doesn't make you God, Commodore.*"

"You've got guns," Steve replied. "I gave you two pistols for light clearance. Which as far as I can tell you haven't used and, yes, I'll take those back as well. So it's up to you and your crew. You're either in or out. You want to take off, we'll accept the pistols back, fill your boat and you can take off. But that's it. Or you can work the problem. Or you can turn over your boat. Or, hell, you can take off right now and I'll spot you the pistols. What you *cannot* do is continue to draw on supplies while not contributing. So I'm giving you two weeks. Start working the EPIRBs instead of hanging out on the back side of the island and playing Bermuda vacation or no more supplies. Do I make myself clear?"

"*I hear you.*"

"To all, make this clear," Steve said. "Make it clear to the people you pull in. You're either working to help, somehow, or you're not. If you're not, you get to go hang out on a sort of beat-up boat with a lot of other useless people. We'll feed you. That's it. How you get along otherwise is up to you. If, like the *Knot*, you've got a boat, you can go away. But we're not going to supply people with diesel and other support who are not working the problem."

"*You know there's fucking zombies on these boats, right?*" a voice screamed.

"*No shit, Sherlock...*"

Steve leaned back as the voices overlapped.

"*'Commodore,' this is the* Knot. *We'll take the supplies. We're done with your shit.*"

"Roger," Steve said. "Come into harbor. One fuel load and one ton of supplies, *Victoria*'s choice. If you come back for more, you trade your boat and join the lost and useless. This captains' conference is now closed."

He leaned back and shook his head.

"That could have gone better," Steve said.

"He picked a bunch of losers just like him," Mike said. "I

think you were right the first way round. Just because they're onboard, doesn't mean they get the boat. I mean..." he said, looking around.

"Your boat, Mike," Steve said, grinning. "Nobody has an issue with that. Hell, if you want to doss on the *Large* nobody's going to have an issue. I don't think. You going to have problems with the *Knot*?"

"I don't think so," Mike said, shrugging. "Can I have one of those shotguns?"

"How 'bout an AK?" Steve said. "They're about useless for clearing and people are afraid of them."

"That'll work," Mike said. "I don't see them getting uppity with an AK staring them in the face."

"How well do you trust your crew?" Steve asked.

"Fine," Mike said. "It's like training cats but they're learning. I mean, the basics. I wouldn't trust them running this at sea but until we can find a main transfer coil for it, it's not going anywhere."

"I'll leave you two AKs," Steve said. "Have the supplies ready to load. Don't let them board and if they have an issue with that, you've got the AKs. Make sure there's no fuel in this one, either."

"I'll do better than that," Mike said. "I'll pull the mains breaker."

"Do we have any idea where they got vaccine?"

Frank Galloway was the National Constitutional Continuity Coordinator. Prior to that he had been Under Deputy Secretary of Defense for Nuclear Arms Proliferation Control.

The post of National Constitutional Continuity Coordinator had been created in 1947 after it became obvious that the entire upper echelon of government could be taken out by one atomic bomb. There was a chain of civilian control that went deep. This was not the "presidential succession" defined in the Constitution, but a guarantee of continued civilian control of the military in the event of global nuclear war or, say, laughably, a zombie plague. The NCCC's job was to keep things in some reasonable order, or restore order, so that there could be an election again.

Right now, he was stuck sixty feet underground in Omaha, Nebraska, surrounded by zombies.

Shortly after 9/11, the various departments that the NCCC succession went through had taken to quietly rotating people into secure points around the U.S. Not only the DoD had such facilities. They'd become a bit of a cachet in the inner circles of government. You weren't *seriously* important unless you had a secure facility. During the Cold War, in the threat of imminent nuclear obliteration, only the Department of Defense, the President and Congress had secure facilities.

By the time of the H7D3 virus even the *FDA* had one.

Of course, wouldn't you know, the only ones that *hadn't* been taken down by the virus were the Hole and CDC. Which left one Frank Galloway, career DoD nuclear war specialist, as the NCCC. Just ahead of the surviving senior officer of the CDC who was *also* on the list. And they came after all the state governors.

It didn't help that he was only thirty-three. His Russian counterpart was nearly seventy and a former KGB nuclear security officer.

"No, sir," Brigadier General Shelley Brice said. The former Assistant Deputy Commander of Strategic Armaments Control was one of the few female generals in the Air Force. A former B-52 driver, she had been part of the movement to recreate Strategic Airforce Command after it became clear that when the Air Force took its eyes off of their nuclear weapons, bad things had happened. Notably, in 2007 an outside inspection by the International Atomic Energy Agency determined that over thirty weapons were "unaccounted for." The head of the Air Force Department was fired and SAC was reborn.

The "rebels" hadn't managed to, quite, retake the high ground but they'd at least gotten full control of the nukes as well as their storied acronym. And they'd gotten the Hole.

And now, well, they'd absolutely taken over the Empire. What was left of it.

She'd been the Flag Duty Officer when the orders to lock down had come in. As far as she could tell, she was now the senior surviving officer in the entire United States military. First Female Commander of the Joint Chiefs of Staff. The Big Cheese. Admittedly, of nothing but some submarines.

Her Navy counterpart was a commander who was now, apparently, the CNO. Or, and this had been a low-level, everybody recognized as sort of pointless discussion, a boomer commander in the Pacific might be since he had the local guy by date of rank. Actually, *six* boomer commanders had him by date of rank.

There was also an Army colonel who was a pretty decent sort and damned good at poker and a Marine lieutenant colonel she suspected had been shoved off to a nothing post because nobody in the Marines could understand how he made lieutenant colonel in the first place. And the fact that he used to not only be a nuclear weapons maintenance officer but security commander for a storage facility sort of scared the shit out of her. Total flake.

"There were the news reports that some groups had been producing clandestine vaccine from human remains," the flake said. Lieutenant Colonel Howard Ellington twitched right after speaking, one of his habits that had Brice right on the edge of murder.

"CDC?" Galloway said. "Comment?"

"It was doable," Dr. Dobson said. "And, quietly, it was recognized in the immunology community that some people were doing it. By that I mean people with degrees who were in some sort of position to get the...materials. Which, admittedly, was being an accessory to murder. Given how things ended up going...I'm not going to point fingers or condemn. It wasn't even particularly hard to do, and much, much faster than the alternatives. Frankly, if we'd just...processed those who became full neurological from the beginning we probably could have stopped this in its tracks. But nobody, then, was willing to even consider it. In retrospect..."

"That's a hindsight I'm not sure I want to explore," Galloway said.

"We may have to, sir, with respect," General Brice said.

"Explain," Galloway said.

"If we're going to get vaccine to the uninfected crews... There aren't a lot of other choices," Brice said. "I don't see anyone being able to produce the...Dr. Dobson...?"

"What the general is saying is that the attenuated vaccine is *relatively* easy to make," Dobson said. "Not easy, and there are dangers. But it's doable. Whereas the crystal formation serum... We've got some here. Now. But it is exceedingly unlikely they have either the ability or the equipment to build it. And from the sounds of it, killing infected does not really bother some of them. Frankly, Mr. Galloway, getting the attenuated virus from infected homo sapiens is the only valid choice in terms of vaccine for the crews."

"There's one problem I'd like to bring up," Commander Louis Freeman said. "Using an untested vaccine produced by people whose credentials we don't even know on our last remaining operational military arm raises some issues."

"You think?" Galloway said, chuckling.

The one of the things going for the NCCC, in Brice's opinion, is that he had a great black sense of humor.

"Then there's the whole chopping off people's heads to make it, Commander. I'm cognizant of the issues, Commander, and we'll cover them if and when we get to that point. But since the agenda for the rest of the day is watching the world not miraculously spring back to its feet, I'm declaring a blue sky discussion. Dr. Dobson, you know, more or less, what is required for... attenuated vaccine?"

"Yes, sir," Dobson said. "General lab equipment. A controlled source of radiation such as an X-ray machine. Infected spinal cords. And a blender."

"I think I know where the nukes can get some radiation," Brice said.

"*Controlled*," Dobson said. "I'm not sure exactly how much you can release from a nuke's engine or how you'd do it. But the most important part is that it be *controllable* and *precise*. If you get too much, you do too much damage to the virus and it's useless. Too little and you infect those you're trying to vaccinate. That was one of the major mistakes that drug dealers, who were selling virus that was, in fact, attenuated, made. Some of them infected their customers, others gave them 'vaccine' that wasn't much more than tap water with some random organic material in it. On the other hand, some of the materials collected off the street might as well have been made here. It was that good. *Controlled*."

"There's a way to do a release," Commander Freeman said. "How controlled?"

"The radiation dosage for creating the primer is forty-three millicuries per second per milliliter in a standard microtube," Dobson said. "For the booster, thirty-seven millicuries. If you're off by as much as a millicurie or a tenth of a second, you get either useless or infection. That's the danger of attenuated virus."

"Damn," Galloway said. "What would you suggest using if we, and I'm starting to think we can't, use this method?"

"A cesium X-ray machine," Dobson said. "And a lot of prayer. I'd suggest testing specific lots of the vaccine on specific crewmen. Absent them having picked up a microbiologist along the way or having someone familiar with successful attenuated vaccine production..."

CHAPTER 22

"Fish or cut bait?" Steve asked. "You want it or no?"

The 67-foot Bertram Convertible had taken a beating from the three zombies that had survived. It looked as if there had originally been six. But according to Stacey none of the damage was critical and it was basically a good boat.

"You missed your calling in life," Blair said, shaking his head at the feces all over the saloon. "You should have been a yacht broker. It's going to be a hell of a lot of clean-up."

"If you don't want it, I'll find somebody who does," Steve said. "That's not being a prick. But if you don't take it, somebody will. Sophia would take it like a shot."

"Oh, I'll take it," Blair said. "I'm tired of getting beat to death on the *Endeavor*."

"How are you with Sophia taking the *Endeavor* over?" Steve asked.

"Today?" Blair asked. "I'd like to take both into Bermuda and get this one cleaned up before changing over."

"I can live with that," Steve said. "Your crew could use some in-harbor time. By the way, if I haven't said this, you're doing a hell of a job. But after?"

"I'm good with Seawolf taking it," Blair said. "She's young but she's good. What about the other captains?"

"You heard the vote the last time," Steve said, shrugging. "There's not anybody else with the same level of experience. Not that we've got right now. Maybe later. The problem's going to be a crew."

"You're the history teacher," Blair said, grinning. "That was always a problem for captains. Was before the plague. Good crew, anyway. Watch she doesn't steal yours."

"Which she probably will," Steve said. "Okay, somebody's got to drive this into Bermuda. Then get to work on it. When you're ready to change over, give me a holler. I'll make sure the rest of the captains are good with Seaw—Sophia taking over."

"Almost got you there," Blair said, smiling.

"Da, you've got a call from the Sea Fit," Sophia said, over the radio.

"Gotta go," Steve said. "Good luck." He stepped into some shit and shook his boot. "Seriously, good luck."

"Thanks."

"Sea Fit, Wolf," Steve said. It was just easier that way.

"You're going to need you and Cooper*'s team on this one,"* Captain Sherill said. *"Big Coastie. And I mean* big. *One of their Famous class. More like a destroyer."*

"Oh, crap," Sophia said.

"Cooper, are you monitoring?" Steve called.

"Roger. Location?"

"Three one point nine one five by seventy point seventy-five two."

"Roger," Steve said, looking at the spot. "Be there in about... three."

"Cooper will be about six," Chris sent.

"Victoria, Wolf, over," Steve said. He sighed and shook his head. *"Victoria,* Wolf, over."

"Uh... Victoria...?"

"Tell *Victoria* actual to expect company," Steve said. "Get the *Large* warmed up. We may have some customers."

"Sorry, what?"

"Tell Mike *Sea Fit* found a cutter," Steve said carefully. "Did you get that?"

"I... what's a cutter?"

"Is there any possibility I could speak to Mike?" Steve said, calmly.

"Yeah, hang on..."

∽ ⊖ ∾

"He's going to go back to Bermuda and kill *everybody*," Fontana said. He had his feet kicked up on the helm of the *Cooper* and was enjoying the radio play.

"Mild Steve?" Chris said, turning the big boat to head to the reported location. "The guy who put a gun to Jack Isham's head and pulled back the hammer?"

"Faith says when he gets real polite it's bad," Fontana said.

"He's going to flip his lid," Bundy said.

"Bet you a dollar," Fredette said, trying not to laugh.

"Where are you going to get a dollar?" Bundy asked.

"We're eventually going to have to work with these jokers, aren't we?" Commander Bradburn said, leaning back in the conning chair. Pretty much the whole sub was listening in. There wasn't much else in the way of entertainment.

"I will not go over there and kill everyone," Steve said calmly. "I won't. Human life is precious. At least, uninfected human life..."

"You said you wanted to save the world, Da," Sophia said, then paused. "Da?"

"Yeah," Steve said.

"What's that?" Sophia said, pointing to port.

Steve pulled down a pair of binoculars and examined the splash of spray on the horizon. They'd seen whales and even dolphins aplenty in their voyage. Lots of birds. Flying fish. But never something scooting along on the surface more or less parallel to them and putting up a whisp of spray.

"That..." Steve said, lowering the binoculars, "is interesting."

"What is it?" she asked.

"What it is is something you didn't see," Steve said. "Just... we're going to forget we saw it for now. I'll talk to you about it later. Okay?"

"Yes, Da," Sophia said, looking at him.

"That is... important," Steve said, getting up and walking off of the bridge.

Bundy looked at the frequency monitor and ran back a recent recording.

"*Submarine paralleling the* Tina's Toy, *this is Commodore Wolf,* over. *Submarine paralleling the* Tina's Toy, *this is Commodore Wolf, over...*"

"Damn," Fredette said. "Short-ranged hand-held."

"CO?"

"Damnit," Bradburn said.

"Apparently they're not quite as incompetent as all that."

"Thank you, XO," Bradburn said. "Drop the aerial. Make your depth one hundred meters. Come to course one nine zero. Quarter speed..."

"Bloody hell," Steve snarled as the ESM mast disappeared below the waves. "For this I paid my bloody taxes?"

"Okay, this is going to be a bitch," Steve said, looking up at the massive cutter.

"There's a real easy place to board on the side," Faith pointed out. "At least we're not going to be climbing ten stories or something."

"Note the surviving zombies on the helipad?" Fontana pointed out. "We got anybody but the three of us?"

"Sophia," Steve said. "She can be my number two. You guys get things worked out?"

"He's more or less trained," Faith said, absently, looking through the binoculars.

Fontana and Steve traded a look as they both tried not to laugh.

"I know you're trying not to laugh," Faith said. "Apparently you don't get dry humor. Yeah, he's good to go, Da. I say we come close alongside and try popping them with an AK."

"You know how well that went the last time," Steve said.

"I'm pretty sure I've got this rolling thing down," Faith said.

"The only people who have ever gotten 'this rolling thing' down were the Jedi Knights," Fontana said.

"Jedi Knights?" Faith said, lowering the binos and looking at him in puzzlement. "I'm talking for real, not science fiction."

"It's the nickname of SEAL Team Six," Steve said. "Alas, I think Faith is right. But *I'm* going to try it and I'll use the M1."

"I've been to sniper school," Fontana said. "Maybe—"

"Sergeant Fontana," Steve said. "If anyone is going to kill his crew and sink his boat, it should be the captain."

∽ ◌ ∾

Steve waited until the boat was on the uplift and stroked the trigger.

"High," Fontana said. "Again."

"I'd rather be high than low," Steve said, jacking another 7.62 round into the chamber. The weapon was a Springfield Armory M1A rechambered for 7.62x39, something that the gunsmith who did it considered very near sacrilege. But Steve was a big believer in ammunition commonality. He just couldn't find any AK variants he considered accurate enough. "High means they don't come back at us at high velocity."

He waited, then fired again. This time he scored a hit.

"He's down," Fontana said. "Chest hit."

The problem was the low rail on the side of the flight deck. It was barely knee high on the zombies but it was high enough that the flying deck of the *Toy* was barely at the same level. And it was steel. Hitting it would have the round come back at high velocity. And, of course, both boats were rocking in the swells, which weren't minor at the moment.

One of the zombies tumbled off the flight deck trying to reach the yacht and splashed into the water.

Apparently, it wasn't the first time. A shark closed in before the zombie had surfaced.

"I suppose we could try to lasso them off," Fontana said.

"No," Steve said. "Sophia," he said, keying his radio.

"Da?"

"Close approach. As close as you can get and not hit the cutter."

"Shorter range, more accuracy," Steve said as the yacht started to pull away for a closer run. "And maybe some of them will try to jump."

"Maybe I should tell Faith that," Fontana said, standing up.

"Okay," Steve said, taking another zombie down. "This is fish in a barrel."

"More like zombie chumming," Fontana said. "You should see the water."

The human body, contrary to Hollywood action films, tends to fall face forwards when shot. Some of the zombies had tumbled over. One had tried to jump. She hadn't made it. Most that were shot tumbled over the side.

"I'm trying not to remind myself that these are U.S. Coast

Guard personnel who are merely infected with a horrible plague,"
Steve said, stroking the trigger. "By preference, I'd have preferred
to bury them wrapped in flags, not in the belly of a tiger shark."

"There are probably some survivors who are not zombies,"
Fontana said. "Hopefully they'll understand..."

"Okay...Bloody," Steve said. They'd checked three of the on-
deck hatches. All were sealed and had some sort of electronic
lock on them. They were also quite resistant to a Halligan tool.

"There's a set of clothes over here," Faith said, picking up the
uniform. "It's got an ID on it. Would that work?"

"Is it a universal?" Fontana asked, taking the ID and examining it. "And the answer is yes," he said pointing to the small
chip on the badge.

"But will it work?" Steve asked.

"No," Fontana said, swiping the badge. The lock remained red.

"Okay, let's look for others," Steve said. "The lock-down may
be based on seniority or other access. We'll gather them up and
check them all..."

"Try this one," Fontana said, handing it over.

"A lieutenant's didn't work," Steve said. "Why would a chief
petty officer's?" But when he tried it the lock went green.

"It's a Coastie thing," Fontana said, shrugging. "Navy, too. A
chief outranks a lieutenant any day."

"What's a chief?" Faith asked. "What's a lieutenant for that
matter?"

"Any zombies?" Steve asked, banging on a hatch.

He was rewarded by the beginning of "shave and a haircut."

"Close your eyes," Steve shouted. "Understand? Close your eyes!"

He undogged the hatch and tossed in a chem light.

"Use that to adjust your eyes," Steve said.

"Thanks for finally coming," the man at the hatch said. "Jesus,
where have you guys *been*?"

"It's a long story," Steve said. "But we're not Coast Guard or
Navy. Just a volunteer civilian group. You need water?"

"The worst sort of way," the guy replied. "We've been carefully
recycling piss for...well, for a long time."

"Bottles," Steve said, tossing them through the door. "I'm going to keep clearing. I'll be back in about five. I need to make sure this area's clear."

"Roger."

"Who's senior?" the respirator-clad man said. The voice was muffled from the respirator but he had a Commonwealth accent. Bobby couldn't tell which. Possibly Irish.

Petty Officer First Class Bobby Kuzma was the senior of the six survivors of the USCGC Campbell, WMEC-909, slumping on benches in the crew mess, so he raised his hand.

The man was just about covered in lights, which were still painful to Kuzma's eyes. From what little Bobby could see, he was just as covered in armor and weapons ranging from some sort of AK variant shotgun to a large hunting knife. He even had the head of a Halligan tool sticking up over his shoulder with the tool in some sort of holster.

Another armored figure—a woman, from the walk, but it was hard to tell—entered behind him.

"I found a cache of sunglasses." Woman. Young. That was all Kuzma could make out.

She started to hand them out. A while back, before the world came apart, Bobby would have thought it idiotic to wear sunglasses in the mess. Now, even with the lights off, they were a welcome relief from the lights the members of the group were wearing.

The first man shut off a couple of the lights and came over to Bobby.

"Need to talk," he said, holding out his hand. "Can you walk?"

"I can walk," Bobby said, but he took the hand.

The man led him down the crew mess and then pulled off his mask with a grimace.

"Ugh," the guy said, grimacing. "We use these for the smell. I'd say let's go outside where it's a little better but I don't think you can handle the light, yet." He pulled out a canister of Vicks VapoRub, rubbed it on his nostrils, then held it out to Kuzma.

"You get used to it," Bobby said, waving his hand.

"Two things," the man said. "More. First, I'm Steven Smith. Australian by birth, naturalized American citizen, former Aussie para, former history teacher and currently, and I put quotes on this, 'commodore' of a flotilla of small boats clearing this patch of the Atlantic. I'm called Captain Wolf or Commodore Wolf and the group has named the flotilla Wolf's Floating Circus. Basically we range between Bermuda, where we're using a disabled ocean-going tug as a supply base, and the coast of the U.S. We're actually just around Bermuda right now because there's only six of us and one of them's a wanker who isn't worth the cost of fuel. It's an all-volunteer effort, which is a bit like herding roos. Which, trust me, are *worse* than cats. I tried it one time as a lad.

"So, to what happens next," Smith continued, "the normal next thing is we get you over to the boats, give you a scrub-down and get some chow in you. Usual sort of at-sea rescue thing except the scrub-down part. That was originally because we feared the virus, these days it's because it's, well, become tradition, and people tend to be ready for a shower."

"Very ready for a shower," Kuzma said carefully.

"And since you were by yourself in the compartment you need to get used to using your voice again," Steve said. "And light. That takes a few days. I said that was the normal thing we do. The issue, here, is that this is the biggest boat we've cleared and it has about ten bloody million compartments..."

"You're not sure it's clear," Kuzma said.

"I'm fairly sure we got all the zombies," Smith said. "If there are more survivors, they're not making noise when we do. They could be too weak. Most likely..." He shrugged.

"Wait," Kuzma said, looking at the group. "*Six*? That's *it*? We had a hundred personnel and refugees!"

"That explains the children," Smith said. "I am very sorry for your loss."

"So...are you assisting the Coast Guard?" Kuzma said. "I need to get back in communication, report in..."

"I think I may have missed some of the important bits," Steve said. "Actually, I was waiting for you to get your wits to the point. The point is that there *is* no Coast Guard. Or, rather, you're it. As far as I can determine, based upon radio reports and local conditions, you're now more or less the commander of the United States Coast Guard, which consists of you and those other five persons."

"That's..." Bobby said, sitting on the table and shaking his head. "That can't be. No..."

"I cannot prove it to you at this moment," Smith said, shrugging. "We are in a dark hangar on a boat in the middle of the ocean. But if there were a Coast Guard, I'd assume they would find and clear their own vessels, first, just to have the trained personnel. You can feel free to verify it in various ways once you get your feet on the ground. We'll, at some point, get you back to Bermuda. You can see the harbor. And the zombies. We find boats. Feel free to take one over to the mainland and see for yourself. There are no official governmental broadcasts. There are no land areas not held by the infected and we have thus far found no evidence of formal governmental activity."

"Jesus Christ," Kuzma said, looking at the blood-smeared deck. "How long?"

"It is the fifteenth of August," Smith said. "I've found some watches amongst the crew's belongings, you can verify that at least."

"Jesus..." Bobby said. "That long?"

"Petty Officer," Smith said sharply. "As I was saying, we normally let people get their feet under them for a few days. I know you are tired. Exhausted. Malnourished and dehydrated. But we either get assistance from some, preferably three, of your crew to clear the remainder of the boat or let it go for now. I'm not saying that it's a requirement. And, frankly, I don't see finding any more personnel. Not alive."

"Did they all zombie?" Kuzma asked.

"Do you really want to know this?" Smith asked.

"Yes," Bobby said.

"We don't have an accurate count," Smith said. "Frankly, we don't keep an accurate count of dead and wounded and methods on large vessels such as this. There aren't enough of us yet to take the time. But, no, many were infected. Some appear to have died of the infection or possibly from violence by other infecteds. Many...were trapped in compartments without stores."

"Oh God," Bobby said, hanging his head again.

"I don't know if it makes it better or worse for you," Smith said. "But at a certain point, many committed suicide. And did so in some very...honorable ways. But they did so as an alternative to starvation or dehydration. Which, frankly, is why we do this. And we don't count the dead because it takes *time*. And the living deserve our time more. So the question is, do you wish us to continue the sweep? To do so, we will need assistance. We've swept all we can find."

"I'll help," Kuzma said, standing up and swaying. "As long as I can. I guess asking you to...collect the dead...?"

"There are, currently, one hundred and twenty-six survivors known to us," Steve said. "One thirty-two counting your group. Only forty-six of which are willing to actively volunteer to the extent of manning boats supplied and supported by us and clearing life rafts. We have an additional six or so who are willing to go into cleared vessels to recover materials or get them operational. I have exactly *three* personnel willing to participate in active clearance, fighting zombies in the dark in confined spaces, as it were. Three more will if pressed. Would you care to answer your own question, Petty Officer?"

"No, sir," Kuzma said. "I mean, yes, sir. I understand."

"There are, literally, not enough of us left to bury the dead," Smith said softly. "That is the world into which you have been reborn. What you make of that is up to you."

"How the hell did we miss this area?" said "Shewolf" in a muffled voice.

Kuzma's "clearance specialist" was a thirteen-year-old girl. Tall for her age, tall for a girl, period, and clearly strong: she was carrying about a hundred pounds of weapons, ammo and gear. But still a thirteen-year-old girl.

"The layout of this boat is screwy," Kuzma said weakly. He leaned up against a bulkhead for a second. He knew he'd get his strength back eventually. But lagging behind a thirteen-year-old girl who was weighed down like an infantryman was embarrassing. "The design looked great on paper but it's not what you call efficient."

"Okay," Shewolf said, banging on the hatch. "Zombies, zombies, zombies! Hello!"

"You sure about that?" Kuzma said, his eyes wide.

"Let them come to you," the girl said. "Bring them into your zone of fire, don't go into theirs."

There was an odd thump from the door, then more.

"And we have a winner," Shewolf said. "I need you to back up into that cross corridor. In fact, I need you to back way the fuck up."

"Why?" the petty officer asked.

"Because if there's a bunch, I'm going to have to back up," the girl said. "And you're not moving real quick. So back *way* the fuck up. And around the corner so you're less likely to get hit by bouncers."

Kuzma backed into the cross corridor, flashing a light around to make sure there weren't zombies there. He had a pistol but he wasn't sure that he could even raise it much less shoot straight. God, he was tired.

Thinking about what the girl had said, he backed farther into the corridor. The bouncer's point was important.

"Olly-olly-oxenfree! Come to momma...!"

Kuzma heard the hatch undog, then slam back on its latches.

"Fudgesicle!" the girl shouted, followed by a series of rapidfire shotgun blasts.

Shewolf backed into the cross-corridor, dropped her shotgun on its harness and drew her pistol with lightning speed.

"Say hallo to my leetle friend!" she shouted, double tapping. She pivoted into the corridor, backing towards Kuzma, clearly covering him. "*You* want some?"

Infected came around the corner after her, lunging at her as she expertly double tapped. The worst thing, for Kuzma, was that he recognized most of them. Some of them were refugees the *Campbell* had been ordered to rescue in the early days of the plague. They were probably how the plague had gotten onboard. Others were fellow crew members, bearded, filthy, naked, covered in sores, feces, vomit and dried and fresh blood. Houston P. Barnes, who had just reported to the *Campbell* before the outbreak but whom he'd known for years. He had bits of flesh in his unkempt beard and then his face buckled under when the second .45 round hit him. Tommy E. Craddock, Jr., "don't forget the junior," one of his closest messmates. He clutched at the round that hit him in the chest, howling the weird cry of a wounded zombie, half keen, half snarl, then was stopped by another round to the forehead, which left a round, blue hole.

"You gonna back up or not?" Shewolf screamed. Her pistol locked back so she tossed it forward onto a dead body and ripped another from her chest holder. The plethora of weapons was starting to make sense.

Bobby couldn't back up, couldn't lift his own weapon, all he could do was stare mutely at the black tide pouring down the corridor.

And then it was done. A refugee was the last, dropping more or less right in front of him, so fixated on the light-covered girl she hadn't even noticed the frozen petty officer.

"That was almost too exciting," the girl said. She reloaded both her weapons, retrieved the dropped pistol, reloaded that, then hefted her shotgun. "Real zombie apocalypse moment there. You done with your break?"

"I think I'm done," Kuzma said. "I think I'm just...done."

Bobby sat on the flying deck of the *Toy* watching the dinghy coming back from the *Campbell*. He'd been in similar dinghies hundreds of times doing inspections of boats just like this one. In fact, he was pretty sure they'd done a stop on *this* boat. But when they were done, they went back to the cutter. They always went back to the cutter.

This time he wasn't going back. He was never going back. After the scene in the corridor, he was never, *ever* going back. Not love nor money nor orders could make him go back aboard the WMEC-909, United States Coast Guard Cutter *Campbell*, "Queen of the Seas." He wished he had a Harpoon missile to sink her like her previous namesake.

"You going to be okay?" Captain Smith asked, sitting down next to him. "I hear you had a little ZA moment."

"That's your daughter?" Kuzma asked tonelessly. Shewolf was riding back in the dinghy. Second on, last off. The helmsman must have said something funny because the thirteen-year-old was grinning with her fine, blond, blood-splattered hair blowing in the freshening wind.

"Yes."

"Is she...okay?" Kuzma asked. "I mean..."

"Do you mean is she freaked out by what happened?" Smith asked. "She said it was almost worse than New York. But not quite. If you mean is she insane? She was a fairly normally adjusted girl before the plague. She never threatened to bomb her school or shoot it up. She played soccer and was starting to date. She chased boys, sometimes literally. But she'd always quip that the worst thing about a zombie apocalypse would be pretending you weren't excited by the prospect. So...she was fairly well adjusted to the previous world. She is well adjusted to this one. So, yes, she is okay. She's even sensitive, which is hard in this job. She hates to shoot the children and lets others do so when possible. I take it you're *not* okay."

"No," Kuzma said. "Not okay. Glad to be out of there. Just... glad to be out."

"I am sorry that you observed the termination of your shipmates," Smith said. "That is a very close bond."

"I had to shoot some myself, getting to the stores locker," Bobby admitted. "But . . . that was bad."

"A large group of apparently uninfected had locked down in another stores locker," Smith said. "And then apparently had taken insufficient precautions to prevent spread."

"And then eaten each other?" Bobby asked.

"More or less," Smith said. "Which was why there were so many survivors. Zombie survivors, that is. I take it you don't want to participate in the salvage operation?"

"Salvage?" Kuzma said. "You can't salvage a U.S. Coast Guard cutter!"

"And there were survivors onboard," Smith said, nodding. "But salvage it we must. For the small arms locker if nothing else. Petty Officer, I left New York with seven thousand rounds of double ought buckshot and a thousand rounds of frangible. For what I had originally planned that would have been more than enough. For this? I'm down to four thousand rounds. I'm halfway through my supply, more or less, and I have an ocean of ships and boats to clear. I can find diesel, food, water from recyclers, even parts. But munitions? Weapons? If not from your storage locker, then where?"

"That's a tall order," Kuzma said, breathing out hard. "I mean . . . Will we help? Yeah, of course. But turning over the contents of a 270 to civilians . . . ? If there ever *is* a Coast Guard again, I can't see them not hanging my ass for that."

"Well, I already purloined one thing from your boat," Steve said. "Step out on the foredeck with me, Petty Officer."

Steve and Kuzma walked up to the front of the boat and Steve pulled out a Coast Guard walkie-talkie.

"I presume this doesn't use civilian frequencies?" Steve asked, holding it up.

"No, sir," the PO said, his brow furrowing.

"U.S. Navy, this is Commodore Wolf on Coast Guard frequency. I know you're not going to talk to me, but will you talk to a Coast Guard petty officer? Here's PO One Kuzma, spelling, Kilo-Uniform-Zulu-Mike-Alpha. Turning over now."

"It may take a bit," Steve said. He handed Kuzma the radio and walked aft.

"What now?" Scholz asked.

"Get me the Hole," Bradburn replied.

CHAPTER 23

"*PO Kuzma, this is the U.S. Navy,*" the radio squawked five minutes later.

Kuzma had started to wonder if it was all a hoax and looked at the radio as if it was radioactive.

"Kuzma to calling station, who is this?"

"*A submarine, obviously. Answer these questions without thinking. Mother's maiden name?*"

"Thomas," Kuzma said.

"*Birthplace.*"

"Mine? Burlington, Kansas. Hers? Peoria."

"*First college attended.*"

"University of Kansas," Kuzma said.

"*Verified. Stand by...*"

"*Petty Officer, it's good to hear that some of you survived,*" a new voice said. "*This circuit isn't secure, so there are some things you're not going to be told. To give you two other answers, so you know I'm looking at your service record, you enlisted on April twenty-second and you hold the USCG rescue medal with two stars. What I'm going to tell you is that this is the highest level commander you're going to talk to for... well, until someone finds a higher level one.*"

"Yes, sir," Kuzma said. "So . . . It's really all gone?"

"More or less," the voice said. *"But you, or rather, and I quote, Commodore Wolf, called us, not the other way around."*

"Yes, sir," Kuzma said. "The . . . commodore, and he really doesn't like to be called that, sir, he's asking for materials from the *Campbell* for his . . . mission. Specifically, they're low on shotgun rounds. And he'd like to off-load fuel and supplies and generally, well, strip her, sir. I'm not . . . I can't authorize that. I can see his reasoning. We can't man her as is. But . . . . I can't go with that, sir. I'm not even sure I can go with a voice on a radio even if you are looking at my service report."

"How about if I can tell an attack sub what to do?" the voice said. *"Is that sufficient authority? I'd rather not surface the sub just to show off, but if I order it, it will."*

"So do I turn over the stuff?" Kuzma asked.

"What do you think of Commodore Wolf?" the voice asked. *"Is that even his real name?"*

"No, sir," Kuzma asked. "It's his handle. He's a former Aussie para, or so he says."

"Who are Seawolf and Shewolf?" the voice asked.

"His daughters, sir," Kuzma said. "And that's part of the screwy part. Sir, none of these people really know what they're doing. I mean, Seawolf is fifteen, for God's sake, and she's up for her own boat. Shewolf is one of the people who cleared the boat. She's *thirteen*. I mean she's big for her age and she knows how to handle guns, but . . . Honestly, sir, I . . . I helped clear the boat with Shewolf and . . . She's scary. But the boats? None of these people have so much as a captain's license, sir. And . . . I can see what they're doing. I think we should help. I'm not so sure about . . . I'm not sure about anything, sir. And, sir, I just got out from clearing the boat and it was . . . Christ, sir, it was really bad. It's just . . . I don't even know if I'm coherent, sir . . ."

"Petty Officer," the voice said, sharply. *"Calm down. You're doing great. You're a god damned credit to the Coast Guard that you can be* this *coherent after what you've been through. Okay? Calm down. You're doing fine."*

"Yes, sir," Kuzma said. "Sir . . . There really isn't *anything* on land?"

"Family?" the voice asked, softly.

"Yes, sir," Kuzma said. "My . . . I have kids, sir."

"*So do I,*" the voice said. "*They were in D.C. I was . . . not. Petty Officer Kuzma, go get Wolf, then stand by. It appears I need to talk to the commodore.*"

"Yes, sir," Kuzma said. "He seems like a good guy, sir. But . . . I mean they really don't know *nothing* about the sea. I'm surprised any of them have survived at all. These are the kind of people that we usually rescue. Not the other way around."

"*We are living in strange times, Petty Officer,*" the voice said. "*Get the commodore.*"

"Wolf."

"*So you're a commodore?*"

"I'm in command of six small boats," Steve said calmly. "And a support vessel. In the World War Two British Navy I'd be a Reserve, Hostilities Only, Lieutenant Commander or so. I was given the moniker by my next senior captain and it was voted upon, against my wishes, by the captains' board. Feel free to call me Mr. Wolf or Captain Wolf. May I have a name?"

"*Mister . . . Blount? My mother's name. It's not a huge security issue. We are in contact with all the rest of the remaining head-quarters, such as they are, and they know who I am.*"

"God," Steve said, his eyes closing. "You're the NCCC."

"*You're well versed in security issues.*"

"I was a history teacher," Steve said. "Including twentieth century. My master's in history was on the defense of Malta during World War Two. I thought *that* was bad. If the NCCC is talking to *me* . . . That's even worse than my worst nightmares. That means this little flotilla really is *it*, doesn't it?"

"*You're . . . unfortunately perceptive. There are other forces, but . . .*"

"The subs aren't infected but they also don't have vaccine," Steve said. "I've had time to think about this, sir."

"*You're Australian?*"

"I'm a naturalized American citizen, sir," Steve said. "But at this point, I think borders are a bit passé. Be that as it may, I'm an American. Passport and everything. Two children who are quite American."

"*From what I've heard, the best of America,*" the NCCC said.

"Fought their way out of the last concert in New York," Steve said. "A tale I'd be more than happy to tell as soon as we can get you out of whatever fortress you're in."

"*Come again?*"

"My plan had been to just survive," Steve said. "Keep hiding. Find a place my family and I could survive. Let someone like, well, you, sir, handle this. But... you save one person and it gets addictive. And this situation... annoys me, sir. I... shortly after we took the *Toy*, I told my wife we were not going to bow to the zombies, sir.

"So, yes, my goal, not plan, goal, is a zombie-free world. I'll start with the U.S. So that wasn't a joke. Say the goal is to get to the point where a lightly armed convoy can pull up with buses and deliver vaccine to your people, and then you can take over and I can go fishing. Don't ask me what the *plan* is, though. I didn't know I was going to find a Coast Guard cutter. I don't know what disaster or success is going to occur next. All I can do is work the goal. Sir."

"*Ambitious. Do you think you can do it?*"

"I've only got a few boats, sir," Steve said. "But if I have the CG personnel behind me, officially, it will help. I've got one active duty special forces sergeant, but I'm going to need more help from surviving military. The sub personnel, especially, as soon as we can produce vaccine. I'm going to need their technical expertise if this is going to work."

"*About that,*" the NCCC said. "*We picked up the snippet where some was mentioned. Might I inquire where you secured it?*"

"I don't know," Steve said. "Can I get a written pardon?"

There was a long pause.

"*Were you... active in producing it?*"

"I was not someone who... acquired the materials," Steve said cautiously. "I knew someone who was. And I know someone who was involved in production of vaccine."

"*Attenuated virus vaccine? Successfully?*"

Steve thought about that for a long time.

"Yes."

"*Know someone? As in they know how to produce it? Have done so? And are available?*"

"Yes, although absent that pardon you're going to have to break out thumbscrews to get me to say who. And thumbscrews won't work."

"*Stand by.*"

∽—⊖—∾

"That is better than we could have hoped for," Dr. Dobson said. He had been brought in on the conversation early on.

"I still don't think some drug dealer..." Commander Freeman started to say.

"Wolf, despite his grandiose name, does not sound like a drug dealer," Galloway said, holding up a hand.

"Captain Wolf? Blount, over."
"Wolf."

"First of all, since I didn't cover it. No, there will be no charges. Can I absolutely guarantee that someday in the fullness of stupidity, some group will not bring charges of crimes against humanity for production of attenuated vaccine from human spinal cords? No. We are human and such things happen. What I can guarantee, and I'll get someone to send you a facsimile of a document to the effect, is that to the extent I have the legal power to do so, I will retroactively permit the production as well as authorize future production for the good of the United States and humanity. That way if there is ever an ICC again we can both *hang. But right now, without vaccine we are truly stuck. I won't ask you to reveal much about it but we need to get some issues straight. Doctor?"*

"This is Dr. James Dobson. I'm the Acting Director of the CDC. Can you detail, at all, the nature of the person you have who is familiar with production of attenuated vaccine? What are his or her qualifications?"

"None, essentially," Steve said carefully. "They were recruited by a clandestine but highly professional lab to assist in the production. They were the primary laboratory technician for the production of the vaccine my family used and currently has. We only have a few remaining doses, which I'm using for clearance personnel since they are more likely to get blood contamination. It works. None of us have contracted the disease and my daughter, handle Shewolf, contracted the virus after only the primer but survived. It was touch and go but she made it."

"Sounds like his wife was the lab tech," Brice said, grimacing. "That had to be cold."

"Can you define 'highly qualified'?" Dr. Dobson said. "In a way that..."

"Fully prepared lab including Scanning Electron Microscope and

all that sort of stuff," Wolf replied. *"Run by a Ph.D. in microbiology. I hope you won't mind if I avoid the name. But he used to work for you, Doctor. He was a consultant for a ... well-heeled group."*

"Corporate lab," Dobson said, grimacing. "The FBI was aware they were around. New York, L.A. and San Francisco were particularly rife with them. They produced the vaccine for senior corporate officers and support. But they *were* professionals. But a lab tech ... that's not the same as the doctor ..."

"Could he or she do it again?"

"The problem is, as you probably know, Doctor, quality control," Steve said. "The doctor running the lab did the quality assurance. I was not directly involved. But I understand that getting the strands just right is critical. Not too much radiation, not too little, no contamination. And we sure as hell can't do it with what we've got. We'll need something resembling a lab and a good X-ray machine for sure. I don't suppose any of the subs have one?"

Galloway looked at the Navy liaison who shook his head.

"They have an X-ray machine but insufficient lab equipment and materials to do production much less quality control."
Steve looked at the deck and wanted to throw the radio as far as he could.
"Stand by, please."
"Roger."

"Dallas," Galloway said. "Can you observe the subject?"

"Roger," Bradburn said, looking at his screen. He'd popped the periscope up for the chat. "Transferring ..."

"That is a man in deep thought," Galloway said, looking at the video. The presumed "Commodore Wolf" was just standing there, looking at the deck. Then he straightened up and keyed the radio.
"Blount, Wolf, over."
"Go ahead."
"The way this was going to go was that I was just going to do one thing after another and hope that nobody big enough to stop

me would get in the way. Not that those things were going to be as bad as, say, a zombie apocalypse. But they were going to get right up some people's nose. And they were going to be to my plan and intentions. Example. I can go loot that Coastie vessel. I really do need the ammo. The Coasties might get it in their noses, but they don't have any guns. And from what my daughter has told me and I saw, they're not going to be much use clearing any time soon. If ever. I suppose you could torpedo my boats, but that wouldn't get you anywhere.

"But at a certain point I'm for sure going to need military personnel. A lot of military personnel. I'm probably going to need a working helo carrier. I'm going to need Marines. The problem, and I'm laying it on you since I'm thinking you're not really busy and I am, is how to do that. Because I said that I've got a goal. I don't know when I'll secure that goal but it sure as a billabong is dry isn't going to be tomorrow. And I won't secure it, ever, without your support. But you don't know me from a wallaby. Somebody else might muckle this out, I suppose. I can find a boat for these Coasties and they can muckle it, maybe. Right now, I don't care. I'm tired. Myself, a green beanie sergeant and my thirteen-year-old bloody daughter just cleared a bloody cutter and rescued your bloody Coasties and we used a bunch of priceless ammo doing it. I'm tired. I've been doing this for weeks with no bloody support and no real reason for anybody to do it but me asking them nicelike.

"I'm going to seed the cutter, mark it, and when you decide if the Coasties are going to work with me or not, get back to me. If not, I'll find them a boat, hell, I have a spare I can't use, and they can do whatever they'd like with it. Rescue, clear or go bloody pirate. But I'm not going to try to read the mind of some bloke I've never met on the radio. I'm going to stop doing that today and I'm not going to do it tomorrow. Or a year from now. So when you figure out how we're going to work together, or if we're going to work together, have your bloody sub come by and say hello. That's not being impolite but I really don't have the time for this. And I'm tired. We usually give people a few days to get their wits back. If you don't want to work with us, I'll give the Coasties the Large in three days and you can do whatever you'd like. Wolf, out."

"That is a man on the ragged edge," Brice said quietly.
"A paladin in hell," Ellington said.

"Excuse me?" Galloway said. "I understand the words—"

"Oh, my God," Brice said, shaking her head. "Congratulations. You get the geek win for the *week*, Colonel Ellington."

"Some context?" Galloway asked tightly.

"Colonel?" Brice asked. "Would you care to explain?"

Ellington twitched and looked at her helplessly.

"General?" the NCCC asked.

"It's from Dungeons and Dragons, sir," Brice said, smiling tightly.

"Seriously?" Freeman said, snorting. Then he paused. "General, how did you...?"

"Air Force Academy, *Commander*," Brice said, smiling at him coquettishly. They'd learned by now that when when the acting CJCS went "cute" that they were about to have their heads handed to them. "Is that a *problem*?"

"No, ma'am," the commander said, holding his hand up to his mouth to hide the grin.

"There is a picture in one of the D and D books, sir," Brice said, turning back to the NCCC. "A knight in armor standing on a precipice wielding a sword against a horde of demons. The caption is 'A Paladin In Hell.'"

"Thinking about it, that does sound rather apropos of Commodore Wolf," Galloway said, nodding at Ellington.

"Every material, every person, has a breaking point," Ellington said, staring into the distance. "Fighting the darkness forces one to either be the light or embrace the dark. Every paladin finds his precipice."

"Colonel?" Brice said carefully as the silence dragged out. "Marine!"

"Ma'am!" Ellington said, snapping upright.

"Colonel, I'm not sure where you just went," Brice said. "But we need you present in *this* reality. Or do I need to call the medics?"

"No, ma'am," the colonel said sharply. "Present and accounted for, General. My recommendation is a Naval Captaincy, sir."

"Excuse me?" Galloway said.

"You're joking, right?" Commander Freeman said tightly.

"Granting the commodore a Naval Captaincy would allow him to command military personnel as well as direct civilian technical experts, sir, thereby reducing his overall difficulty load. Furthermore, absent finding and rescuing a higher ranking military officer, which would require in all probability the clearance of a Nimitz-class aircraft carrier or better or more likely the clearance of a major ground base, he would outrank any of the current submarine commanders. The captaincy would be contingent upon allowance of communications by professional officers to assure some semblance of reasonable command responsibilities. Absent that choice, he could outline his plans such as they are to the submarine commanders and upon developing some method of vaccine production turn it over to them. Sir."

"A captaincy?" Commander Freeman snapped. "A *captaincy*? Are you *insane*? To some unknown Australian pirate *wannabe*? For that matter, Under Secretary Galloway does not have the *authority* to grant a captaincy!"

"As a matter of fact—" Brice said.

"I do, in fact, Commander," Galloway said tightly. "It's in the fine print. I can even give a brevet to flag rank. Obviously, it has to be approved by the Senate in time. But for that we'd have to *have* a Senate."

"I . . ." Freeman said, his face tight. "I was not aware and meant no disrespect . . . sir."

"Colonel Ellington, thank you for that novel suggestion," Galloway said. "That language is not to suggest I am dismissing it. It is, however, I feel, premature. Right now we have a virtual unknown whose only claim to fame is rescuing a few people including some Coast Guard personnel and possibly knowing how to produce vaccine. I would say that we need more CV than that before making such a significant decision. That is all."

"Yes, sir," Ellington said, then twitched.

"As for Commander Freeman," Galloway said. "I can understand your distaste for the very idea. You are a professional naval officer who has spent many years honing his expertise and the idea of just handing a commission, much less a captaincy to, as you put it, a pirate wannabe, is obviously distasteful. I'll remind you that various persons were given ranks to which they were not 'entitled' during World War Two, a much less serious catastrophe than the one in which we are currently engaged."

"I recall the story of your grandfather, sir," Freeman said. "But with due respect, they weren't given *commands*, sir."

"As I said, it is premature," Galloway said. "And this discussion has been contentious and, yes, tiring. We have time to consider even the subject of the Coast Guard personnel and the cutter. Let us use it."

"Bureaucrats," Steve said, tossing Kuzma the radio. "They're trying to figure out what to do. I said I'd give them three days."

"Okay," the PO said. "What are we going to do in the meantime?"

"I'd run you back to Bermuda and put you on the *Large*," Steve said. "But it's a six-hour steam both ways and there are EPIRBs. So just chill and we'll go rescue people."

"We can help, sir," Fore said. "That's the best part of our job."

"Just rest," Steve said tightly. "You're all knackered out. Which is normal. You'll recover. I was wrong to use you to clear when you'd just been rescued. Besides, usually there's nobody *to* rescue. It'd just be nice to have somebody I could trust at my back. But until the Powers-That-Be speak I can't even trust *that*."

"Da," Sophia said. "While you were on the horn we got a call. There's another yacht. Sixty-footer."

"Joy," Steve said. "How far?"

"About two hours."

"Make for it," Steve said.

"It's . . . getting dark, sir," Kuzma pointed out.

"Odd thing at sea with no clouds," Steve said. "You can really tell when the sun's going down, PO." Steve winced. "Sorry, I'm still bloody furious at that bugger on the radio."

"I understand, sir," Kuzma said. "What I was pointing out is that it's getting dark as in 'are you going to do a boarding in the dark?'"

"Why not?" Steve asked. "These things tend to be bloody dark belowdecks, anyway. Really, it's easier in the dark 'cause you don't have to let your eyes adjust."

"Oh," Kuzma said, blinking rapidly. "How many boardings have you *done*, sir?"

"I don't know," Steve said. "I'd have to check the log. Probably not as many as you. But probably a few more that had zombies on them. No worries: usually these sixty-footers are fairly straight-forward. It's the doing them by *myself* that's getting tiresome . . ."

Kuzma moved up to the flying bridge to observe the evolution.

"If you want to tell me anything, go ahead," the "commodore's" daughter said, a touch nervously.

"You've done this a few times before?" Kuzma asked.

"Yes, sir," Sophia replied. "This is my seventeenth approach to a yacht this size. For larger than this we usually use the dinghy."

"You come directly alongside?" Kuzma said.

"Yes, sir," Sophia said. "If you'll hold on a second. I don't see any on the deck, Da!" She picked up the intercom. "Horn, horn, horn…" she called, then hit the foghorn in three short blasts. She waited a moment, then hit two more. "That usually brings them out if there are any that can get on the deck."

"Come alongside!" Steve yelled.

"Roger, Da!"

She moved up to the yacht and let the wind carry her in the last few feet as the crew put balloon fenders over the side and hurled grapnels to bring the two yachts together.

"We had problems getting those right at first," Sophia said. "The balloons. You've got to get them at just the right height."

"Yes," Kuzma said. He didn't mention that he'd have actively advised against tying two boats together in six-foot swells.

"Tied down!" Paula called.

"Is that your mate?" Kuzma asked.

"Well, technically Da's the captain, Mom's the first mate and I'm the second. Paula's sort of my mate if you will."

"Was she a boater? Before?" Kuzma asked.

"Ran a T-shirt shop," Sophia said. "Pardon, this is a bit tricky."

She engaged power to the engines, carefully, reversing to port and forward to starboard.

"It's easier to hold them together if they're into the swells," Sophia said. "And the ropes don't snap as much. Well, except when I'm doing this."

Kuzma tried not to flinch as he saw the strains being put on the three-quarter-inch lines that were used on the grapnels.

"Lines part often?" he asked.

"Yeah," Sophia said. "All the time. If we don't use a boat we salvage all the ropes."

When the two boats were arrayed, "Wolf" leapt from one boat to the other. He was wearing body armor with a standard Class III PFD on top. His only weapon appeared to be a pistol. He dropped the PFD on the aft deck and entered the interior of the captured yacht.

"Worry about him when he's in there?" Kuzma asked.

"Not as much these days," Sophia said. "But, yeah. It's worse with the big ones."

"Top deck is clear. Evidence of zombies but none found. Going below."

"Not 'infecteds'?" Kuzma asked.

"They're humans," Sophia said, shrugging. "Not walking dead. More like evil, weaker, insane chimps. But it's easier to think of them as zombies."

"Ever killed one yourself?" Kuzma asked.

"We made the mistake of going to the last concert in New York City," Sophia said. "They had their first real power outage during it. The concert was using generators. And lights. The zombies closed in. So...yeah. Don't ask how many. I stopped counting after three or four. The next day, they blew the bridges, my uncle took off for his secure point, and we sailed out."

"Sailed?" Kuzma asked.

"We were on a sailboat Da bought when we got the word," Sophia said. "We loaded it up with stores and we were careful with them but we finally ran out. So we found the *Toy*. Tina was still alive and Da just...changed. We started doing this."

"You weren't afraid of the flu?" Kuzma asked.

"We got vaccinated in New York," Sophia said carefully. "Since you're still sort of a cop, you'll allow me to take the Fifth on any more discussion of that, okay?"

"Okay," Kuzma said. "But some of that stuff..."

"It was for real," Sophia said, tonelessly. "Let's just say my uncle had some connections. And, yes, it was the kind made from people's spines. And, yes, we knew it. Now can we change the subject or are you going to arrest us?"

"No," Kuzma said, shaking his head. "I wish I had some. I wish *we'd* had some."

"Yeah," Sophia said, shrugging. "Put it this way, NYPD was vaccinated *up*. Take my word for that. They and their families. Which took, by my count, about six thousand spinal cords."

"Holy crap," Kuzma said, his eyes wide. "Seriously?"

"Really should drop the subject," Sophia said. "But, yeah, I'm sure. You could only get about ten units per infected. The count I got was thirty thousand vaccinated. And you needed primer and booster. Sixty thousand units. I don't know where they were doing it, but they had to have had an assembly line that made Auschwitz look like Central Park."

"One zombie, already dead, in the engine room. I don't think this one is operable. Boat's clear. Call your Mom..."

"Wolf, Kuzma," Kuzma said. "Mind if I accompany?"

"Up to you," Wolf replied.

"Grab a respirator," Seawolf said.

"Respirator?" Kuzma asked.

"For the smell."

"You get used to it."

CHAPTER 24

"Once upon a night we'll wake to the carnival of life," Steve crooned to the blaring music, his feet propped up on the flying bridge and just enjoying the ride. "It's hard to light a candle, easy to curse the dark instead..."

Sea Fit always seemed to find the big ones. And this time Captain George was being cagey. He'd just said "you're going to need all your clearance teams."

Steve, after some thought, had centralized the "clearance teams" on the *Toy*. It just made sense. Captain Blair had picked up a former Army cook who was comfortable enough to do clearance on small boats. But right now, hard clearance was still relegated to Faith, Fontana and himself. And that way they had all their throw-weight concentrated.

He kept his voice low: singing wasn't one of his gifts. But he could hear Faith caroling along in a high, perfect soprano, and even a deeper and not-bad tenor from Sergeant Fontana. They were busy prepping gear on the aft deck. If the rolls bothered them it wasn't apparent. He heard Faith laugh about something and wondered, mildly, if putting her alongside the older and presumably heterosexual SF sergeant was a good idea. He wasn't a jealous, angry father type by any stretch and trusted his girls to make reasonably intelligent decisions. But Faith was still a bit young to make mature and intelligent decisions regarding romance and, face it, both his daughters were hotties. The main issue he had wasn't if something happened. He knew Faith generally knew the guidelines on that sort of thing. They'd had discussions on the subject. And in Fontana's position, the temptation had to be fairly high. The real issue was when, not if, something went wrong and dealing with the aftermath. Faith was both passionate and, at this point, about as deadly as they came.

It didn't, for now, appear to be a real issue. But it was just another nagging problem at the back of his mind.

Like the Coasties. The "headquarters" hadn't gotten back to them at the three-day limit. The sub was still out there. It even maintained the same general position relative to his boat. The ESM mast was scooting along the surface, five klicks or so, port, forward. Just in case he got a call, he guessed.

He'd put the Coasties on the *Large*, since they had some people who could figure out the systems, and pointed out that they didn't really have the fuel to use it, then showed them the flotilla's usage. The Coasties were ... coasting. They were being useful, helping out on the *Victoria*, working on boats, but until they got some orders they couldn't really do much.

They'd gotten two more boats up and doing rescue/clearance. Blair was over on the *Changing Tymes*, now, and Sophia had taken over the *Worthy Endeavor*, taking most of his crew with her! And they'd found a captain—with an actual ticket and everything, all ocean, all tonnage—Geraldine Miguel, as a survivor on the 72-foot *N2 Deep*. After taking a little break in harbor and getting her boat cleaned up, the tough "forty-something" captain had immediately headed back out to sea. And on her first day, with a crew drawn from the women and the "sick, lame and lazy," had cleared ten life rafts and rescued six survivors. She'd do.

He paused in his ruminations and picked up his binoculars, peering into the distance. The *Toy* was a yacht, not a sportfisher, so it didn't have a tuna tower. Which slightly limited the distance at which anything could be spotted. That depended upon the conditions, of course, but in general, height equaled how far you could see at sea.

That also meant that up on the fly bridge he could see farther than from the helm. Which meant he was the first to spot the target.

By the same token as having a higher spot to look from, being higher above the water meant you were more visible. And this boat was visible from too far away. Then the music cut off.

"Captain Wolf?" the helmsman called over the radio. "I think I've spotted it on radar...?"

His new helmsman, Gustav Fleischmann, had had some experience with small fishing boats. Graduating to the *Toy* was an adjustment and he was still unsure about all of the readouts. But he could and would drive a boat and he seemed fairly reliable. Sure of himself...not so much. Then again, Steve wasn't so sure of him and generally took the boat for close maneuvers.

"Roger," Steve said. "I've got it on visual."

He wanted to curse. The boat could be a gold mine or a bust. But it was even larger than the *Large*. Much larger, as he finally spotted Sherill's 35-foot Bertram alongside. It looked like, well, a toy boat. In fact, the boat was much, much larger than he'd realized. It wasn't a boat, it was a...Small cruise ship? Megayacht? He wasn't sure.

He flipped channels for the flotilla frequency.

"*Sea Fit, Toy,* over."

"Sea Fit, *over,*" Sherill answered back immediately.

"*Fit,* you sure know how to pick 'em."

"*You like? We get part of the swag, right? If you've got it, we'll continue.*"

"Oh, no," Steve said. "This is an all-hands evolution. All boats, relay, proceed to location of *Sea Fit* for all-hands clearance." He paused for a moment, then keyed the radio again. "*Fit*...Is that thing listing?"

"*Yeah,*" Sherill replied. "*And you gotta see why...*"

"Bloody buggers..."

The megayacht was...massive. As long as the cutter, with some of the same lines, but...prettier. It was anything but utilitarian. And it was, indeed, listing.

On the starboard side of the yacht was a "boarding and support center" that was basically a *door* in the hull of the boat that dropped down to water line. There was also a boarding ladder down from the promenade deck, which was above the height of the *Toy*'s flying bridge.

The reason for the list was immediately apparent. There was

a heavy hawser pointed straight down from the boarding area for "support boats." Attached to it, as was apparent from looking down through the crystal-clear water, was a sportfisher, probably as big as Sherill's Bertram or a tad bigger. About sixty feet down. Bobbing up and down from the swells. Underwater.

"I can't believe this thing hasn't capsized," Sherill said over his loudspeaker.

The yacht also had a contingent of zombies. But they were sort of background to the big fishing boat attached to the much bigger ship.

"Well, that there's a puzzler," Fontana said, looking over the side of the *Toy*. He spit in the water. "It's so clear I sort of thought it would keep dropping."

"You don't realize how clear till you see something like that," Steve said.

"And them," Faith said, pointing to the circling sharks.

"Okay, here's the puzzler," Steve said. "The way the zombies are now, they're easy meat."

They were lined up on promenade deck, their arms waving and reaching for the nearby boat. There was a waist-high railing but there was plenty of room above it for a shot. Of course, there was a steel bulkhead behind them, which meant that any round was going to bounce. At least any that went through.

"Bouncers," Fontana said.

"Move back to the aft deck," Steve said, pointing but not looking. He was still considering the sunken boat. "The problem being that someone is going to have to go down there and release that thing. If you try to cut the hawser...You don't want to get close enough to cut the hawser. It'll snap back like a sixty-foot taipan and twice as deadly. That means raising it or releasing it. Raising it...no. However, there is, unless I'm mistaken, a quick release on it. So...hook up a line, pull and it goes into Davy Jones's locker."

"Makes sense," Fontana said. "Except for the being sixty feet down and we don't have SCUBA gear."

"That is not an issue," Steve said. "I am an expert free diver."

"And then there's *them*," Faith said, pointing to the sharks again. "You know, the *sharks*. The man-eating sharks. The man-eating, probably-been-surviving-on-zombies-that-fell-off sharks?"

"Right, those," Steve said. "About those..."

∿—⊖—∽

"You sure about this?" Sherill asked.

Some people tended to call him "Captain Gilligan" for his vague resemblance to Alan Hale, Jr. He had the same blue eyes, thinning blond hair. As he was getting his beer gut back, the resemblance was increasing.

His devotion to the *His Sea Fit* was almost doglike. He'd already lost three crewmen who couldn't take the constant pounding of being on a thirty-five-foot sportfisher, in deep ocean, day in and day out. Thirty-five-foot sportfishers were not designed for long-endurance, at-sea operations. Captain Gilligan didn't seem to care. You'd pry him out with a crowbar.

"If they don't leave," Steve said, sitting on the bulwark of the aft deck of the *Fit* wearing swim fins and goggles, "no."

The sharks were still circling below, but with luck, that was going to change soon. There was another shot from the aft of the boat and Steve vaguely heard the ricochet go by overhead. There was a flush-deck at the rear of the yacht, which had the infecteds right at waterline. Whether they dropped in the water or not, the blood from them should attract the sharks.

"You'd better not shoot my boat," Sherill said.

There was a splash in the distance, and first one of the larger sharks then the entire group headed aft.

"Unlikely," Steve said. "Angles are wrong." Of course, they were probably going to be putting holes in the yacht, but he figured it could probably take it. The "boarding support area" was halfway underwater and the yacht hadn't sunk.

He took a deep breath and slid quietly over the side.

He porpoised down into the depths, spinning in a three-sixty to keep an eye around. In his left hand he had a light line with a spring clip on one end. The other hovered over his H&K.

While there had been snorkels, swim fins and masks aplenty among the boats, not one single speargun had been found. Steve was hoping, really hard, that he wasn't going to have to test if you could fire an H&K USP .45, with octagonal barrel and Austrian engineering, sixty feet underwater.

He hadn't had much of a chance to do breathhold diving in a while. Most of the times they stopped, there were sharks around the boats and zombies to kill. People to save. Even Jew Bay was a no-go zone. In fact, he hadn't had a lot of time for anything but the Program in a while.

But while he'd grown up on a station, it was close to the coast. And he'd grown up swimming and free diving. This was home territory. Including the sharks, which in Australia were just one of those things like box jellies, spiders and snakes you had to put up with.

When he reached the hawser he put his right hand on it and followed it down to the latch point. The hawser wasn't tied to the fishing boat. It was connected to a quick release latch, which was, in turn, connected to an apparently massively strong davit.

Steve felt like he was out of air but knew it was just CO_2 build-up so he let out some air as he carefully connected the clip to the quick release. That was as much as he could handle on one breath so he started back up. He spun around, again, looking for potential threats but the sharks were busy feasting at the aft of the boat. His motions were smooth and regular, just another healthy, happy fish in the water. Nothing to attract them.

His heart beat faster as a massive hammerhead came coasting down the length of the megayacht. It seemed in no hurry to get to the feeding frenzy aft. On the other hand, it didn't turn towards Steve.

He surfaced and swam, splash free, to the dive platform on the rear of the *Sea Fit* and pulled himself completely out of the water, sprawling out on the platform.

"You okay?" Sherill called from the tuna tower. He was holding a rifle in his hands.

"Fine," Steve said. "Is that for zombies or sharks?"

"Yes!"

Steve breathed deeply and waved with two fingers for Sherill to back the boat closer to the megayacht. The less lateral distance he had to cross the better.

This time he slipped off the dive platform face down to get a better head start. He spun in place and then tried not to panic as the massive hammer came coasting towards him. It had apparently decided that the other boat was probably going serve up tasty zombies as well.

Steve decided to just keep heading down. Hammerheads were known to attack humans and this one was obviously accustomed to feeding on infecteds. But they were also fairly smart for sharks and also tended to focus on distressed fish, birds and mammals. Steve's movements were regular and steady. It should ignore him. Should.

He kept an eye on it as he headed down the hawser to the line. The medium-weight nylon was more or less negatively buoyant and hadn't gotten far from the hawser. Steve got ahold of one end and moved away from the hawser. As soon as he was clear, he sped up, swimming away from the boat and the quick release as fast as possible, the line wrapped around his left hand.

He felt the shock of the line going taut and looked back. The quick release had surrendered, finally, and the boat shot into the depths as the hawser snapped upwards.

Pulling Steve along with it. Which had been part of the plan.

Unfortunately, the sharp movements excited the hammerhead, which headed for the only reasonable source of protein in view: Steve.

The shark came in at lightning speed but Steve had had a master's course in drawing and firing fast at this point. He fended the charging hammerhead away by placing the barrel of the H&K against its port hammer and pressing the trigger as it rolled to take a bite of tasty human.

The gun did *not* explode and the hammerhead did *not* take well to being shot in the head by a polymer capped, expanding, .45 caliber ACP. It spasmed and dashed away in a corkscrew, its tail lashing furiously.

Unfortunately, it was now "a distressed fish, bird or mammal." Sharks sense such movements and are attracted to them. And while there were tasty zombies at the aft of the boat, there were also a lot of sharks. So some of the ones on the edge of the pack banked away and headed towards the new source of potential protein.

Which meant right at Steve.

He wasn't sticking around to watch or anything, but the sharks were coming in from near the surface. The hammerhead was tracking down and forward on the megayacht, and that meant that the sharks' path led them right to Steve.

Who they passed without note. He was still being calm and regular in his movements and they didn't see him as easy prey. Five, six, nine sharks darted right past him in pursuit of the massive hammer as he calmly made his way to the surface.

"I thought you were a goner, there," Sherill called. "They were too deep to shoot."

"If you'd shot one of them I *would* have been a goner," Steve muttered. If one of the charging sharks had been shot as well, all the rest would have closed in with Steve as tasty snack in the middle.

"What?" Sherill asked, starting to climb down.

"Easy peasy," Steve said, decocking the H&K and taking a series of deep breaths. "No worries, mate."

"Okay," Fredette said, shaking his head and listening to the take from the captains. The increasing number of boat captains in the "flotilla" gossiped like old women on various frequencies, which made keeping up with the goings-on of the group easy. "This guy is flipping insane. Diving into a feeding frenzy to release a boat and then taking out a shark with a pistol?"

"If it's crazy and it works, it ain't crazy," Bundy said, shrugging and making a note. "Note to sonar. That weird transient was the sound of a forty-five being fired sixty feet underwater..."

"Don't forget the whole 'into a shark' part," Fredette said. "That probably changed the acoustics from just firing it."

"Good point..."

Galloway raised an eyebrow and looked at Commander Freeman.

"His own subordinate skippers call him 'Captain Insanity,' sir," Freeman said, defensively.

"Not to influence the discussion or anything," Brice said, holding up her hands. "But I'm starting to like this guy."

Freeman looked at his monitors and sighed.

"Sir, we may have a destabilizing element in the equation."

"Which is?" Galloway asked.

"Passive sonar on the *Dallas* indicates an approaching Russian Typhoon."

"They're sending a boomer?" Brice said, blinking. "A *boomer*?"

"Their fast attacks are not as well designed for long endurance as ours," Freeman said. "It's possible that they don't have a fast attack to close the position. Acoustics indicate it is probably the *Servestal*."

"Sounds like time to talk to Sergei again," Galloway said, grimacing.

"Slippery," Steve said as he jumped off the dinghy onto the boarding platform. The dinghy was going up and down in five-foot regular seas whereas the boarding platform was hardly moving. He'd done it so many times, he really didn't notice. "Watch your step."

He'd actually landed on the chest of one of the dead infected. He also didn't really notice that except one detail.

"Is it just me or is there a preponderance of women?" he asked, catching the line thrown to him.

"We'd noticed that," Fontana said. "And for all they were zombies...kinda pretty ones."

"Men," Faith said, stepping easily onto the flushdeck. "Da, this is one of the easiest boardings we've ever done."

"Noticed," Steve said. "But if you slip overboard it will go quickly to one of the worst," he added, pointing to the still-circling sharks.

"So, you seriously shot a hammerhead with a forty-five?" Fontana said, taking point. There were stairs up to the promenade deck to either side of the landing. He took port just because. There also appeared to be some sort of pop-out door but there were no obvious external controls.

"Wasn't my first option," Steve said, as Faith took starboard. "And I'm not sure whether to trust the gun again. We need to be *really* careful on fire discipline on this one. I think it's going to be as bad as the cutter."

"Well, it's got all the usual zombie mess," Fontana said, looking over at Faith. "Ooh, look, there's movement to my starboard!"

"Very effing funny, Falcon," Faith said. She looked through the heavy glass doors at the interior and shrugged. "I dunno, a little paint, some carpet..."

"A *lot* of carpet," Steve said. "I think we need to start clearing freighters to look for carpet."

What appeared to be the main saloon was about sixty feet long, two stories high and had once been a vision in fine wood bars, tables and white carpet and equally white sofas and chairs. There were also plasma screens freaking *everywhere*. From the looks of it, some of the windows could double as smart-screens. The central bar was a vision of cream, silver and blond wood with "*SOCIAL ALPHA*" emblazoned above along with what appeared to be the logo for Spacebook, the social networking site. Someone had defaced it, apparently tried to strip off the platinum, and since it was above most of the damage, that had probably been an uninfected human.

Half the plasmas were obviously trashed. The floor was covered in the usual mix of blood, decomposing flesh and feces. So were the sofas, chairs, tables and the fine wood bars. There were bullet holes in half the windows. There were at least nine chewed corpses in view.

"All of the booze is gone," Fontana said, looking behind the central bars.

"Maybe they figured out how to break the top of a bottle," Faith said, stepping gingerly around the central bar to starboard and sweeping from side to side. The room had no interior light but they were still getting good radiance from the tinted windows. She checked behind the bar on her side, leading with her Saiga. "Cleaning this up is going to be a bitch and a half. But I think it might be worth it."

"The problem is, again, fuel," Steve said.

"There's that small tanker Sophia found," Fontana said, sweeping to port again.

"Let's say I'm a little uncomfortable clearing a tanker," Steve said, hefting his Saiga. "Especially one that has been sitting without spaces being vented. All I can see is Faith shooting a zombie and the whole thing going boom. Then there's the problem of getting it running and getting the fuel from it to the other boats. In mid-ocean."

"All problems we're going to have to figure out," Faith pointed out. "We're going to need the fuel now or later."

"Open hatch to the interior," Fontana said, pausing. The scattered bars were designed to get people to flow in a freeform manner. They also tended to restrict line of sight. Which he wasn't enjoying.

"Olly olly oxenfree!" Faith shouted. "Zombies, zombies, any zombies home?"

"I wonder how far that actually carried?" Steve asked.

"Far enough," Fontana said, as the laser dropped onto a zombie's chest.

"Wait!" Faith said delightedly.

"Why?" Fontana asked. The zombie was in pretty bad shape and it wasn't closing fast, but it wasn't like he wanted him to get to melee range.

"Oh, my God!" Faith squealed as the zombie charged. "Do you know who that is?"

"No," Steve said, still covering the rear. "You going to shoot or Fontana?"

"Mike Mickerberg!" she said, pulling the trigger on the Saiga twelve-gauge. The former internet billionaire was splattered all over the deck of his megayacht. "Clean-up on Aisle Nine!"

"That's getting old, Faith," Steve said. "And who?"

"The guy who invented Spacebook! Duh."

"Well, even if we had the equipment we couldn't use him for vaccine," Fontana said.

"Why?" she asked, heading to the next hatch. "He'd infect people with horrible apps?"

"Actually, I was wondering if he had a spine," Fontana said, then looked down. "Yep. Sure does. Amazing..."

"Don't step in him, Da," Faith said. "You might get Slimelined. *HELLO!* ANY ZOMBIES IN THERE? ZOMBIES, ZOMBIES, OLLY-OLLY OXENFREE!"

CHAPTER 25

"I'm starting to think there was a mutiny," Steve said, stepping over the corpse. This man had been wearing body armor and he would have been facing a similarly clad man farther down the corridor. Both had rifles by their bodies, one an M4, the other an AK variant, and there were casings scattered along the corridor.

"Looks that way," Fontana said, turning the smaller man over. His legs and face had been chewed off but the armor had kept his torso intact. Except for the decomposition. "Ugh."

"What?" Faith asked, looking down. "Clean it up and it's pretty good gear. Well, except the holes that are in it."

"It wasn't the body or the gear I was going ugh about," Fontana said. "Socorro Security. Evan Socorro's company."

"Context?" Steve asked.

"There are contractors and contractors," Fontana said, continuing the sweep. "Despite its rep, Blackwater wasn't actually that bad. They had something resembling quality control. Triple Canopy? Very good. At least their primary operators. And they pick good associate operators."

"Primary, associate?" Faith said. "Bosses and subordinates?"

"Generally, but not exactly," Fontana said, banging on a hatch. "You can call it racist, but primaries are all from developed nations.

Generally. Associates are guys hired from developing nations. Associates are cheaper and generally not as well trained. Not always. Some groups use former Ghurkas for associates or even primaries. There's one run by a former Ghurka that does shipboard security."

There was no response so he entered the compartment. There were several bodies in there but none had been chewed. Some men, some women. Most had been shot in the head.

"So what's with Socorro?" Steve asked.

"I won't get into my *personal* issues with former Special Forces Major Evan Socorro," Fontana said. "Although I had personal issues with Socbreath. Which term came from his tendency to . . . fellate highers from SOCOM. Pretty much anybody who worked for him did. But he finally got a chain of command that, officially in writing, asked how an asshole, and a not particularly competent asshole, got to be a major in the Groups in the first place and he got out. And started his own security company. He had some assbuddy primaries that were mostly not former military, just call them gun geeks. Some of those guys are fine. A lot of them weren't military 'cause they couldn't make the grade. 'How soon do I get to kill somebody?' couldn't make the grade. That's the kind he liked to hire. Then instead of hiring good associate contractors like, say, former Peruvian mountain commandoes or El Salvadorans or even some of the SA or Angolan 'bleks' he picked West Africans."

"Bloody hell!" Steve said, looking around a corner. "Seriously? More here."

"Is that bad?" Faith asked. "I guess so."'

"Think child soldiers whose 'military experience' consisted of rape, loot, pillage and burn," Steve said. "Again, there are good West African troops . . ."

"For values of good," Fontana said. "I think 'good' for even their elite is a stretch."

"But the majority are pretty damned bad," Steve said. "By any definition of bad you'd care to name. Competence, ability, discipline. I'm surprised anybody would hire a group like that."

"They were cheap," Fontana said, shrugging. "He didn't pay his primaries at full standard rate and his associates got paid dirt. So he could shave a few bucks off a contract."

"Looks like the client got what he paid for," Faith said, pointing to a hole in the bulkhead. "Steel. I'd say . . . seven six two?"

"Yeah," Fontana said, staring at one of the female bodies. "I think these were potential infected that were terminated. I don't see any bites but that might not have been how they were chosen. And..."

"The women have all been raped," Steve said. "From the ligature marks."

"Oh, God," Faith said, grimacing.

"*If one holds his state on the basis of mercenary arms, he will never be firm or secure; because they are disunited, ambitious, without discipline, unfaithful; gallant among friends, vile among enemies; no fear of God, no faith with men; and one defers ruin insofar as one defers the attack; and in peace you are despoiled by them, in war by the enemy,*" Steve said.

"Da and his quotes," Faith said. "Which one is this one?"

"Machiavelli's *The Prince*," Fontana said. "I know some good guys who are contractors. And some good companies."

"So you're facing a zombie apocalypse where every reasonable person foresees a potentially permanent breakdown in law and order, and you bound onto your megayacht, load up with models, then hire a security company filled with freaking *West Africans*?" Steve said.

"Well, no," Fontana said. "*That* was stupid. You might as well put a steak around your neck and go jump in a tiger pit."

"So..." Faith said. "Guy's smart enough to build and run a billion-dollar company. How come he makes that mistake?"

"Situation he's in is a tough call," Fontana said. "I mean, in normal times no way that you'd have to deal with a take-over by your security. There's laws. Bad things *will* happen to them. Post-apoc? Don't ask me what I would have done if I was the guy running security, had all the guns and all the people who knew how to use them, and the boss was now utterly useless."

"I'll keep that in mind," Steve said.

"Different situation entirely," Fontana said. "And I'm not Socorro."

"I'm not talking about that," Faith said. "I can see that problem. I mean, I've been nervous about all the new people. Not you, Falcon, but... You know, who do you trust? I guess I'm wondering how a guy like Mickerberg could have picked somebody even I would know not to trust?"

"You're thirteen but you've got the background," Steve said. "Your mom and I gave it to you. I don't know a lot about the guy, but I got the impression of intelligent liberal, one each. To them, everybody who knows how to use a gun looks the same. There's

278 John Ringo

no difference between Sergeant Fontana and Kony in Congo. He probably just told one of his staff to find a security company that could supply security and picked one of the lowest bidders."

"We're all babykillers after all," Fontana said, banging on a hatch. "Hello! Any babies to kill in there?"

"If there were any survivors, that would not be very reassuring," Steve pointed out.

"No, just zombies," Fontana said, looking in. "Dead zombies."

"Sure they were zombies?" Faith asked.

"They're naked and some of them are chewed," Fontana said, closing and marking the hatch. "I hope like hell they were."

"Da, I'm starting to think that zombies aren't the worst things in the world..."

The cabin on the top deck was nearly the size of the main saloon, with a panoramic view of the surrounding ocean, a massive in-deck hottub, a wet bar big enough for a public bar and a bed that could hold forty. At a guess, there had once been a good bit of gilding, from the looks of where stuff had been ripped out. There was also a huge stack of Mountain House boxes and five-gallon containers of water.

The solid steel door had been cut through by a welding torch. On the bed were ten women, naked, their hands bound behind their backs and shot in the head. At the head of the bed was a male corpse, unbound, also naked, with the top of his head blown off. All of the bodies had been gnawed by ferals, but they hadn't died from the zombies.

"Major Socorro," Fontana said, smiling thinly. "We meet again."

"How do you know it's him?" Faith asked. The body's face had been chewed off.

"Right height, right build and I know how he was about women," Fontana said. "There's rough and then there's batshit."

"Holed up to wait for the zombies to take over," Steve said. "Probably with the pick of the prettier women. Then when the mutineers burned through the door he shot them and himself?"

"Looks that way," Fontana said, wandering around the suite. "What's missing are the weapons and ammo."

"And the gilt," Steve said, pointing to where something had been prised from the walls. "You know, modern sportfishers don't sink very readily. They've got buoyant foam inserted everywhere..."

"Zombies are taking over, the mercs load up the one away-boat with all the gold and all the guns?" Fontana said. "Overload the boat?"

"Which explains why it went down like a stone," Steve said, shaking his head.

"You know," Fontana mused, "billionaire like this probably had *real* gold. I mean, bars, coin..."

"Jewelry," Steve said. "And not costume."

"Did we just drop a treasure ship in five thousand feet of water?" Faith said. "*Please* tell me we didn't drop a treasure ship in five thousand feet of water..."

"Yeah, you did."

James Michael "call me Mike" Dugan, assistant engineer, had been found hiding in one of the yacht's cavernous storage lockers along with a female Indonesian cook named Eka Sari. They'd been brought up on deck and were sipping soup in a relatively undamaged portion of the promenade.

"We could hear them talking about it," Sari said softly. "When they were speaking English."

"It wasn't real clear that Socorro had taken over at first," Dugan said. "Mick was always sort of standoffish with the crew. But then Socorro took over his cabin and the...Africans started going nuts. Mick had brought a bunch of his friends and execs along."

"And women?" Steve asked.

"Yeah," Dugan said. "Lots of girls. Mick hadn't been seen for a week. I mean, I didn't interact with guests but—"

"I did," Sari said. "And there were questions. All of Mr. Mickerberg's food was being taken to him by security, 'for his safety.'"

"Then...Socorro had all the guests brought up on deck and the Africans separated out the men and women, and the women who were...older," Dugan said. "And the Africans shot 'em. Right in front of God and everybody. Told us if we didn't follow his orders, we'd get the same. Then the party started..." he said, glancing quickly at Sari and then away.

"Rape," Sari said, looking at the deck. "Much rape."

"Told you Socorro was batshit," Fontana said, shrugging. "I think he hired the Africans 'cause they were the only guys he could find as fucked up as he was."

"Then people started going zombie," Dugan said. "And it really hit the fan. There was some sort of a split in the gang. We heard Socorro was killed, the leader of that faction, guy named Meloy, went zombie and the Africans, those that hadn't turned, started loading the away boat. With, like, every bit of treasure they could get their hands on. And there was a lot. It was about that time that I...went into the compartment and sealed the door. Turned out Sari was already there..."

"I had hidden when the fighting broke out," Sari said.

"There was a pause there," Steve said.

"What pause?" Dugan asked.

"Before you hid in the compartment," Steve said. "You skipped a step."

"I sort of locked the engines down and turned off the lights," Dugan said, grinning thinly. "And locked down the engine room doors. I was the last surviving engineering officer. That's what got them to leave the ship; no lights, no power, drifting. I figured, turn everything off, lock it out, hide in the compartment, wait for them to leave and then come out."

"Good plan," Fontana said drily. "Except for the zombies."

"Yeah, them," Dugan said, shrugging. "Thanks for clearing them off."

"Mr. Dugan, you know the laws of salvage," Steve said. "Any live survivors means it's not salvage. Our...approach is slightly different. We allow survivors equal shares on all portable wealth of the boat. The boat is property of the flotilla as well as half of the materials. We give... When there is a survivor or survivors who can run the vessel, we generally allow them to keep it if they want to join the flotilla. Or if we don't need it. In the case of this, let's say we'll be extremely lenient in that regard. But if, as you've indicated, it's still probably functional and has some fuel...I think this, we may need."

"So...That sort of makes you pirates," Dugan said.

"Needs must is the best I can say," Steve said. "Okay, flip it around. You take the boat. It's not salvage. It's not entirely clear, by the way. Are you going to finish clearing it?"

"Uh..." Dugan said. "Can I get some help?"

"No," Fontana said. "I mean, face it, you already did."

"So even passing that," Steve said. "Your stores will eventually run out. Where are you going to get more? Where are you going to get fuel?"

"You can't run this without support," Fontana said.

"On the other hand," Steve said, "we can't run it at *all*. You and a Coast Guard petty officer are the first qualified engineers we've rescued. I doubt that however many manuals she reads, my wife can even start the engines on this thing."

"Not the way I buggered the computer controls she can't," Dugan said.

"So, obviously, we need your cooperation and I hope support," Steve said. "This is well set-up to be a floating command and support ship. We need somewhere to put the refugees, give them a few days rest before we give them the choice of helping or being put into Coventry."

"You can get to Coventry?" Dugan said.

"There are two sailboats we floated in Bermuda harbor," Fontana said. "Which is filled with sharks that have gotten used to snacking on uncoordinated zombies. Anybody who doesn't want to help out we drop on those. They're hellholes, really, but there's nothing else to do with them."

"Most of them are less sick, lame and lazy than tired and afraid of the sea," Steve said, shrugging. "And there's no great benefit, to their eyes, to bouncing around in tiny boats in a big sea. I think that some of them would probably go for being on this one. Even if it's not in the big room."

"Cleaning this up . . ." Dugan said, shaking his head. "When I went to ground it had gotten bad, but not this bad."

"That's the price of getting out of Coventry," Steve said, grinning mirthlessly. "And the price of remaining out is continuing to provide support to a reasonable standard."

"I can run the engines," Dugan said. "For as long as they hold out. And they're good, don't get me wrong. And new. But I can't con this thing. Where you gonna get a captain?"

"What do you think?"

Despite her surname, Geraldine Miguel could have been from Missouri. She had that Midwestern look. Blond hair, blue eyes, Scandinavian facial structure. She was actually from Texas, a ninth-generation family that went back to the pre-Republic days. Most of the line, however, was Germanic rather than Hispanic, which explained the looks.

"I think it's going to take a hell of a lot of crew," Geraldine said, looking around the still-dark helm. "And one hell of a lot of cleanup."

"I have a cunning plan for that," Steve said as the lights came on and the panels started to light.

"Which involves?" Geraldine asked.

"Using an enemy."

CHAPTER 26

"Sea Hooky, Tina's Toy, over," Steve said. *"Sea Hooky, Tina's Toy,* over."

"Are you sure this is a good idea, Steve?" Stacey asked.

"No?" Steve said. "But it's the best idea I can come up with."

"What do you want, Smith?" the voice growled over the radio.

"I want to meet you out here," Steve said.

"Fuck you, bite me and go away."

"You're about out of fuel or already out of fuel," Steve said. "You're fishing for your dinner and not catching a lot of fish. I'll trade you a half a tank of gas to come out to this location. When you get here, I'll throw in a load of supplies. The gas is just to be able to get out here. Or you can keep fishing for yellowtail."

"Yellowtail isn't bad eating."

"When you're catching any," Steve said. "It gets tiresome as sushi. I want to make you an offer I don't think you'll refuse."

"What offer?" Isham asked suspiciously. *"And why are you so nice all of a sudden?"*

"Because before you were a pain and a problem I did not need," Steve said. "Now you are a potential asset. I'll even lend you a respirator."

"Toy, Cooper. Are you serious?"

283

"You want these headaches?" Steve asked. "You're the second choice for this."

"No way," Chris responded.

"So there's a hook," Isham said.

"Actually, I can see you seeing it as a positive," Steve said. "You're also going stir-crazy with nothing to do. I want to offer you an opportunity."

"This is going to be a doozy, ain't it?"

"You son of a bitch," was the first thing Isham said as he stepped onto the flush deck.

"I feel the same way," Steve said, holding out a respirator. "Take a walk with me."

"I know you don't want me to captain this thing," Isham said, putting the respirator on. "How the hell do you use this thing?"

Steve showed him how to fit it.

"You could barely figure out how to steer it," Steve said, walking up the back deck. "However, part of the opportunity is being able to sleep on it in a very comfortable cabin."

"One that stinks," Isham said, looking at the saloon. "Jesus, this is a wreck."

"And someone needs to clean it up," Steve said. "Some *ones.* It will take a lot of people to clean it. *And* to run it."

"So you can have the big yacht?" Isham growled.

"So that we can use it as an at-sea support base," Steve said. "Somewhere for the refugees and the crews to fall back on for rest and refit. I don't know if you'd realized it, but there are storms that are about to start sweeping down on this area. We're going to have to leave soon. Our crews aren't good enough, our boats aren't good enough, to survive the North Atlantic in winter. Or a bad tropical. We need a base. The *Large* isn't big enough."

"How are you . . . ?" Isham said, shaking his head.

"I'll provide plenty of answers," Steve said. "But I want you to follow me and see something first."

"Dead bodies," Isham said. He'd seen quite a few on the way down. Since he hadn't been working with the flotilla he'd had to stop and try not to puke at the first few.

"Both in body armor," Steve said. "Because there was a mutiny by the, well, mercenaries the owner hired. He wasn't killed. They deliberately infected him with the zombie virus."

"Jesus," Isham said. "Sick. What's your point?"

"This is why I threw you out," Steve said, pointing. "And why I've thrown others out. What they wanted was the power and control. It's what you want. But they couldn't say 'I've been given x amount of power and control and I'm fine with that.' They wanted all the pussy and all the booze and all the gold. And they each wanted all of it."

"I wasn't going to rape your daughters, Smith," Isham said.

"But you would have had others following you that would," Steve said. "Or would try. Everyone talks about Faith but I would not suggest it with either one. This is the darkness that every one of us has in us, Jack. And this is what happens when we let that darkness loose. Fontana has it. I have it. And you have it but you use other means. What I understand, what Fontana understands, is that when you let it loose this is the result. No man can trust another. You desire power, control, prestige. I'm willing to give you those. But. The moment that I suspect that you are going in this direction... Then I will kill you, Jack. Without hesitation and without warning. This will not happen on my watch."

"You still haven't said exactly what you want," Isham said.

"I want you to be the XO of the flotilla and of this boat," Steve said. "The operations officer, if you prefer. I want you to, first, get this place cleaned up. We'll recruit the people in Coventry for it. Which is part of the challenge because they're not exactly self-starters."

"God, no," Isham said, grimacing.

"They're who we have," Steve said, shrugging. "You're a micro-manager. This will give vent to that. Then find the ones that can do jobs, actually do them, and set them to it on this boat. Others will be sent onboard that are actually skilled. I want this to be turned into a support boat, not a floating palace. And we need to get the resupply system under control, repairs to the boats, division of materials, organize salvage teams... That will all be on your shoulders. Something for you to do, Jack. Prestige, power, control."

"And the second I let it go to my head I get a bullet in the back of the head?" Isham said with a dry laugh.

"I won't say that we're not playing fast and loose with the law of the sea," Steve said. "But the law has always held that sedition, mutiny if you would, is grounds for the death sentence. Try to use the authority I'm giving you to take over and, yes, I will put a bullet in your head. Not because I want the power and authority and control. Because I know it will lead to this," he said, pointing at his feet. "I don't know if you understand that. If you ever can."

"I can't exactly mutiny if you've got all the guns," Isham said.

"There will be guns," Steve said. "I'm about done waiting for whoever that is on the phone to make up his mind. If I don't get a call, soon, I'm going to strip that damned cutter without permission and damn to them. And one point to this is a place to put materials."

"You really have been talking to Washington?" Isham asked.

"Washington is gone," Steve said. "You know that. I heard about your trip to the coast. I don't know *who* they are. Just that the subs, or *some* subs, follow their orders. Jack, I need someone to ramrod this, to get it done. You're a get-it-done person. Can I trust you not to knife me in the back?"

"You're so trusting," Isham said.

"It is a well-known fact that Australia is a nation populated entirely by criminals," Steve intoned. "And criminals trust no one."

"Funny," Isham said.

"So you want the job?" Steve asked.

"I dunno," Isham said, rubbing his head. "Lemme see the cabin."

"It got trashed out by the mutineers but not the zombies," Steve said.

The starboard side cabin was the size of a small home with a magnificent sweep of windows, and a bathroom that was worthy of any palatial home. On the other hand, some of the fixtures had been ripped out.

"Gold?" Isham said, fingering a hole in the alabaster counter top where a faucet had been pulled out.

"Probably," Steve said.

"I don't suppose it's still onboard?"

"Funny story that..."

Steve turned the *Toy* away as the *Alpha* dropped anchor in Jew Bay and headed for the *Livin' Large*.

"*Livin' Large, Toy,* over," Steve called.

"Toy, Livin' Large. *Just had to one-up us, over?*"

"Something like that," Steve replied. "Coming alongside for a chat."

"Hey, Steve," Kuzma said, shaking his hand.

The petty officer looked much better than the last time Steve had seen him. And he had to admit that the Coasties had been a real help. Most of the refugees were being slowly moved back to Bermuda harbor. After a few days' rest out of the waves they were given the choice of joining the flotilla or going to Coventry. Those who volunteered for the flotilla had stayed onboard the *Large.* The Coasties had been managing that process, taking some of the burden off of Steve.

"How's the personnel situation?" Steve asked.

"Nominal," Kuzma said. "Until we get more boats, we've got more volunteers than we've got slots."

"Good," Steve said, hooking a finger. "That's going to take some work. Any of them skilled?"

"Two sailors," Bobby said, shrugging. "Deckhands, not captains, but they know deck work and some mechanics. But I've got one kid you need to meet. I mean, you stopped by, want to cover that?"

"Let me meet the 'kid,'" Steve said.

"Lance Corporal, this is Commodore Wolf," Kuzma said.

The lance corporal jumped off his bunk and came to attention.

"Lance Corporal Joshua Hocieniec, sir, pleasure to meet you!"

Hocieniec was slightly under normal height, almost skeletally thin and darkly tanned, a sure sign of having been in a raft or lifeboat rather than stuck in a compartment. He didn't have a beard, which had become common in the flotilla, but he did appear to have a five-o'clock shadow.

"As you were, Marine," Steve said.

The crew room was neat as a pin. There was clear evidence of zombie damage but it had been scrubbed to the walls and the Marine's blouse was washed and neatly hung on the wall. He'd even polished his boots.

"Where'd you come from?" Steve asked.

"Life raft, sir!" Hocieniec barked.

"The *Iwo Jima*," Kuzma said softly. "Only guy in the life raft."

"Sir..." Hocieniec said. "I swear, it was abandoned!"

"Start from the beginning," Steve said, sitting down on a chair. "Or, rather, what happened in general?"

"We were in lockdown, but the bug got onboard somehow, sir," Hocieniec said precisely. "Just the flu at first, then people started to turn, sir. We tried to maintain control but... My team leader, Sergeant Fry, he turned in the middle of a clearance, sir, and then he bit PFC Conner. Finally, the acting CO ordered abandon ship, sir. I...the boats were going over the side, just...going, sir. I couldn't even find a boat and I was clocking out, running out of ammo, sir. And I'd got the flu. I didn't know when I was going to turn, sir. I went over the side and into the drink. I was floating when I spotted the raft, sir. I climbed aboard. I tried to paddle to some other guys who were afloat but the wind was blowing...sir, I did absolutely everything I could, sir..."

"Calm down, Lance Corporal," Steve said. "No worries, as they say in my homeland. Nobody was able to hold onto anything. Generals, admirals, captains and commanders weren't able to do more. And I'll note that 'commodore' is an honorary title in my case." He considered the Marine for a moment. "How are you doing? What's your condition, in your opinion?"

"Ready for duty, sir," Hocieniec said. "I understand you need clearance personnel. I am ready to fight zombies any day you say, sir."

"Here's the deal," Steve said. "You might have heard rumor we're in contact with higher. They haven't called back in a while, but the subs, which is how we communicate with them, are still out there. So, presumably is this unknown 'Headquarters.' They haven't given me the right to *order* military personnel to provide support. But they know that military are working with us and haven't objected. The situation is ambiguous. But we've got an SF sergeant, active duty, doing clearance. I don't see them objecting to a Marine. However, it's up to you. I can't order you to do it. That being said, if you agree, it's like enlisting. You then do follow the orders of whoever is assigned over you. You may just be trained in clearance by a thirteen-year-old female. Think you can handle that?"

"I've...heard about Shewolf, sir," Hocieniec said. "Shouldn't be a problem, sir."

"Do you have a handle, Lance Corporal...Hoochken—"

"Hocieniec, sir," the Marine said, his face very clearly not smiling. "Hooch or Burma, sir."

"Burma?" Steve asked.

"If I don't shave three times a day I get a shadow, sir," Hooch said, rubbing his chin. "Burma Shave, sir."

"All right, Burma," Steve said, sticking out his hand. "Welcome to Wolf's Floating Circus."

"How's the weather report look?" Steve asked. "If it chops up this is purely going to suck."

The ship wasn't a tanker. It was an oil rig support ship. Which in a lot of ways was better. Support ships were designed with massive tankerlike bunkers because, oddly enough, oil rigs had to be resupplied with diesel. But they also had deck cargo room and some even had machine shops. This could be a real find. There being a few little issues. One of them was not whether it had diesel. They knew that because they could smell it. That was one of the issues. There was a leak somewhere.

The other issue was what was on deck. Besides lashed down cargo, there were two zombies. And between the hydrocarbons and not knowing exactly what was in the cargo on the deck, they couldn't exactly shoot them off.

"It's good," PO3 Ruth Gardner said. "Again."

For this op, Steve simply had to have some trained people. While Isham cleaned up the *Alpha*, he'd pulled Geraldine and Dugan off to come try to recover the support ship. But he'd also had to dip into the Coasties for support. Ruth Gardner was a fueling expert, called POL in the military. She was trained in unrep as well as "issues" with fuel and fuel systems. What she *wasn't* trained in was *repairing* fuel systems. Different MOS. Dugan was pretty sure that if it was repairable at all he could do it.

"I'm okay with input on how to do this," Steve said. "'Cause I'm sort of buggered."

"I've got an idea," Fontana said. "But I don't know if it's a good one."

Steve was just fine with "normal" danger, like, say, a zombie apocalypse, for Faith. This was something different. So he'd dropped Hocieniec off on the *Endeavor* with Faith to go do some light clearance and brought along Fontana.

"Which is?" Steve asked.

Fontana went over to a bag of gear he'd brought along and rummaged through it. After a moment he brought out a machete in a sheath and drew it with a flourish.

"You're joking," Gardner said, munching on a cracker.

PO3 Gardner was pregnant. So were many of the women. There had been a noted sociologial response to societal stress called "the replacement factor." After major disasters, women had a habit of getting pregnant at a higher rate than during good times or during the stress period. The post-war Germany was noted as an example as well as post-Black-Plague Europe.

In the case of the zombie apocalypse, it had much more to do with men and women trapped on lifeboats and in small compartments with no access to contraceptives and exactly zero to do. In a few cases, that had definitely been due to force. Those men were on a special boat in Coventry. There were a few cases were the jury was still out. In Ruth's case, like the young lady found with Fontana, there seemed to be no issue. The only real issue was that she was found in a compartment with two other, male, Coast Guardsmen and she honestly had no clue which was the father. The "dads" didn't really care. They were both good-naturedly arguing over who was the "real" prospective dad.

"In 1994, eight hundred thousand people were massacred in Rwanda," Fontana said. "Mostly by having an arm hacked off by a machete and being left to die. These zombies are not walking dead."

"No," Steve said. "But they do spread a blood pathogen."

"I've been exposed at this point," Fontana said. "And I'll wear raingear. 'Cause clear sky or no, it *is* gonna rain."

"The question is how you're going to get up close enough to chop off an arm," Steve said, conning the inflatable closer.

The supply ship had a midships deck that was, for a ship its size, remarkably low to the waterline. Steve couldn't see how it wouldn't get swamped in heavy seas.

Low did not mean flush to the waterline. It was well above Fontana's reach while standing on the deck of the fifteen-foot, center-console inflatable.

"No offense, but I'm not going to step up on the pontoons," Fontana said, looking up at the zombies. They weren't howling or keening, but they were drooling.

"Not with those down there," Steve said, gesturing to the now-familiar sharks.

A wave caught the inflatable and pushed it closer to the ship. As it did, one of the infecteds saw its chance and jumped over the low side-rail with a shriek.

Keeping your feet on a small boat was a skill that everyone in the flotilla had mastered at this point. And Fontana had spent two months on an even smaller raft before being rescued. He easily backed away as Steve reversed to avoid the zombie. But it had leapt well out and still managed to sprawl face down on the foredeck of the boat.

Fontana stepped forward and cut down as the zombie was pushing itself to its feet. There was a sound very similar to a frozen melon being hit by a large knife.

"That's one," Fontana said, levering the machete out of the infected's head.

"It's times like this I wonder how my children are doing...." Steve said.

"How do you like being back on the *Endeavor*, Hooch?" Sophia said, sitting down at the dinette.

"Better than a life raft, Skipper," Hooch said.

"I can't believe Da stuck me on this tub," Faith said, crossing her arms. "Especially with *you*."

"Is that seditious speech I hear out of you?" Sophia said. "That's lashing round the fleet."

"You and what army, Tiny?" Faith said. "Try it, and while I won't exactly mutiny, you're going to have to learn to swim *really* hard."

"So, what's the op?" Hooch asked quickly.

"General clearance," Sophia said. "There are plenty of boats that can and do pick up life rafts and lifeboats. Those that have survivors, about one in ten, they just pick 'em up. Like, say, you. Which was what we were on before. But when they spot boats like, well, this, most of them don't have the guns..."

"...Or the guts," Faith said, picking at her fish.

"Or the experience or the, yeah, guts to go clear them," Sophia said. "Which is where you come in."

"Roger, Skipper."

"*Skipper*," Faith said, under her breath. "Heh."

"Faith," Sophia said. "You can cop attitude in front of my crew. They all know us. You can even do it with Hooch. Hooch, we're sisters, that's all this is."

"No, I get it, Skip," Hooch said. "I've got two sisters and they—" He stopped and his face worked.

"I'm sorry for your loss," Sophia said, frowning. "We really... Our family is the only family that hasn't lost people to the plague. It's hard for us to truly understand. But... I'm sorry for your loss."

"It's..." Hooch shrugged. "I'm not going to count them as lost until I can't find 'em, Skip. Simple as that. But about the two of you. It's sort of... comforting. Listening to sisters argue is sort of like being back home. Doesn't bother me."

"I get it," Sophia said. "But, Faith, don't give me crap, at least at first, if we find survivors. If there's an emergency, I don't want them doubting my orders. I can't have that. We can't have that. Okay?"

"You and what army?" Faith repeated. "Yeah, yeah, got it."

"Seriously."

"I said I got it," Faith snapped. "What is it about 'got it' you don't understand?"

"You can just *feel* the love," Paula said, laughing.

"I just love you so much, sis," Faith said. "You're just the biggest baddest captain of a *dinghy* in the whole fleet!"

"I sooo want to rename it *Minnow*," Sophia said. "Next time we get time, I swear. But it's mine, all mine."

"The captain she was a mighty sailing man," Paula caroled. "The mate, that's me, was brave and true..."

"Hey!" Patrick called from the helm. "I thought *I* was the mate?"

"We're all mates," Sophia said. "Well, actually, I think me and Paula are sheilas."

"God, I hope so," Hooch said. "'Cause you look like sheilas. And one deployment to Okinawa was enough..."

CHAPTER 27

"Hydrocarbons, sure enough," Gardner said. Her voice was barely audible between the silver suits they were wearing and the air-pak. She knew this so she tapped Fontana on the shoulder and made sure he saw the blinking indicator. "Take off your mask in here and you're going to hit the deck, fast."

"No worries," Steve shouted. "The same could be said for the zombies. There is some good news."

"And one spark and we're going to go sky high," Fontana noted. He used his hand to bang on the next hatch. "Anybody home?"

There was an answering banging, regular, not frenzied like zombies.

"I knew we forgot something," Steve said. "Spare air."

"How many!" Fontana shouted. He put his ear to the hatch to hear the reply. "I think they're saying four."

"Stand by here," Steve said. "I'll take Gardner back to the ship. But I'm not sure how to...We'd have to *fit* them..."

"They must have a clear, or reasonably clear, air supply in there," Gardner said. "And if there are females, they're probably pregnant. Not good to have them exposed. I suggest we run blowers down here and clear out this passage, *then* extract them."

"And we get blowers, where?" Fontana asked.

"There are some on the cutter," Gardner said.

"Which we already had to do a six-hour run up to and a seven-hour run back," Steve said. He was either going to have to figure out how to tow the damned thing or strip it soon. That was one of his nagging issues.

"It's a supply ship," Fontana said. "Would they have some?"

"We can try to ask," Steve said.

"Do you have blowers?" Fontana said. "Blowers! Where are the blowers? If they're answering, I can't hear. They're saying something..."

"We passed an aid station," Gardner said, pointing back the way they came.

"Which would have blowers?" Steve said.

"No," Gardner said. "But it might have a *stethoscope*."

Fontana ripped off his mask and leaned into the hatch.

"Where do you have air blowerthisairyoucan'tbreatheitwhere ARETHEAIRBLOWERS!"

"OW!" Gardner snapped, holding her ears that the stethoscope was inserted into. "That hurt!"

Fontana quickly redonned his mask and took a deep breath.

"Wow, that really is foul."

Gardner waved a hand for silence as she listened.

"Ask them if they said 'locker by engineering'?" She pulled the stethoscope away from the hatch and covered it with her hand.

"LOCKER BY ENGINEERING?" Fontana shouted through his mask.

"Yeah, that's it," Gardner said, nodding and taking off the stethoscope. "Okay, you can bellow as loud as you want, now."

"You got a clue how to use these?" Steve asked, looking at the fans and big, coiled duct stuff. Mechanical wasn't his gift any more than singing was.

"As a matter of fact, I do," Gardner said. "But I'll need some help moving them. Oooh, oooh, My. Poor. Pregnant. Back."

"There's a reason Sadie is back on the *Large*," Fontana said.

In the end, Gardner did pretty much all the work but the toting. And in thirty minutes, they had the blowers evacuating and replacing the air in the corridors to the survivor compartment.

"How long?" Steve asked, looking at the descending sun. It wasn't red. Which wasn't necessarily a bad sign. A bad sign was if the *dawn* was red.

"When this says it's okay," Gardner said, holding up the hydrocarbon meter.

"Picky, picky," Fontana said. "*Women!*"

"You know, Fontana, on a boat like this I know ways to *just* catch *you* on fire. Ah, God. Not now..."

"What?"

"I gotta puke again," she said, hurrying to the rail. "Be right back."

"You gonna be okay?" Faith said as Hooch puked over the rail.

"Jesus," he said, shaking his head. "Sorry, that's not what... I mean..."

"I'd say I puked the first time but I didn't," Faith said, then shrugged. "I mean, I *have* puked. Trust me. But I've seen worse than this. You should have seen some of the stuff on the *Alpha*."

"How many of these have you done?" Hooch asked. The scene in the lower deck was fucking awful. The male of the group, presumably the dad, had survived. By feeding on his family in what had been the master's cabin. From the looks of it, they'd all zombied and had been fed on one by one. As he'd killed them he'd brought them down into the cabin as a nest and slept with the dead and decomposing corpses. Hooch had managed to hold it in until he noticed one really totally "what the fuck?" detail. At the head of the bed, not covered in filth, almost like a little shrine, was a teddy bear. Like somewhere in the thing on the boat's brain it almost remembered that it had somebody it cared about. It just couldn't recognize that it was the tiny little corpse it was feeding on.

"People keep asking me that," Faith said. "I need to get a count..."

"Five," Steve said, nodding. "That's not bad for a boat this size. Come on, we'll get you over to the rescue boat."

"Wait," one of the men said, holding up his hand. "I'll stay onboard."

"Why?" Fontana said.

"If we leave the boat it's salvage," a woman said.

"Heh," Steve said, grinning. "It's salvage already. You're not going to get screwed, but you kind of want to sit down and have a chat about the new reality."

"You do, you really do," Gardner said. "And I'm saying that sort of officially as a member of the Coast Guard. In fact, as far as we can tell, I'm the number four senior United States Coast Guard officer. 'Cause there's only *six* of us left."

"What?" the man said, his face going ashen.

"Just come on over to the boat and get some fresh air," Steve said. "We're not going to pirate your boat."

"Not *exactly* pirate," Fontana said. "Hey, I wonder if I'm, like, senior NCO of the Army."

"In that case, I think Hooch is the commandant..."

"How much fuel in the tanks, Hooch?" Faith asked, looking at the form. She was letting him do it for the experience. Besides the post-clearance tasks were getting old.

"Like, half a tank?" Hooch said.

"But dead batteries," Faith said. "Okay. Hey, Paula! Toss me the slave!"

"Slave cable?" Hooch asked.

"Got it in one," Faith said as Paula hefted the cable up from the other boat's engine room. "*Vicky* makes it up from cables and stuff they find. They do a little salvage in the harbor when the zombies aren't real active or off boats they can get to that don't have any. But it's stuff like this. I mean, I've had a couple of other people say they'll try out clearance and they see one boat like this and give it up. It's not just the zombies."

"Who clears 'em out?" Hooch asked.

"Oh, the crews do," Faith said. "If you want a new boat, that's the catch unless it's a hand-me-down like the *Endeavor*. Okay, engineering deck hatch is over *here*..."

"This is confusing," Hooch said, looking at the electrical panel.

"Confused the shit out of me the first time I looked at it," Faith said, throwing a breaker back and forth. "But this isn't complicated. The *Large*, the *Vicky*, that fricking *Alpha*. *Those* are complicated." She hit the "Start" button and the engine started whining. "Come on, baby..."

The engine rumbled to life, and she grinned.

"And we have a working boat," Faith said. "I think we get some sort of spiff for that but I don't really know what it is."

"Spiff?" Hooch said.

"Bonus," Faith said. "Like, extra rations or booze or something. Speaking of which." She keyed her radio. "You want the good pickins, come and get 'em. And it works."

"Awesome," Sophia replied. *"Maybe I'll ask for an upgrade."*

"Might want to look at the master cabin before you say that."

"Oh, my God," the man said, his face white.

"I know, zombies, right?" Faith said to the "captain" of the "prize crew." The group was made up of recent rescuees, mostly from life rafts, who had volunteered to join the flotilla. "They're worse than a rock band. Just try to avoid the crap. The flying bridge isn't too bad and it's a nice clear day. All you've got to do is run it into Bermuda. The course is laid in on the GPS. Just follow the marked route. That's the current channels, whatever the markers might say. Don't necessarily follow the markers. They're getting filled up. Follow the marked route, got it?"

"Yeah," the man said.

"If you get in trouble, we're always up on sixteen," Faith said. "Don't go into the lower decks unless you've got a really strong stomach. The Marine with me puked; put it that way."

"Who cleans these up?" the guy asked looking at the feces- and blood-smeared interior.

"First test of a captain in the flotilla," Faith said, grinning. "Can you find a crew who's willing to clean the boat?"

"You drink, Hooch?" Sophia asked.

"There's two reasons for my nickname," Hooch said.

"Twenty-five-year-old Strathisla," Sophia said, handing him a highball half full of dark whiskey. "One of the real reasons to be a clearing boat."

"And stuff like this," Faith said, admiring the new gold and diamond tennis bracelet on her wrist. She'd had to "extend" it with a bit of parachute cord since it was for a much smaller wrist. "Especially since I don't drink."

"This is authorized?" Hooch asked, taking a sip of the scotch. "I'm not really into scotch but that's pretty good."

"And enough of it and you forget what you see," Sophia said, taking a pull. "Balancing doing this job half-hammered and just doing it is the tough part. And we're authorized one-third of the salvage from cleared boats as the clearance boat. We really don't have the room for it. Basically, we can take anything we can carry."

"Hell, *you* don't even *clear*," Faith said. "What do you see that's so bad? And *I* don't *drink*."

"Remember that raft with the kids in it, Faith?" Sophia asked, taking another drink.

"Yeah," Faith said, looking at the deck.

"Kids?" Hooch asked.

"Life raft," Sophia said. "Two kids. Maybe six and eight."

"Zombies?" Hooch asked.

"No," Faith said. "That was the tough part. They *hadn't* zombied. There was no saltwater still. I mean…"

"There was a *pack* for one," Sophia said. "It had been opened. But the still was gone. Maybe they could read the directions, set it up, but didn't hook it up right and it drifted away. But it was gone. They'd died of dehydration."

"Oh…crap," Hooch said.

"That one still…" Faith said, her face working. "I mean, they must have tried really *hard*. They at least got the still out, you know?"

"Empty rafts," Sophia said. "What happened? Who knows. Rafts with zombies and bits of the rest of the crew. Lifeboats with corpses and one zombie. Or even that's dead. Just putrid bits of meat and intestines all over the fucking place…" She took another hit of the scotch and breathed it through her nose. "So I'm fifteen and I'm shooting for cirrhosis of the liver by thirty. Sue me. We *earn* this."

"We barely touched the *Grace*'s tanks," Isham said, looking at the computer. "I mean, the *Alpha* took them down but less than a quarter. There's three times a fill-up for the *Alpha* in *Grace*'s tanks and the *Alpha* wasn't dry. And we've filled the *Large*. I figured with the Coasties on it, they weren't going to up and run off with it."

"We were just preparing for a supply run when the word broke about the plague," Victor Gilbert, First Mate of the Offshore Support Vessel M/V *Grace Tan* said. "We sort of packed along our..." He stopped and his face worked. "We packed along our families. Just a little...cruise..."

"Mr. Gilbert," Steve said, handing him a glass dark with whiskey. "The same thing *would* have happened if they were on land."

"Yeah," Gilbert said, taking a drink. "But I wouldn't have had to watch my wife and kids turn. You know?"

"I'm one of the few who doesn't," Steve admitted, shrugging. "Luck. Planning."

"Bloody-mindedness," Isham said.

"That as well," Steve said. "Issues?"

"No," Isham said. "Just keeping it in mind."

"So I ended up in the compartment with Stella, Larry Ashley's wife and...Christ, Luis is Jeff Busler's kid. Jeff was the deck boss. Larry was maintenance. And Sharon, she's Chad Wilborn's daughter, and Rich, he's Sherri and Bob Tilley's son, Sherri was the systems tech. Nobody has anybody."

"No," Steve said, "You all have each other. Captain Gilbert, those are the *only* children except Tina we've found. Alive anyway. This plague may or may not have wiped out civilization, but it *has* wiped out an entire generation."

"Yeah, but there seems to be a new one on the way," Isham said, chuckling.

"Pardon?" Gilbert said.

"Ahem," Steve said. "I'm not going to pry, but I suspect Stella is pregnant?"

"How'd you..." Gilbert said, his eyes flaring. "Look...!"

"No worries, mate," Steve said, shaking his head. "Just about every woman who was in a compartment with a man is pregnant. And we can usually sort out the rapes from the other."

"Vic," Isham said to the still visibly upset captain. "Take a deep breath. What Steve is saying is that it's how things are, now. Part of the new now. Hell, there's even a meme."

"Meme?" Gilbert said. "Like LOLCats or something?"

"Sort of," Steve said. "I wouldn't be surprised if someone hasn't photoshopped it onto a picture of a pregnant woman. The saying is 'What happened in the compartment, stays in the compartment.' Goes two ways. There's stuff that happens that you're really ashamed of. On boats, in compartments. Having to kill somebody who turned."

"Or, hell," Isham said, "there's one boat where there was a

death that people just don't talk about. It came out slow, they sort of hemmed and hawed..."

"And the response is, what happened in the compartment, stays in the compartment," Steve said. "If there's a complaint, we investigate it. To the extent we can. But... Stella hasn't even hinted it was rape..."

"It wasn't, honest," Gilbert said, holding up his hands. "Hell, it just sort of..."

"You can talk about it if you want," Steve said, shrugging. "Or keep it in the compartment. But you don't have to be *guilty* about it. Yes, her husband was recently dead. So was your wife. The 'right' way, even if you'd liked each other before, was to 'wait a decent period.' You were alone in a compartment with *nothing else to do* and death all around you."

"Except the kids in this case," Isham said.

"We waited till they were asleep and did it real quiet," Gilbert said. "Sue me."

"Again and again if necessary," Steve said. "*No worries.* One of the women from a life raft, the man with her had to kill her *husband* when he turned. And she's pregnant and they're a couple. Humans adjust to the incredible. The survivors do. And one of the ways we adjust is things like 'What happened in the compartment, stays in the compartment.' Nobody but the people in the compartment, life raft, what have you, can really judge. It is one of the reasons that people in unusual jobs are given different courts than common citizens. Seamen have their own courts. Military. Because there is a reality to 'You weren't there. You can't know. You can't understand.'"

"And then there's the prison thing," Isham said, smirking.

"Prison thing..." Gilbert said, then grimaced.

"What happened in the compartment," Steve said.

"Stays in the compartment," Gilbert said. "Got it."

"So, seriously, no issues," Steve said. "The real issue is that while we're starting to find some professionals, most of our crews are not professional seamen. Most of our *captains* are not professional seamen. And we have a real, critical shortage of engineering personnel. Even mechanics. So when something breaks on a boat, the crews are generally stuck. And although most of them have been through storms, it's mostly been while stuck in compartments or puking up their guts and holding on for dear life in lifeboats and rafts."

"No storms while you've been doing this?" Gilbert asked.

"Nothing serious," Steve said, shrugging. "High summer and we've only had one tropical come up this way. That was before we started clearing and it was only a storm by the time it got here."

"I remember that one," Gilbert said.

"Me, too," Isham said.

"So we're going to have to move," Steve said.

"Move?" Isham said. "Why? We've got a good harbor here."

"You've got *Bermuda* harbor," Gilbert said. "Which is an *okay* harbor. You get hit by a really hard, late-season I'm-going-to-rip-you-a-new-asshole hurricane, this is *not* the harbor you want to be in."

"And with the ships, absent a truly excellent harbor, it's better to be at sea," Steve said. "If you've got the right crew. Which we don't. And the small craft... There's a reason they call it a 'small craft advisory.' Between the late-season hurricanes that we're going to get soon and the diurnals and winter storms... I'm thinking Canary Islands?"

"Good choice," Gilbert said, nodding. "We're going to have to fuel. I mean, the *Grace* has plenty for herself and probably enough for a while for the small boats. But not to constantly refuel the *Alpha*."

"Could you tow a full-sized tanker?" Steve asked.

"Yes," Gilbert said. "But I'd need a tow crew who knew what they were doing."

"How about a guy who knows what he is doing and some people willing to learn?" Steve said, grinning. "Because that is the best you are going to get for any job in this flotilla."

"What fun, what fun," Gilbert said, grimacing. "In that case, I can try. But I'll be perfectly content to cut it loose."

"Works," Steve said. "I think we're going to have to leave the *Vicky*. I really should have gotten Mike in on this. But you've got quite a few accommodations, from what I saw."

"We could have carried a lot more people than we did," Gilbert said, then sighed. "I don't think that would have been a good idea."

"There were few good choices," Steve said. "As I said, my family was lucky. Although," he added, shrugging, "the basic plan would have worked. I wouldn't have been able to do this without one aspect, but... Be that as it may, we can put more people on the *Grace*. We can put people on the *Alpha*. I'm willing to

push it to the first diurnal, or if we see a cyclone coming this
way. For the diurnal we'll bring the small boats in. But when
either happens, we are upping stakes and heading away from the
northeast Atlantic."

"There are still a lot of boats and rafts out there," Isham
pointed out.

"And we can't rescue *anyone* if we're dead," Steve said. "I am
audacious, not stupid. Thereafter we will head to the Canaries
and do this same thing, more or less. There are distress beacons everywhere and only we few, we happy few, to clear them.
Depending on how many EPIRBs there are in that area, we may
cut back across the ocean to the Caribbean in winter. I would
like to be off of Cuba by January. But I do not want to do that
at the cost of leaving many behind. Which means we need more
boats and more captains. Despite that, I'm going to start shutting
down the thirty-fives, including the *Endeavor*. And I'm going to
drag Captain Sherill out if it's the last thing I do."

"Good luck," Isham said.

"Sherill?"

"Fully rated captain," Steve said. "Who is totally stuck on his
tiny little Bertram thirty-five. Used to run freighters for Maersk
and chucked it, had a hissy fit as he puts it, for being a charter
captain out of Charleston. Doesn't want the responsibility. I'm
going to have to convince him otherwise."

"Like I said," Isham said. "Good luck."

There was a knock on the door and Isham looked at Steve.

"Enter!" Steve called.

"Commodore," the young woman said nervously. "Sorry, but
Captain Sherill is calling and he says it's urgent."

"Speaking of Captain Gilligan," Steve said. "Where's the radio
room on this tub?"

"What's up, Gi... *Sea Fit*?" Steve said.

"*You need to get out here,*" Sherill replied instantly. "*Now.*"

Steve was used to the irascible skipper's usual tones. Desperately
serious was a new one.

"Details," he replied.

"*You know how you're always talking about people dying waiting
for rescue in compartments?*"

"Yes," Steve said.

"It's a cruise ship. I'm watching that in real time. Get in your fucking tub and get your Aussie ass and all the guns you can find out here. I'll help clear this one. There are people still alive in their staterooms and they're looking at me. I'm making a banner that says 'Help is on the way. Hold on.' Get out here, Wolf. Now."

"All ships, relay that information to all receiving stations," Steve said. "All vessels converge His Sea Fit's location. Large, time to earn your munificent pay from your friendly Uncle. And time to fish or cut bait on the arms locker. Victoria, begin transfer all personnel and mobile equipment to Grace. Endeavor, Endeavor, Endeavor, Commodore, are you in radio range, over?"

"En—vo—proce—Sea-fit..."

"Endeavor's about twenty miles away, Commodore," Sherill called. "Their response was proceeding our location."

"Begin surface clearance," Steve said. "Do not do entry until I arrive. Relay that, Sherill. Commodore moving to location now. All vessels: don't spare the horses. Wolf, out."

He looked over at Isham and Gilbert.

"Get all of Victoria's personnel and stores on your boat, Gilbert," Steve said. "And any of the SLLs left. When you're cross-loaded, head to the location. Isham, tell Captain Miguel to make ready for sea."

"Are you taking this?"

"No time," Steve said. "I wish I had something faster than the Toy."

"That tears it," Galloway said.

"Sir..." Commander Freeman said.

"I'm not talking about the captaincy, Commander," Galloway said. "But we're also not going to stand by and let who knows how many survivors die sealed into a cruise ship. Get me the Dallas and Charlotte..."

CHAPTER 28

"Time, time, time," Steve said pushing the throttles of the *Toy* forward again. It didn't give him any more speed. "Ask me for anything but—"

He stopped speaking as an attack boat made a fast surface off his starboard bow at about a thousand yards. He noted in the back of his mind that they'd surfaced upwind.

"Tina's Toy, USS Dallas, *over*," the radio crackled.

"Steve!" Stacey screamed from below.

"I see it," Steve said, picking up the radio. "Wolf Actual, over."

"*Wolf, all possible support has been authorized for this operation,*" the *Dallas* said. "*USS* Charlotte *is in the process of taking the* Campbell *under tow to bring it to the cruise ship. We cannot supply clearance personnel but access to all USCG materials are, say again, are authorized and USCG personnel are to place themselves, temporarily, under your command for clearance and rescue support. We don't have much in the way of shotgun rounds but we're going to float what we have off in a boat, as will Charlotte upon arrival, to assist your clearance teams. Current weather report is no fronts or tropical activity for this area for a minimum of ten days. Some convection storms are possible but they are scattered. We will be monitoring all area channels but are now authorized to direct communicate. We will be taking over Marine Channel Thirty-Three. We will continue to give what support we can without being contaminated. Do you have any questions at this time?"*

"Not that I can think of," Steve said.

"We will draw ahead of you and drop off a radio on a float," Dallas said, speeding up.

The *Tina's Toy* was a fairly fast yacht. Not a racing yacht but no lubber. The *Dallas* just left it behind. On the *surface.*

"That radio is for your use and your use only, Commodore Wolf," Dallas continued. *"Higher would like to have a secure chat. Proceeding to the* Sea Fit's *location. Good luck, Wolf."*

A bright orange buoy ejected from a launcher and the *Dallas* slipped below the waves. Steve was pretty sure by the time it disappeared it was going faster than a cigarette boat.

Stacey sat down next to him and wrapped her arms around him. Her eyes were misty.

"We're in contact," Steve said, hugging her.

"That's not what I'm crying about," Stacey said.

"What's wrong?" Steve asked.

"Nothing," Stacey said, hugging him again. "The commander of a U.S. Navy nuclear submarine called you 'Commodore.' And I don't think he even realized he'd said it."

"Oh, that," Steve said, slowing the boat as Pat pulled out a boat hook to catch the buoy. "No worries, wife o' mine. I'm sure he's regretting it already."

"Where do you want me to put it, Faith?" Sophia asked.

"How the fuck should *I* know?" Faith said. She sounded desperate. There was reason to be.

The cruise ship was massive. Really, seriously, stupidly huge. The boats around it were so many mice, no, *fleas* circling an elephant. A wounded and still bleeding elephant. Because rising as high as a skyscraper, or so it seemed from the waterline, there were staterooms. With exterior balconies. And on at least a dozen of those there were people watching the circling craft. People who looked like survivors of the death camps. Most of them couldn't even stand. They were leaning against the railings, just staring with glassy eyes at the help just a few hundred yards away.

One of them on a lower balcony lurched to his feet and started to climb the rail.

"No, no, no," Faith shouted.

"No! No! Sharks! Sharks! Sharks!" Sophia shouted over the loudhailer.

The man couldn't seem to hear or understand. He more fell than dove over the side.

Hocieniec started firing from the aft deck but there was no way. There were sharks everywhere. It was unlikely that he was the first person who'd taken that way out in preference to starvation or dehydration. The man didn't even scream as he was taken under.

"Why, damnit, why?" Faith shouted. She picked up the mike for the loudhailer. "STAY WHERE YOU FUCKING *ARE*! WE *WILL* COME FOR YOU. JUST *HOLD ON*!"

"How?" Sophia asked. "There's no entries. And that promenade..."

It wasn't really a promenade. It was the lifeboat deck. And that was fifty feet above the flying bridge of the *Endeavor*.

"How the hell am *I* supposed to know?" Faith repeated.

"You're the entry specialist," Sophia said calmly. "I'm trying not to stress you. I really am asking."

"Hooch!" Faith shouted. "How would the Marines board this thing?"

"A helicopter!" Hooch shouted back. "Or a boarding ladder."

"There's a helo on the *Alpha*," Sophia said.

"You know how to fly one?" Faith asked, somewhat hysterically.

"Faith, take some breaths, Sis," Sophia said calmly. "We're going to do this. We are."

"Okay, okay," Faith said. "We get a grapnel up. Then...I dunno, maybe with some knots in it or something?"

"There we go," Sophia said. "It's going to be a bitch to climb."

"Yeah," Faith said. "Especially in armor. And if we drop in the drink... Shit..."

"Keep going," Sophia said.

"Well..." Faith said, then stopped. "Or maybe we could ask the sub if *they've* got an idea."

"What su—" Sophia said, looking around, then stopped.

"*Local Wolf Squadron boats, USS* Dallas. *Looking for the boarding action commander. Please switch to Channel Thirty-Three. All captains may monitor but request not break. Again, USS* Dallas *looking for boarding action commander. Shewolf, you on the* Endeavor, *over?*"

"So we're Wolf Squadron, huh?" Sophia said, picking up the radio and handing it to Faith. "Faith, honey, take a deep breath and don't get hysterical when you're talking to him."

"I'm *not* the boarding action commander," Faith said. "That's Da."

"You're the closest," Sophia said. "Want me to take it?"

"No," Faith said, her face firming. She took the radio and cleared her throat. "Thirty-three?"

"You're on," Sophia said.

"*Dallas*, Shewolf," Faith said. "Over."

"*Shewolf, we've been monitoring your squadron's communications. Your reputation precedes you. The man who is filling in as President says that the moment he meets you he's going to cover you with so many medals, you're not going to be able to move. Of course the same can be said of everyone in this squadron. But we know you're the squadron's premier clearance specialist. This has got to be a nightmare for you. Over.*"

"Got it in one," Faith said. "Over."

"*We can't get out of this tin can. We're still uninfected and can't change that for any reason. But we are going to do everything else we can to help. Have you discussed how to do entry?*"

"Roger," Faith said. "All we've got so far is throw up a grapnel with a knotted rope. Lance Corporal Hocieniec is still not really in shape. And I'm not what you call a great climber. That completely skips the whole man-eating sharks part. And the zombies at the top. Still thinkin' it, over. Over."

"*We have an assault boarding ladder,*" Dallas replied. "*We will float that off along with all of our onboard shotgun ammo and the shotguns. We use nine mil onboard. Can you use that, over?*"

"Not really," Faith said. "Limited guns for it and we carry mostly forty-five. We're okay, for now, on forty-five. The shotgun ammo is, yeah, going to be helpful. But," she unkeyed the mike for a second. "Hey, Hooch, you know how to use an 'assault boarding ladder'?"

"Yeah!" Hooch said. "Sort of. I mean, I've seen it done."

"*Dallas*, we may need somebody to coach us through using an assault boarding ladder, over," Faith said.

"*We'll do that, Shewolf,*" Dallas responded. "*The tough part is the throw. It's got a double line. You get the grapnel up, make sure it's on, then pull in on one of the lines. That pulls the ladder up and it hooks in at the top. Then it's just a matter of climbing the ladder. Stand by . . . .*"

"Roger," Faith said, shrugging at Sophia's look.

"*Shewolf, have your boats pull back. We're going to do a close approach and send up a party to clear off some of the zombies from your boarding area. We may, say again may, be able to get the ladder in place for you.*"

"*Don't* get yourselves contaminated doing that," Faith replied, sharply. "You're the closest thing we've got to home left, *Dallas*. Look...Just. Standby."

"*Roger, Shewolf.*"

"Hooch," Faith called. "They want to shoot some zombies off the side and maybe get the boarding ladder in place. I'm afraid they're going to get contaminated."

"They've got suits like moon suits onboard, Faith," Hooch called back. "And a machine gun. I think they can do it. The question is, can they get the zombies up to the boarding area?"

"*Dallas*, you sure you can do this and not contaminate yourself?" Faith asked. "'Cause I just thought of something."

"She's more worried about losing a sub than her own life," Galloway said. "I *am* going to cover that girl in medals. So help me God."

"*What is your suggestion, Shewolf?*"

"We've got some vaccine," she said, looking at Sophia. "It's still good, right?" she whispered.

"Should be," Sophia said. "We even stabilized it."

"Not a lot left, but enough for a small team. We'd really appreciate the help with the boarding. But I'm worried about the rest of your crew getting contaminated. So...your guys clear the group off. Get the ladder up if they can. Then put them off in a lifeboat or something. We'll get them some vaccine. It's supposed to take two weeks to work. But they can't get the blood pathogen except with a bite or getting blood in a cut. And if that's all you get, well, I survived after just the primer. So all they get, maybe, is the flu bug. And we'll keep away from them so they shouldn't get that. I guess you can float them rations or something. So...they hang out until they're boosted. Ten days on a raft. Most of the...squadron has done two months. If you can spare them and if somebody wants to volunteer. And if that makes any sort of sense. Over."

"*Interesting plan. Considering that, Shewolf. Being discussed by experts. We have volunteers either one way or both. Have your boats clear back from the port side. We are going to do a close approach for direct fire.*"

"Roger, *Dallas*," Faith said. "Thanks. Really, really appreciate it."

"*Hey, you've got the tough part, miss.* Dallas *out.*"

"Squadron, this is Seawolf," Sophia said over the flotilla net. She engaged the engines to full and turned to port as she said it. "Clear the port side, say again, port side of the ship. *Dallas* is going to do a 'close approach for direct fire.' Get way, way back. In fact, get forward and way back or on the far side of the ship. Ricochets from machine-gun fire can kill you at a mile."

"*You girls just know too damned much about guns,*" Sherill growled. "*Moving around to the far side. I do want to watch, but not enough to get hulled.*"

"*We* were *approaching your location,*" Chris called from the *Cooper.* "*But on consideration, I'm stopping about five miles out. Nice to see the bloody USN decided to finally show up to the party.*"

"*Navy's here?*" someone called. "*Hallelujah!*"

"Submarine," Sophia said. "It can't do much but fire from range. They're not contaminated and don't want to be that way. But, yeah, we've got some support. Finally."

"*Chuck, switch to twenty-three and I'll fill you in,*" Chris said. "*I was monitoring the conversation.*"

"*Be nice to get some help. Switching.*"

The "radio" was a blue satellite phone with no markings on it. Steve set the *Toy* on autopilot and hit the only number listed.

"Strategic Armaments Control, is this Commodore Wolf?"

"Roger," Steve said.

"Stand by, please."

There was a click.

"Wolf?"

"Roger."

"This is quote Blount, Commodore. My actual name is Frank Galloway. Prior to the Plague, I was one of several people rotated to secure points to act as NCCC in the event of something like, well, this."

"Zombies high on the list of possible problems?" Steve asked.

"No," Galloway said. "Not really. And to give you an idea how bad it is, I was number one hundred and twenty-six on the list. The current Commander of the Joint Chiefs is a brigadier and you can guess how low the rest of the people are. The reality is that there probably are other survivors higher up the chain. There may even be functioning secure points which have just lost commo. But..."

"But possibly not," Steve said.

"CDC is still there as well. And several other nations have maintained at least one functioning fraction of their former government. Russia, notably. One of the reasons we haven't called you back is that we've been getting... flak from the Russians. They're insisting on equal access to the vaccine."

"I don't have an issue with that," Steve said. "I mean... I'm not some sort of tranzi, but right now there's no real point in worrying about borders. They're basically gone."

"My Russian counterpart is an interesting chap," Galloway said. "He's stated that Russia is no more and that it is again the Soviet Union and that absent supplying all of his "nuclear wessels" with vaccine, *immediately*, he will solve our zombie problem with nuclear strikes."

"*What?*" Steve said.

"I'd appreciate you keeping that to yourself, Commodore," Galloway said. "As I said, the reason you've been out on a limb is that we didn't have a secure line. I had considered this method earlier but it was not... I should have done it sooner. I apologize. While this is not exactly a busy job, it's not all beer and skittles."

"Going to have to leave that in your lap, sorry," Steve said. "Any idea if this cruise liner has an X-ray machine?"

"It does," Galloway said. "But the overall lab supplies and equipment will be minuscule. And the nearest hospital ship with one is in the very south Atlantic. It was on its way from the IO when the plague broke out. And it managed to *still* get contaminated. Do you think you can clear a land area?"

"Depends on how large," Steve temporized. "And right now, no. But I have some notional plans for clearing, say, small towns that are remote from major infected presence."

"Guantanamo Bay, Cuba, had barely nine thousand personnel," Galloway said. "However, it had been upgraded to support not only the detainees but as a support base for disasters in the Caribbean region. Also... sometimes there were refugees with medical conditions from those disasters who needed a better hospital. If there wasn't a hospital ship available, they could be treated at Gitmo without bringing them to the U.S. So a second hospital was built, which has a full epidemiological lab. It should have everything you need to produce attenuated vaccine. However, there is a significant infected presence on the base."

"I think I can clear it," Steve said, rubbing his chin. "Possibly. Probably."

"How?" Galloway asked.

"Well, you have information I need," Steve said. "Is there a large source of fifty-caliber ammunition somewhere nearby? At sea, I mean. I'm thinking of a SeaLift ship. There aren't any on the AIS I've got. But that's not complete. AIS stops working when the ship does."

"Standby... There is a Marine amphibious assault carrier, the *Iwo Jima*, approximately eight hundred nautical miles southeast of Bermuda. According to my senior Marine, that would have a large store of fifty caliber. You need fifty caliber to take Guantanamo, I take it."

"Mount fifties, water cooled, at the level of the docks," Steve said. "Make lots of light and noise overnight. Open fire at dawn. Then continue clearance on land. If there are survivors on the *Iwo Jima*... That would increase our chances. So far we've only found the one life raft from the *Iwo*. Most of them probably went east of Bermuda, and we've been searching west. God knows I could use some Marines. As well as trained Navy people."

"The question of your ability to prepare the vaccine has been raised again. Is your tech... Without naming any names or... Oh, skip that. Can he or she do it?"

"Quality control is the issue," Steve said. "We have the recipe, if you will. But the doctor checked the quality and we won't have the materials or equipment he had. Then again... we don't know what we're going to get off this cruise ship. In terms of help, that is. There are people alive."

"Yes, we're getting a live feed from the *Dallas*," Galloway said.

"Some of them could be doctors," Steve said. "Biologists or MDs. Possibly. Or not. That's the problem with making plans with this job. You never know what you're going to get. You change your plans on the basis of whatever shows up, however it shows up. Fortunately, my master's is based on that."

"Excuse me?" Galloway said.

"Have you ever wondered why my daughter is called Faith?" Steve said.

"I had assumed you were a fan of *Buffy the Vampire Slayer*," Galloway said. "Or at least that was suggested by one of my advisors."

"Never saw it until after she was born," Steve said. "My master's was on logistics in a low-support condition, specifically keeping the Gloster Gladiators flying on Malta during the Siege."

"I have a lot of history, but... Standby... Ah, my senior Air Force advisor just filled me in. Faith, Hope and Charity. I see."

"Three obsolete biplanes faced down the Luftwaffe for nearly two years and kept flying, sir," Steve said. "Their crews had to make parts from scrap metal. Parts would come in for Hurricanes. Hurricanes. They didn't see their first Hurricane until 1943. So they would rework Hurricane parts to work in Glosters. They would beg, borrow or steal. Rework, refit, literally use chewing gum. When they *had* chewing gum."

"That makes sense," Galloway said. "I guess you are well prepared for your current situation."

"Does your Air Force advisor know which aircraft had the most kills, sir? That never missed so much as *one* battle?"

"She admits that as a bomber pilot she'd sort of consider them the bad guys, so, no."

"Put it this way, sir," Steve said. "Whenever they went to battle, they always had Faith."

"We decontaminated everything," Sophia said over the loudhailer.

The submariners had taken the "lifeboat" alternative. Although it was a Zodiac with an outboard.

They waved as the packet of vaccine floated towards them.

"Thanks for the assist," Faith said, waving back. It had been quite an assist.

First the *Dallas* had approached to within a few hundred meters of the cruise ship. The sub was also dwarfed but the sail was fairly high. Then a team clad in MOPP gear came out on the sail. The team first mounted their machine gun, then set off multiple flares as well as repeated blasts from a loudhailer. The combination had drawn a large herd of zombies to the lifeboat deck.

After there was a fair concentration, the team opened fire.

Much of the fire had struck the side of the ship, but quite a bit managed to hit the zombies. It had taken about thirty minutes of short bursts and two barrel changes, but they finally cleared all of the obvious infecteds from the lifeboat deck.

Then the team clambered down, got out the Zodiac and the boarding ladder and approached the ship. Getting the line up would probably have been the tough part for the Wolf crews. The submariners made it look easy. Among other things, they used a line thrower. But Hooch had explained that that was not usually considered "the easy way."

With the ladder in place they backed off to pick up their vaccine.

"We got to get in there before more zombies come around," Faith said.

"Da said wait till he got here," Sophia said.

"Bring us in close," Faith said, picking up the radio.

"Toy, *Shewolf.* Da, you there?"

"Roger," Steve said. "Closing your position. ETA, one hour."

"*Da, the* Dallas *cleared off a deck and put in a ladder. If we wait, the zombies are going to come around again. You know how they are. Permission to, I dunno... 'Get a foothold' is what Soph just said.*"

Steve thought about that and looked at Stacey. She was looking at him and bending her head as if waiting for a punch.

"Do you have a back-up plan?" Steve said.

"*No, but I've got lots of guns and knives and a machete. I'm still looking for a chainsaw.*"

"Sir," the chief of boat, senior NCO, of the *Dallas* said, standing at parade rest. "Might I suggest, with no disrespect, that it is *unseemly* for a commander in the United States Navy, skipper of this *mighty* engine of war, to literally roll around on the deck laughing...?"

"*Authorized.*"

"*And you had better be okay when we get there or I'll tan your hide!*"

"Yes, Mother," Faith said. "Shewolf out. Hey, Hooch, let's LOCK AND LOAD!"

"Let me go first, at least," Hocieniec said.

"Hooch, you're a Marine," Faith said, tightening the strap on her helmet. She was wearing what had become her standard "extreme zombie fighting" kit. Tactical boots and tacticals. Firefighting bunker gear. Nomex head cover tucked under the collar of the bunker gear. Full face respirator. Helmet with integrated visor. Body armor with integral MOLLE. Knee, elbow and shin guards. Nitrile gloves. Tactical gloves. Rubber gloves. Assault pack with hydration unit. Saiga shotgun on friction strap rig. A .45 USP in tactical fast-draw holster. Two .45 USP in chest holsters. Fourteen Saiga ten-round 12-gauge magazines plus one in the weapon. Nine pistol magazines in holster plus three in weapons. Kukri in waist sheath. Machete in over-shoulder sheath, right. Halligan tool in over-shoulder sheath, left. Tactical knife in chest sheath. Tactical knife in waist sheath. Bowie knife in thigh sheath. Calf tactical knife times two. A few clasp knives dangling in various places.

There was the head of a teddy bear peeking out of her assault pack.

"And you're a grown-up. That says you should go. But you're also not back in shape, it's been a while since you've done a boarding ladder, you're still in training at zombie killing and I've done these things a few times lately. Just make damned sure the soft part of the boat stays under the ladder. And if I drop in the drink, you'd better get me in fast. 'Kay?"

"No, but...I guess you're in charge."

"Damn straight," Faith said, clipping the safety line to her waist. "And no paying attention to my butt. Keep your mind on the job."

"Yes, ma'am," Hooch said.

"Here goes nothing," Faith said, jumping up and grabbing the ladder.

"*Faith, you've already got company,*" Sophia called from the *Endeavor*. "*One. Male. Decent shape.*"

"No worries, mate," Faith muttered to herself. "I hate heights."

"*Make that two.*"

"Easy. As long as I don't look down."

"*Four.*"

"Six a dollar."

"*Five...*"

"Target-rich environment."

"More..."

"You have got to be shitting me," Faith said, keying her radio and whispering. She was nearly to the top of the ladder.

"*I think they're feeding on the ones the* Dallas *shot.*"

"Okay," Faith said, looking up at where the grapnel was connected to the bulwark. She could hear them. "Okay. What's my back-up plan? Oh...fuck it." She keyed her iPod and rolled over the bulwark.

"Oh, shit, no," Sophia said as Faith clambered the rest of the way up the boarding ladder and rolled over the side of the ship. She could see more zombies moving towards the piles of dead. "No, no, no."

Faith straightened up and started firing her Saiga to aft. Which was great except for the zombie that appeared from behind cover to her rear and tackled her.

"HOOCH, GET UP THERE!" Sophia screamed over the loudhailer. The Marine started to climb the ladder, painfully slowly.

Faith suddenly reared up into sight again, a pistol in her hand and firing into the deck. She stomped once or twice, then turned with her back to the landing ladder and fired one-handed to aft, where the zombies were closing, and pulled another pistol out and fired forward, turning her head from side to side like she was watching a Wimbledon match. She was missing a lot, but zombies in view were dropping. Unfortunately, not enough, and she got dog-piled.

Then she was up again, with a pistol in one hand and a kukri in the other. She slashed down with the kukri, kicked again, shot a couple more and then went down. Again.

And back up. This time with the Saiga. Got two more. Went down.

Back up, holding a zombie over her head. It had a tactical knife in its eye. The zombie went into the drink. And she went down again.

And up again, Halligan tool in a two-handed grip, pounding down. Tackled.

"Okay, this fucking sucks," Faith panted over the radio. There was a background of constant snarls. "Trying to reload your fucking pistol with a zombie biting your fucking ass fucking sucks... Quit chewing my *ass,* you dummy...."

There was an "open circuit" button on the radios for hands-free operation. Sophia realized that had happened to Faith's radio in the scuffle and her sister didn't realize that she was broadcasting.

"Careful, careful, Faith, don't shoot yourself in the ass. That would be embarrassing—" There was a shot. "Dinkum...I'm wearing fucking bunker gear, you dumbfuck." Two shots. "You cannot *bite* through it. And that's my *shin pad*!" Another shot. "Oooh, I'll call you melon head. Let go of my arm or I'm going to...Oh, *there* you are, my rugged Nepalese beauty. What were you doing hiding under there? Come to Momma... *There*, I cut off your *hand*. Happy now? Are you *ready*?"

Faith came up with a zombie on her back and shrugged it off, spinning in place with the kukri and cutting its throat as she fired her .45 into the back of one grabbing her waist.

"I AM SICK AND TIRED OF THESE MOTHERFUCKING ZOMBIES ON THIS MOTHERFUCKING..." She screamed at the top of her lungs.

Hocieniec cleared the railing and finally saw what was going on. He clearly was frozen trying to figure out what to do, pull zombies off Faith or engage the ones still closing. Faith swung the Halligan tool, jamming the claw hammer into a zombie's skull, then overbalanced and went down again.

"GET THE OTHERS," Sophia boomed. "FAITH'S DOING FINE."

Bradburn waved a finger at the periscope repeater.
"COB."
"Sir?"
"Remind me never to piss that young lady off."
"Yes, sir."

CHAPTER 29

"Dibs on direct commission."

Lieutenant Colonel Justin Pierre had been missing meetings due to a recurrence of, of all things, malaria. He'd picked it up in Afghanistan. Doctors at Walter Reed thought they'd gotten out every trace with a new drug regime but it turned out they were, well, wrong. Which hadn't been spotted before he was put on this assignment or he'd never have had it. In fact, malaria was now one of those things that were grounds for medical retirement. Or, possibly, a letter of reprimand since you were supposed to take prophylaxis medication.

Colonel Pierre had not been lax in his use of prophylaxis medication. He had ended up way in the back of nowhere and cut off for about thirty days until he could E&E to friendly lines. Unlike the SEALs who had ended up in a similar situation, his team had never made the news. Probably because he had managed to extract all of them without any deaths. Wounded, yes, but they had an Eighteen Delta with them. Regular medics and corpsmen were trained to stabilize a patient until they could be evacuated. Special Forces medics were trained to heal people. They admitted they were not doctors, nor anywhere close, but Sergeant Ford had gone above and beyond.

However, they were planning for a seven-day mission. Not thirty. *All* of them had gotten malaria.

But he was back in the saddle and determined to get that girl as a commissioned officer in the United States Army.

"I'll throw in submitting a Memo for Record to the CJCS that they waive normal restrictions against women attending advanced combat schools, set up a quicky Q course and automatically pass her."

"She's thirteen, Colonel," Brice said drily.

"I think the youngest officer the U.S. Army ever commissioned was fifteen," Pierre said. "I can gin up a recommendation to the Joint Chiefs that given current global conditions we can waiver some people."

"That's a lot of waivers, Colonel," Freeman said. "Besides, I think all things considered, she's more the SEAL type."

"Got any available SEAL instructors?" Pierre said. "I'm a qualified Q course instructor."

"Actually I was thinking Marines," Mr. Galloway said. "Colonel Ellington. I now have a better appreciation for your paladin in hell metaphor."

Galloway looked over at Ellington and saw that the colonel's face was covered in tears.

"Colonel?" Galloway said carefully.

"She reminds me of my wife, sir," the colonel said. "She was a lieutenant in the MPs when we met."

"I am..." Galloway said. There was an unspoken rule against speaking about family. At least in these sort of circumstances. "Sorry. I hope to have the opportunity to meet her someday."

"That would be difficult, sir," Ellington said. "She was killed in Iraq. Long before this...debacle. Suicide bomber. I was standing about ten feet from her. Facing her, sir. They...picked parts of her out of my face at Walter Reed, sir." He pointed to an odd bump on his face. "Then again, parts of her are still with me, sir. They believe it is a portion of a tooth. My wife had beautiful teeth."

"Holy fuck, Ellington," Brice whispered. "That wasn't in your service report. Just that you'd been hit by an IED in Iraq."

"That was personal rather than professional," Ellington said with a shrug. "She essentially shielded me from the blast. I survived. She did not. It was tough, but we'd arranged to be on the same team, doing analysis of the Iraqi WMD program. She was commanding the security team. She was always—" His face tightened and he breathed hard.

"I am a Marine officer. I am versed in combat. But she was the *warrior*, sir, General. I was, am, a geek. I can fight. I have proven that. I have direct combat action in Iraq. But she was the *warrior* of us, Mr. Under Secretary, General Brice. She was our warrior half. Colonel Pierre, my wife was an Army officer. I would not prevent that young lady's career in the Marines in any way. She would make a fine Marine. I would also not be upset if she chose the Army. Some Marines might. But I have known the warrior women of the Army and they are fine warriors. Honorable and courageous warriors, all."

"Thank you, Colonel," Pierre said. "I wish I had met her in my career. Mr. Under Secretary, a serious suggestion?"

"Yes?" Galloway said.

"I would recommend that a recording of this be downloaded to all the still in-contact submarines," Pierre said. "There is damned little, currently, to build morale. Perhaps put it together with earlier bits such as Miss Smith's response to her father's question about back-up plans."

"That, Colonel, is a really sensible suggestion," Galloway said. "Commander, can we do that, bandwidth-wise?"

"Not an issue, sir," Freeman said. "And, yes, I'd agree it's an excellent idea. It sure as hell raised *my* morale."

"Let's hope her father is as heartened," General Brice said. "I'm betting he hits the roof."

"You okay, Faith?" Steve said, clearing the landing ladder. You couldn't walk on the deck for all the bodies. He literally had to jump into an open ribcage to get off the ladder. When he'd gotten into contact with Sophia she'd been really noncommittal about how things were going. "Faith's still there. No bites." Now he knew why.

"No worries, Da," Faith said, shrugging. She was absolutely covered in blood. "Fair dinkum scrum. Hooch handled it just fine."

Hocieniec's gear, while blood-splattered, was *splattered*, not *covered*. For that matter, parts of Faith's heavy battle gear were *torn*. There were teeth marks everywhere. And she had some knives missing from their sheaths. And her machete was on the deck, bent. And her Halligan tool had matted brain matter and hair on it. It was long and blond and for a second Steve wondered if she'd somehow ripped some of her own hair out with it. Except hers was thoroughly covered by her gear.

"Trixie got a little messed up," Faith said, reaching back to pat the teddy bear. "Trixie's going to need a nice hot bath after this, isn't she? Trixie says she got a little frightened but she'll be okay. She shut her eyes during the bad parts."

Steve had seen enough zombies dead from wounds at this point for a twenty-year career. And he knew wounds even before this apocalypse. Zombies were cut, smashed, bashed in heads; all the shot wounds had speckling around them from close or direct contact shots. Angles were *insane* on some of them. Shots down into the shoulder, which could only be done from...

"Okay," he said. "No worries. Thanks for holding the high ground. You need to take a breather for a bit?"

"What I need to do is ammo up," Faith said. "But I think most of my mags are so...messed up that they sort of need to be cleaned first. And I'm down to less than one mag of Saiga."

"Pistol?" Steve asked.

"Uh, I'm down to three rounds."

"I think that Fontana and I will hold this position while you go wash down your gear and ammo back up. Can you keep going? Seriously?"

"Try to hold me back, Da."

"These doors are locked," Fontana said, pulling at the hatch. The massive construction was one of the doors to the lifeboat deck and it was positively unwilling to open. A Halligan tool wasn't going to scratch it.

"Crap," Steve said, looking around. "That means another passcard hunt."

"Isn't this Chris's boat?" Fontana said. "Does he still have his?"

"I don't know," Steve said, keying his radio. "Sophia, all the exterior hatches we've found are locked down. Call Chris and ask him if he still has his passkey or whatever for the boat. And tell him we're probably going to need his help finding our way around. *Dallas*, you monitoring?"

"*Roger, Wolf actual.*"

"Tell the Coasties as soon as they get here they're to coordinate the evacuation teams. These people are going to need wheelchairs, stretchers, something. And right now getting them off the boat is going to be a professional evolution. They'll need to primarily provide expertise and security. We'll clear the zones, then they can come in and get the people. Copy?"

"*Coast Guard personnel to organize evacuation and maintain security presence, Wolf teams to clear.*"

"Roger," Steve said. "As soon as we can get a master key or something."

"*Wolf,* Dallas, *over.*"

"Go ahead, *Dallas,*" Steve said.

"*Retransing a call from the* David Cooper, *over.*"

"Go ahead retrans," Steve said.

"*Wolf, Chris. Got in position to observe. First of all, you know this was my ship, over.*"

"Roger, over," Steve said. "What can you tell us, over?"

"*Good luck. The* Voyage *is one of the largest liners in the world. Getting into it was only the first problem. The Staff Side Acting First intended to do a complete lockdown after all lifeboats were away. A complete lockdown closes and locks all interior doors and hatches including room doors in both directions. The only way to override it is from the central control, with the right codes or correct passkey, or using passkeys locally. Then it gets complicated. I've sent my key over for Faith to bring over to you. But it will only open certain internal common doors and doors specifically related to my job. I can move in all common staff areas and in all the kitchen and supply areas. It won't, for most important example, open cabins. There was no reason a chef should have unrestricted access to the cabins.*"

"Buggers," Steve muttered.

"*You're going to have to hunt for a senior Staff Side officer's key . . . Standby.*"

"Roger," Steve said, looking at Fontana with a quizzical look. There'd been something in Chris's voice.

"*I didn't really talk about leaving . . .*" Chris said. "*Or about before, much . . . By some sort of horrible coincidence you boarded right where I left. There was a . . . break . . . Standby, please. Sorry, Wolf . . .*"

"Take your time, Chris," Steve said.

"*Steve, Paula, breaking in.*"

"Go, Paula."

"Look for the body or remains or clothing of a female senior Staff Side officer in that area," Paula said. *"First name is Gwinneth, don't recall last, Third Officer, Staff Side. Last seen directly opposite boarding area of Lifeboat Twenty-Six."*

"Cooper *again*," Chris said. *"With that key you'll be able to access all areas except those specifically locked down by higher. That's only going to be bridge and possibly engineering. If you can find Gwinn's badge— That'll do the trick. If not... you're down to cutting torches. All the doors, including cabin doors, are steel."*

"Roger," Steve said, gesturing at Fontana with his chin. "Any way to upgrade your key?"

"Only with power to the systems," Chris said. *"And you'd need to find and get into the Staff Side office... Break... Steve, I really don't want to come over there. Can't describe how much. But..."*

"Once we're to that point, I'm going to need you to liaison with the Coasties on clearing," Steve said. "But if you're talking now, no. We can probably find the cabins that are occupied on our own. We're going to need help when we start clearing the crew areas and the working areas. But by then maybe we'll have found a map or something."

"Roger."

Fontana came back shaking his head. No badge.

"Cooper, for what it's worth, it's not here. She's not here. Will your badge get us into the interior?"

"All common areas," Chris replied. *"Passenger and crew and most support supply areas. Food at least. But you're going to be buggered getting to those passengers in cabins."*

"What about security, over?" Fontana asked.

"Security officers should, repeat, should have access to cabins. Also some housekeeping will access some but not all. Did you find a security officer?"

"Minimal clothing and materials cast-off in this area," Steve said as Faith clambered over the side. "Faith's here. We're going to continue this operation."

"Again, good luck, Wolf."

"Thanks, *Cooper*," Steve said.

"Chris said this isn't going to get us in the cabins," Faith said, handing him the card.

"Where there's a will, there's a way."

∽ ⊖ ᥱ

"Zombies, zombies, zombies," Faith said, banging on the hatch with the butt of her Saiga. "Customers." She worked a stethoscope in under her gear and listened. "Okay, *lots* of customers."

"Okay," Steve said, trying not to snarl. They hadn't even gotten off the *lifeboat deck*, yet. This was the third hatch they'd tried and they all had "multiple customers" lined up. "Faith, Hooch and Fontana, form a line, five meters that way," Steve said, pointing forward. They'd gotten away from the entry area and the deck was mostly clear except for the usual fecal matter and occasional gnawed corpse.

"I will pop the hatch, then run like a bugger your way," Steve said. "Do not fire until I clear the defense point. Let me make this very clear: Do *not* shoot me."

"Sir..." Fontana and Hooch both said.

"Yes, one of you probably should do it," Steve said. "But I'm going to. That's an order. Just form up and don't shoot me."

"Try not to, Da," Faith said, walking forward. "Just better run like a roo."

"Weapons pointed down," Fontana said when they'd lined up. "Locked and loaded, off safe, fingers off the triggers. Take position, prepare to point." There was a large gap between himself and Faith. "Faith, locked and loaded?"

"Ready."

"Hooch?"

"Prepared, Sergeant."

"Ready when you are, boss."

Steve took a deep breath and keyed the door. It popped open slowly, fortunately, and he turned and started running like a scared roo.

"Don't look back," he muttered. "Don't look back."

He didn't really need to. The howls of the zombies told him everything he needed to know.

"Oh, run faster, Da," Faith said.

Ten meters didn't seem very far unless it was the distance your da had to run to outrun a pile of zombies that was, if anything, larger than her reception party. Da was loaded down with weapons, ammo and equipment. The zombies were not. They'd been slowed opening the heavy hatch but they were now catching up.

"Fire!" Fontana said, putting words to action with a blast of 12-gauge into a zombie's chest.

Steve skidded to a stop and turned around, then lunged to fill the gap in the line. There were at least fifty zombies in the group that had been following him. They were tripping over the bodies of the leaders but that wasn't stopping them, just barely slowing them down. He lifted his shotgun as he joined the line and pulled the trigger. It wouldn't move. He grimaced, jacked a round into the chamber, took it off safe and pulled the trigger again. *That* time it worked.

"Back step," Fontana called. "Stay on line."

"I'm out," Faith said, pulling a pistol.

"Going pistol," Hooch said. Ten rounds goes fast when it's a zombie horde.

"Shit," Steve said. One of the zombies was still wearing body armor and a riot helmet. No pants but body armor. And shotgun and .45 did poorly against body armor.

The zombie zoomed in on Faith and tackled her. It had apparently figured out how to lift its face shield to deliver a bite and bit down on the juncture of her neck and shoulder.

"Fuck!" Faith said. "Not again!" Her hand scrabbled for a weapon. "Pistol...won't work...Kevlar...Knife...!" She reached down to her leg, pulled out a nine-inch Gerber Commando and started to stab the zombie repeatedly and rapidly in the back through its armor. "I looove youuuuu toooooo..."

The wave had receded; the security zombie was pretty much the last.

"Reload," Fontana said. "Faith, you going to get back to work any time soon?"

"He's heavy," Faith said, pushing the dead zombie off. "Use a little help here."

Steve lifted the security guard off his daughter by the neck of his armor and gave her a hand up.

"*That* is why I hate mall cops," Faith said, pulling out the knife with a twist and wiping it down with a rag.

"For future reference," Fontana said. "The pistol would have worked. He had his arms up. Stick the barrel in the armpit."

"Point," Faith said, putting the knife away. "But I was pissed off. I couldn't tell if he was trying to eat me or...something else."

Steve rifled through the pockets on the armor and came up with a security card.

"Tada!" he said, waving it.

"Cross-load ammo and reload magazines," Fontana said, pulling off his assault pack. "Hooch, Faith on guard. Wolf and Falcon to load. Commodore, I would recommend, despite that card, that we remain together as a four-man team until we're sure that we've dealt with all similar large groups."

"Agreed," Steve said, pulling out ammo and reloading his Saiga mags. He'd never pulled his pistol. He held out his hand for Faith's and started loading hers. "What could we have done better?"

"The overall plan was good," Hooch said. He'd turned to face forward while Faith covered aft. "Except for one thing. I think in future with large groups and multiple possible entries...Or... I understand the thing about bringing them to you, not going to them. But... Maybe open the hatch, *then* call for zombies?"

"If you have reason to suspect a large zone with multiple zombies, open the hatch, back off and then draw them to you?" Fontana said.

"Reasonable," Steve said.

"It's not really relevant here," Fontana said. "But the one rule of *Zombieland* I'd like to bring up is always have a way out. Preferably with a way to lock it behind you."

"What if we run into more security zombies?" Faith asked. "I tried for a leg shot but missed. Sorry."

"Shooting a person in the leg is tough," Fontana said, closing up his assault pack and handing Hooch his refilled magazines. "Melee weapons?"

"If you're talking about a machete," Steve said, standing up, "I don't think so. Kevlar takes stabs, and it will cut, but I don't see cutting through it with a machete."

"Machete or a kukri takes off their arm," Faith said. "With enough force. And I still say a chainsaw is the way to go."

"They're heavy," Fontana said. "And if you tried to cut a security zombie with one the kevlar would jam the chain."

"Come up," Faith said, making a motion of cutting up between the legs.

"Ooooh," Hooch said, grabbing his jewels. "There's things you just don't *say* around guys."

The area the zombies had come from was a corridor about

ten meters wide with *more* hatches off of it. There was a faint light area where the exterior hatch was open, but most of the corridor was shrouded in darkness. It was impossible to tell how long it was but at least there weren't any zombies immediately coming into view.

"Where to?" Fontana asked. They'd decided to go for the quiet approach and see how it worked.

"Sweep this," Steve said, pulling out a taclight. The powerful hand light carried to the far end, but barely. Turning around, the same happened. The corridor was as long as a football pitch. "Bloody hell. Falcon, Shewolf, forward. Hooch, on me. Pick up any cards you find. Meet back here."

"We need some cave lights," Fontana said, sweeping the taclight on his Saiga from side to side. "This ship is too big for taclights."

"No shit," Faith said, then tapped hers. "I think mine took a beating. I'm going to need to switch it out."

"I've got a spare," Fontana said.

"So do I," Faith said, stopping and pulling of her ruck.

"You guys had more Surefires than any one group should own," Fontana said. "Not that I'm complaining." He not only had one on his rifle, but two duct-taped to his body armor facing forward and another in a helmet mount.

"Da always complains through movies, you know?" Faith said. "The idiot going into the basement in the horror movie with the light that doesn't work pisses him off. We've got flashlights all over the house at home. And if we had to drop in the dunny in the dark he wanted plenty of light. But we never figured on clearing a bleeding cruise ship! What are cave lights?"

"You know those million-candlepower portable spotlights on boats?" Fontana said. "Like that, but head lights and hand lights. Smaller, too. They'd fill this up with light."

"There," Faith said, standing up and shaking her shotgun. "Better."

"Must have been bad if you busted a Surefire," Fontana said.

"Fair dinkum scrum," Faith said. "And I don't think it's busted. Just messed up. This isn't somewhere I want my taclight going out."

The end of the corridor was a blank wall covered in instructions on boarding lifeboats. This was clearly the preboarding assembly area. All the hatches were either inboard or outboard.

While there were plenty of "remains," there were probably four times as many bodies as there had been zombies; all the zombies had been at the hatch. They picked up three security cards and moved back to the rendezvous.

"What now, sir?" Fontana said, handing over the cards.

Steve checked through them and stuck them in a pouch.

"No Gwinneth," he said. "No senior officers." He contemplated the hatches lining the corridor.

"Eenie-meenie-minie-mo?" Steve said.

"I was expecting something Australian," Hooch said. "Like, um, g'dye or something."

"Australians use it, too," Steve said. "It's a mnemonic of the Celtic numbering system. But that's not important. The real question is, do we use this hatch that is in the light or one of the ones that is in darkness? If we use this one, it will automatically attract zombies when we open it. If they haven't already gathered from the noise. If we use one farther down either way, we might have the element of surprise, but we'll be fighting in the dark *and* silhouette."

Faith pulled out her stethoscope and checked the door.

"I don't hear anything," she said. "But these are thick doors. No banging, no scratching."

"I'd say this one, sir," Fontana said. "First, we're here. Second, we can see our exit."

"Fair dinkum," he said. "*That's* Australian, Marine."

"Roger, sir," Hooch said, chuckling.

Like the exterior hatches, it had massive double doors designed to open outboard. He swiped the reader with the security guard's card, and while the light went from red to green, the hatch didn't open.

Faith flipped out her Halligan and applied the prybar to the hatch, which popped open slightly.

Steve held up a hand, then waved to Hooch. Once it was moving, the hatch opened easily.

The room revealed beyond was apparently vast and entirely dark. It appeared to be an arena with a square deck in the middle.

"Is that a pool?" Faith whispered, pointing her taclight at the deck. "Or a basketball court?"

"I think it was an *ice rink*," Hooch said. "No zombies, though."

"Really?" Faith said. "OLLY-OLLY-OXENFREE!"

There was a widespread and growing growling and howling, and heads started popping up all over the arena. The zombies turned their heads away at the bright lights after months in darkness, but they also stumbled to their feet and started to close on the hatch.

"Back up," Steve ordered, snapping up his Saiga and shooting the closest zombie. "All the way outside. Exterior deck. Maintain formation. Back aft on exit."

"Thanks a lot, Faith," Hooch snarled.

"This was the *plan*, right?" Faith said, firing steadily. "Come get some, zombies!"

"This would have been the perfect time for some seven six two," Fontana said.

The good news, this time, was that the zombies were half blind, and instead of coming in a mass, were trickling out. In large numbers and clots, but not fifty in a bunch.

"Fontana, Hooch, reload," Steve said, going to pistol.

"Up," Fontana said. "Reload."

"Okay," Steve said. "We have something resembling a method for outer clearance. What did we do right and wrong? Faith?"

There had been nearly as many zombies in the arena as in the outer corridors. And in much better shape. When the wave had stopped they closed and latched the door to get some time for cross-load and another AAR.

"I shouldn't have initiated without warning?" Faith asked.

"I'm going to put that in the area of a boo-boo," Steve said. "But, yes, only initiate zombie call with warning. Hooch?"

"I fumbled my reload," Hocieniec said. "I'm not that used to this AK system. Like it. Don't get me wrong. These things are the shit. But I'm still getting used to the system."

"Two things," Fontana said. "Our store of twelve is low and so is forty-five. We're fighting in fairly big areas, and while this would be a weapons switch, I suggest we change out for your AKs. Seven six two would work just about as well as shotgun, we have more seven six two, this is one of the few areas where it will make sense—and my shoulder is getting pounded by this twelve," he added with a grin.

"Whiner," Faith said, grinning back.

"Makes sense," Steve said. "You said two."

"More, really," Fontana said. "The initiation. Okay, so the

zombies apparently spend a lot of time sleeping. We need an initiator. My first thought was a flash-bang but we don't have any and it would probably be overkill. It would have been fun to toss one in the middle of that arena, mind you. But overkill."

"There is no such thing as overkill," Faith said. "There is only 'Open Fire' and 'Reloading'! That that never caught on as a bigger meme than LOLCats just says it all about people..."

"Hush," Steve said. "Continue, Sergeant."

"I'd suggest a whistle."

"Makes sense," Hooch said. "May I suggest, with due respect, that the commodore handle that?"

"Bite me," Faith said, shaking her head. "It all worked out okay. But, yeah, Da can get his little whistle. You be coach."

"Will do," Steve said. "More, Sergeant?"

"We probably should take some time and sit down with Chris and discuss the layout of this place. We should have known that door would lead to an arena. I mean, we could have gone back on deck, called him and asked him. He might not have known exactly but he probably would have had some idea. Also, and we should probably cross check this, it makes sense that the lifeboat hatches would open on large gathering areas. Thus another reason for the seven six two."

"I'm fairly terrified of bouncers around all this steel," Steve said. "I admit that's because I caught one myself once upon a time. But rifle rounds just keep going."

"Again, in this type of environment," Fontana said, waving around. "This deck is fairly smooth walled. We should be able to fire, parallel to the ship, without fear of bouncers. We'll have to retreat outside before engaging with rifles."

"Rifles *and* these?" Hooch said, patting the Saiga. "We're already fairly Ramboed up as it is."

"No," Fontana said. "We'll have to either use the rifles in close or use pistols on the retreat."

"Two sets," Steve said. "You and I will take the AKs. I've trained with them almost exclusively since I got out and fell in love with the bloody things. Hooch and Faith will maintain the Saigas despite Hooch's discomfort with the reload. They will cover on retreat to exterior with us as back-up if necessary, then we'll switch roles. And we'll rehearse it first."

"That sounds like a plan, sir," Fontana said.

CHAPTER 30

"Back on the *Campbell*," Gardner said nervously. She had a 10mm and a shotgun the Smiths had "borrowed" when they cleared the Coast Guard cutter. And they'd searched the whole ship for infected. But getting back on the ship was giving her flashbacks.

The ship was being towed by a submarine of all things. They'd taken a 24-foot inflatable to make the rendezvous and pick up critical medical supplies. Everything else could wait until it was in place near the liner.

"It'll be okay, PO," Seaman Jeff Woodman said. "We just get the saline and go."

"Easy enough," Gardner said. She keyed open the deck hatch, started to step across the coaming, then stopped. "What the hell?"

The floor was swarming with black bugs. There were so many it looked like the deck was black and moving.

"Oh . . . gross!" Woodman said. "Where the hell did they come from?"

"Jesus Christ," Gardner said quietly.

"What?" Woodman asked. She was shining a light into the interior. He craned his head around to look.

On the deck was a skeleton. Some of the bugs seemed to be fighting for the last scraps of flesh but pretty much everything but

334

John Ringo

bone and some scraps of skin and hair were gone. Bugs were even crawling in and out of the eye sockets, cleaning out the brains.

"Holy crap," Woodman said, "I don't want those getting on me!"

"I just figured out what they are," Gardner said, stepping through the hatch after a flash around with her light. Every step caused a crunch. "And they won't bite."

"They stripped that guy to the *bone*!" Woodman said.

"That's what they do," Gardner said, bending down and picking up one of the beetles. It skittered along her arm and she shook it off. "They're carrion beetles."

"Carrion?" Woodman said. "So they eat people?"

"They eat dead flesh," Gardner said. "I'd heard Wolf say he'd 'seeded' the boat. I didn't know it was with these."

"Wolf did this?" Woodman said angrily. "To *our* people?"

"Six of us came off, Woodie," Gardner said softly. "Ninety-four and twenty-six refugees didn't. You've carried bodies. You know how heavy they are. Now . . . they're not."

"That's horrible," Woodman said.

"No," Gardner said, flashing her light around. "It's efficient, simple and brutal. It's Wolf all over if you think about it. These things only eat dead flesh. They may get into some of the electronics but those are mostly thrashed by the infecteds, anyway. It cleans the boat out of the main issue, the dead meat on the dead people. If we ever get around to clearing this out, all we'll have to do is bag the bones."

"We won't know who's who," Woodman said.

"Does it matter?" Gardner said. "There's a big thing, it's called an ossuary, in France. All the guys who died in a certain battle in World War One. They buried them, waited for bugs like this to do their work, then dug them back up. All of certain bones are on the left, all the others are on the right and the skulls are in the middle."

She picked up the skull of the former Coast Guard crewman and looked at it as beetles poured out.

"I don't know who you were but you were my brother," Gardner said. "This way, I know I can give you a decent burial. And I will remember you. Now, we've got a mission to complete, Woodman, and people waiting on us. Live people. Let the dead bury the dead."

∽⊙∾

Chris hadn't known the boat like the back of his hand, but he'd been able to determine the areas on the other side of several of the doors. The one they'd chosen was the "lobby" area between the, yes, bloody damned skating rink and the even more bloody damned "four-hundred-person theater." Steve was starting to think that whoever had conceived this bloody beast had more megalomania than Napoleon.

About half the doors were to stairwells to the passenger cabins. Steve was torn between wanting to clear the major areas and concentrate on the passenger cabins. But the way their fire had to be echoing in this ship, the passengers *surely* knew they were on the way. And he wasn't sure he yet wanted to clear stairwells possibly filled with zombies.

"We'll open and attract from, not clear, this area," Steve said. "Then the theater. Then start on the passenger zones."

"Roger, sir," Fontana said, shaking his head at the pile of ammo boxes. They'd gotten boats alongside and brought up more people, including some "trained" seamen who were willing to go into "non-zombie" areas. With their help they'd brought all the ammo up onto the deck well away from the zombie bodies. Steve had also had them bring up some of his "little friends," and they had been scattered on the bodies. And the team had gotten a bite to eat and rehydrated. Time to get back to work.

The outer doors were already open. Faith checked the door, shook her head, put away the stethoscope, then pulled out the Halligan tool. This time Fontana and Hooch were on either side of the door, ready to pull.

Steve swiped, then pulled back to cover.

Faith popped the door, stepped back and started to put the tool on the deck. But there seemed like time so she stowed it away in its holster.

Steve realized that they'd made a mistake. Not a major one, but a mistake. He either should have had Faith take one of the rifles or have Fontana handle the Halligan. The shotgunners were the first line of defense with the riflemen backing them. It was a minor point. There was, again, silence and darkness on the far side of the hatch.

The foursome lined up in the hatch, and Steve lifted the whistle and blew.

Again there was a gutteral howling from the interior. They

immediately started to back up and were to the exterior hatch before the first zombie appeared.

"Wait," Steve said, taking the shot.

"I thought you said shotgun in here?" Faith complained.

"It was a clap shot and we're conserving shotgun ammo," Steve said. "Rotate for engagement."

They continued to back down the deck and stopped at the point they'd planned. And waited. There were sounds from inside the ship but no zombies appeared.

"I think they stopped for a snack," Faith said. It was hard to hear with all the gear on their heads.

"Bloody stupid..." Steve said. He lifted the whistle and gave another blast on it. That got some coming around the corner and he and Fontana began to engage.

The crackle of semi-automatic fire started to draw the zombies. But slowly. They came out even more slowly than at the theater, and the two riflemen continued to pick them off as they stumbled, mostly blind, into the light, looking for the source of the sound and thus food.

Finally there were only the growling sounds echoing from the hatch.

"Faith?" Steve said. "Don't want you whining—"

"Going pistol," Faith said. She started to reach for her .45, then pulled out one of the 10mms that they'd gotten off the Coast Guard cutter. They'd left the arms room alone but any weapons on the deck were considered fair game. "Cover me, Hooch."

"Got it," Hocieniec said, following her to the hatch.

Faith fired several slow and deliberate shots into the darkness and downward. Then she shifted up and shot twice more.

"I know this is a more powerful pistol," Faith said, reloading and putting the weapon away. "But it really doesn't *feel* that way, you know? We gonna close these doors? I'm not moving the bodies."

"Next time wait till they're clear of the doors, then," Hooch said. "Cover me."

"Ready?" Steve asked.

All four had switched back to shotgun after clearing the lobby and theater. Now it was time to start working up to the passenger cabins. That meant clearing the stairwell to the first three levels of passenger cabins.

According to Chris, there were two sets, inboard and outboard. Based upon what they'd seen with the exterior ones, there might be as many as fifty survivors. Spread over an area the size of a skyscraper.

But first they had to clear the stairwells.

"Been that way," Faith said. She'd insisted on point.

Steve keyed the door, which popped open, dropping a decomposing corpse at her feet. It was wearing bermuda shorts and a flowered shirt. It was unchewed.

There were scratch marks on the inside of the door.

"Shit," Faith snarled. "Shit, shit..." She turned around and walked to the far bulkhead and started kicking it. "Shit, shit, shit, shit, SHIT!" Then she reached behind her to cover the teddy bear's eyes. "Don't look, Trixie. It's not nicey."

Fontana looked at Steve, who held up a finger. Hooch had turned away as well. Steve was nodding his head as if counting time.

"Faith," Steve said as softly as he could through the respirator. "There are people who need saving upstairs. Do you need to head back to the boats?"

"Just give Trixie a second, okay, Da?" Faith said. She kicked the bulkhead a couple more times, then stuffed the bear's head down into her assault pack. "I think Trixie needs some sleepy time." She pulled off her outer glove, then reached into a pouch and pulled out an iPod. She put in the headphones, consulted the playlists, then turned it on. Last, she turned around and walked across and into the stairwell.

"What are you waiting for, an invitation?"

Robert "Rusty" Fulmer Bennett III had gotten over regretting this "pleasure cruise" a long time ago. How long he wasn't sure. His buddy, Ted, had suggested they go halves on a room "'cause chicks on cruises are easy." He hadn't managed to score before the news announced a plague on land. Then the word went around—rumor at first, then confirmed by the ship's crew—that the "Pacific Flu" had gotten onboard. Things kind of went downhill from there.

When they started getting really bad, the crew had passed out cases of bottled water and cans of food to each room. The cans were Number Ten cans and "you get whatever we have." There was one case of liter bottles of water per person and three

Number Ten cans. That made two cases of water and six cans in their room.

Rusty was a big boy, over three hundred pounds and six foot seven in his stocking feet. He could go through two number ten cans of food in a sitting. One of the reasons he wanted to do the cruise was the all-you-can-eat buffets.

But he also wasn't an idiot and had watched enough zombie movies that he realized that they might be stuck in that room for a long time.

Then there was the fact that they'd been handed six number ten cans of some weird-ass bland paste. It said "hummus" on the side and had a smiling picture of some terrorist-looking mother-forker spooning the stuff up and grinning like he'd just bombed a church.

So Rusty put them to the side and hoped they wouldn't have to eat it. And then Ted turned. He hadn't even shown any signs.

By the time the overworked security guards got there, Rusty had Ted tied up in some torn sheets and he'd managed to avoid getting bitten. Barely. He'd nearly lost it when Ted went. They had been friends since they were in grade school. But, face it, the reason they were friends was that Ted was the geek, Rusty was the muscle. If Rusty had turned, Ted wouldn't have stood a chance.

Rusty and Ted hadn't been able to afford the expensive cabin with the ocean view. So they'd been watching the occasional zombie go for a couple of days. The ship was still serving, some. And Rusty had gone out a couple of times. But he sure wasn't cruising for chicks. Just storing up fat and hoping like hell he wasn't going to go zombie. The zombie plagues were the worst. Twenty-eight days and it was all going to hell.

Then the "abandon ship" call came. Rusty tried to get to the lifeboats but there were zombies in the corridor. So he ducked back into his cabin and tried to figure out what to do. Then the doors locked and that was that.

He'd drunk an entire bottle of water and filled it from the tap. He kept doing that for two days, drink the water, fill up the bottle. Drink the bottle, fill up the water. While the zombies howled in the mall. He could watch them. That was about the only entertainment.

Then the power failed and while he could still watch the zombies

there wasn't any more water. Along with the water stopping working, so did the shitter. That was okay, he wasn't pooping much.

He'd conserved. He'd sipped even when he was desperate with
thirst. He'd heard you could drink piss. When he filled a bottle,
he drank that instead of water till it got dark and nasty. Then
he'd sip water. . . .

He could see the days go by but his iPhone ran out of power
pretty quick and he had no idea what day it was. He had no idea
how long he'd lived in that cabin. When he got up, he'd eat a
teaspoon of that terrorist stuff, which somebody told him was
made from ground-up chickpea, though the guy called it "gar-
banzo beans," drink piss and then a capful of water to wash it
down, then sit and wait for all the zombies to die or somebody
with, you know, guns to come along.

The ones in the hallway stopped making noise after about two
weeks. He was surprised it was that long without any water. But
he still couldn't get out 'cause the door was locked and it was,
like, steel. He'd pulled off the veneer to check.

He was thirsty all the time and he was down to pure piss in
the bottles. And it turned out that piss turned. It was starting
to smell like ammonia or something.

The zombies had, like, moods. Sometimes they'd be quiet,
sometimes it seemed like for days. Then they'd get active and
usually start fighting each other. He started calling them "orcs"
'cause they reminded him of those movies with the hobbits.

Then the day came when he could hear them getting really riled
up. He could barely pay attention. He couldn't really remember the
last time he'd gotten out of bed. He knew he was getting bed sores
but it was just too much trouble to get up. But he could hear the
zombies making noise and some sort of odd thumping. It was different but he really couldn't care less. There'd been thumps before.

Then the door opened. He heard it but he realized he couldn't
even move his head.

"Another terminal," a muffled voice said. It sounded like a
chick but he'd had that dream before.

"I'll check."

A bright light was flashed in his face and he flinched. That
hadn't happened before.

"You're *real*. . . ?" he croaked.

∽ ⊖ ∾

"I need a stretcher team," Faith said over the radio. "Some big guys. Even as a skeleton, this guy is big." She unkeyed the radio. "I thought he was a deader. My bad."

"Just drink," Hooch said, giving the guy a sip of water. All the survivors looked like they'd been in the death camps but this guy was particularly bad if for no other reason than being so big to begin with. His feet were hanging off the end of the bed. "A couple of sips. Your body needs to get used to it again."

"You're really real?" the guy croaked again.

"We're really real," Hooch said. "Sorry it took so long but the world's gone to shit. We're going to get you over to the boats in a bit. Tell them to bring an IV or this guy's going to go into shock."

"Bring an IV," Faith said. "Cabin three-nine-eight-four. Hooch, we need to keep clearing."

"Can you hold the bottle?" Hooch asked, putting it in the guy's hand. "We need to keep looking for survivors. Don't die before the medical team gets here, okay? Don't give up."

"I won't," the guy said. "Thank you. Who are you?"

"Wolf Squadron," Hooch said. "Long story. They'll explain it later. Just hang in there. We're going to prop the door. We've cleared the zombies."

The guy just barely nodded and tried to raise the water bottle. He couldn't even manage that.

"Straw," Faith said. She'd spotted one in an old Coke bottle. She cleaned it off, put it in the bottle and propped it where the guy just had to turn his head. "Can you do it now?"

"Yes," the guy said. "Thanks."

"Just hang in there," Hooch said. "You made it this long. Don't give up."

"Not gonna," the guy said. "I want to kill zombies."

"Okay, now you're talking my language," Faith said, patting him on the shoulder and sticking the straw between his lips. "We'll talk in a couple of weeks."

Rusty couldn't *believe* how good water tasted. It was, like, *orgasmic*. He didn't have to worry about drinking too much. Every time he took a sip he had to let his body and brain settle down from the intensity of the experience. Sip, fireworks. Sip, twitch.

Sip, more fireworks. There were, like, stars in his eyes. Then he realized it was a flashlight.

"Son-of-a-bitch," a voice said. "The guy doesn't have any veins to put a stick *in!*"

"Let me try it," another voice said.

"Like you know how any better than me. Hey, guy, this is gonna sting a little."

Rusty felt the needle go in but he'd just taken a sip of water and the fireworks sort of made it unnoticeable.

"Shit..." Another probe. "I cannot find a vein..."

"Let me..."

Rusty wasn't sure how many times they tried to put an IV in but he did notice that he was out of water.

"Water?" he asked. "Bottle...?"

"Yeah, got it," the guy said. Unlike the first two, who had been covered in weapons and what looked like firefighter gear, not to mention gas masks, the guy was wearing a raincoat and a gas mask but that was about all. He pulled the straw out and got another bottle, then inserted the straw back in Rusty's mouth.

"Finally," the second guy grunted.

The sensation coming up Rusty's arm *couldn't* be an IV. It felt like somebody had shot him up with freezing cold Coke. Then it spread through his whole body. He wasn't sure he was going to survive the rush. He groaned.

"You okay?" one of the guys said. "You know, that's like the stupidest thing I've ever said."

"It's right up there," his partner said. "Let's get him on a stretcher."

"Should we call for help?"

"Seriously? I think this guy *might* weigh ninety pounds."

Rusty was in a haze the whole way out of the cruise ship. He could sort of recall swaying in the air. And the feel of wind. It was cold after so long in the stuffy cabin. They'd wrapped a blanket around him but his feet stuck out.

He saw people climbing up ladders on the side of the ship and had a vague impression of what looked like charter fishing boats or something.

Then he was in a room in a boat that was bobbing up and down. A girl with black hair was holding onto his IV bag. She was a girl, too young, but she was the prettiest girl in the whole wide world.

"I need another bag," the girl said. "This one is nearly out already."

"Going to have to wait," a male voice said. "We don't have any. They've got some on the *Grace*."

"I don't think this guy can wait," the girl said.

"What's your name, angel?" Rusty said.

"Tina," Tina replied. "You're on the *Changing Tymes*. We're going to take you over to another ship called the *Grace Tan* in just a little while."

A stretcher was set down next to his holding a woman who looked like one of those survivors from a death camp. Her skin was pulled back against her cheeks and she was, really, literally, skin and bones.

"Can you hold two?" one of the stretcher bearers asked.

"I can for a while but we need some way to hold them up," Tina said. "And more. This guy needs another one!"

"We're running out," the stretcher bearer said, shrugging. "I'll see if I can find something to rig up..."

"...I said we need more IVs. These people are so gone..."

"We'll float everything we've got off. *Charlotte* is about two hours out with the *Campbell*. They have plenty..."

"Roger, *Dallas*. Thanks again for the assist..."

"*Dallas*, Squadron Ops, tell the *Charlotte*, we're sending an inflatable up to pick some up. We'll handle the boarding..."

Rusty wanted to hold on. He was afraid if he closed his eyes he'd die. But finally they closed.

The passenger cabin areas didn't really involve "clearing." It just involved opening the cabin door and seeing if the people inside were dead or alive.

"I can kill zombies all day long," Faith finally said, shaking her head at the door. "And I'm fine with this. But Trixie cannot walk into one more cabin and find a family dead of starvation."

"Tell Trixie that's fine," Hooch said. "I've got this. You and Trixie guard the door."

"Sorry, Hooch, but—"

"Faith, you've got nothing to apologize to anyone, ever," Hooch said, going in the cabin, then coming back out. "Empty."

"Really?" Faith said. They'd found some like that.

"Shhh..." he said, leaning forward and whispering. "That's all Trixie needs to know."

"Okay," Faith whispered, nodding.

"You know your daughter's going a little batshit, right?" Fontana said, checking the corpse for pupil response. It seemed like some of them weren't even decomposing they were so dried up. But this was a corpse.

"I've noticed," Steve said. "The question is if it's functional batshit or nonfunctional batshit."

"There's a difference?" Fontana asked as they checked the room across the hall. There weren't any surviving zombies, period. And the only human survivors were those who had been very very careful using their supplies. And there weren't many of those.

"One of my grandparents had been a prisoner of war during The War, as it's referred to Down Under," Steve said, closing the door on the dead. "To his dying day he never drank more than one cup of water with breakfast, one with lunch and one with supper. That was exactly all he drank. Doctors told him it was bad for him. He didn't listen."

The next room contained a family that had zombied. Or at least some of them had. One young male was still wearing scraps of clothes. All the corpses except one had been thoroughly gnawed.

"And he had about a million other quirks. Like reading so slow it took him a year to finish a book. He'd read one word, savor it like the water, then read another. He'd developed what looked like batshit habits that kept him alive and sane in the camps. This world isn't going to get any better soon. The question is if Faith's response is a functional one or if it's going to cause a real split personality. Because, right now it's the only armor her brain has against this horror. And, face it, whereas Granpa's batshit was weird in the normal world, Faith's going to have to grow up in this batshit world."

"She's only thirteen," Fontana said, walking into the next room. That was the pattern. Fontana took outboard, Steve took inboard. "Ever thought about, you know, pulling her back? We've got the Coasties now to help with clearance."

"The Coasties have other skills," Steve said. "And when they say 'clearance' they mean rounding guys up, searching for drugs and maybe getting shot at. They don't mean blowing their way through zombies."

"They're still adults with some weapons training. Got a live one. Not thirteen-year-old girls."

"On the face of it, you're right," Steve said. "I should pull her back. You wanna tell her? Medical team to cabin two-nine-seven-four."

"No," Fontana said, giving the woman some water. "Hey, you're gonna make it, okay? Just hang on. We've got medical teams on the way."

"Th'nk u . . ." the woman whispered.

"Just sip the water . . ."

"So, about Faith," Fontana said. "The zombies don't bother her. Much. *This* shit is killing her."

"I know," Steve said. "But the damned stretcher teams will barely come up into the dark areas. And they won't go anywhere we haven't cleared for zombies. Even when all the zombies are dead. Find somebody who'll do this besides you, Hooch, me and Faith and I'll send Faith zombie hunting."

"Get the Coasties," Fontana repeated. "This is their kind of shit."

"I will," Steve said. "When they get here. Some. Some are going to have to help with just keeping these poor bastards alive. We'll go back to heavy clearance. But for now, we're all we've got."

"And we can't do this all day and all night, twenty-four seven," Fontana pointed out.

Steve reached up and changed the frequency on his radio.

"*Dallas*, you got me?" Steve asked, walking into the exterior cabin. There was a body on the bed. He pointed.

"Gone," Fontana said. "No pupil response."

"Dallas *here*."

"Can you retrans to squadron ops, over?"

"*Roger.*"

"*Squadron ops. Jesus, Wolf . . .*"

"Yeah," Steve said. "Isham, we're going to call this at twelve hours from when we went over the side. Whenever that is. The clearance teams that is. If the Coasties are on site by then I'd like them to manage the recovery work. But nobody works on it for more than twelve hours at a time. The clearance team is going to need some bunks on the *Alpha* or the *Grace*. And somebody who has a clue about gear to get this shit cleaned up. All that we're going to be able to do for the next... God knows how long is clear, eat, sleep and clear. Can you manage that?"

"*I've got it under control, Wolf*," Isham replied. "*I'll get all that set up.*"

"All the zombies are dead in the passenger cabin areas," Steve said. "We're getting about one survivor per ten cabins. As soon as some of the Coasties get on site, have them replace Faith and Hooch. Then us. Faith and Hooch go down for longer than we do. We'll both start again tomorrow at the same time but get them replaced *as soon as possible*. We are going to be clearing this... floating den of horrors for a long time. We need to think about how we're going to sustain this."

"*Roger*," Isham replied. "*Got all that.*"

"Thanks," Steve said. "Wolf out."

He changed the radio back over to the medical channel, then shrugged.

"Best I can do," Steve said.

CHAPTER 31

"Any decisions you need me to make?" Steve asked as he stepped off onto the flush deck of the *Alpha*.

The waves were chopping up and the deck was awash but he didn't really care. It would clean some of the crap off his boots.

"None," Isham said, shaking his head. "It's not a power grab. Everything that can be got under control is under control. Just... trust me on that and get some rest."

"I want to drink myself to sleep," Steve said.

"Hang on," Isham said. "Hang on to that grab rail and just stand there. We're going to wash you down out here."

"Makes sense," Steve said. He was covered in wet-weather gear top to bottom. "The guns are going to need—"

"To be cleaned off in fresh water, dried really well and then lubed up really well," Isham said, backing up the stairs. "Just let them wash you down..."

"Steve," Stacey said, hugging him. "Oh... God..."

"It's bad," Steve said, nodding. "I'm really regretting bringing Faith onboard."

"She's having a lot of problems with the—" She stopped and grimaced. "She likes the zombie hunting..."

"I'm going to switch her to that as purely as possible," Steve said, nodding. "I mean, there are horrors to that. But this has been... Different."

The cabin was excellent. Steve wasn't sure how Isham had procured the materials to return it to, if not its former glory, then back to very liveable. But it was nice. And the meal that had been waiting for him after his long, hot shower looked really, really good. He wasn't sure that he could eat it, though.

"You have to eat," Stacey said.

"Reading my mind?" Steve asked, smiling faintly.

"Always," Stacey said.

"Talk to me about something," Steve said, taking a forkful of the dish. He wasn't sure what it was but it was excellent. "When did Chris go back to being a cook?"

"That's Sari," Stacey said, smiling.

"The one that was on here?" Steve asked, then winced. The horrors of the *Voyage* had nearly blotted out how bad the *Alpha* had been when they boarded.

"She's a really good cook," Stacey said. "And Mike is oversee-ing the maintenance on the weapons and gear. I made sure they were all clear. He knew how to clear them but I checked first. He's going to fine-tooth them."

"How's Isham doing?" Steve asked. "This is the sort of thing I need to talk about."

"Doing fine," Stacey said. "He found one of the SSLs who's a premier scrounger who turned up, among other things, boxes of Cuban cigars. Isham's up in Mickerberg's old office smoking big black cigars and running things like he's General Patton. It's funny to watch in a way. I think until this came up he really wasn't... in the game? But now he is. And he's doing a good job at it."

"Keep an eye on him," Steve said.

"I am," Stacey said, shrugging. "But when we had a moment alone *he* brought it up. And he pointed out that you're the one with the subs backing you. That headquarters gave you the authority. Not him. He said 'Broken down and busted or not, I'm not going try to buck the United States Government. It's still got nuclear weapons.'"

"Now that sounds like it might be honesty," Steve said.

"Okay, wow," Faith said, shoveling down the breakfast. "This is really good. Do I want to know what it is?"

"Eggs," Sari said, laying the plates out for the clearance team. "With more eggs."

There were the scrambled eggs, which were awesome, a really good canned fruit salad and fried potatoes. There was even fresh baked english muffins. With butter.

"It's got a bit of a fishy taste but a good one," Fontana said. "What's the meat? It tastes like...lobster?"

"Scrambled eggs with lobster," Sari said. "And some secret ingredients."

"I'm going to let you keep the secrets," Steve said, looking out the window of the "dinette." The small compartment—relatively small, it being the *Alpha*—had a good view of the growing flotilla of boats working on the *Voyage*. He could even see the *Campbell* drifting in the distance. The *Alpha* and *Grace* had rendezvoused with it overnight and transferred clearance materials as well as medical supplies. Fortunately, it had lots of both. The cutter had seemed like a big ship when they first cleared it. Now they had a new appreciation for "big." But for its relatively small size, it was absolutely packed with disaster material. Which made sense given its jobs.

"Today is pure clearance," Steve said.

"Oh, thank God," Faith said. "Wait— Zombie killing clearance or checking cabins clearance?"

"Zombie killing clearance," Steve said. "We're going to sweep all of the remaining untouched areas on the port side cabin zone, then work our way across the ship and sweep the starboard side. If we run into survivors doing that—unlikely—we'll call for extraction or extract them ourselves. The Coast Guard personnel are going to manage the extraction in cleared areas and provide security. That's mostly for the people doing the actual removal."

"I can handle that," Faith said. "Sorry, but I'm just—"

"Nothing, at all, to be sorry about, Faith," Fontana said. "This is getting to *me*. And I thought I'd seen pretty much every horror possible in Iraq and Afghanistan. The fact that you're not completely round the bend is pretty remarkable."

"I know the Trixie thing is freaking people out," Faith said, shrugging. "But..."

"It's a way for you to compartmentalize," Steve said, nodding. "People who do this sort of thing have to do that. Everyone does. You just happen to have an outward expression. The question, since you raise it, is are you going to be okay continuing?"

"I'm fine if it's killing zombies," Faith said, shrugging. "And I can handle the usual sort of stuff. But Hooch had to take over checking the cabins. I...I can't do that right now. Even finding live ones... Half the time I was like: What's the *point*?"

"We've lost some," Steve said. He'd had a quick briefing that morning before breakfast. "And according to the doctors at the CDC we'll probably lose some more over the next week. But most of them are making it. We're saving people. But for today... We'll just blow some zombies away."

"That'll help," Faith said, grinning.

"Weaponry," Steve said. "There are some large areas we'll be clearing. Despite my fear of bouncers, I think we need at least one rifle. There are sure to be more security zombies and we need to start conserving our shotgun rounds to the extent it's possible. Sergeant Fontana, you'll carry that."

"Roger, sir," Fontana said. "Any word on the ammo from the *Campbell*?"

"We got a resupply of two hundred rounds of shotgun," Steve said, grimacing. "That was all that was in the ready locker or found scattered onboard. There's a magazine but it's apparently a vault. And nobody can find the keys. And since it's a magazine—"

"You can't exactly cut it open with a blowtorch," Fontana said.

"There's a team looking for the keys at the moment," Steve said. "According to what I got, there should be two thousand more rounds of twelve-gauge in there. Another reason to use the rifles whenever possible. We have, also, a limited amount of seven six two but we're currently better on that than on shotgun. So when it's possible, Sergeant Fontana will take the shot. Please make sure that all rounds go into the target."

"I will," Fontana said. "But you get bouncers from shotgun as well."

"They tend to be caught by the body armor," Steve said. "And the spots not covered by armor that are likely to kill us are small. With the exception of the face, of course. Which is why, in addition to all the other stuff we're carrying, we're going to be adding ballistic face shields. The *Campbell* had six onboard. They've already been mounted to the helmets.

"Kuzma has set up a freshwater decontamination shower on the lifeboat deck, forward. If we get as bloodied up as we did yesterday, Faith, we'll run through that. There's also a forward support post set up with food, water and ammo, and we can drop back to it and take a break. One thing we're going to have to look for is a forward point that we can set up as a permanent secure point on the *Voyage*. Not too big, not too small, some exterior light and most of all secure.

"That's all I've got for now. Let's eat."

"Just sip," the lady said, putting a straw to his lips. "It's chicken broth..."

Rusty still could barely do that. He was feeling better. Not human but all the water they'd been pumping through him was helping. He still could barely lift his arms.

"Thank you," he said, leaning back on the pillows when the small cup of broth was down. He was so far gone, he actually felt full. "Are you a nurse? And where...?"

"Okay, first of all, you're on a support ship called the *Grace Tan*," the lady said. "I'm Amanda. No, I'm not a nurse. We've only got one nurse survivor and she's organizing this. I'm a survivor like you. I was on a lifeboat. I was on the *Voyage*, too. The way things worked out...I'm glad I made it to the lifeboat. But a lot of those..." She shook her head.

"So...is it the Navy or...?" Rusty asked.

"It's a long story," Amanda said, smiling. "If you feel you're up to some reading, they've made a little pamphlet..."

"I can't believe we're trying to unrep from a cruise liner," Gardner said.

Unrep, or "underway replenishment," was a tricky business in the best of times and circumstances. The basic idea was to create sort of zip-lines between two ships and slide stuff back and forth. Simple on land. Two rocky points tended to stay reasonably the same distance apart down to the subatomic level. Ships, however, did not. So what usually happened was that your package, be it ammunition or food or toilet paper or, God help them, people, tended, if the ships closed, to go into the drink, or if they separated, be flung upwards at a high rate of speed. In extreme circumstances the package could fail to choose between being crushed as the too-close following ships collided or being flung upwards, the rope part, and go flying into the far distance.

One unfortunate, and extremely disliked, lieutenant commander in the Navy in the 1960s had all four happen on a single attempt at moving between a destroyer and a carrier. The lieutenant commander was first dunked, then popped back out rapidly enough to thoroughly dry the ropes as they hyperextended. This, of course, had the effect of bouncing him up and down like a tightened rubber band. He was then dunked, again, repopped, at which point the carry line parted, throwing the unfortunate officer upwards in a ballistic arc. The lieutenant at the conn of the destroyer panicked, ordered a radical course correction to starboard, towards the carrier, just as the officer landed in the water between the two vessels, which promptly collided. The lieutenant commander was assumed to have been crushed as his body was never found. The irony that the lieutenant commander, the carrier vessel battle group's inspector general, had just written a scathing report on the conn training of the officers of the destroyer was not lost on the incident report board.

Thereafter the Navy went to all helo or boat transfers for personnel at sea.

"You know we just hit the four hundred mark?" Steve said, keying the double doors.

"Four hundred days?" Fontana asked, popping the hatch with the Halligan and moving back.

"Four hundred people," Steve said. "Four hundred known survivors of humanity. Plus the Hole and CDC and whoever they're in contact with."

"Holy crap," Faith said softly.

"I know it's not a lot," Steve said, shining his taclight around the cavernous room. A zombie in the distance growled, then howled. It couldn't even be seen, but it alerted others, who stumbled to their feet and headed to the lights. "But we're getting there. Back to defense positions."

"Not that," Faith said, taking up her position behind a counter. "That room. What was it?"

"Casino, I think," Fontana said. He began slow-aimed fire at the blinded zombies stumbling through the door. He already had four magazines laid out on the counter.

"It's *huge*," Faith said, sticking a finger in her ear to cut down on the cracks from the AK.

"Should have seen the ones in Vegas," Fontana said.

"Maybe someday," Faith said. "When I'm, like, ninety. Zombie clearance, Vegas."

"Resident Evil: The Cruise Ship. You can see the game, right?" Hooch said.

"I think we're playing it," Steve pointed out.

"How come when I'm shooting, my ears don't ring?" Faith asked, tagging a zombie in the chest as it tried to figure out how to get around a roulette table with a Surefire in its eyes. "*The beauty of this ride ahead...*" Tap, tap...

The zombies were having trouble with the complex layout of the casinos. Casinos were designed to get people to change directions so they'd go "Ooooh... I bet I can win *that* game!" The zombies could see the lights, they just couldn't figure out how to *get* to them. Then, all of a sudden, they would. For that matter, it wasn't always clear to the clearers where the open areas, or the zombies, were.

Clearing them out was a painstaking process of zombies howling and thrashing in the darkness. When they could, they took the zombies at range.

Faith had had to break out the kukri. Twice.

"Aural damping," Fontana said.

"Checking right," she said, shining the light around the other side of the roulette table. For some reason, the chewed-up people just weren't horrible anymore. She could even slide her eyes right over the kids. "There's an answer? I was sort of asking one of those rectangular questions."

"Rhetorical," Fontana said, chuckling. "Clear left. Clearish. I think we're going to have to sweep and resweep."

"Works for me," Faith said. "Hang on, stumbler coming around my side." She took the shot. She'd stopped double tapping to conserve ammunition but the .45 round was usually good enough with one shot. It didn't kill the zombies immediately, but they bled out pretty quickly. "Reloading. Hang on. Da?" she said, over the radio.

"*Go.*"

"I'm running out of forty-five mags. I've got ammo but I don't exactly want to reammo in here."

"I've got mags," Fontana said.

"Like I'm gonna use a Colt if I don't gotta," Faith said. "I could also use a break."

"Roger. Pull back to the entrance."

"This does get the adrenal gland, don't it?" Fontana said, firing twice in rapid succession. "They just seem to come out of nowhere."

They'd learned when they cleared the theater to shut the door behind them. It meant they didn't have a way out. It also meant they didn't have leakers that suddenly appeared when they thought they were at a "secure" point.

"And I think if we're going to keep clearing this thing we might as well all go to carbines," Faith said, starting. She fired two rounds into a body on the floor. "It moved. I swear it did."

"How long can I stand under here?" Faith shouted as the water from the fire hose poured over her.

"As long as you want!" the guy manning the system wasn't Coast Guard. She didn't even recognize him. "It recycles!"

"Cool," Faith muttered, giving him a thumbs up. She was just going to stand there for a while then.

"Be careful not to fire in the direction of the other team," Fontana said nervously. "And watch the bouncers."

"No worries," Faith said, hefting the AK variant. The Arsenal SLR-107 would only have been vaguely recognizable to Mikhail Kalashnikov. It had an improved safety, AR buttstock, rail with lights and Trijicon TA11F. But the guts were still the reliable system Kalashnikov had stolen from various WWII assault rifles, then refined. "I have fired this thing before..."

A zombie charged out of the shadows to her right and she turned and double tapped it in the chest. The rounds continued through the body and bounced off a bar on the other side, and pinged off into the darkness.

"Oops," she said as the infected collapsed on the floor.

"You hit?" Fontana asked.

"No. You?"

"I'm good."

"I hate full metal jacket..."

∽ ⊖ ⌒

"Okay, okay, okay," Faith said. "I just . . . *Seriously*? An indoor *pool*? Seriously?"

The cavernous room was marked "spa." Faith had always wanted to go to a spa. She'd sort of envisioned small rooms with hot tubs and massage tables or something. She'd always wondered what a "walnut scrub" was.

There were hot tubs scattered around in various styles. There were Roman baths, Japanese baths, stone flagging and walls. The ceiling, far, far overhead, was a massive skylight that gave them an unfortunately clear view of the interior.

Zombies would eat each other for food. All they really *needed* to survive was something resembling water. And the "spa" had had *lots* of water.

So there were *lots* of zombies, and although they'd been awakened by Steve's whistle, it had echoed in the cavernous interior and they weren't sure where to go. The room was lit well enough the team had turned off their taclights. Not to mention, there were pools of water all over the place so even the zombies that noticed them were having a hard time getting to them.

Except for the close ones.

"I'm really glad we went to rifles," Faith said, targeting one of the nearer zombies. It was having to go around a counter to get to them and she got it with a deflection head shot on the run and it dropped out of sight.

"Nice," Fontana said, taking two more down.

"Is it just me, or was that *exactly* like shooting a duck in an arcade?" Faith said. She fired at another one but missed. "We going to move forward?"

"Yes," Steve said, firing. "But one team. Head for that high ground over there."

The "high ground" was what had probably been an indoor waterfall.

"Hug the wall," Steve said. "Take them down as they come to us. Don't engage over twenty-five meters unless I say so."

"What's the fun of that?" Faith asked.

"I'd like as many of the rounds to go *into* the zombies as possible," Steve said.

"Don't shoot till you see the reds of their eyes," Fontana said. "Gotcha."

⁘ ⊖ ⁙

The one problem with the "high ground" was that once they'd gotten up there, all the zombies could see them and closed in. And they couldn't exactly retreat.

"This is getting sort of hot," Fontana said, doing a fast reload. He had to pat for magazines until he found one.

"Hot, yeah," Faith said, firing steadily at the mass of infecteds clawing their way up the former waterfall. "But it's not in the dunny, yet."

"Dunny?" Hooch asked.

"Aussie for a latrine," Steve said.

"What is, in your opinion, in the dunny?" Fontana said. "'Cause I could sure use some time to reload mags."

"Being in the dunny isn't no time to reload magazines," Faith said, reloading. "Being in the dunny is all your knives are stuck in bodies, you're tripping over your mags and brass and your Halligan tool is bent."

"I can't wait for you to get legal so I can propose...."

"We in the dunny, yet?" Fontana asked as he stuck the pry base of his Halligan into a zombie's eye.

"Nope," Faith said, pounding one on the head with her AK. "I haven't had to shoot one off me and I've yet to pull a knife..."

"...dunny yet?" Hooch yelled, sticking his bowie knife into a zombie's stomach and ripping up.

"Halligan tool bent?" Faith asked, firing into a zombie's head. Another one grabbed her legs and her feet slipped out from under her. The zombie dragged her down the rocks of the waterfall as she kicked at it. Others piled on, trying to bite through her armor.

"Shit, shit, shit," Fontana said.

"Okay," she yelled. "*Now* we're getting there!"

"We're going to have to melee down to her," Steve said, smashing his Halligan into a zombie's head.

"We're barely holding here," Fontana said.

"When we've winnowed them down..."

"Nice thing about being in a scrum," Faith said as Fontana dragged her out from under the bodies. Steve was doing the same thing for Hooch. "You don't have to worry which direction you're aiming and there's no real way to miss. *That* was in the dunny." She looked around, sitting up, her legs still covered by zombie bodies.

"Hey, look, the waterfall is working again. Sort of..."

Day Four

Faith stood under the decontamination shower and made a motion with one hand for "more..."

Day Six

"Okay, seriously, like, how many of these damned things *are* there...?"

Day Nine

"*This* is why I hate five five six." Faith fired three more times. "Oh, just *die* already!"

As the supply of rounds for the Smiths' AK variants dwindled, they had switched to the Coast Guard M4s, which used the much smaller 5.56mm round. The arguments for or against 5.56 were complex but the fact that it generally took multiple rounds to stop one of the infected was notable.

"You need to shoot them in the head," Fontana said, double tapping a zombie.

On the other hand, a team had finally found the key for the *Campbell*'s ammunition magazine, which had a *plentiful* supply of 5.56.

"The United States started to go downhill when it changed from a round designed to kill the enemies of our glorious republic to one designed to piss them off," Faith said, shooting a zombie five times, then walking up and shooting the still-thrashing infected in the head. "Seriously, just die, okay?"

"Seriously, it's legal to marry at fourteen in Arkansas."

"Fine," Faith said, double tapping a zombie that had reared up out of the darkness. "If we clear Arkansas by the time I'm fourteen we'll talk."

"That's not fair..."

Day Eleven

"Okay," Faith said, laying down fire with the MG240 off the *Campbell*. "*This* is more like it!"

They'd finally cleared the "passenger" areas all the way to the top of the ship. The top deck was mostly open and a perfect place to use a machine gun. Especially from the top of a water slide…

"Happiness is a belt-fed gun," Fontana said, grinning. "Remember, short controlled bursts or the barrel will overheat."

"That's *got* to be a design flaw. What's the fun of short controlled bursts…?"

"Eh," Faith said, stepping out of the stairwell. "Back in the dark again."

The passenger areas were entirely clear. Except for the few emaciated survivors in the cabins, there had been no uninfected individuals.

Now it was time to work on the crew areas.

"I'll clear if we find zombies," Faith said. "But if there's nobody who answers a knock, I'm just going to let somebody else check the cabin."

"Hopefully down here they'll all have died of dehydration," Steve said. "The zombies, that is."

"Trixie doesn't want to know about the cabins," Faith said.

"We get it, honey," Fontana said. "We'll check the cabins."

As a senior maintenance officer, Robert "Rob" Cooper didn't have access to all the supply areas. Technically. But as a senior maintenance officer what he did have was a lot of friends willing to look elsewhere when he turned up with a dolly. Besides, everybody was doing it. Everybody knew that things were going to shit—you only had to be around one person who "turned" to realize that this was really and truly bad—and everybody was stocking their cabins.

Rob didn't stock his cabin. He stocked a maintenance locker. For one thing, it was closer to the supplies area. For another it had a white water line running right through it that was below the line of the water supply. And it wasn't anything tough for a guy who'd worked his way up as an engineer to run a quick fitting into the line. In other circumstances, that would be an automatic firing offense and really, really stupid.

After two months in the darkened maintenance shack, he was sooo glad he'd ignored both regulation and "common sense."

And so was Gwinn.

He'd run into the Staff Side Third Officer while trying to

make it to the lifeboats. Unlike a lot of the Ship-Side officers, he'd stayed on the ship with the passengers. Right up until the "abandon ship" call, which had been made by Staff. And when he'd headed to the lifeboats, in a zombie apocalypse, he'd gone prepared. The crowbar was how he'd beat his way most of the way to the lifeboats before finding out, from Gwinn, that they were all gone.

She'd protested heading to his hide-out. She'd been bitten at the boats and then again from the zombie he beat off of her. Then there was the blood splatter from the beating. But he'd insisted. He didn't know why even then. Maybe it was the thought of such a pretty lady becoming a zombie or being eaten by them. And he kept in the back of his mind that he had a crowbar and a bunch of painting plastic if it came to it. But in the end she'd accompanied the burly fifty-three-year-old engineering officer into the bowels of the ship.

It had been fortunate he'd brought her with him. They were halfway to the forward maintenance shed when the full lockdown hit. Even *his* card didn't work, which pissed him off. Maintenance, as he mentioned to her at the time, was *supposed* to have access to the *whole* ship. *Especially* in an emergency. But Gwinn's continued to work all the way to the shed.

It had been touch and go with Gwinn. She'd gotten *real* sick. Fortunately, he had plenty of water to feed her and a pretty decent supply of medicine. He'd had a lot of friends in the crew.

But she was a tough lady. Easy on the eyes until the lights cut out on day three. Easy on other areas as the months went by.

The "months" was starting to be a problem. He'd thought he'd stocked enough food for pretty much any reasonable period. And they'd been careful with it. But he realized that it was no five-year stock. Eventually, they were going to run out. And being in a compartment, even one as large as this, with anyone, even someone with as much common sense and decency as Gwinn, occasionally made you contemplate the crowbar.

"I spy with my eye..." Rob said.

"If you ever want to have another of something that *also* starts with a B, don't even think about it," Gwinn said.

"Queen bishop to Knight four."

"Queen to rook five. Check."

"Your bishop is at king six, right?"

"Right."

"Damn. King bishop to—" He paused as there was a strange sound in the distance. "You know, even if all the zombies would go away, fixing this thing is going to be a shipyard job."

"I doubt there's much use for a—" She stopped as there was a distinct, rhythmic, clanging in the distance. "Was that . . ."

"Shave and a haircut?" Rob said, rolling to his feet. He didn't even have to fumble his way around the compartment anymore. He walked to the hatch and started banging on it regularly. "Come on!" he said, banging harder. "I don't care if you're fucking pirates!"

"I sort of do," Gwinn said, then paused. "No, I've changed my mind. I'm fine with pirates."

"Nothing," Faith said, lowering the steel pipe. "You wanna check it?"

They'd found some survivors in the crew cabins. Some of them weren't even in horribly bad shape. The crew had, it turned out, been stocking up. And several of the cabins that were empty had quite a bit of stores. Some of them even had stuff that was sort of comical in a black way. One of the stewards' quarters had five pounds of caviar in it. Fontana had pointed out that caviar was originally designed to be long storage and was a good source of protein. Faith had learned two things that day. That and beluga caviar was icky. Even on some really expensive kind of cracker.

"Roger," Fontana said, keying the lock. As he did, there was a distant clanging.

"Customers?" Faith said. "Seriously?"

"Sounds like it's coming from forward," Fontana said, moving down the corridor. "Try it again."

Faith banged on the walls, hard, and was rewarded with more banging.

"Guy's in good condition," Faith said.

"This way," Fontana said, continuing.

They followed the sound around a cross-corridor to a door marked "Forward Maintenance Support."

"Figured it would be a food supply locker," Fontana said, keying the door. He'd stood to the side to keep from blinding the people. He popped a chem-light and tossed it through the door.

∽ ⊖ ∾

Rob had put his arm over his eyes when the door clicked to keep from being blinded. He heard something rattle on the floor and, Gwinn's comment about pirates still in mind, panicked that it might be a flash bang.

"That will help your eyes adjust," the guy on the other side said. "Just slowly let them creep open. How many?"

"Two," Rob answered. "You Coast Guard?"

"Wolf Squadron," the guy said. "We've got some Coasties with us but it's mostly a volunteer civilian effort. You sound in good shape."

"Stocked up," Rob said, shifting his arm just enough to get a little light. It was blinding and he quickly covered it again. "And there's a water tap in here. Can we get out, now?"

"Wait for us to finish clearing this area," the guy said. "Get your eyes a little adjusted. You know of anyone else in this sector?"

"Other than the infecteds?" Rob said. "No. And all those are dead up to the main sector hatch. There are some on the other side."

"That hatch four-six-one that leads up to the main passenger area?" a female voice asked.

"Yeah."

"Took care of that for ya," she said coldly.

"If you guys can walk we'll finish clearing, then come back for you," the guy said. "Just hang in there another fifteen minutes. No more. Oh, if you hear us banging, bang. This place is a fucking maze."

"If we do get lost," the woman said, "you can actually self-extract if you've got the strength and the guts. It's clear. We've spent two weeks and nearly ten thousand rounds making it that way."

"We'll wait," Rob said. "Fifteen minutes?"

"Should be about that," the guy said. "Be back."

The hatch shut and locked and Rob cracked his eyes again. If he looked away from the chemlight the light was only slightly blinding.

"Rescue," Gwinn said, wonderingly. He hadn't seen her in months and chemlight wasn't usually considered romantic but she was the prettiest thing he'd ever seen in his life. Like him she was stark naked. The compartment had been so warm and stuffy, they'd stopped wearing their clothes after the first couple of weeks.

Rob went over, sat down next to her and put his arm around her shoulders.

"We've got fifteen minutes," Rob said. "I wonder how we could spend the time."

"You old goat," Gwinn said, shaking her head. "Maybe by getting dressed?"

"Spoilsport."

"Sunglasses," the guy said, sticking a pair through the cracked hatch. "We're using taclights. You're going to need them. And for outside."

"Outside," Gwinn said, wonderingly. "What's the weather?"

"It's kicking up," the woman answered. "There's a front that's headed down. We may have to suspend ops depending on how bad it gets. *Don't* look directly at the lights." She opened up the hatch, then paused. "Son of a— Are you Third Officer Gwinneth Stevens?"

"Yes," Gwinn said, holding up her hand to the lights.

"Son of a gun," Fontana said, laughing. "Chris said you got bit."

"Chris survived?" Gwinn said. Her hand flew to her belly and she looked at Rob.

"Miss Stevens," the woman said carefully, "Chris was on a small boat for two months. Uhmm..."

"Don't sweat what happened in the compartment," the guy said. "You're not the only one who has been friendly with others, Miss. We've got a saying—"

"What happens in the compartment, stays in the compartment," the woman said.

"He found someone?" Gwinn said. She couldn't decide if she was hurt or relieved.

"Sort of..." the woman said. "He really didn't talk about the boat until we had to board it. We didn't even know about *you* two until... He told us to look for you, your body anyway, for your access card," she finished, pointing at the card on her lanyard. "And I'd been around him lots of times. Which, by the way, meant he was really broken up about it. If he'd gotten over you completely he'd have talked about you. That's how it works, mostly."

"Look," the guy said. "Can we get you two topside and figure out the social-political issues later?"

"Mind if I bring my crowbar?" Rob said. "Just in case?"

"You don't get to use it on Chris," Gwinn said.

"Not gonna," Rob said. "I'm afraid he's gonna want to use it on me."

When they reached topside and the twosome were shielding their eyes from the light, Faith reached for her radio, then paused.

"How do I do this, exactly?"

"Better you than me," Fontana said.

She switched frequencies and looked around. Sure enough the *Cooper* was right off the ship, taking on more survivors. There had been three passengers for every crewman on *Voyage* but about twice as many crew as passengers had survived.

"*Cooper, Cooper,* this is Shewolf for *Cooper* actual, over," Faith said.

"*Cooper, actual, over.*"

"Talk to him, girlie," Faith said, holding out the radio.

"*Chris . . . Chris, it's Gwinn . . .*"

"The Assault Carrier *Iwo Jima* is in the Bermuda High so it's out of the storm belt," Steve said as the *Toy* was tossed by another wave. "We need the ammo, we need the guns and with any luck at all, there will be some surviving Marines . . ."

He spun the boat to the south and put the hammer down. Behind him the boats of Wolf Squadron formed themselves into a ragged line and followed. There were ships to clear.

Two miles to the north, the cruise ship rocked on a darkling sea silent as a tomb. . . .

TO BE CONTINUED

PLAYLIST

NAME	ARTIST	ALBUM
"Meadows of Heaven"	Nightwish	*Dark Passion Play*
"Cool Change"	Little River Band	*Little River Band: Greatest Hits*
"Becoming the Bull"	Atreyu	*Lead Sails Paper Anchor*
"Vater Unser"	E Nomine	*Das Testament* (German Bonus Tracks)
"Into the Nothing"	Breaking Benjamin	*Dear Agony*
"Roland the Headless Thompson Gunner"	Warren Zevon	*A Quiet Normal Life: The Best of Warren Zevon*
"Immigrant Song"	Led Zeppelin	*Mothership* (Remastered)
"Storytime"	Nightwish	*Imaginaerum*
"What Have You Done" (U.S. Edit)	Within Temptation featuring Keith Caputo	*The Heart of Everything* (Bonus Track Version)
"Stand My Ground"	Within Temptation	*The Heart of Everything* (Bonus Track Version)
"Fade Away"	Breaking Benjamin	*Dear Agony*
"Anthem of the Angels"	Breaking Benjamin	*Dear Agony*

"If I Can't Dance"	Sophie Ellis-Bextor	*St. Trinians* (Original Soundtrack)
"On My Way to Satisfaction"	Girls Aloud	*St. Trinians* (Original Soundtrack)
"E Nomine"	E Nomine	*Das Testament* (German Bonus Tracks)
"The Howling"	Within Temptation	*The Heart of Everything* (Bonus Track Version)
"Vampire Club" (Twilight version)	Voltaire	*Spooky Songs For Creepy Kids*
"Lights Out"	Breaking Benjamin	*Dear Agony*
"Miami 2017"	Billy Joel	*The Essential Billy Joel*
"Skye Boat Song"	Moira Kerr	*Celtic Soul*
"Declaration of War"	Hadouken!	*Music for an Accelerated Culture*
"I Will Not Bow"	Breaking Benjamin	*Dear Agony*
"Sophia" (Radio Edit)	The Crüxshadows	*Sophia* (Maxi Single)
"Mein Herz brennt"	Rammstein	*Mutter* (Double CD Tour Edition)
"Tears"	The Crüxshadows	*Wishfire*
"Last of the Wilds"	Nightwish	*Dark Passion Play*
"Honor"	Atreyu	*Lead Sails Paper Anchor*
"Rule the World"	Kamelot	*Ghost Opera*
"(Don't Fear) The Reaper"	Blue Öyster Cult	*Super Hits*
"Warrior"	Disturbed	*Asylum* (Deluxe Version)
"Seraphs"	The Crüxshadows	*Wishfire*
"Tubthumping"	Chumbawamba	*Tubthumper*
"I Want My Tears Back"	Nightwish	*Imaginaerum*
"Winter Born (This Sacrifice)"	The Crüxshadows	*Ethernaut*

"The Warrior Song"	Warrior Project	*The Warrior Song* (Single)
"Genocide"	Hammerfall	*Threshold*
"Ready to Die"	Andrew W.K.	*I Get Wet*
"Ghost Opera"	Kamelot	*Ghost Opera*
"Bye Bye Beautiful"	Nightwish	*Dark Passion Play*
"Danse Macabre in G Minor, Op. 40"	Slovak Radio Symphony Orchestra & Keith Clark	*The Best of Saint-Saëns*
"Amaranth"	Nightwish	*Dark Passion Play*
"Reign of the Hammer"	Hammerfall	*Threshold*
"Citadel"	The Crüxshadows	*Ethernaut*
"Excuse Me While I Kill Myself"	Sentenced	*The Cold White Light*
"Lord's Prayer"	E Nomine	*Das Testament* (German Bonus Tracks)
"Glory to the Brave"	Hammerfall	*Glory to the Brave*
"Per l'Eternita"	E Nomine	*Das Testament* (German Bonus Tracks)
"Last Ride of the Day"	Nightwish	*Imaginaerum*
"Homeward Bound"	US Navy Band Sea Chanters Chorus	*Homeward Bound*

"Last Ride of the Day" is, more or less, the "anthem" of this series:

Riding the day every day into sunset
Finding the way back home.

http://www.youtube.com/watch?v=ZTN5E5fReSc